Second Contact

and other stories

Gary Couzens

Elastic Press

This collection copyright © 2003 by Gary Couzens

"Subject Matter" copyright © 2003 by Gary Couzens. Originally published in Roadworks. "Tell Me That You Love Me" copyright © 1993, 2003. Originally published in Loving, September 1993, under the pseudonym "Rosetta Newman". "Eskimo Friends" copyright © 1997, 2003. Originally published on PC disk in Cluster #2 and reprinted in Roadworks #1. "Second Contact" copyright © 1994, 1998. Originally published in a different form in The Magazine of Fantasy & Science Fiction, March 1994 and in its present form in Gravity's Angels (TParty Books, 1998) and online in The Storyville Anthology. "Second Contact Revisited" copyright © 2001. Originally published online in The Storyville Anthology. "The Day of the Outing" copyright © 1999. Originally published in Roadworks #6. "Thunderhead" copyright © 1995. Originally published in The Third Alternative #6. "This Flight Tonight" copyright © 1994 by Gary Couzens & D.F. Lewis. Originally published in Substance #1. "Amber" copyright © 1999. Originally published in Roadworks #5. "Drowning" copyright © 1991, 2003. Originally published in The Ebb Tide and Other Stories from Cornwall (Weavers Press, 1991). "Half-Life" copyright © 1996. Originally published in The Magazine of Fantasy & Science Fiction, August 1996. "Straw Defences" copyright © 1996. Originally published in Psychotrope #4. "Miss Perfect" copyright © 2002. Originally published in Crimewave #6: Breaking Point. "Eggshells" copyright © 2003. Originally published in Roadworks #15: Slow Burn. "City 101" copyright © 2000. Originally published online in Cascade. "Migraine" copyright © 1996. Originally published in Substance #4 and online in Dark Planet. "A Night Away from Home" copyright © 1996. Originally published in Urges #3. "Four A.M." copyright © 1995. Originally published in Peeping Tom #20 and reprinted in Not One of Us #22. "A Giant Amongst Women" copyright © 2003. Previously unpublished.

All rights reserved. No part of this publication may be reproduced, stored in a retrieval system, rebound or transmitted in any form or by any means, electronic, mechanical, photocopying, recording or otherwise, without the prior written permission of the author and publisher. This book is sold subject to the condition that it shall not by way of trade or otherwise be lent, resold, hired out or otherwise circulated without the publisher's prior consent in any form of binding or cover other than that in which it is published.

ISBN number: 0-9543747-2-X

Printed by Blitzprint, www.blitzprint.com

Published by:
Elastic Press
85 Gertrude Road
Norwich
UK

ElasticPress@elasticpress.com
www.elasticpress.com

For Mum and Dad, Robert and Mandy, David and Holly

*

Acknowledgements

The oldest stories in this book were written in 1990, and I'm writing this in December 2002. That's a long time and many people to thank. No doubt I'll miss someone out but if I do, apologies – consider yourself there in spirit.

For general help and encouragement, for being there when needed, or for specific input into particular stories, I'd like to thank: Tiffany Bradford, Mark Collins, Maria Contos, Pam Creais, David Critchard, Trevor Denyer, Barbara Harrison, Phil Heinricy, the late Jane Holbeche, Tony Lewing, Des Lewis, Fred Marden, Peter Middleton, Rosetta Newman, Martin and Mary Owton, Rosanne Rabinowitz, Suzanne Shaw, Clare Stevens, Valerie Thame, Sara Townsend and Chris Harlow, Val Waters, Cheryl Wright, and the members of the Farnborough, Fleet & District Writers'Circle, the T Party Writers'Group, the British Fantasy Society, and Storyville.

Thanks to the editors for accepting the previously-published stories here:
Allen Ashley, Paul Beardsley, Mark Beech, John Benson, Andy Cox, Trevor Denyer, Stuart Hughes and David Bell, Ian Hunter, Lorna Read, Justina Robson, Kristine Kathryn Rusch, Eileen Shaw, Jason Smith, Lucy Snyder, John T. Wilson. Thanks also to Ellen Datlow and Terri Windling and Gardner Dozois for honourable mentions.

Particular thanks go to Pam and Barbara for consenting to make fictional appearances as themselves in "Subject Matter", to Des, for making the co-writing of "This Flight Tonight" such an enjoyable experience, and for giving his permission to reprint the story here. And finally for Andrew Hook for taking on this project.

The Tall Person's Club of Great Britain, mentioned in "A Giant Amongst Women", is a real organisation, and their 1994 convention did indeed take place in Docklands. The organisation can be contacted at: The Richmond Business Centre, Greyhound House, 23-24 George Street, Richmond, Surrey, TW9 1HY, U.K. Phone 07000 TALL-1-2 (07000 825512). Website at www.tallclub.co.uk

Table of contents

Subject Matter	1
Tell Me That You Love Me	13
Eskimo Friends	17
Second Contact	33
Second Contact Revisited	47
The Day of The Outing	53
Thunderhead	67
This Flight Tonight	75
Amber	89
Drowning	99
Half-Life	111
Straw Defences	117
Miss Perfect	123
Eggshells	133
City 101	175
Migraine	179
A Night Away From Home	209
Four A.M.	219
A Giant Amongst Women	227

Subject Matter

Ros goes into Bracknell Town Centre on her lunchbreak. Christmas decorations blink with strained jollity, yellow and red against a grey sky. Ros has set herself a list of tasks for the next hour: pay her phone bill at the bank, buy presents. She likes browsing in bookshops, window-shopping.

Stop there. Freeze-frame. This is how I first picture Ros, catching sight of her reflection in a shop window. She wore her dark-brunette hair long for some years, but decided – less a whim than addressing a worsening annoyance – to cut it short. She liked the result; it suits her, she's been told.

When you look in a mirror, what do you see? A face you've grown up with, that's changed with you. Do you like it, hate it, feel resigned to it? When I was tall enough to look in the wall mirror at my parents' house, I thought: *Is that what I look like?*

Ros has that memory too. She saw, sees, an oval face, blue eyes, a light dusting of freckles, high cheekbones and a pointed chin. She thought: *I'm not pretty.*

Not plain, either. Presentable, given effort. She'll admit to being overweight, but not so much as to be obese. She tries not to worry about her weight – the stress she could put herself under could do more damage than a few excess pounds – but it's depressing when her jeans are too tight.

Characters grow by accretion: a gesture, a turn of phrase, a quirk. I have to make them seem part of a whole, not a collection of discrete traits. Externals sometimes arrive with an initial image: let's return to Ros gazing in that shop window.

She was always tall for her age, tall for a girl. She stopped early at five feet eight. Some of the girls she towered over at school are now Amazons around the six-feet mark. She has a mesomorphic build and is not flat-chested: she takes a 38C. She's wearing a long coat over a white top, heavy royal-blue skirt and thick dark tights.

At the end of her lunchbreak, tasks completed, she goes back to the office.

*

Ros works for a software company, spending most of her time manning the technical helpline. After several years, her telephone manner has a practised smoothness. Sitting across the desk from her is the only other woman in the office, Joanne, who wears short skirts and has a coffee mug which says *Psycho Bitch from Hell*. Joanne has a natural flirtatiousness that Ros envies. In every office Ros has worked in, the gender that is in the majority tends to dominate the tone. In this very male place, much of the talk is of football, in which Ros has no interest; when the talk shifts to movies, she is more able to join in. As if thrown together by circumstances, Ros and Joanne sometimes go out together in the evening, to a pub, or for a meal, or to a film. Ros has an invitation to Joanne's hen night next month.

Ros lives in a flat in Harmans Water, a suburb of Bracknell, within reach of a modern-design pub, a church and a parade of shops, a bus or train journey from the town centre. When Ros gets home at six o'clock, she finds John, her boyfriend, has let himself in. He sits in the front room, practising chord progressions on his acoustic guitar.

"Hi," he says, looking up. "Want a coffee? Kettle's just boiled."

Ros goes to her room to change out of her work clothes into an old shirt and a pair of leggings. One of John's shirts lies on the floor abandoned, arms spread as if in surrender. She wishes he'd pick up after himself.

This is her room. Her refuge. She considers herself sociable, but only if she can have times when she can switch off the outside world like so many lights. Times when no-one can care what she does, how she looks, how tidy the flat is or isn't.

I have, she says in one of her pronouncements to herself, *to strike a balance.*

Now, of course, there is John. He doesn't officially live here; he shares a house in Wokingham with three other men. She's stayed overnight several times but has always been conscious of a lack of privacy: John's housemates leaving and returning at all hours, sometimes with friends, John's band practising. And thin walls: she wonders if everyone in the house can hear their lovemaking.

John spends the night at her flat more and more often; he now has a key. Sleeping in her double bed, changing her refuge from within.

*

One night in bed, resting on his elbow, John says: "You know, Ros, what would you say if I wrote a song about you?"

"Why would you want to write a song about me?"

He glances away. "I'd have thought you'd be flattered."

"Actually, I'd find it a bit strange more than anything." She sits up. "Do you know what I mean?" She leans forward, loops her arms about her knees. "I just have this picture of someone singing this song about me. I mean, people listen to it and suddenly they know all these private things about you."

John sits up too, rests his arm about her shoulders. "If you're not happy about it, Ros..."

She pouts. "For all I know, you've written this song already."

"I'm sure you've written about me in those stories of yours. You're in no position to talk."

"I suppose not. Who did that song called 'Rosanna'?"

"Toto. Don't tell me you like that crap."

"It's okay. We used to dance to it at sixth form discos. That's about Rosanna Arquette, the actress."

"I know who she is. She was in that shitty Jean-Claude Van Damme film we saw. She took her clothes off."

"You would remember that. What I'm trying to get at, she was going out with the guy who wrote the song. She isn't now. What must she feel when she hears that song now?"

"Same as you'll feel when a certain album comes out with a certain song called 'Rosetta' on it." (Rosetta is Ros's full given name.) "Come on, Ros." He kisses her on the cheek, his arm slipping about her waist.

*

A story is a pattern of significant events, or at least significant detail. But in our lives there is always downtime between significant events, filled with actions both habitual and unexpected. Between the significant events in her story – the story that tells her – I wonder what are those actions in Ros's life. What goes through her mind when she takes a bath, say? Or on the daily bus-ride to work? Or when she makes love with John?

I'm sitting in a restaurant overlooking Leicester Square. It's the early evening, a busy time: waitresses scurry back and forth like rabbits. Their uniform is a plain white top and a short black skirt, the zip positioned exactly where you would imagine the cleft between the buttocks to be.

Across the table from me is Pam, whom I've known for several years. We talk freely, about people we know, shared interests, more personal matters, just like any other good friends. But, I wonder, if it wasn't the real-life Pam but the fictional Ros sitting opposite me now, at this table, sharing a meal before we go to see a film? How differently would the conversation proceed? Different friends in common, different shared interests – different touchstones. A voice on the phone – "Hi, Gary, it's me" – presaging different things each time.

But Ros doesn't often come to London. Occasionally, yes, to shop, or to see a show. But she doesn't work here (as Pam does) or visit the city habitually (as I do, mostly for film press-screenings, sometimes socially). In such small ways do characters assert their independence.

*

Ros lies supine on a couch, nude, her arms resting behind her head. At first David adjusted the position of her arms and legs, small increments Ros couldn't see the sense of. Now that is done, she lies as still as possible while he draws her.

"Get the reference?" David asks.

"No, I don't, sorry."

"*The Naked Maja.* Goya. You must have seen that one. *La maja desnuda.*"

"Oh, I know what you mean." A distant memory from her mother's art books.

The heating in David's small front room is on full blast. Ros is warm enough, though her nakedness prevents her becoming so warm that she might fall asleep. She's aware, too aware, of how her breasts lie, their weight, the large mole just at the top of her pubic hair, the breadth of her hips.

"How's John?" asks David, a pencil held crossways in his mouth.

"He's much the same. He's fine."

"He's a good-looking guy."

She chuckles. "I won't tell him you said that. He'd die if he thought another man fancied him."

"I can dream, can't I?" David pouts campily.

David is a friend of a friend; Ros met him at a party. She doesn't remember how the conversation got round to the subject, but he asked her straight out if she'd consider posing for him. Intrigued by the idea, she did, clothed at first. Posing nude seemed a natural progression: she'd done it before as a student, to earn extra money. She trusted David: he was openly gay, so they knew there'd be no misunderstanding. John wasn't happy with the idea, but she went ahead and did it anyway.

David works as an illustrator, but the drawings of Ros he does for his own interest at weekends. She's seen others he's done: still-lifes, nudes of Tony, his present boyfriend, some of these sexually explicit.

"Women artists seem to like painting circles," he says. "Not sure why – it's a sort of female shape, I guess. Circles and tunnels." He pauses, shades a small area, then continues: "My sister, when she was pregnant, she used to draw nothing but circles. They got bigger and bigger the fatter she got. Tony and I went to the Mapplethorpe exhibition at the Hayward the other day – there was this Arts Council exhibition upstairs. There was this cave entrance thing, like a shrine, made out of fibreglass. It looked just like a giant vagina. A woman did that one."

At that moment, there's a knock on the door.

"That'll be Tony. Okay, Ros, take five." David leaves the room. The door opening. "Hi!" The sound of a kiss.

Ros sits up, yawns and stretches, cracking the knots in her legs. She loops her arms about her knees for a moment then stands. She puts on the dressing-gown David provided: it's too big for her, scratchy on her skin, smelling of aftershave. She reaches across for the novel she's reading, Stephen King's *The Dark Half.*

She walks round to David's easel and looks at the uncompleted drawing. It's merely a suggested torso at this stage.

David and Tony come into the room. "Hi, Ros," says Tony, shorter and younger than David, his hair in a buzzcut. "David working you hard, is he?"

Ros smiles thinly: Tony makes this joke every week.

As the two men talk over Tony's day, Ros sits back down on the couch. The Mapplethorpe catalogue is on a table next to her. She opens it at random to a full-page monochrome print of a black man's buttocks, large in close up, their owner barely visible leaning away from the camera.

"How about that, then?" David says, glancing over Ros's shoulder. He points to the print and says to Tony: "Wouldn't you want to shag that?"

*

Ros doesn't keep it a secret that she writes, indeed that she's had short stories published. But her writing is a small secret part of herself, the only part she exerts complete control over, that for better or worse, is hers alone. Acceptances and rejections are less important: she'd continue writing regardless. Oh, there are certainly suggestions, undoubtedly meant to be helpful. *Why don't you write for Mills & Boon?* is one. *But I don't read Mills & Boon,* is her answer. The chairman of her local writers' group, a retired army officer who has published many stories in women's magazines, suggested she tried *Loving.* After reading several issues, she sent the magazine a story – and it was accepted. Many rejections followed, but so did three more acceptances.

Write about what you know: the standard advice. But the protagonist of that first story was pregnant, which she's never been. Two of the others were narrated by men, which she hadn't been sure she could do convincingly. The last and to her mind best was the only one in any way autobiographical: it concerned a woman in an affair with an older married man. *But in my case it wasn't an affair,* she thinks, *more a one-night stand.* She and a manager one Christmas, both very drunk, barely able to consummate their adultery, red-faced with embarrassment the next day at work. But no-one said anything, and his marriage continues. They say hello, or merely nod, whenever they meet, professional to a fault.

Ros continued submitting to *Loving* out of loyalty, but it was clear that romance was a genre uncongenial to her. *Too dark,* one rejection slip read. Happy endings seem false to her more often than not. No other women's magazine accepted her. She's now writing a teenage horror novel: another suggestion, certainly a commercial one, but one she's comfortable with.

She works on it at the PC in her bedroom, when she has time alone. But with John in her life at the moment, she has less and less of that.

*

Barbara and I leave the train at Bracknell, walk five minutes down a shallow hill, then a left turning to The Point, a leisure centre, a ten-screen cinema being our goal.

Barbara is one of my longest-standing friends. Despite being old enough to be my mother (her daughter is actually ten months older than me), she's like a sister to me, the sister I never had. We're a platonic couple, though I don't doubt there are rumours to the contrary – which might have been true at one point. But if we had slept together, would we still be friends?

After the film, we walk through Bracknell High Street.. Time and again, I see Ros, or women who could be her. Avatars. We've been to the cinema she goes to: on her own, if no-one is willing to accompany her. There's the Barclays cashpoint she uses, the Our Price she buys CDs from, the Hammicks where she browses through books, the W.H. Smiths inside the Princess Centre where she buys magazines and stationery. The old-world pub where she and her work friends go sometimes in the evening, in the shadow of the steel and plate-glass office block: oasis of old in this New Town. The routine landmarks of her life.

And here is the place where I first saw her, standing on or very near the spot where I am now, gazing at her reflection in a shop window. Behind the glass, rows of dresses, shop assistants as attentive as bees.

Ros is here. She is real.

*

A week before Christmas, Ros changes into her black party dress, sleeveless with half-inch-wide shoulder straps. She thinks: *Do I look fat in this?*

As she fixes her earrings, John comes in.

"Mmmm."

"How do I look?" she asks.

"Pretty fucking sexy."

She makes a moue as she puts on her lipstick.

The party is being held by friends of John he knows through the band: she's of course invited as his girlfriend. *You know - John's Ros.* She wonders if she'll know anyone there.

Ros is standing by the side of the room, helping herself to a glass of wine, conscious of how tight her dress is. One man gazed blatantly down the top of her dress: material for whatever fantasy he is brewing. She turned hurriedly away: she'd rather not know what that is. She suspects he'd try to hit on her if John wasn't there. Near to her is a tall woman with long fair hair, so slim – her hips mere points in her tight skirt – that Ros wonders if she is, or was at one time, anorexic. The woman smiles at her.

John, standing nearby, introduces them. "Lorraine, hi, this is my girlfriend Ros. You've got something in common: you're both writers."

And he goes away, leaving them together. "Hello, Ros." Lorraine is so quietly spoken that Ros has to lean forward to hear her over the mostly seventies and eighties music coming from the sound system. She offers Ros a cigarette; Ros declines. "What do you write? Have you had anything published?" Ros tells her.

This is obviously intended as a prompt, as Lorraine leans back and says: "That's good going. I write poetry myself. I've just had my first collection published."

"Congratulations."

"It's called *Marilyn Monroe in the Bathroom.*"

"I'm sorry...?"

Lorraine giggles: Ros senses the nervousness behind the bravado. "I thought that would be a catchy title."

"It certainly is."

"What I'm getting at" – Lorraine's hands cartwheel – "well,

take Marilyn Monroe, she's more than just a woman, she's an *image* of a woman..."

"An icon?"

"Yes, that's right, that's it." Lorraine's fingers brush Ros's elbow. "One created by men, mind you, though I'm sure she colluded in it to some extent. But we forget there was a real woman behind it all. Someone who clipped her nails, shaved her legs, saw herself in the mirror when she'd just got out of bed and hadn't put her makeup on, went to the toilet, had her period...that's what I'm getting at."

By the end of the evening, Ros has Lorraine's card in her handbag; she's given Lorraine her name, address, phone number and email as well. Lorraine suggested they send each other samples of each other's work; she will send Ros details of a women's writing group she knows.

At Ros's flat, as they are undressing for bed, John says: "I knew you and Lorraine would get on."

"She's...quite an interesting person." Ros isn't sure how to put it. She can't rid herself of the suspicion that Lorraine was trying, or will try, to make a pass at her.

John doesn't seem to notice her hesitation. "It wasn't so bad, was it? You got to talk to someone."

"She's probably writing a poem about me right now."

Naked now, she climbs into bed beside him. "Hey," he says, and kisses her: on the lips, on the forehead, on each breast.

She's oddly detached as John moves on top of her, as she parts her legs and he enters her. It's as if she's part of their lovemaking and is watching it at the same time: her eyes closing, a bead of sweat breaking and running down his back, her sighs and gasps, his tension and release.

The Rosetta in John's song, the Ros-image David is painting, even Lorraine's hypothetical poem. Each of them, derived from her, not the whole of her. A surface: she is their subject matter. But if she is written by them, how much is she her own person?

*

I am writing about Ros. She is a character in a story written by me. What life she has is granted by the scratch of pen on paper, or 1s and

0s in a computer program. The person created by words, residing in the space between them.

But I am the same. Or I could be. Somewhere someone is bringing me into existence.

I don't hear the sound of fingers on a keyboard.

*

One evening, Ros is alone in her flat. John is out with the band, a boys' night out: he'll struggle home tonight or tomorrow, hung over. She's going to spend the weekend with him and his parents: they're a pleasant enough couple, but somehow she's not looking forward to it.

There's nothing on TV, so she's sitting in front of her PC, Radio One in the background, tinkering with a short story. It's an idea she's had for a while, one proving stubbornly hard to crack.

She saves and closes the document, opens a new one. A blank white screen. She must write something, anything, even complete gibberish, to clear the block.

She lets her mind wonder. *What if – what if I were a man, not a woman? What would I look like?*

Men are on average five inches taller than women, she types. Where did she hear that? Somewhere – she's got a good memory for odd facts like that. She continues: *I'm 5'8" so therefore I'd be 6'1". That's tall enough, not too tall. I'd hate to be a short guy.*

She continues typing.

*

The phone rings; I pick it up.

"Hi, Gary - it's Ros. Did you get the review? I emailed it half an hour ago."

"Yeah, it's just arrived." I know she wants to chat; terse, businesslike phone conversation seems unnatural, even bordering on rude. "You didn't like *The Island of Dr Moreau,* I take it?"

"No I didn't. Not even Val Kilmer in a sarong could save it for me." She chuckles. "I do pick them, don't I?"

"The review's fine. It'll go in the next issue. Thanks."

"Oh good. I haven't got fed up of seeing my name in print!" she laughs.

I meet Ros outside Bracknell Railway Station. She's in a coat, scarf wrapped about her neck against the November chill. She's wearing the thick skirt she wore to work. Her nose is red; she sniffs into a handkerchief. She looks up as I leave the platform. "Gary...? Hi."

"Hi. You're looking well." We kiss.

We walk through the bus station into the town centre.

"Is Pizza Hut okay?" she asks. "We've got an hour before the film starts."

"I'm easy. You live here. You choose."

"Pizza Hut it is then."

For a moment, her reflection in the shop window, elusive in the darkness.

I follow her into the restaurant and we wait to be seated.

Tell Me That You Love Me

"Do you love me?"

"Hmmm?"

"Do you love me?" I ask again.

"Shhh," he says. His hands are cold on my shoulders. "Of course I do. Do you doubt me?" He kisses me.

*

I'm sitting at my PC. I don't notice Leigh, the supervisor, standing over me.

"Excuse me, Charlotte," she says. "Could you come into my office for a moment, please?"

I follow her. She's a short woman in a pinstriped trouser suit, rounded figure, rounded face, fair hair pageboy-cut, wide mouth painted red. She's two years older than me.

She closes her office door behind us. "Take a seat." She sits behind her desk, fingers interlaced on the wooden surface.

"Charlotte," she says. "In confidence, is everything all right?"

"Yes." I smile, shrug nervously.

"I'm glad. But one thing I must say – there's your work life" – a hand gesture, like a karate chop, to emphasise her point – "and there's your personal life." Another karate chop. "They're separate things. Or they should be. If you're having trouble at home, leave it there. If you're having an affair" – and she gazes directly at me, can surely see me blush – "then that's your business, but have it in your own time. I've noticed – or rather, it's been brought to my attention – you've been making a few personal calls. Now, I don't mind the odd one or two, I'll turn a blind eye to that. But if I were you, I wouldn't abuse it, or you'll end up spoiling it for everyone."

She places a stack of reports on the desk in front of me.

"As for these," she continues, "there are a few – how shall I put it? – *errors* in these. I mean, my job is on the line here." She smiles wryly. "Do I tell my boss Charlotte was in love when she wrote these?

How far would that get me?"

As I return to my desk, I suppose I should feel chastened. Leigh's little talk should sting, like a slap in the face. But now I have Michael, nothing can hurt me.

*

Saturday is shopping day, when I can best leave the house, and when Michael can leave his wife and children.

I load my shopping into the back of the car and drive to our meeting place. It's a bright summer day. I pull up outside the flat. It's owned by a friend of Michael's, who lends it to him for his Saturday afternoons, as a favour.

I sit in the car and wait for Michael. My lover. I curse myself for arriving early. Michael is one of those people who are habitually late, who eat away your time. But I know he won't let me down.

*

It wasn't as if I was saving myself. I was very shy in my teens, I never went away to College or University, and as I was living at home with Mum I didn't have much in the way of opportunity. I had male friends, most of them through work. I was close to some of them, if platonically. I could have gone out nightclubbing every Friday night, like someone I knew in the office. Like her, I could have woken up each Saturday morning in a different bed. But where was the romance in that? That seemed too relentless for me: relief, scratching an itch. That was for teenagers to experiment with; I'm twenty-eight years old and more is at stake.

And then I met Michael.

Let me describe him. He's just over average height. I'm tall, which makes us the same: five foot ten. He's broader-shouldered, heavier-built than me, with dark curly black hair and a tight beard. He has blue eyes. He's thirty-six years old, married for twelve, with two daughters aged eight and four.

We'd been going to the evening class for a few weeks before we spoke. That happened on an evening when we ended up sitting next to each other during the coffee break. He cycled to the class (his wife used the car in the evenings). After the second time we'd chatted, I followed him as he unlocked his bike. He said, "Do you want to go for a quick drink, Charlotte? I'm not in a hurry to get home."

So we did. And again the following week. He knew I wasn't married, guessed I didn't have a boyfriend. As we talked, he put his hand on my knee. I tensed at first but didn't protest, let him gently rub it under the material of my skirt. He'd got to me: I'd become attracted to him without realising it. The following week he became bolder still: as we stood by my car, he kissed me. As we embraced, he moved his hand up to my breast.

I thought, *This is what it's like to be seduced.*

I drove to a layby and we made love on the back seat. We didn't even get completely undressed.

*

We're lying in bed on our sides, face to face. He glides his hand along my side, down the dip of my waist, over the curve of my hip. My fingers toy with the hairs on his chest. He takes my hand in his and guides it down his body, leaves it there. Under my touch he's becoming aroused again.

I used to be shy about nakedness. When we first came to this flat, I walked around swathed in a towel. Michael laughed. "What are you hiding for? You've got a lovely body. You've got nothing to be ashamed of."

So I dropped the towel. And now we're naked together. It seems the most natural thing: I know every inch of his body, he of mine.

As I stroke him, I straddle him. He leans his head back and sighs: "That's so good." He reaches up and places his palms on my temples, my hair loose about my face. "Take it," he says. "It's yours." And I gently take him inside me.

I always used to wonder, when meeting strangers, how much different they would look when naked, in bed, making love to someone. Face flushed, nostrils flared, mouth open in climax. Now others can wonder the same about me. How different do I look?

*

After work, I go home to the house I've lived in for twenty years.

I was a late, unexpected baby. A change baby: Mum was forty-five when she had me. I have two sisters and a brother, the youngest ten years older than me. I could have gone away to University (I may still do so one day) but Dad had died and Mum had her first stroke and I couldn't just leave her.

These days Mum is still alert, though confined to a wheelchair. We have a home-help during the day. I take over in the evening.

"You don't want to sacrifice yourself for me, Charlotte," she said once. I smiled and said nothing.

I can't abandon her. It's painful having to keep Michael a secret from her (from everybody). She's turned to religion in the last few years, and I know that it would hurt her to find out her youngest daughter is having an affair with a married man. Adultery. The Seventh Commandment. *Thou Shalt Not.*

*

Time to go. I step into my knickers and pull up my leggings. I'm standing in front of the full-length mirror. Michael stands behind me, still naked. He puts his hands on my shoulders, gently massaging them then moves his hands down to cup my breasts.

"I can't make it next Saturday," he whispers. "I promised the kids I'd take them to the beach."

I look up at him; perhaps my expression betrays some hurt.

"Don't worry, Charlotte. I'll make it up to you the week after."

I nod. I turn away from him, bend over to pick up my bra, put it on. I pull on my T-shirt over my head, shake out my hair and tie it in a ponytail.

Outside, we embrace and kiss.

"Do you love me?" I say.

"Shhh, of course I do," he says. "Why, do you doubt me?" He moves his hands to my bottom, squeezes my buttocks together.

"I love you," I say.

*

Michael, and the part of my life he belongs to, is shut off from the rest of my life. He's in a compartment to himself. One day I want to let him in to the rest of my life, but not yet. People will be hurt. This may be forced upon me, but I hope not. I want to declare my love when I'm ready.

He carries pictures of his wife and children in his wallet. Perhaps that love may revive. Perhaps not.

We can't go on this way forever.

But don't talk about such things. Tell me that you love me, and it'll be all right.

Eskimo Friends

The man wouldn't leave me alone. His breath stank of alcohol.

"Look, please go away," I said.

It was past midnight and I was cold. Under the coat I only had on the thin black minidress and tights I'd worn at the party. I thought of making a run for it, but I wouldn't be fast enough in my heels. I stepped backwards one pace, towards the road.

A car pulled up behind me. Tim leaned out of the window. Alison, what the hell are you doing?"

I said nothing.

"You can't walk home at this time of night. Get in." He unlocked the door. I climbed into the front passenger seat and fastened the seatbelt.

The man was still standing on the pavement, the darkened shop window behind him, his heavy-jowled face bearing an expression of bewilderment.

Tim leaned across me. "Look, mate, fuck off, will you. She's with me." He wound up the window and restarted the engine.

I leaned away from Tim, rummaging in my handbag for a cigarette.

"Open the fucking window if you're going to smoke," said Tim.

I inched the window down and lit my cigarette.

"What the hell were you playing at, Alison?"

"Tell Alan to keep his hands to himself. What's it to you anyway?"

"You're pissed as a fart. I'm taking you home right now."

And he put his hand on my knee, his fingers resting against my inside thigh. He drove fast - too fast - down the main road. The vibration of the suspension was making me feel queasy.

It was quiet at this time, with straggles of two, three or four on their way home from pubs and parties; it was too early for the nightclub crowd. I glanced out of the window at the people we passed, quick and blurry under streetlights. My head was swimming. It was unpleasantly warm in the car with the heating on full-blast. Tim was right: I had drunk too much.

He pulled up outside my house. He took hold of my hand as I climbed out of the car. As soon as I set foot on the pavement the cold air hit me: I stumbled and reeled sideways into next-door's fuchsia bush, slipping down so my bottom hit the icy paving slab hard. I vomited all over the front of my coat.

"Jesus Christ," said Tim.

He took hold of my arm and lifted me up, my heels skittering on the concrete.

"The least you can do is say thank you," he said.

"Thank you," I muttered.

He put his hand into the small of my back. I took some tissues out of my handbag and wiped my mouth, then the worst of what I'd brought up, balling up the tissues and dropping them into the wheely-bin outside the front door. There wasn't too much damage: I hadn't eaten a lot.

"I'm sorry," I muttered.

"That coat fucking stinks. Put it in the wash."

I rummaged in my handbag for my front door key. It took me several attempts to get the door open. I'd never been this drunk before, ever.

Tim took hold of my hand and led me to the nearest room. By chance, it was mine. He shut the door behind us and took hold of my shoulders. I struggled as he tried to put his hands on my breasts.

"Don't tease. I can't stand girls who tease."

He pushed me down so I was lying half on, half off the bed. I didn't put up a fight. He fumbled with the zip of my dress, swore, and left it half undone. I was lying on my back, gazing up at the ceiling. He pushed up my skirt and tugged roughly at my knickers and tights. I closed my eyes. It was over very quickly.

I lay there, my stomach churning, wondering if I was going to be sick again.

"Thanks, Alison," he said. He kissed me on the cheek. I turned my head away, felt him stand up, his weight lifting from me. There was the sound of his zip being pulled up, then he turned and left.

If it hadn't been for the alcohol, I wouldn't have slept at all. I woke at six o'clock with a hangover, my head throbbing, my mouth dry as sandpaper.

How had I let myself get into this state? I never got drunk, not this drunk. In fact, I had a reputation for the exact opposite. A *sensible* girl. I'd been called that all my life, more often than I'd liked.

There was no-one else awake at this time. In any case, it was less a household than a collection of students under one roof. Rachel was almost certainly spending the night with James, her boyfriend. She had been at the party; she'd no doubt have things to say to me when she got home.

I lay in the bath, water and bubbles up to my chin, my short mid-brown hair flat against my scalp. My skin felt tender with shame - I'd been extremely foolish. I'd got very drunk, more than I'd ever been. What were people thinking of me? And Tim, who I hardly knew, had had sex with me. I hadn't consented to it, but I hadn't fought him off either. He'd taken advantage of my drunkenness.

I was unattached. I'd had relationships, in Sixth Form and in the Hall of Residence, but in many ways I'd felt relief when they were over: I could go back to doing my own thing. I didn't have to fit myself around another person.

But now this had happened.

I scrubbed at myself, anxious to remove the sweat, and any trace of him. Salty tears ran down my cheeks. He had left bruises and scratchmarks on my buttocks and inner thighs.

I lay in the bath until the water went cold. Marcus, the gay man who used the upstairs room only to sleep or play his drum & bass collection a little too loud, knocked on the door. "Hurry up, whoever's in there! Is that you, Alison? I need to use the bathroom!"

I closed my ears, held my nose, and sunk my head under the water.

"He did *what?*" Rachel was incredulous. "I can't believe he'd do a thing like that. It's fucking unforgivable."

She'd come home in the afternoon. She'd seen me sitting in the front room on my own, trying to read that day's *Observer*. I was in a thick jumper and my leggings were tucked into woollen socks and slippers. Even so, I still felt cold; the house's heating was inadequate. "Hi, how are you feeling, Alison?" she'd said brightly as she came in. "Hung over? You were really really pissed, you know."

I'd looked up and met her eyes. My expression must have been clear enough, for she said: "Oh shit, what's happened?"

She held me as I rested my chin on her shoulder and sobbed.

Now we were sitting in my room. We'd gone there to talk, for privacy.

I remembered brief moments of the party. Dancing. Loud music. But much of what happened between nine o'clock and just before midnight was a blank. I knew I'd chatted with Tim, but I had no recollection of anything either of us had said. I remembered Alan's hands on my breasts, my slapping him around the face, then turning on my heel, snatching my coat and walking out the door. And what had happened from then on.

"I thought you'd taken something, you were so out of it." Rachel's voice hardened. "But that's no excuse. What he did was despicable."

I shrugged, and lit another cigarette.

"I don't know how you can be so calm, Alison. You've got to take action."

"I don't want to make a fuss. I just want to forget it."

"'Make a fuss'? *Alison* - you've been *raped.*"

"He'll say I agreed to it, I consented. It'll be his word against mine."

Rachel threw up her hands in exasperation. "*Jesus.*"

To tell the truth, I didn't know myself why I was so calm. I was on edge, certainly, but that had more to do with the time of the month. Perhaps I'd just been numbed. All I felt was the soft throb of the scars the experience had left: the real hurt was hidden behind them.

The following day, Rachel and I left the Students' Union building. She wrapped her scarf about her neck: at five feet eight she was four inches taller than me, and bigger built. She had a tightly-permed auburn nimbus of hair, her bright red lipstick offsetting her fair, lightly-freckled skin. With her thick coat and her full-length skirt that belled out about her legs as she walked, she looked her size. I felt safe with her around.

"Alison!"

We stopped in our tracks, turned in unison. It was Tim. I felt my cheeks burn with embarrassment. He looked very different in the hard clarity of daylight, somehow diminished. His high cheekbones gave him a gaunt, hollow-cheeked look. His fair hair was uncombed and his forehead wrinkled with anxiety.

"Alison, I've got to talk to you!"

I stared back at him, not saying a word.

"Alison, I don't know what came over me. I - I did a dreadful thing... I'm sorry - "

"Fuck off, lowlife," said Rachel. She strode away. "Come on, Alison."

"Alison, *please* - " He seemed about to burst into tears. For a moment, despite myself, I felt sorry for him and was going to stay and talk.

"Alison! Come on! We'll be late!" Rachel called, already halfway down the path to the Arts Faculty buildings.

"You hurt me, Tim," I said, in a half-whisper, but loud enough for him to hear. "You took advantage of me."

"Yes, I know. I can't say how sorry I am."

I didn't reply, turning to follow Rachel.

I had no lectures the following day, so I lay in bed until ten reading *To the Lighthouse.* I spent the rest of the time tidying my room, listening to Radio One. The heating had been fixed, so I was wearing a T-shirt and an old well-worn, faded but comfortable skirt.

I was sitting in the front room, drinking coffee, eating my lunch from a plate resting on my lap, when Rachel came in. She was very pale.

"What's up?" I said.

"Alison, it's Tim."

"What about him?"

"He's dead."

"Dead?"

"He killed himself. Last night."

I looked down. "Oh shit." I remembered the state he'd been in yesterday. He'd been all but pleading with me to forgive him. I hadn't done that, but I'd hoped for a reconciliation.

"I mean, the guy was a bastard, to do what he did to you," said Rachel. "But I didn't expect him to do *this*. What would make him kill himself?"

Two grandparents aside, this was my first experience of death and I suspected it was much the same for Rachel. Neither of us had known Tim well: he was a friend of a friend, someone who was around. Whatever we had said to each other at the party had been the first extended conversation I'd had with him - and the last. Most people I knew liked him.

"Alison, it scared the shit out of me," said Rachel.

It was my turn to hold her.

By the end of the evening, which several of us including Rachel and myself spent in the bar, I knew more details. Tim's suicide was the topic uppermost on our minds. That night I dreamed of what may have happened. I dreamed of him stepping into a hot bath and with two quick strokes of a razor opening the veins on both his wrists. When he was found, the water was cold and deep red. He hadn't left a note.

I woke in the early hours of the morning, sweating and trembling and crying, my nightdress sticking to me in patches.

I went to the funeral and sat on my own at the back of the church. I would have liked Rachel to be with me, but she'd refused to go. She'd urged me to stay away. But I went all the same. The woman in a black veil, bent over and sobbing, was Tim's mother, supported on either side by his father and sister.

Some of Tim's student friends were there too. One of them was his ex-girlfriend. Her name was Lorraine: she was tall, about five feet ten, and so slim I wondered if she were anorexic. She was wearing a white top and a long narrow black skirt, and her blonde hair was gathered up. Standing a couple of rows behind Tim's family, she seemed very calm, but I wondered what was going through her mind as she watched the coffin disappear for cremation.

We met outside. "You're Alison, aren't you?" she said. She was very quietly-spoken; had there been any background noise, I would have had to strain to hear her. "I recognised you from the party. It's good of you to come along."

I said nothing.

"Do you need a lift back?" she said. I'd taken the bus here. "We've got room in the back."

We stood in the lane outside the church, both of us smoking.

"He went home with you, didn't he?" she said. "After the party."

She had been there, I now remembered - but how did she know? Tim had picked me up on the road outside, half a block away. I'd only told Rachel what had happened. Had Tim boasted about his conquest? I doubted that, considering his remorse two days after the event. Or had someone in my house heard creaking bedsprings and put two and two together - had the story got out that way? *That was quick,* I thought. *Who else knows?*

Lorraine gazed down the road at the approaching car, framed by trees like interlaced skeletal fingers, the tarmac carpeted with copper leaves. "You know," she said. "That makes us Eskimo friends."

"I'm sorry...?"

"It's an American expression. Someone who's slept with someone you've slept with."

But it wasn't the same for you as it was for me, I thought.

She took one final drag on her cigarette, then ground it out underfoot. She looked directly at me, her blue eyes unblinking.

"Something happened at that party, didn't it?" she said. "Something got out and we can't get it back in again."

The car pulled up at that moment, and I couldn't ask her what she meant.

That evening, as I was cooking dinner for myself, Rachel came in. She tugged off her scarf, dumped her bag on the floor and sat heavily on a chair, puffing out her cheeks. She rested her feet, still in ankle boots, on another chair, her skirt hanging like a banner. "God, what a shit day I've had!" She described it to me as I stood stirring the soup. "Mmmm, that smells nice. Do you want to borrow my lecture notes?"

"Yes please."

She stood behind me. "How did it go?"

"Sad."

"There was a card going round, you know? I signed the card."

"I thought you hated him. You wouldn't give him the time of day."

"I hated what he did. You don't speak ill of the dead."

I shrugged.

She stood up, a quizzical expression on her face. "You know, you're the calmest of the lot, Ali. You're a real stoic."

"I don't like fuss. I never have."

"You should have seen the atmosphere in the department the last couple of days. Some of them were crying their eyes out. No-one could understand what made him do it."

"Was it guilt?" I turned to face her. "Let's get this straight, Rachel. He didn't rape me. I was too drunk to do anything, but I let him do it. He didn't force himself on me."

Rachel stood in the centre of the room, mouth open.

"The only thing is," I went on, "did he think he had?"

"I did tell him to fuck off, after all. I feel really shitty now."

"Don't be. Rachel, we'll never know what made him do it. We can't know what was going on in his mind."

"Cheers," she said, and gave me a big hug.

After a pause, I asked: "What happened at the party?"

"It was just like any other party, Ali. Why? You were very pissed. I though you were going to fall out of your dress at one point."

"I don't get that drunk."

"Well, you did - what's the problem? We've all been there. You know, I thought, there's a girl who needs to let her hair down and you probably do hold yourself in too much, don't you think? Anyway, I didn't see you much until the end, when Alan had his hands on your tits. You slapped him and stormed out - that's all."

The following day I was walking along the pathway from the Arts Building to the Students' Union. There was frost on the ground and I was wrapped up warmly: coat over woollen jumper, thick skirt over tights.

Approaching me was Lorraine, walking in step with a man I didn't know. When she saw me, Lorraine stopped in her tracks and broke into a broad grin. "It's my Eskimo friend."

Eskimo as in bloody cold, I thought, shivering.

The man who was with her didn't bat an eyelid. I wondered if she had a reputation for eccentricity. "See you later, Lorraine," was all he said. She didn't reply, merely nodded.

"So, how are you?" she said to me.

"Cold," I said. "Aren't you?" She seemed underdressed: a coat over a white blouse and black waistcoat, and a long black skirt with a pleated split at the back. Her hair was loose to her shoulders.

"I never feel the cold," she said. She lit a cigarette and offered me one. Smoke mingled with clouded breath. "Would you like to have lunch with me?"

She held my place in the queue while I used the Ladies'. The Union building's heating was on full-blast. The heat sat heavily on my chest, making me breathless; I broke into a sweat. There was a flu virus around, and many of those who weren't at home in bed were nursing colds. The hot, soporific air seethed with infection.

Lorraine and I found a table by the window. She ate a salad while I'd gone for something hot and substantial: steak and kidney pie, potatoes and green beans.

"So, how did you meet Tim, Alison?"

"At the party, I suppose. I'd seen him around before, but I'd never spoken to him." I told her about how I'd been accosted by the drunk on the street and how Tim had picked me up in his car. I didn't go into detail about what had happened when we got home.

"So it was a one-night stand." Half a question, half a statement. I guessed I wasn't alone in finding Lorraine hard to read sometimes.

I shrugged. "I suppose so. I was too drunk to do anything much." I grinned sheepishly; her expression did not change.

"There wasn't any hope of it continuing?"

"I doubt it." I shrugged again. If Tim and I had met under different circumstances - who knew? Tim had been handsome and I wasn't immune to good looks. But it was a first impression. First impressions were seductively easy, and I never trusted them. Too many such men turned out to be superficial on deeper acquaintance. But by then - sometimes - we'd slept together. Was sex enough? Something inside me said: *Not always. It doesn't have to be.* "It's academic now, isn't it?"

Her eyes met mine. "Tim and I were together for six months." It was as if I'd called the strength of their relationship into question.

"You must have been very close."

"We were." She blinked: a full stop. She glanced away. "He was a beautiful man. If anything, he looked better naked than with his clothes on. Most men don't."

I'm not sure I want to know this, I thought, but I said nothing.

"If it's any of my business, Lorraine," I said after a pause, "why did you split up?"

"We were still friends. Sleeping with someone changes a friendship. So does no longer sleeping with someone you've had a sexual relationship with. Don't you agree?"

"I guess so." I didn't exactly have a wealth of experience to draw on.

"Tim had a darkness in him. It didn't show, and I may have been the only one to see it. His family may have seen it, I don't know. He didn't know how to deal with it." Her eyes met mine again. "That's what killed him." She glanced at the remains of her salad; she'd been picking at it. "I'm a nervous woman, Alison. That's why I smoke - I need to have something to do with my hands. I suspect you're much the same. That's my curse, I'm too sensitive. I know too much about how people are feeling, I *have* to."

After a pause, I asked her: "What happened at that party?"

"There was a bad atmosphere. I could feel it, people being unnecessarily nasty to each other. So much bitchiness. I saw one woman throw a wineglass over some guy - her boyfriend, I guess. Then he slapped her. She was in tears. A couple of days later, I saw her, she had a black eye. It was like something was in the air, I knew it would end badly."

"I don't remember any of this."

"I remember you. You were dancing very energetically, but I didn't sense you were enjoying yourself. You seemed a bit too grim, too determined."

"I was drunk. I've never been that drunk. I don't know how I did it, unless someone slipped me something. I was only on white wine."

"Was that malice?"

"I suspect it could've been someone's idea of a joke, don't you?"

"Yes, but a joke is an act of aggression. That would be in keeping."

I let myself into the house. As I cooked myself dinner, Rachel came into the room. I hadn't seen her since yesterday - she'd spent the night at James's - but one look told me she was ill. She wore a jumper over her nightdress and was carrying a box of tissues. Her eyes were bloodshot and her nostrils inflamed.

"Hi," she said palely. "I heard you come in."

"Rachel, you look *awful*."

"I feel like shit. Don't come too close, I'd hate it if you got it too."

"Shouldn't you be in bed?"

"I've been in bed all fucking day. I'm burning up. I can't keep anything down, it just comes out of both ends."

"Do you want me to call the doctor?"

"Thanks, I'll see how I am tomorrow. I just wanted to chat to you. The house has been empty all day - I'm getting fucking stir crazy."

"I met up with Lorraine today."

"Who's Lorraine?"

"I met her at the funeral. She used to go out with Tim."

Rachel stared at me. "*Alison* - This is getting too weird for me. Do you compare notes or something?"

I smiled. "She calls me her Eskimo friend."

Rachel snorted. "I don't understand you sometimes, Alison. I hate to speak ill of the dead, but I wouldn't want to have anything to do with Tim if he'd done that to me. And that includes getting pally with his ex fucking girlfriends." She picked up the copy of the local free weekly paper, lying on the table. "Jesus, you can't get away from him. He's on the fucking front page."

"Let me see."

She thrust the paper unceremoniously into my hands. Tim's story was a long article, with quotes from his parents and sister and some student friends (not Lorraine). Everyone said how he seemed to enjoy life; no-one could understand what had made him kill himself. If he really did have a darkness inside him, only Lorraine had noticed or else no-one was telling. I had a vague memory of dancing with him, but all I remembered was his bad temper and his sexual aggressiveness, which I'd capitulated to. In a way darkness was all I'd seen of him, but not the kind that would have killed him.

My eyes wandered over to the other item on the front page. A murder enquiry. A fatal stabbing on the High Street. *Only five minutes away...* I thought with a shudder. The victim's picture nagged at me: I'd seen him somewhere before. It was when I read the time of the murder - just after midnight, the previous Saturday - that it clicked.

I had seen him before. He was the drunk who had accosted me.

"*Shit*," I said.

Rachel looked up. "What's the matter?"

I told her.

"There really must have been a bad atmosphere that night," I said, half to myself, echoing what Lorraine had said.

Rachel sneezed into Kleenex, wiped at her nose. "Don't be silly. It's just a coincidence."

At the end of the article, there was a request for anyone who'd seen anything to contact the Police Station. "Perhaps I should do that."

"Alison, why? You didn't see it happen."

"I did see him, though. It could only have been minutes before he died."

"Yes, but you didn't see it happen. You don't want to get involved with the police. We don't want them sniffing round here."

"Why should they?"

"Why? Use your head, Alison. There's drugs around the place.

And there's Marcus too, he's screwing a guy who isn't eighteen yet. Can't you think about other people for once?"

"What do you mean by that?"

"Don't be so fucking pig-headed. That's your big problem." Before I could react - I felt as if she'd slapped me - she touched my elbow. "Sorry, didn't mean that, it's the flu talking." She grimaced, then stood up.

"Where are you going?"

"The loo. I've practically been *living* in there today, you know."

I did go to the Police Station.

Rachel hadn't come out of her room again before I went to bed. In the early hours of the morning I heard her heavy-footed tread on the floorboards: she went into the kitchen to wash out the plastic bowl she'd been sick in. She didn't emerge for breakfast. Either she wanted to lie low until the illness ran its course or she was tacitly acknowledging it was best we didn't see each other for a while. Probably both. I'd known there would have to be tensions now and again; they were inevitable. But I did wonder if I might have to find someone else to share a house with. Lorraine, perhaps.

Lorraine went with me to the Station. Despite my resolve, I was nervous, so I was grateful for her support.

I was interviewed by two officers, a man and a woman.

"Let me get this straight," said the policeman, red-faced, large and balding. "He accosted you, then your boyfriend drove up - "

I glanced across at Lorraine. She gave no reaction to that. "That's right," I said.

"And that's the last you saw of him?"

"That's right."

"Why weren't you in your boyfriend's car in the first place?" asked the policewoman, bespectacled, about Lorraine's height but nowhere near as slim, her brunette hair gathered up in a plait. "Why were you walking home on your own?"

By not demurring at being called Tim's girlfriend - and in front of Lorraine, too - I'd trapped myself in an untruth. "I - we - we'd had an argument."

The policeman wiped his forehead. "Oh God, not *again*. It must have been a good night for domestics."

"Is your boyfriend willing to be interviewed?" asked the policewoman.

"He's dead," said Lorraine, quietly but firmly: it was the first time she'd spoken. "He's the student who killed himself. He's on the front page of the *Echo.*"

The policewoman couldn't hide her discomfiture: she blinked rapidly, looked down. "I'm so sorry."

"I used to be his girlfriend too, you know," said Lorraine.

They thanked me for coming forward. As it happened, I needn't have done so. Other witnesses had made themselves known. The man had got drunk and argued with his girlfriend. (According to her he was a virtual teetotaller.) He'd left her house and was on his way home when he met me. Then he'd stumbled on a fight outside a pub; due to his drunkenness he'd lost his way and wandered into the roughest part of town. One of the men fighting had turned on him and stabbed him.

"Are you okay?" said Lorraine, outside. "You're shaking like a leaf."

"Something did happen that night, didn't it?"

"Yes it did." She looped her arm through mine.

Something had indeed happened. As well as the murder and the domestic arguments the policeman had referred to, the Samaritans had reported an exceptionally busy night. Cases of vandalism had also increased. Perhaps the outbreaks of bad temper, the uncharacteristic drunkenness - both mine and the murder victim's - were part of the larger picture.

Like a drop of ink in water. Concentrated black at the centre, greyer as it diffused. Was it all over now? I thought of something descending that Saturday night, feeding on what it had stirred up, then moving on. I hoped it had been appeased.

"Was it here?" said Lorraine.

I looked around. "Oh God, yes it was." The DIY shop we were standing outside was now busy, bright, doing its trade. At the time, of course, it had been shut, unlit, silent. But it was the same shop. It was here, almost exactly on this spot, where the man had accosted me.

This was where it had all began, nearly a week before.

Suddenly, to my surprise, I burst into tears.

Lorraine put her arms about me, embraced me. "There," she said. "Let it out. It's over now."

"I hope so," I sniffed.

"I hope so too. We're in this together." She patted me on the shoulderblades, kissed me on the cheek. I sensed passers-by staring at us. A woman asked if something was the matter.

Lorraine took charge. "It's all right, thanks - she's had a bad week." She led me away from the spot. "Come back to my place, I'll make you dinner."

My Eskimo friend. My friend.

Second Contact

Wednesday 11th August 1999. It is not Judgment Day.

As the train pulls into Penzance, Mary Beth yawns and stretches. She hasn't slept well in the hard narrow seat. Her clothes - UCLA sweatshirt over T-shirt, jeans - are gritty and grimy from dried perspiration and two days' wear. She reaches up for her backpack. Dizziness as she stands: breakfast and coffee will cure it. She undoes the rubber band holding her hair back, shakes her hair out, then ties it again in a ponytail. She strides down the platform, her ticket ready for inspection. It's still cool at this time, 8.30. Salt is in the air; seagulls squall. She visits the restroom to wash under her arms, clean her teeth, freshen up.

Tonight she'll sleep better: she's booked ahead at the Youth Hostel here in Penzance. It'll be hot today, few if any clouds. She won't be disappointed. No clouds will hide the Sun, not today of all days. Britain's notoriously unpredictable weather won't spoil everything.

She goes into the small station buffet and on impulse buys a newspaper. She's made a point of disregarding the news during her two months in Europe, especially what's been happening back home - strife and race riots. Too depressing - she'll bone up on all that when she returns to California in September. She sits down at the corner of a table with a Brunch Muffin and a plastic cup of coffee almost too hot to touch. Travelling on a budget: it appeals to her ascetic side, and keeps her slim.

Mary Beth left Amy, the College friend she was travelling with, behind in London. Amy hadn't wanted to come with her to Cornwall: London was much more interesting. "I can see it on TV," she said. "You'll get a better view that way."

"It's not the same," said Mary Beth.

So Amy went with her to Paddington, saw her off on the overnight train. They kissed, embraced, promised to meet up again at the end of the week. Mary Beth waved at Amy as the train pulled out;

just as Amy slipped out of sight, Mary Beth saw her turn and walk away down the platform. *It's all or nothing now,* she thought. This was why she'd insisted on being in England in August, rather than anywhere else in Europe. Mary Beth's obsession, as the much more sanguine Amy put it.

In the news-stand, the local paper has a large headline:
ECLIPSE DAY!

As she sits at the table - alone now except for a late-thirties man with thinning hair sitting opposite - an elderly man strides past and slaps something onto the table. Both Mary Beth and the other man look at it simultaneously, catch each other's gaze, smile.

The elderly man has left a crudely-printed flier on the table: *REPENT FOR JUDGMENT DAY IS AT HAND,* it says.

Mary Beth glances about her. It's a weekday morning in Penzance; men and women are travelling to work. Children are out of school for the summer. She is just one amongst many to pass through this station. There is nothing unusual about today. Except for one thing, there will be nothing unusual. It is not Judgment Day.

*

Clive sips his coffee and idly watches the young American woman. A student, obviously: he got her nationality from her accent when she spoke to the woman behind the counter. She must be about twenty, he guesses; five foot ten tall, tanned, honey-blonde hair tied back with a rubber band.

Their eyes meet. "Hi," she says.

"Hello. You were on the train, weren't you?"

She nods. "It was so *uncomfortable.* Jeez."

"Wasn't it just. And I had a sleeper. So much for British Rail."

"Do you come from London?"

"Well, the Home Counties, actually. Surrey. How about yourself?"

"L.A. I'm on vacation. In Europe for three months."

There's a pause, then Clive says: "You're here for the eclipse?"

She nods, her mouth full of Brunch Muffin.

"Me too. I'm going to take the bus to St Just. You'll get a better view of it from there. The path of totality goes through it. It's a church town, twenty-five minutes away."

"Sounds a neat place."

"It's quite pretty, I'm told. It's been developed a bit in the past few years, though."

And so they tacitly agree to travel together. Clive guesses she senses he's no threat to her. She's intelligent, and her intuition is sharp. He radiates no sexual interest in her.

He said goodbye to his lover Mark at Paddington. They'd spent the evening watching *Nashville,* as ever one of Clive's favourite films, in an all-but-empty London cinema club. The print was faded and scratched, and jumped in places, but the film is an old friend; Clive's memory filled in the blank spots, resonated with familiar scenes, settled into the characters' interlocking stories as if into a comfortable, well-worn chair. It had been several years since he'd seen it, but it's a film that he's marked stages in his personal development by, in the way it changes at each viewing. His only regret is that he wasn't old enough to see it on its first release, in a virgin print.

They kissed goodbye on Paddington platform. Mark would be visiting a dying friend in the North, while Clive made his pilgrimage to Cornwall.

Clive's parents woke him one night in July 1969, just short of his fifth birthday, to watch live coverage of Neil Armstrong making one small step for a man. To his chagrin he doesn't remember that, although he remembers watching later Apollos on TV. And all the space missions after that: Apollo-Soyuz, Skylab, the Space Shuttle. This total eclipse will be the only one visible in Britain during his lifetime, and he's made a pact with his younger self to witness it. He's taken time off work to do just that.

He and the American leave the station buffet, walk outside into the car park. It's a quarter to nine, and the sky is brightening. He points out to her St Michael's Mount, still wreathed in morning mist. He is the host, she the guest in his country; he feels obliged to show her the more famous sights. The sun is still full: first contact, when the Moon's disc clips the Sun's, is an hour and three quarters away. Perhaps he'll show her around Penzance first before they take the St Just bus in time for second contact, when the eclipse becomes total, at 11.10.

"I'm Clive, by the way." He extends his hand.

She takes it. "Mary Beth."

*

"Ready," says Tom the director, and the red light on top of the camera turns on.

Diana imperceptibly breathes in and says: "Thanks, Michael. It's ten o'clock here in Penzance. The eclipse isn't due to start until 10.30, but already crowds have gathered for this rare astronomical event." She steps to one side and turns her head. The camera follows her gaze and looks over the railings to the narrow beach - if beach isn't too grandiose a word. Nearly five hundred people are standing on the pebbles, looking up at the sun, holding up squares of smoked glass to test them, or projecting through telescopes onto white card. The tide laps about the ankles of those furthest out, but they're oblivious to it. Some are sitting on the sand, others in swimsuits squatting in the water. At the far end, a small group of women are sunbathing topless.

"This is Diana Mathis, BBC News in Penzance."

The red light goes out, and Diana sighs audibly. "Shit! I've got a fucking ladder!" She bends forward, picks at her tights with her fingers.

"It didn't show," says Tom.

Diana looks up. "Good." She straightens. "I haven't got a spare pair on me. There's no way we've got time to buy one." She glances down ruefully at the ladder, tugs half-heartedly at the hem of her skirt in an effort to cover it. "Oh *fuck* it."

"You were good, Di," says Tom.

"I should fucking well hope so," says Diana. "I've done it long enough." She glances up at Tom; their eyes meet briefly. A flicker of a smile. Professional to a fault while at work; she prides herself on that. Even though every member of the crew knows she and Tom are lovers.

Diana straightens, lights a cigarette. She never smokes on screen; she remembers the furore when a children's TV presenter was filmed unawares doing it. But there's a few minutes that can be snatched before they have to film again, when she has to readopt her public face. Fortunately no-one stares at them, or tries to get in the way of the camera. And no-one questions the presence of a black woman amongst three older white men.

TV crews will be numerous today. The BBC itself has two at the ready: one at St Just to film the eclipse itself, plus Diana's to get the human interest angles.

"Don't all relax at once, guys," she says. "We've got that village to do next. Got some locals to talk to. Eleven-fifteen and it'll all be over, and we can get a drink. Or several."

*

Adrian pushes the last newspaper through the last front door on his round and cycles down Trezillan's narrow high street to the corner shop. He secures his bicycle and goes in.

He sees Morwenna talking to someone so he lingers at the door. The man is tall and about Morwenna's age. You can tell from the way she's laughing, from the way she's leaning forward intently that she fancies him. She's wearing a flimsy summer dress and you can see the top of her cleavage. Adrian looks down and uncomfortably shuffles his feet.

Morwenna looks up and sees him standing there. She waves at him. "Hi, Adrian!"

The man straightens. "Well, I'll see you this evening, Morwenna."

"Sure."

Adrian expects them to kiss, but they don't. The man walks past him without saying a word. The doorbell *tings* as he goes out.

"Well, that was quick," says Morwenna. "You've finished your round already. Good boy. Give you a kiss."

She comes out from behind the counter and stands next to him. She's still taller than him, but he's growing fast. She's much too old for him of course, but he knows he's in love with her. She shakes out her long frizzy red hair. "It's going to be a *wonderful* day." She's standing by the window where the sun comes in: it makes her dress translucent and you can see her knickers. She's not wearing a bra.

Morwenna Hughes was her father's last child, late and unexpected. From what Adrian can gather, she lived for a while in Truro with a married man. But that didn't work out, so she came back to Trezillan and runs the corner shop now that her father has retired.

She stretches her arms out behind her head, her back arching slightly. She reminds Adrian of a cat luxuriating in the sun. He wonders what she looks like naked.

"What are you doing this morning, Adrian?" she asks.

"I want to watch the eclipse," he says.

"Mmmm, so do I. Should be good." There will be a fete in the village hall and grounds this morning. Mrs Weldon, the local councillor, has used one of her contacts; the BBC are sending a crew to film the eclipse from Trezillan. "Tell you what, is your Mum going?"

"No, she's at work."

"Oh, that's a pity. I'll run you up there if you like."

"Yes, please."

"Just help me shut up shop. I need a wee." She leans forward, touching his upper lip with her forefinger. For a moment he thinks she's wiping a smudge off his cheek, just like his mother used to do. "Coo, look," she says. "You're growing a moustache."

As he waits for her, he feels in his pocket for the scraps of old photographic negative the papers and TV said he should use to view the eclipse. He glances at the rack of cards. It's Morwenna's birthday next week; she'll be twenty-five. He must buy her a card, but how can he do that without her knowing? There's no other place in the village to buy them. And would she pay more attention to him? She's twelve years older than he is. No chance.

*

At 10.30am the eclipse becomes partial. Through most of Britain it will be no more than that. But in Cornwall it continues its advance, a semi-circular bite widening, black spreading over fire yellow. People look up at the sun, then take it for granted as they continue their tasks. But more and more abandon them as totality nears. The beach at Penzance is filled with watchers; it's too crowded to move. Some swim out and tread water to get a better view, squares of photographic negative on chains about their necks. A teenage girl faints in the heat and an ambulance man forces his way through the press of people and carries her out. They sit her on the steps leading down from the pavement, her head resting on her knees.

*

When Clive and Mary Beth leave the bus at St Just, the eclipse is only just partial, a black mouse-nibble at the top. They walk towards the town centre, across the green with its grey stone war memorial, into the square. The pub is open, earlier than usual, and the outside chairs and tables are already full.

They go into the corner shop and buy packets of crisps to munch. Mary Beth buys a bottle of mineral water, Clive cider. At the edge of the square a portly middle-aged man has parked an ice-cream van. They buy a cornet each. Clive hasn't eaten ice cream in years; it's the traditional Cornish variety. The cold shocks the inside of his mouth; he eats the ice cream in quick gulping bites before it melts.

"You ever been here before?" asks Mary Beth.

"No, never. I've been to Penzance, years ago, when I was a child." He rubs his chin, the prickly stubble. Different from the picture of professional respectability his work colleagues see. He'll spend a day unshaven, just for once.

"I've never been to Europe before," says Mary Beth. "And when I heard there was going to be this eclipse, I just had to come along. I'd never seen one."

"It'll be quite a spectacle."

"Sure." She touches him lightly on the elbow. So self-confident. That is what he likes about her but wonders most at. Perhaps it comes with being American, he thinks: a self-confident race. It took him years to gather any sort of poise: he had shyness to overcome, and had to accustom himself to being gay.

They walk past the pub and down a side street towards a small church. Just before it is a graveyard. Already there's a crowd, some of them sitting on the headstones. People of all ages from babes-in-arms to a ninetysomething woman in a wheelchair. Most of them have smoked glass or photographic negatives, some of them have telescopes set up to project the sun's light onto card. They've passed several TV crews on the way here, but many other people have their own cameras, still or cine, or camcorders. Others are sitting on the ground with instruments Clive can only guess the function of. There are journalists here, too, who'll send their copy through by cellfax when it's all over. He instinctively feels inside his grip for his own camera, to check it's still there. They sit down on the grass verge. She pulls her sweatshirt off over her head, drapes it over her shoulder. Clive notes the beads of perspiration on her upper lip, the damp dark circles under the arms of her T-shirt.

"Is that your lunch?" he asks, looking at the bag of crisps, the bread rolls and cheese.

She grins. "I don't eat much."

"Travelling on a budget. I used to do that. A good way to crash-diet."

She nods, grins. Then she asks: "Where did you go?"

"Oh, France, Germany, Italy, Switzerland..."

"I've been there, too. There's some neat places there. I'd like to see Eastern Europe if have the time."

"Well, you've got plenty of time to do it in, Mary Beth. That was when I was a student, myself."

"Before you settled down?"

"I'm not married, if that's what you mean."

"I figured you weren't."

"I'm gay, actually."

She raises her eyebrows. "Really? Oh, fine."

They sit in silence for a while. Clive's words have inhibited Mary Beth. She hadn't realised he was gay, but perhaps that was why she felt safe with him. It's not that she's unused to homosexuals: there are enough of them at college, after all, some of whom - of both sexes - she counts as friends. Just a little disappointment: she has found him attractive, in a middle-aged kind of way. But it was only an idle fantasy: she's committed to Todd, halfway across the world now. They're already living together and, when the next semester starts, they'll announce their engagement.

She loops her arms about her legs and draws them in to herself, resting her chin on her knees.

"Have you got a boyfriend?" she asks.

"Yes, I have. His name's Mark. He's five years younger than me. He's gone up North. A friend of ours is dying of AIDS."

"I'm sorry. Todd's the same. He had to stay behind; his Mom's very ill. Cancer."

"I'm sorry for you both."

Connections. Things in common. Mary Beth likes to find them. The similarities between her, a twenty-year-old Californian heterosexual woman and this at-least-fifteen-years-older English male homosexual. The coincidence of objective and meeting. The randomness from which your life coalesces, the unknown strange attractors that shape it. *I sound like Todd, explaining what he does to me,* she thinks. Todd is a mathematician working in Chaos Theory. She met him at a faculty dance and was attracted to him immediately. He's tall, six four, tanned and blond, archetypal beach-Californian. She carries a photo of him in her backpack.

"You know," Clive says. "I've heard so much about this eclipse. I used to be really into astronomy when I was younger. They all mentioned this eclipse in Cornwall in 1999. I just had to go and see it. Judging by Penzance and here, it looks like lots of people felt the same."

"Well, it is a rare event."

"The only total solar eclipse visible from the British Isles since 1954, and it'll be a long time until the next one. The newspapers and TV have been full of it." He remembers an animated diagram on one of the TV programmes, inscribing the Line of View on a map of Cornwall from north of Penzance to south of Truro.

"Jeez, I never realised it was such a big deal," says Mary Beth. "Suppose I should've guessed."

*

The van bumps as it goes up the hill towards Trezillan. "Fucking backwater," Diana mutters. "It's in the middle of fucking nowhere." She takes a long drag on her cigarette.

"Well, we're on the right track now," says Tom. "We won't miss anything."

"Why couldn't a local crew do this?" Diana goes on. "They'll at least know where the tinpot little place is. Oh, no, Diana'll do it. Good old Di. Give her the shit no-one else wants."

"We're here," says Tom. They pull up in the carpark by the village hall, on the edge of the green. A space is reserved for them. Stalls have been set up; music plays from a ghetto blaster at one end. It's mostly women here, Diana notices: women with young children in tow, women who don't work outside the house.

She renews her lipstick and steps out of the van. Tom goes back to help with the camera and sound equipment. Diana stands at the edge of the green; a fiftyish woman in a dark suit strides across the grass towards her.

"Diana Mathis?"

"Yes, that's me."

The woman extends a hand; Diana takes it. "Good morning, Ms Mathis. I'm Margaret Weldon, the local councillor. We're very privileged to have you here."

Diana smiles. So many people thought the presence of a TV camera was doing them a favour. She knows this woman pulled a few strings to get the BBC here; the event will add to her prestige. "Well, it's not every day this sort of thing happens."

Margaret Weldon smiles broadly. "Yes, it is rather exciting, isn't it? I didn't realise they were quite so rare. And it's such a lovely day for it, too..."

The woman is much too fluttery for Diana's taste. She continues talking as she leads Diana and the crew to the main marquee. "Do have a look around if you have time. We do take pride in our unspoiled little village. And I'd be very grateful if you'd have lunch with me."

Silly old cow, thinks Diana. *She probably doesn't get too much excitement in her life.* The soundman makes a chatterbox gesture behind Margaret Weldon's back. Diana grins, and puts her finger to her lips.

At the other side of the green, Morwenna parks her car. She and Adrian walk across the grass to the stalls, Adrian one step behind.

"Now, you stay with me, young Adrian," she says. "I am responsible for you. Your Mum doesn't know you're here."

"I can look after myself."

"You say."

"You're being bloody bossy," Adrian pouts.

Morwenna stops, turns, extends a finger. "Look, Adrian. You're with me now. Don't make me angry."

"All right."

She takes his hand and continues walking. So embarrassing. Morwenna is treating him like a child. He's thirteen; he's not a baby any more. He takes his hand away.

"Okay, suit yourself," she says. "But don't leave my sight."

They pass in front of one stall, a tombola. The middle-aged woman behind it says: "Hello, Morwenna! Aren't you running the shop today?"

"It's shut for the morning, Eileen," she says. "I decided. Special occasion."

"Who's this young man?" says Eileen, squinting past Morwenna to Adrian.

"This is Adrian. He does my paper round. He did it in record time this morning."

"Hello," says Adrian flatly.

"Well, the BBC have arrived," Eileen adds. "Over there, by the marquee."

Morwenna looks, shielding her eyes from the sun with her hand. Adrian follows her gaze. A tall black woman is speaking to Mrs Weldon. Something about the visitor fascinates him: the expensive suit, the twitchy manner. A city dweller, not at ease in the country. You don't see many black faces in Trezillan.

"That's Diana Mathis," says Eileen.

"She looks prettier than she does on telly," says Morwenna. "Come on, Adrian, let's get a bit nearer. We might get our faces on the news."

Over by the marquee, Diana tells Tom: "We'll get a few overviews of the crowd. If we can interview you, Mrs Weldon - "

"Call me Margaret. Certainly."

"We can do that any time. I'd like to talk to some of those people out there."

"I'm sure that can be arranged."

"And one of the k - children, too. That'd add a nice touch."

"That won't be any problem."

"We won't get in anyone's way."

*

The eclipse reaches fifty percent partial, and more; the Sun has become an increasingly thinning crescent. The sky over Cornwall has darkened, and will darken still more as totality approaches. The temperature has dropped; birds stop their wheeling in the sky and fly to their evening perches. Noisy children become quiet and still.

*

As he talks to Mary Beth, Clive senses that for once, their bodies do not matter. Masculinity and femininity no longer apply, no longer inhibit. A pure meeting of minds, and at last his body can be ignored: the rough stubble, the expanding waistline, the thinning hair. He imagines his body hair melting away, his penis shrinking inwards; her breasts reabsorbed into her body, her vagina closing up. But he opens his eyes again, and difference is still apparent: the swell of her breasts and hips, the white ridge of her bra through her T-shirt. The ground is still hard on his buttocks. The body can't be wholly ignored.

Although he has a lover of two years' standing, sex for him has always mattered less than companionship. He knows not everyone shares his view: certain past lovers certainly didn't. But companionship is what he has, if only briefly, with this young American woman, and sexuality cannot muddle the equation. But he won't see her again after today; before long she'll be halfway across the globe, in another continent. He can buy her lunch, back in Penzance; perhaps they'll exchange email addresses. Perhaps.

Near to them, a small black and white portable TV is sitting on the grass, a lead running back between the gravestones and over the wall to a nearby car engine. Clive hasn't paid much attention to it, but occasionally lets himself be distracted by it. He watches an interview with a German man talking about how he was at the '91 Pacific eclipse and the '94 South American amongst others; how he does not tire of watching eclipses and how everyone should witness one at least once in their lives - it's a religious experience.

Clive nudges Mary Beth's elbow and points at the TV set. *That's what it's like for me,* he thinks, *something like that.* Mary Beth looks up at him and smiles warmly.

Clive takes another swig of cider. He remembers when he was Mary Beth's age, when he'd be sitting somewhere like this of a weekend, a man beside him, slipping slowly into an amiable tipsiness. Alcohol always makes him expansive, and in an excess of goodwill he slips his arm about Mary Beth's shoulders. Normally such a gesture would horrify him: in the past, before public attitudes eased, he wanted to publicly embrace his lover, kiss him, the way he's seen heterosexual couples do, but he knew full well he couldn't. But she doesn't resist, accepts his gesture as if he were a favourite uncle. She'll stay with him today for as long as she can: she'd prefer that to exploring St Just, Penzance, Land's End on her own. Perhaps they'll keep in touch; already she regards him as a friend.

"And now over live to Diana Mathis in Cornwall."

"Thank you, Michael. Well, I'm here at Trezillan village green, and we're not far from totality now. Adrian - " and she turns to a young boy, nearest the camera - "Isn't this an exciting event?"

The camera moves in to a close-up of the boy, who is in his early teens. Clive doesn't hear what the boy says, and only marginally registers his strong Cornish accent. *I must have been like that, years ago,* he thinks. *In my case, the Moon landings; in his case, this. He'll never forget this day. He hasn't become cynical, not like me, not like that reporter. She's seen it all, possibly seen too much. So she doesn't see anything at all. Tomorrow she'll be interviewing an old lady who's rescued a cat. It's all one long blur of news. Other people's lives don't impact on her outside her own little circle, nor on me. But at least I'm aware of it. But I don't know quite what to do about it.*

The sky is darkening, as the sun is reduced to a thin tiara round the black disc of the moon. The seagulls are silent, mistaking the darkness for night. In St Just there is no activity now: cars have stopped on the main road, even in the village centre, and the drivers are looking out of their windows at the sun. Totality is very near. Mary Beth leans forward, puts her sweatshirt back on, settles back into the crook of Clive's arm.

"It's a beautiful sight," she says.

"I'm glad it's come out this way," says Clive. He has taken out his camera now; it rests on his lap, ready. "What a disappointment if we couldn't see the Sun. If it were overcast."

"The sky'd still go dark."

"But it wouldn't be the same."

Mary Beth looks up again. The Sun is a fingernail-paring now, slipping inexorably into total eclipse.

"There it goes," a man somewhere in the crowd shouts out.

At the very last moment, the Sun flares in a brilliant point of light at the edge of the Moon. The diamond-ring effect, the last stage before second contact. When the Sun disappears the crowd cheers and applauds.

"Make a wish," Clive mutters in her ear.

Mary Beth does.

*

Total eclipse. Portent of millennial disaster, or the time when, as they say, in its special darkness you can see yourself more clearly? As thousands of people in Cornwall, and millions more live on television, watch, at 11.10 British Summer Time Total Eclipse 1999 begins.

The sky is night-dark, and there are stars. Venus, Jupiter and Mercury are visible, their positions carefully noted by the astronomers present. The Moon is unyielding black, a hole in the sky. Around it is the opalescent ring of the solar corona, rippling like a net curtain. A red-orange prominence spark-spits out into space. Another curls round and joins itself: the hole formed is large enough to contain the Earth. A minute passes; two. For the two minutes and twenty-three seconds of totality cameras click and whirr. People look up, holding hands in silence. And then a point of brilliant light bursts out at the side of the Moon, and grows brighter. Third contact. The corona is no longer visible, and the stars have gone out. Already the sky is lightening.

It is over. It is not Judgment Day.

Second Contact Revisited

St Ives, Cornwall, Friday 6 August 1999, 8.45 pm.
It took a long time getting here: four trains and a taxi, eight hours. But now I am here, I leave my suitcase in my hotel room and walk down the hill into the centre of St Ives for something to eat. I'm not in the mood for a sit-down meal; a takeaway will do, then a bath and bed.

Were this home, I'd expect most of the shops to be shut by now. But the streets of St Ives are still busy, the narrowness of the roads and pavements making them seem more crowded than they are, almost claustrophobic. Many shops are open past their advertised closing times. Every third shop, it seems, sells food: takeaways, restaurants, pubs. Eventually I buy a steak-and-ale pasty and eat it on the move, back up to the hotel.

There's a sense of expectation: if anything, by next Wednesday, there'll be even more people crammed into Cornwall and South Devon.

*

Church Crookham, Hampshire, mid 1970s
There's a boy who's ten years old, a bright boy who does well at school, who has his circle of friends but will never be Popular with a capital P. He's very interested in space – the earliest world events he can remember are the last three Moon landings – and wants to be an astronomer when he grows up. He is a science-fiction fan, watching *Dr Who* from the age of six and *Star Trek* for about as long.

One birthday he was given a small refractor telescope and some evenings he stands out in the back garden looking at the Moon, trying to identify the various craters and seas. The astronomy books he reads from the library talk about how an eclipse happens: the Sun, Moon and Earth are in alignment. The Sun is 400 times larger than the Moon, but averages 400 times further away. This coincidence means that every eighteen months or so, visible from somewhere on Earth, the Moon's disc covers the Sun and the eclipse is total. The books say that the next total solar eclipse visible from mainland Britain will be on 11

August 1999. Somewhere in the back of his mind he decides he will be there, in Cornwall. He will be thirty-four years old then. It's a long time in the future.

*

That was me, of course. I didn't become an astronomer; in fact, my interest waned during my teens, though it has never been totally extinguished. As for science fiction, I graduated to the written variety via an Isaac Asimov short story collection which I took on holiday at the age of thirteen. For the next few years I read virtually nothing else, but even as a teenager I think I read with some discernment: as a result I have a solid grounding in the classics of the genre up until the end of the 1970s. At about that time I lost interest; mainstream fiction seemed much more relevant to me then. I returned to science fiction, fantasy and horror in my mid twenties, but now as part of a wider spectrum of reading.

I began writing fiction myself at the age of thirteen, starting a novel which I completed six months later at fourteen. Since then, with occasional gaps (such as exams) I've been writing fairly consistently in my spare time. I have less of that now, of course, and more distractions, and I've never been very disciplined about a writing routine.

"Second Contact" was written in 1991. The Cornish eclipse had been at the back of my mind for some time, but how would I write a story about it? I often find you need two ideas to produce a story: in this case, the event provided the content. The second idea, when it occurred to me, provided a structure.

Robert Altman directed *Nashville* in 1976. Instead of a linear plot, the film follows twenty-four characters for two and a half hours as they interact during a Nashville political rally. It's undoubtedly one of the great American films of the 1970s, but unlike Clive in "Second Contact", I don't number it amongst my all-time favourites. But what I took from the film was its structure, which seems almost free-form, but is actually tightly organised. My idea was to tell "Second Contact" via a miniature version of this structure. There are four viewpoint characters (plus some sections in an omniscient voice).

In choosing my four viewpoint characters, I deliberately tried to come up with as much variation as possible. Two are male and two are female; one is not English (Mary Beth), one is not heterosexual (Clive), one not white (Diana), and one not an adult (Adrian). The characters were meant to have equal weight, but Clive all but took over the story. He's one of my earliest gay characters, though not the first one. Nor is he autobiographical, any more than any other character (though some elements, such as being woken to watch the Apollo 11 Moon Landing, are true). I prefer to see him as a version of a part of myself.

Mary Beth got her name from an exchange student I met at University, but was probably more directly based on Americans I met while Interrailing. Adrian is one of my few child/teenage viewpoint characters, while Diana remains the only ethnic-minority person I've ever used as a viewpoint. She was partly inspired by *Viz* magazine's Roger Mellie, a foul-mouthed TV presenter himself based on a famous, clean-cut TV personality overheard effing and blinding in the BBC canteen.

The story is written in present tense. I could write almost anything in this tense as it seems quite natural to me. (When I've kept holiday journals, they're written in the present as well.) Sometimes I have to make myself use past tense when it's appropriate, but here I think it works, for a story reliant on mood and characterisation rather than plot. In fact it has neither plot nor ending in a conventional sense.

At the end of September 1991, I spent a weekend in Cornwall. Like my characters, I took an overnight train on the Friday night, arriving in Penzance at 8.30am. I spent the day wandering around Penzance and took a bus to St Just, where there was a wedding going on. I spent the night at the Penzance Youth Hostel, then took the train back on Sunday. All this time, I made notes and took photographs.

Then I wrote the story, in two sittings. The first draft, under the working title "Not Judgment Day" (a name which is still reflected in the story's opening and closing paragraphs), came in at a sparse 4000 words. As I had hopes for this story, I remember feeling disappointed. But that was raw material to be shaped on the second draft, where I also fed in information on eclipses which I'd read in an astronomical magazine, from an account of the great Caribbean eclipse of earlier that year. This, plus further detail, expanded the story to its current length of 5600 words. The sections involving Adrian had to be rewritten as I'd made a mistake so obvious that no-one had spotted it: in August, British schoolchildren are on holiday.

I sent "Second Contact" to *Interzone* with all fingers crossed. It was rejected with the comment "engaging and excellently written, but too mundane to count as SF". At around the same time, a long story had come back from *Fantasy & Science Fiction* (sent there because I couldn't think of anywhere else to send something that exceeded 15000 words) with the comment from the then editor Kristine Kathryn Rusch: "strong writing – please send more". If I'd received a plain form rejection I might not have responded, but "Second Contact" was the best story I had available, so I sent it. And on 14 July 1992, I received an acceptance letter, contract and cheque in the post.

F&SF published "Second Contact" in the March 1994 issue. Two reviews I read (*Locus* being one) implicitly questioned it being in the magazine as it was neither fantasy or SF. I disagree, though I accept that it's very borderline as SF. Firstly, it has a near-future setting, which becomes an alternative past after the event. Secondly, it is specifically about the effect of a scientific phenomenon, albeit a real one. Even so, it made *Locus's* Recommended Reading List for 1994 and Gardner Dozois gave it a Honourable Mention in *Year's Best Science Fiction.*

When "Second Contact" was republished in the T Party anthology *Gravity's Angels,* I revised it slightly. This was mostly to correct a few timing inaccuracies, but mostly to cover the fact that in 1991/2 I knew nothing about the Internet. Now, when Mary Beth and Clive exchange addresses at the end of the story, they are email addresses.

Now, as the day approaches, I have a sense of finality, of closure. I am trying to finish off existing novels and stories, so that I can move on to new ones, whatever they might be. Perhaps it's Millennial, maybe because it's my thirty-fifth year, halfway through the Biblical span. Or both. But when the eclipse happens, and my fiction becomes reality, I have a sense of a circle closing.

St Ives, Wednesday 11 August 1999
At 8.00am, on my way to a hotel breakfast, I look out of the front door

at grey clouds stacked like slates. It's as the forecast said. Saturday was overcast and rainy, but the days in between were hot and sunny, with broken cloud. But a Low has come in from the Atlantic.

After breakfast, I walk down to the Malakoff Gardens, by the bus station and overlooking Porthleven Beach. About twenty people are here; there are far more in the hill in the distance. I have my solar viewer and my pinhole camera (two pieces of card, one with a small hole in it), but already I sense that I won't need them. I've bought a copy of *The Guardian* on my way here, and on the front page is a photograph (syndicated to at least two other papers), of astronomers setting up their equipment just outside Truro.

This eclipse has caused a lot of interest, as well it might: the last one visible from mainland Britain, in 1927, caused the greatest movement of population up to that time, outside wartime. Even so, I do feel some ambivalence: it's as if someone, a band or writer or film director, you've been aware of and following for years has suddenly hit the big time – what was yours, and a few others', is now everyone's. Not that I wish to begrudge anyone the experience.

First contact passes at 9.56, but the sun is still invisible. A couple standing in front of me wonder how they could get to Iraq...

Just after 10.00am, it begins to rain. Not having an umbrella, I go back to the hotel. A family I'd met earlier (we were part of the same quiz team last night), are watching the event on TV. There's a notable difference between TV companies: the BBC has the gravitas of Michael Buerk and Patrick Moore, while Channel 5 has Russell Grant and an item on whether children born during eclipses would have special powers.

I watch the rest of the eclipse from the hotel doorway. Just after 11am, it suddenly becomes very dark and much colder, as if it's night-time. I can barely see those people around me. In the distance, the sky on the horizon has an orange-red glow. The headland is speckled with points of light: flashbulbs. On the TV set is an image of totality, a black disc surrounded by white flame, the solar corona which is invisible from Earth at any other time, and a couple of small red prominences. One minute, two, then appears the diamond ring at the top of the Moon: the Sun shining through a crater or valley at the lunar edge.

And then it's over, fluid anticipation now fixed as memory: light returns and the shadow of the Moon recedes. The people around me are marvelling about how dark it went, and how cold. I've certainly experienced something, even if I didn't get to see totality with my own eyes. Next time, all going well. Even if the next total solar eclipse visible from mainland Britain is in 2090, there will still be many other opportunities to see one elsewhere in the world. Maybe next time, Zimbabwe on 21 June 2001. Or Southern Australia on 4 December 2002. Or the Faroe Islands on 20 March 2015. Or maybe all of them, who knows?

The Day of The Outing

The alarm clock's stabbing bleep. You get up. Have breakfast. Wash your face and clean your teeth. Another day.

You walk the mile and a half to work. You're neither early nor late. Your shoes are shined, your shirt is ironed, your tie is firmly knotted. You are an office worker.

But something is different today. As you hang up your suit jacket and sit down in front of your PC, reach over to your right for the mail and faxes in your In tray, you sense that some of your colleagues - one man here, two men over there in the corner, a woman by the photocopier - are staring at you. As you stare back, they glance away, return to their tasks. Is something wrong you wonder? Have you missed something obvious?

Mary, the Clerical Assistant, empties your Out tray. She glances sideways at you, smiles a small complicit smile, then mutters: "I thought you probably were, you know. Just like my son."

"Pardon?" you say, but she walks away without another word.

It's left to Dawn to ask, as she's known to be friendly to you. Short, blonde and pretty, hailing from Manchester, she's thirty years old, married with three young children. Her desk faces yours. There have been rumours, none of them true, about the two of you, as is the way with large offices.

During the coffee break, she sits next to you.

"Simon, love, can we talk?" she says.

"Sure." You put your newspaper down unread on your lap.

"Simon, are you gay? Be honest with me."

You want to deny it, your insides instinctively clamming up, but you nod.

She touches your knee with her hand. "Don't worry, I won't tell anyone."

"How did you know?" You wonder if some man you've had sex with has spoken to her, somehow met her. But this is unlikely.

"I don't know how...I just *knew*. I'm sorry to be nosey, and I know it's none of my business really, but I had to ask."

"I'd have told you anyway, Dawn." If you'd had to. If you'd had no choice. As now. You can't tell a lie.

"Good." She smiles, pats you again on the knee as she stands up. "Must go, darling. I've got to powder my nose. See you later." A brittleness to her voice: you sense she hadn't suspected, the realisation was a shock to her. She walks in quick scissor-steps to the door.

You sit for a while, unable to concentrate on your newspaper. Words with all meaning blanked out, empty letters. People's eyes on you. You want to stand up and defy them, ask them what the hell they think they're staring at. But you don't. You stand and leave the room.

You gaze at your reflection in the mirror in the Gents'. Your face is no different: just the same as it always was, neither handsome nor ugly. There's a centimetre-wide patch of stubble under your left cheekbone that you missed as you shaved this morning. But otherwise nothing different. No brand on your forehead. But the other man here, washing his hands in the next basin, glances at you and makes a definite step away.

The door opens. In comes Anthony from the postroom, he of the fair curly hair and blue eyes that the women in the office half-fancy or like to mother. You've passed him many times, almost failed to notice him, but today it's different. Now, as soon as you see him, you know in your gut he's like you. He's gay. A look of recognition passes between you both; you begin to tremble, your hand shaking as you fumble with the tap. The man beside you hurries out.

Anthony puts his hand on the latch of a cubicle, turns to you and smiles. The door clicks shut behind him.

You have an erection: full, painful, pressing at the zip of your trousers. Were you at home you might masturbate, but here you press your crotch against the basin hoping that its coolness, even through two layers of fabric, can subdue this sudden access of lust.

For lust it is. Was Anthony inviting you to go into the cubicle with him? You could quite easily have done so. You could have fucked him. But something held you back: not just the illegality of the situation. It would be instant dismissal if you were caught. At seventeen, Anthony is below the legal age of consent. But he has a knowingness beyond his years: you wonder how many cocks he's had up his arse.

Your erection finally subsided, you go back down to the office.

The lunchtime news. The ashen face of the cabinet minister caught in flashbulb glare. He confesses that, yes, he is homosexual; yes, he has lived a lie; yes, he has voted for homophobic legislation. No-one is sure if he will resign - you think he will - but the Prime Minister is quoted as offering him his full confidence and support. Also, reports of unprovoked attacks on gay men: the attackers have told police they just *knew* the victim was... A gay spokesman suspects what has happened - still inexplicable - is some kind of anti-gay plot; he is concerned it provides a licence for queer-bashers. Someone else suggests that some new kind of truth serum may have been released into the water.

There is nothing else on the news. As you walk back to work, three teenage boys shout across the road to you: "Oi! *Poofter!*"

You keep on walking, head down, tense at the prospect of assault.

"Fucking poof!"

A teapot gesture: left arm akimbo, right arm limpwristed.

You shrug, hurry along. Fortunately they don't follow you, just shout: "Hope you die of AIDS, you fucking queer!"

And again, that afternoon, in the Gents: as you wash your hands, a man you vaguely know approaches you.

"'Ere, are you gay?"

You tense. An image of sudden violence: the man pushing your head forward, breaking your nose against the tap, the chips of bone driven up into your brain -

"Yes," you say, your armpits damp with sweat. "Yes, that's right. Yes I am. I'm gay."

You glance at him: late thirties, overweight. And, you sense, heterosexual. You keep your expression blank, in case the slightest smile be construed as a sexual advance.

"Well, fucking keep out of my way," he mutters.

Yes, I'm gay, you think. But that's not all I am.

You go into the office. There's a Post-It note folded in half, held upright by the keys of your PC. You open it - it says simply:
Simon -
Good luck. It doesn't make any difference to me.
A friend.
It's otherwise unsigned.

Dawn gives you a lift home. As she drives, there's silence. You - and, you sense, she - are reluctant to be the first to speak.

Then finally she says: "Well, at least they won't be talking about us any more, will they?" Incongruously, the Mancunian cadences in her voice have broadened in her otherwise neutral accent: you sense she finds this difficult to say. Her attempt at jollity falls flat.

You shrug.

"What are you going to do tonight?" she asks.

"Go out, I guess."

"To a gay club?"

"Well, I might as well. Not be defensive about it, I mean. Now everyone knows what I do in bed."

She shakes her head vigorously. "I don't want to know." You can see she finds the idea hard to cope with.

She pulls up outside your flat.

"Well, now we can both moan about the men in our lives," you say.

Dawn smiles thinly. "And bitch about ladders in tights and chipped nail polish."

Drag is not your scene, but you don't correct her; you're simply glad she's beginning to cope with what she's learned about you. As you unfasten your safety belt, she puts her hand on your elbow. "Simon, take care. I'm *concerned* about you - a lot of us are."

"Thank you, I will." On an impulse, you kiss her on the cheek. You've only ever kissed at Christmas; she hides her surprise with a smile. You wave as she drives away.

A photograph of the headmaster, black and white and blurry as if taken on the run. Round-faced, jowly, balding, deep crow's feet like scratchmarks in putty. As soon as his penchant for young boys was discovered - *you could see it, just by looking at him:* a soundbite - he was dismissed from his post. He is considering legal action. *Prove it,* he says.

What has happened dominates today's news. Many of the great and the good have been forced to admit their hitherto-concealed sexual preferences. Some have resigned; others are quoted as being determined to weather the storm. A trade union spokesman voices his concern that "this happening" will put many members' jobs at risk. Will it be an instant rejection-factor in interviews? What about insurance?

A psychic denies any involvement. A libertarian organisation is scrutinising hours of videotape for evidence of mass hypnosis, subliminal imagery or other tampering.

After half an hour of this you become sated, and turn off the TV just as a panel of experts begin a discussion.

You go out. A packet of condoms and a tube of KY jelly goes in your coat pocket. It's been a while since you've had sex. You've told yourself you can do without it, but something inside you responds to the prospect: you have been starved.

Your answering machine has five messages, four from friends, one from your sister (who, alone in your family, knows you are gay - your stomach clenches at the thought of meeting your parents again, and what will this happening tell you about them?). All are asking after you, anxious. You ring none of them back: that's for later, tomorrow maybe.

The town's gay club, Karina's, is fifteen minutes away on foot. You remember its opening, a year ago. Furious letters and editorials in the (right-leaning) local press. Fulminations about declining standards (after the town's sex shop was forced to close). The actual opening was a comparative non-event. There's more trouble in the pub on the other side of town than with Karina's ostensibly mixed but mostly male clientele.

You've visited the club now and then, nervous that someone might recognise you. (Now you, like everyone else, are out, it doesn't matter.)

As you check in your coat and make your way to the bar, you sense much of the crowd turning to look at you. Have you violated the dress-code? They're checking you out.

"Hello, Simon! How goes it?" You turn, distracted. It's Pete, a large man with a bristly haircut. You've met him before, had sex with him a couple of times. "You okay?"

"Yes. It's been quite a day."

"Hasn't it just. Let me get you a drink. It's payday."

Pete is married with two children; his wife knows about, but turns a blind eye to, his gay lifestyle as long as he plays it safe. Pete hands you your drink. "No room to move in here tonight, eh? No chance to sit down."

"I thought I'd better come along," you say.

"Gesture of solidarity, eh? Show your face. Know what you mean. Stick together after what's gone on, that's why I'm here. You weren't out, were you?"

You shake your head.

"Can't say I was, except to the wife and a few friends. Still, should be able to weather the storm. Not like Matt, poor bastard was on the phone to me earlier, sobbing his guts out. Thinks he's going to lose his job." (Matt is a primary schoolteacher.) "Thinks they think he's going to fiddle with all the little boys, or they're scared the parents'll think so."

At first you consider taking Pete home tonight: at least sex with him will have the comfort of familiarity. But he says: "Not cruising tonight, Simon. Just thought I'd show the old face. Got to get back to the kids - the wife's at her evening class tonight."

You smile. "There's domesticity for you."

He chuckles. "Don't get married." He slaps you on the back.

You buy another drink then turn away from the bar. You see through the crowd, between the heads, the proportionally-small, steamed-up windows. They seem far away, but you could reach them in ten good strides were the floor clear. It's full tonight: you think of what has happened (an event with no name, at least not yet) as something as simple as removing the cork from an overpressurised bottle. You can sense the relief on many faces: whatever may be in store for them - bad as well as good - at least they don't have to *hide*.

Someone taps your left shoulder; you turn to see no-one there. Anthony, in a leather jacket, is standing on your right.

"Well well well," he says. "So we meet again. I haven't seen you here before."

"I haven't been here very often."

"Too *local* for you, is it?"

You say nothing. Unaccountably you feel nervous in his presence, at his self-assurance. He's half a head shorter than you, and plump. Why should you be afraid of him? *Afraid* is the wrong word; more, *wary*.

"You going to buy me a drink, then?" he says, his blue eyes unblinking. "Mine's a Fosters."

As you wait at the bar, you wonder if Someone intends you to end this evening with Anthony. He walked in here as if he owned the place: he must be a regular. Who knows how many men here he's fucked at one time or another? More than you, for sure.

He's turned away from you. Sizing up the talent, you think. You can see why many women at work secretly (or not so secretly) fancy him: blond hair, blue eyes, round pink face. He's undoubtedly a pretty boy. You watch his chubby arse, in tight chinos. You think of pulling down those trousers, planting your cock between those two fleshy globes. You could do worse, far worse.

You carry his drink to him. "Thanks," he says. He disappears into the crowd. "See you later."

At ten o'clock, you decide enough is enough and you go to leave: Anthony is at the door.

"Leaving so soon?" he says.

"Thought I'd better be going," you mutter. "I've got to get up early in the morning," you lie.

"Going home alone? Come, come. What sort of queen are you?"

You want to ask him: *Come home with me,* but nervousness paralyses your throat.

"Come back to my place," he says. "But we'll get another round in first, why not eh?"

Finally, at ten past eleven, you leave with Anthony. It's a cold night, your breath frosting in the air; the chill takes away the light-headedness of four pints.

It's pub closing-time, and you tense as groups of men, many of them holding women's hands or with their arms about their waists, spill out of the doors. If any of them notice you and Anthony, sense you're both gay and take offence...you fear for your life.

"Don't worry," says Anthony. "You're safe. I've fucked at least two guys in that crowd."

"Is there anyone you haven't fucked?"

"God gave me a prick and an arsehole. All I'm doing is using them."

You turn off the main road and follow Anthony through a network of side streets to the house he shares. A large Edwardian house, converted into bedsits. As Anthony lets you in the front door, he whispers: "Try not to make any noise. Jason has to get up early - he and Trish are light sleepers."

"Do they know you're gay?"

He nods. "Uh-huh. I've got a better sex life than any of them."

You follow him upstairs, to his room at the back of the house. He turns the light on. The heating is very low, barely working at all. In one corner of the room, an unmade bed. A gay pin-up calendar is tacked to a board above a desk, and a large stack of copies of *Gay Times*, *Attitude* and *Boyz* tilts alarmingly on the floor underneath.

Anthony shuts the door behind you.

"Talk first or fuck first?"

"Talk first," you say.

"Right, I'll make coffee then."

You sit and drink.

"You know," says Anthony, "I'd never have figured you as gay."

"How do you mean?"

"I never got...that feeling. I'm usually quite good at that sort of thing."

"Now everyone's 'quite good at that sort of thing'."

"That's true."

"Do you know what's caused it?"

"Fuck knows. Some boffin'll figure it out. As I said, I thought you were straight. Maybe latent and ashamed of it, but basically straight."

"Thanks a lot. I knew I was gay when I was ten."

"Me too. Probably even earlier than that."

"I'm sure people thought the same of you."

"Oh yeah, people always assume you're straight unless you're an obvious mincing queen. I'm eighteen in a couple of months. Two more months of pretending I haven't found a nice girl. Have you ever fucked a woman?"

At first you don't want to answer. You remember, back at school, fellow pupils bragging that they'd *done it,* they'd *scored,* they'd *gone all the way.* The shame of admitting you were a virgin (as you were, until you were twenty). "No. Have you?" you ask with strained levity.

"Uh-huh. What's it like? It's different, not as tight as arse. Not my sort of thing of course - not into cunt. But I can see what straight guys like about it." A pause, then he continues: "It was back at school. There was this guy I fancied, captain of the football team. That's how I got into playing football - I was never all that good at it, just okay in midfield - to be near him. When he was in the showers - well, I'm no size queen, but he had this whacking great cock, biggest one I'd ever seen. Hung like a fucking donkey. It was all I could do not to give myself away by staring at it and getting hard myself.

"Anyway, he invited me back to his place one evening, and I slept over in the spare room. Well, this guy was beautiful, but he was dumb as shit. He was terminally straight; I had no chance. As I lay in bed, I heard the door open - it was his Mum, in this skimpy little nightie. Before I knew it, she'd pulled my sheets back, pulled my pyjama trousers down, climbed into bed with me and had my cock in her mouth.

"That was more than enough for me. I fucked her.

"Of course, I did better with another guy in the football team. In that case, I scored - "

"Pun unintended," you say.

He smiles thinly, but you sense he begrudges the interruption to his perfectly-wrought story. "I got him to blow me, and his Dad screwed me. More coffee?"

"No thanks." It's strong coffee, and you know it'll keep you awake all night, your bladder full.

He takes another sip of his drink. "There's another woman I've fucked. Guess who."

"I've no idea."

"I'll give you a clue: works in your office."

"I don't know." Many of the women mother Anthony, but you can't imagine any of them wanting to have sex with him.

"How about, sits opposite you?"

As you realise who he means, you want to resist the thought. But Anthony laughs and spells it out: "That's right, Dawn Stephens."

"I don't believe you."

He grins broadly. "It's *true*."

You don't want to believe him. If you were to turn straight - as you wished through many fraught adolescent nights before you finally accepted you were gay - you would like it to be with Dawn. Is it true you quietly fancy her? You've known some longtime gay men who've fallen in love with women, and straight men who've turned gay, to their great consternation. You know such an earthquake-shift in sexual identity is possible. Would this aura (for want of a better word) that everyone can now see change accordingly? Anthony's revelation (or is it a boast? a tall tale?) has hit you in a tender spot. And he knows it.

"I don't believe you," you say. "Prove it."

He spreads his hands. "How can I? It's not like I kept a pair of her knickers, is it?"

"I can't imagine it. Not *her.*"

"I'll tell you how it happened. I was walking home one night and it was raining, really pissing down. Dawn pulled up in her car beside me and told me to get in. She drove me home. I said thank you (I'm a polite boy) and I asked her if she wanted to come in for coffee. She hesitated, but said yes. Her old man was away on business and her kids were staying with their Gran. It was the first time she'd been on her own for ages.

"Anyway, I made her coffee. She was sitting right there, where you're sitting now. She seemed uncomfortable. I asked her why.

"'I'm all tensed up,' she said.

"'Let me,' I said, and I gave her a shoulder massage. As I did it, I saw she had tears in her eyes. I asked her why she was crying, and she just spilled her guts. Everything had got on top of her. The kids were playing up, she was sure her old man was being unfaithful, and because she was on her own she realised how lonely she was.

"Anyway, by this time I'd put my arms around her. She slipped her arms around my neck in a clinch and kissed me, and took hold of my hand and put it on her left tit. I unbuttoned her blouse. She had a black bra on, one of those tied at the front with one of those little ribbon things. She's actually got very nice tits, quite big - she dresses down too much. She really ought to show them off a bit more. Oh, if you want proof, she's got a mole just under her left nipple.

"To cut a long story short, I fucked her. Only the once, though. It was the right thing at the right time. You couldn't repeat it and we didn't try. We knew better than that."

He could be lying; he could be telling the truth. You don't know. If he wanted to find a pressure point, he's unerringly done so: you consider Dawn a friend and here's Anthony presenting your friendship with her as something very shallow - there's a whole side to this supposed friend you didn't know about. You look at him. His aura shows him to be unequivocally homosexual: no hint of heterosexuality. But can it show such subtle gradations, or have you not yet learned to see them?

"We've talked enough," he says. "Let's fuck."

You stand. Still seated, he pulls his T-shirt off over his head. His hairless chest, the puffy flesh about his nipples.

"Come on then," he says, hands on the zip of his fly. "Get those trousers off."

Getting your rocks off. A transaction: you knew as much before you arrived here. You unbutton your trousers, let them slide to the floor. Your cock is stiffening, pushing out the front of your underpants.

Anthony kneels and reaches up behind you, kneads your buttocks through the fabric of your underpants. He tugs the garment down. He leans forward, his lips curled back over his teeth, and takes your cock into his mouth. You clutch at his scalp, tangling your fingers in his hair as he sucks you and you feel a tightening inside. You put your head back, and close your eyes. You come with a gasp.

Silence. You open your eyes

"Take your shirt off," Anthony says.

You do this, sitting on the end of the bed, as you watch him remove his trousers and underpants. He puts on a condom. "Lie on your front."

You do so, shifting to get comfortable, slightly raising yourself to receive him. He rests his hands flat on the bed either side of you, positions himself and enters you.

He's not gentle as he fucks you. You hear his ragged breathing, his mouth close to your ear. Finally he tenses, then thrusts even deeper in and climaxes with a grunt. He pulls himself out of you and slumps on the bed beside you. You lie there, your buttocks exposed to the air, the fine hairs on your legs rigid in the cool air.

He goes outside to dispose of his condom, then returns. He lies on his back on the bed, his limp cock tilting to one side. He reaches out to his bedside table, takes a cigarette from a packet and lights it. As he smokes, he becomes aware of you watching.

"Yes?" he says. "Do you want something?"

"No."

"Well, get dressed, then. I'll see you in work tomorrow."

Well, you think, you've had sex tonight - that was what you set out to do, wasn't it? You have sex, or can get it - more often than previously, if you put your mind to it. What you don't have is love.

"You know the way out," says Anthony.

The night is cold on your face as you walk the mile home. It's after midnight and the streets are quiet: the pubs have closed but the nightclubs are open for another two hours yet. You're glad of this: you don't want to be picked on by drunks or gay-bashers. A woman is walking in the same direction as you; you cross the road to avoid seeming to follow her. You wonder why you do this: one glance at you - especially after today - would tell her you have no sexual interest in her, and you hope you don't seem threatening. You glance back at her: heterosexual, as far as you can tell. You wonder who she is, how she got here, is she happy? You could ask her, but you don't. You're six feet tall, she five feet four at the very most - who knows what you look like looming out of the darkness? There's still endless room for error.

In your flat you make yourself a cup of decaffeinated coffee as you play back the two messages on your answer machine. There's Dawn, her voice tremulous as it always is on the phone, asking if you want to come to her thirtieth birthday party next month. You can bring a guest. *But I don't have a partner,* you think. The other message is a male voice shouting abuse: "You queer bastard, you'll burn in hell, how many little boys have you buggered today?" You turn it off. Is it someone from work? You hope it's no-one you know: never have you heard bigotry and hatred so naked. Hopefully the caller won't ring again, or you'll have to take some action.

There's nothing that takes your interest on late-night TV. You wish you'd recorded *Newsnight:* hopefully someone might have some explanation for today's event. Someone somewhere, someone more scientific than you, must surely know the answer.

As you lie in bed waiting for sleep, you try to think of nothing, as anything could happen.

Thunderhead

Storm Scene

Lightning, and momentarily the iron-grey sky is white. Less than a second later comes thunder in its wake, an open-throated roar. Rain falls hard and vertical, bouncing pellets off the roofs of parked cars, prickling puddles into hedgehog spines. Trees bend in the whistling howl of the wind.

Flash.

So safe in here. Briony presses her face, her palms, against the window, watching the storm. The crash of thunder. She shivers. Her breath mists a circle on the window. She presses the length of her body against the cold glass, closer still. Her heart is palpitating, her breathing ragged. With the next flash and crash she closes her eyes, her nostrils flared, her lips parted.

In her mind she travels out, through the glass, outside its protection. Where it cannot save her from the lightning searing her sight, the thunder her hearing, so much brighter and louder now. Where the rain comes down on her, reducing her hair to a straggle, filling her mouth and nostrils and soaking through her clothes so rapidly it's as if she's naked. Where she's powerless in the dark and violent heart of the storm. At one with it, its force inside her, its kick inside her brain, its coursing through her body to her fingers and toes. Its full strength would overwhelm and obliterate her in an instant, but a little of it she can take inside her. And control.

Phone Call (1)

"Hello?"
      "Briony...?"
      "Hello?"
      "Briony, it's me – Paul."

"Hello, Paul."
"Are you okay?"
"Yes, I'm okay."
"Thank God. I was afraid the phone lines'd be down."
"No, they're not."
"I can see that. Look, I'm not going to be able to get home, love. No trains are running in this weather."
"Oh, right."
"Look, are you okay?"
"Yes, I'm okay."
"You seem a little...disconnected."
"No, I'm okay."
"Sure?"
"*Yes.*"
"Take care. I'll see you tomorrow."
Click.

Wet Through: A Memory

Briony is at the window, watching the rain, when Paul comes home. He staggers inside, shaking out his umbrella. His hair is flattened, white streaks of scalp visible through the smeared wet black lines.

"Jesus," he says. "*Christ.* What a cloudburst."

He stands on one leg and pulls off his shoe. He tips it up and a thimbleful of water pours out. His clothes are heavy and clinging.

"I'm wet through."

"Stay right there." She hurries to get a towel. He undresses and she rubs him down. The hairs on his arms, his fleshy buttocks, his rounded stomach, lie like smudged streaks. With the wet and cold, his penis has shrunk into itself.

"It's a mess, isn't it? Got caught in the rain." He flicks water at her.

"Hey, stop it! You'll get my blouse wet."

"Then you'll just have to take it off, then..."

Her smile twists up at the corner. "Then you'll just have to rub me down, won't you...?"

"Mmmm, that's a tempting thought..."

The towel is soaked; she fetches a new one and continues to dry him. Through the cloth she feels his limp penis slowly stiffening.

Phone Call (2)

She reaches across the bed for the phone. "Hello?" The voice at the other end is crackly. "Hello?" she says. When he answers, she says flatly: "Hello, Paul." Why is her husband ringing her up now?

The other man has his arms about her. She lies on her side, one leg draped lightly over his hip. He draws her T-shirt and bra-strap away from her shoulder, kisses and nuzzles the bare warm skin. She bats at him playfully with her fingers.

"Yes, I'm okay."

He runs his hands up her sides under the T-shirt, tracing the swell of her hips, the sharp butterfly points of her pelvic bone, the incurve of her waist, round to her back to tug at the tight elastic of her bra.

"No, they're not."

He fumbles with the clasp. Her brow creases in annoyance. *So inept. That wasn't the idea.* "Oh, right," she says. He unhooks it at last, then lifts up her T-shirt and touches her nipple with the tip of his tongue.

"Yes, I'm okay." Annoyance. "No, I'm okay." A soothing voice.

He kneels on the bed and lifts up her legs, resting them on his shoulders. A sudden urge to giggle; she immediately stifles it. Slowly he draws her knickers up, pulling slowly away from the white buttocks, the untanned part of her.

"*Yes.*" Said both to the man on the phone and the man on her bed.

Her Incubus

The other man. His name is Adam. That's what she calls him.

She watches him lying on the bed facing her. She runs her fingers along his side, marvelling at the firmness, the solidity of his flesh. He has blond curly hair and blue eyes. Blue as water, blue as ice.

The texture, the detail... As if he might dissolve into the storm from whence he came.

Her hand rests in the thick mat of hair on his chest, lazily traces a ring about his nipple.

His only garment is a black jockstrap. She runs her hand down his washboard-flat chest, cups the bulge with her hand.

He stands up, turns away from her. With a swift movement he removes the jockstrap. She drapes her arms about his waist, runs her tongue down the base of his spine, kisses and nuzzles his tight buttocks. She reaches round and strokes his jutting penis; at first softly, then more vigorously.

My Adonis. My secret lover.
My incubus.

Storm Warning

It's been humid for days; the sky is a sickly grey. There'll be a storm tonight. The Met Office has issued an official warning: Stay indoors. Do not travel unless absolutely necessary.

Briony drives homewards. Her clothes, so apt earlier, seem unfitting now: sleeveless top, short skirt, sunglasses. Her skirt has ridden up beneath her, and the undersides of her thighs are red and sore from where the plastic car seat has scorched a line across them.

She stops at a petrol station. She fills the tank, then goes in to pay. The man behind the counter is a six-footer, ten inches taller than her. He makes conversation. She's aware he's taking a long look at the tops of her breasts. Caging her with his gaze. She tenses inside: stiffens her shoulders, tautens her chin and cheekbones. Warding-off signals. Is he astute enough to read them?

She pays and leaves, aware of his eyes on her back as she walks away.

As she drives the few remaining miles home, she sees it ahead of her in the sky. The thunderhead. A massy lump of dark-grey cumulonimbus, flattened at the top like an anvil, rimmed with light. The wind is stronger now, as if the thunderhead is sucking everything into itself, into its black heart.

In the Bedroom

Only the bedside lamp is on, its weak-tea light barely filling the room, casting long shadows. They are both naked. She lies on her back on the floor, his head between her thighs.

A lightning flash turns the curtains momentarily white. She hears a splintering and a tearing from outside, then a *thump* that makes the floor vibrate. A tree must have been hit, perhaps that big oak outside. She pads over to the window. But she cannot see out. Tangles of raindrops blur her sight.

He stands behind her, his hand caressing the swell of her hip.

Another flash and the lamp fizzes and dies. Darkness. Not even the red LED display of the alarm clock. The power has failed.

Another flash and she sees his silhouette against the curtain.

She drops to her knees, her buttocks spreading slightly as they rest on her calves. She holds his waist for support. She leans forward, lightly closes her eyes and takes his penis into her mouth.

Spectral Crown

Paul watches through his car window. He has stopped in a lay-by and reclined his seat. He curls his legs up into his stomach, knotting and unknotting his muscles to get comfortable. He clutches his blanket to himself, but the cold seeps into his bones nonetheless.

The radio is useless, unlistenable. Too much static. He thinks of ringing Briony again on the carphone, just to make sure she's all right.

He pictures her: sexy little Briony. Everyone wanted to dance with her at the office party, Briony in heels and that short black dress, two inches of cleavage. Many of them did, slow dance after slow dance. He stood at the side and watched them.

Of course she's okay. She's at home. Safe and warm. It's me I have to worry about.

He's cold. He won't sleep. He has nothing to do but wait.

In the distance he sees the nearby town, a patch of deeper darkness amongst the hills. Lightning curls about the tallest building, a spectral crown.

Climax

Finally he moves on top of her. She slides her legs apart and feels him enter her. His greater weight presses down on her, sinks her into the mattress. Her fingers scrabble on his sweatslick back. She gasps and moans, her eyes closing, her mouth opening, her back arching. Her thighs clasp his waist and he thrusts thrusts thrusts into her. Her climax is a sigh and a scream combined.

Lightning Strike

Paul shivers in his blanket. The storm is overhead now. The lightning flash and thunderclap are simultaneous.

Each flash bathes him in blue light, leaving red and green afterimages.

And then an especially vivid flash, outlining the black bonefingers of a tree. In the distance, an explosion.

The tree is moving.

Impossible. How – ?

He has only a second to realise what has happened before the tree comes crashing down on his car. He feels little pain, just the sensation of his mouth filling with blood which spills over his clothes and the seat.

Aftermath

Briony awakes. She has slept fitfully. She puts on a dressing-gown and slippers and goes downstairs to the kitchen. The electricity is still out, so she lights the gas stove with a match and heats a saucepan of water for coffee. As she drinks it she sits on a stool and looks out the window.

The storm has left its wake of destruction. The patio is strewn with leaves and scattered fragments of the wooden fence. Out in the woods, although she doesn't know it yet, trees have snapped off halfway down their trunks and lie in a heap like so many matchsticks.

Did I do this? Briony thinks.

An Act of God. Force majeure. A wide area is in chaos. Remote villages are inaccessible, the roads cut off by fallen trees, electricity and telephone lines down, gas mains broken. Polythene has been seen blown in the wind, wrapping itself round pylons, causing them to short-circuit.

Briony bends forward, runs her fingers through her hair. Silence, the bone-weariness of exhaustion. The power has had its way with her, toyed with her, left her drained.

Reports of fatalities are slowly coming in. An old woman died when her chimney collapsed. A teenage boy was struck by lightning, the rain dousing his burning clothes. Emergency teams are working overtime to clear the roads, the major ones first. Electricity and telephone services will be restored as soon as possible, but in the more remote areas it'll be several days before it's done.

Briony sits alone.

This Flight Tonight

[co-written with D.F. Lewis]

Ten minutes before he died, Andrew James Crichton selected a drink from the bar. A single Southern Comfort with ice. He pushed away the remains of his in-flight meal and gazed out of the window at the deep blue of the sky. At 30,000 feet he could look down at the clouds, thick and drawn up into ice-cream peaks, or single tufts like cotton-wool.

Five minutes before he died, he continued to sip at his drink. He switched on his laptop. Two minutes later, feeling distracted, he gazed up at the seatbelt sign, which was unlit. He was lost in a reverie for a minute and a half before he returned to the laptop.

He was so engrossed, all he knew was a loud roaring in his ears, intense heat and splintering, and a sense of infinite space around him as he fell.

*

Statistically more people are killed every year on the roads than in the air, but air disasters are more newsworthy. A car accident will normally kill at most four or five people, maybe seven or eight, but unless it's a major pileup it won't make the news. And because it takes place on terra firma, it's more survivable. A plane crash will eliminate more than a hundred people at once, and if your vehicle disintegrates several miles up you have no chance.

*

There's a sick feeling in Jane's stomach as she sits down and fastens her seatbelt. It's not the wine she drunk the evening before, at their wedding reception. After they'd made love, Simon slept easily, strange bed and all, and woke up refreshed. Jane tossed and turned all night. It was the thought of this flight, her first since the bomb which tore apart that 747 and everyone on board. Including her father.

After the take-off, after that rushing of blood to parts of the body gravity normally fails to reach, Jane gains comfort from the ordinariness of her surroundings. A stretched-out hotel foyer. Simon, by her side, leans back. A man, across the aisle, tapping at his laptop. The plane's hum of power, a throbbing which could easily be mistaken for a deep-throated central heating system. She relaxes. A honeymoon is not a time to allow an embolism into the mind: a memory of a father who died after surely comforting himself with similar ordinariness.

*

Statistically more people die before their predetermined mind-stop than otherwise...and so they hover onward like misbegotten memory forces - or anachronistic ghosts - blotting up further thoughts and, yes, memories. They skim and soar in the same air through which sleek metal monsters divert them into a mixed backwash of mentalities.

*

Peter Clayton had risen that morning, not knowing he was to fly later in the day. Business trips were often abruptly arranged by the Director in charge of his area. Based in London, Peter often flies to Birmingham or Manchester or Glasgow or Edinburgh or Southampton. Not for him the nervousness of the infrequent flier; nor the boredom of the long-haul traveller. An hour to check in, an hour to fly, and he is at his destination, fuelled by plastic-wrapped food and airline coffee. All airports are basically the same - the details and language spoken may differ - but there is no plunge into disorientating strangeness. Later in the day he returns, sustained through the tedium of the meeting by company catering - all laid on, of course: keep the important delegates happy.

   Today, Manchester; next week, Dublin, the location of the farthest-flung present, a pretty thirty-year-old redhead called Roisín, representing the company's Irish holdings. A few months ago, in an overnight stop in a Glasgow hotel, in an excess of loneliness he and Roisín made love. A moment in time, nothing more: a meeting of tired bodies and bored minds. Now and then he thinks of her: of her slim boyish figure, her small breasts and tight upward-pointing nipples, the sensation as her legs clasped his hips and he slid warmly into her. *It never happened.* The next morning they went separately to breakfast and were later debating fervently from either side of the meeting table. It never happened: he has a wife and three children he adores. He's forty years old, with thinning hair, a developing spare tyre and a blood-pressure problem; Roisín is ten years younger than him, unmarried but with a live-in boyfriend of two years' standing. The hurt they'd cause if what they did became known, and the consequent misinterpretation: they'd meant no harm, it was just a gesture of friendship. *It never happened.*

*

Jane watches the landscape veer away, as roads become lines and fields green and brown mosaic tiles - a flush of white as they break through the clouds. The sign ahead of her still burns its red message: FASTEN SEAT BELTS. Her hand inches sideways and meets Simon's. He wraps his fingers about hers.

She remembers the dream she had sometime during last night's fitful sleep. She was on a plane similar to this one. She tapped a passing stewardess on the arm. "Excuse me...?" The stewardess turned; instead of her face there was a skull. Jane screamed. She jumped past the stewardess, who reached for her, her bony fingers touching the fabric of Jane's blouse but sliding off as Jane ran up the aisle. She reached the cockpit and tugged at the door -

"Excuse me, Madam, you're not allowed in there - "

- and finally she forced it open. It was noisier in the cockpit, and as she half-stepped, half-stumbled in, the co-pilot turned. His face was another skull. And the pilot's face too. As she stood there and screamed, she saw through the window the plane's nose tilt downwards until she could see no clouds no sky just the ground rushing up faster faster and faster -

She woke up choking back a scream. Simon was there, holding her, soothing her.

"Are you okay?" Simon asks, bringing her back to the present. The sky: an intense unbroken blue. The clouds below: a thick clotted white.

"I'll get you a drink," he says. "You're shaking like a leaf."

As he reaches past her to attract the stewardess's attention, Jane lightly closes her eyes. Her blouse is damp under the armpits, her sweat glands defying her antiperspirant. *Face your fears.* Well, so far she has done this. That was her first take-off. *Overcome your fears.* As if by shining a light on them they shrink, become trivial, instead of letting them lurk in darkness, your imagination doing the rest. She feels light-headed. *It's the pressure: hold your nose and pop your eardrums.* Well, if she is to overcome her fears, what better than an hour-long flight from Heathrow to Dublin? *Short and sweet - soon be over.*

*

Peter Clayton spends the hour's flight reading through the paperwork he'll need to get through before tomorrow's meeting. He breaks for the in-flight meal - lamb chop and creamed potatoes and green beans - and towards the end of the flight gives up reading and stares out at the darkening sky over Manchester. He thinks of collecting his luggage after disembarking, then the bus into the city centre and the at-first-overwhelming largeness of Piccadilly Square, and then checking into the hotel. He'll phone Helen, his wife, then there'll be the evening to kill. Hopefully Roisín will be there; they'll share a drink for old times' sake. Old times: the memory of that never-mentioned, half-denied infidelity.

In fact she's in the queue ahead of him, waiting to register. The only woman there, amidst all the anonymous men in suits. At first he doesn't recognise her, not even when she turns to face him: her hair has been cut to collar-length and she's wearing wire-rimmed full-moon glasses. It makes her look older, more like her actual age instead of just out of her teens. She waves to him and after she's registered walks back down the queue to where he's standing. "Hi."

"Hello Roisín, how are you?"

"I'm fine, thanks. How was your flight?"

"Oh, nothing special."

She touches her hand to his elbow. "You going to have dinner with me?"

"I had something to eat on the plane."

Head-and-shoulders shorter, she gazes up at him with something he reads as disappointment. Atavistic gallantry gnaws at him.

"But I'm still hungry," he says.

She smiles.

The meal doesn't live up to expectations. Roisín, changed into a lavender-coloured top and black leggings, eats voraciously. Peter forces himself to finish his meal, knowing he'll have to do some exercise to burn it off. He feels bloated as he stands up and they move to the bar. He has a second drink although he knows he shouldn't; he feels himself become light-headed.

Conversation remains on the surface: how are his wife and children, how is her boyfriend Seamus (fiancé now), company gossip - the substance of many past face-to-face, phone and email conversations. As he slides into tipsiness, he slips his arm about her shoulders. He senses her discomfort, but she doesn't resist. He thinks guiltily that he hasn't rung Helen, but he feels in no condition to do so. At ten o'clock, Roisín yawns.

"Long day. I need to go to bed."

He escorts her to her room, one floor below his. They say goodbye. He wants to kiss her; he's tempted to reach out and put his hand on her breast. But he knows he shouldn't. And he doesn't.

*

Statistically, Andrew James Crichton was one of those exceptions that prove the law of averages - by accidentally dying at the *precise* moment he was meant to die - which made everybody else on the plane victims of synchronicity, spear-carriers in the unique drama of self-reality.

*

Soon be over. Jane notices that the laptop has ceased tapping.

She glances towards the man whose name she'll likely never know. She can just discern the gold-embossed initials AJC on his samsonite briefcase, its black cuboid untidily tilted on the spare seat next to the aisle.

Probably an executive or maybe a politician. He probably needs to sleep. Such thoughts allow her to maintain equilibrium - as if altruism is an aid to safety.

Planes and spiders, her only known phobias, she thinks. No spiders on planes, though - unless they get in with the food or cargo. *Do spiders have phobias?* Her wandering thoughts are akin to returning to dream, but not quite.

AJC, she sees, is indeed sleeping, just as she must have done when dreaming for real.

Simon too now is sleeping. *Sweet dreams, Simon. Sweet dreams, AJC - whoever you are.*

Soon be over.

*

He should have made a move. Peter Clayton is only Peter Clayton by virtue of his impulses. His whole career up to the age of forty has been a series of unexpected moves from company to company, each one a slight jump up the ladder. His current job in itself comprises surprising changes of plan, with meetings galore abruptly cropping up for the firm's troubleshooter - as he describes himself. He has sometimes spent a whole week chasing meetings without ever attending one of them. Ever a more important meeting around the next corner. Late cancellations. Sudden appointments. Chasing crises. Chasing shadows. Chasing...

Hang his blood pressure! Cabin fever, nothing more.

He needs a cuddle. Roisín now asleep just one floor below. What a waste of resources!

He hears the sound of long-haul aeroplanes plying their invisible paths above the Manchester hotel. Their droning - although a sign of humanity - enhances the night's solitude. He thinks of Helen and the kids, nearly cries - but falls asleep before remembering why he wants to cry.

He dreams of a plane crashing. He watches from a creeky terrain as it banks steeply, then seeming to splutter to a halt. No sooner seen, it slices into some far-off trees with a splintering roar. It is up to him to scramble across the squishy marshes to save any survivors. He is horrified when he arrives on the scene. The flaming trough which the nosecone of the plane has divotted is at least a highrise-block deep. A number of passengers still trying to clamber out, despite the ferocity of the fire: they are flickering shadows, actually part of the living flame. The plane itself seems to have disappeared altogether. Surely it can't have taken off again, after allowing the maimed and half-dead to disembark? The fire-pit created by the crash gradually relinquishes its imitation of a long vertical volcano, but dark perforations and fragile black sculptures of ash still float intermittently upwards from the former core. He squints into the sky where he can just discern the wrecked aeroplane gliding with the large black birds...

Peter Clayton is woken by a soft tap-tap on his bedroom door, as if someone is typing out a message. He hopes it's Roisín with her own share of impulse.

"Come in," he says.

*

As he fell, Andrew James Crichton thought: *Is this what it's like to die?* Deep azure sky above him, sun shining bright on white clouds below. To his satisfaction he learned that what he was always told was true: his life flashed before him. He saw again himself at school, at university; he remembered how he lost his virginity at the age of seventeen; he met again his wife. He saw through a mist of tears his only child Jane pulled bloodily from his wife's vagina, her first gurgling scream.

Then he fell into a cloud.

As far as he could see was greyish white. The only direction indicator was the sun, above him. He couldn't breathe - a burning in his lungs - as he fell. And finally - a matter of seconds in real time - the white darkened, became red, then black, as Andrew died.

Minutes later his body hit the Atlantic.

And, somewhere else, someone drew out his life's thread, lined up the scissors, and cut.

*

Her bladder full, Jane undoes her seatbelt and stands up. She glances down at Simon, asleep now. His head lolls to one side, exposing his double chin. *You really must exercise more,* she thinks. She doesn't want to nag, but she sees Simon in ten years, after his sedentary job has taken its toll: puffy-faced, face mottled with broken blood-vessels, a spare tyre.

She's a little unsteady on her feet, her legs numb from sitting down. The plane is on a tilt: the windows to her right face upwards into the sky, the sun burning out the blue; to her left, she can see through a gap in the clouds the Irish Sea, grey-green flecked with white. She can see individual waves.

She walks the length of the aisle to the toilet. It's occupied. She stands there, stepping aside to let the stewardess pass. The stewardess - Jane can read her namebadge: GRAÍNNE O'HARA, a real Irish name - smiles at her. "All right?"

Purse-lipped, Jane nods, smiles politely in return, and watches Grainne O'Hara's retreating back. Professional to a fault: Jane is just one more nervous passenger. There are probably many like her.

The toilet door opens and a middle-aged man, with thinning hair, overweight, comes out. He smiles encouragingly at her as he returns to his seat.

I must look nervous, thinks Jane as she shuts the door behind herself. She's always been small - her full height is five feet one - slim-built, looking younger than her years. She seems to inspire men to want to protect her, always older men. From her father onwards.

Her father. She rarely thinks of him now. She was six when he died: his face is a vague blur. The man in the old photographs is almost a stranger to her, even in the picture of him with her one-year-old self on his lap. She remembers more vividly her mother, racked with grief, bent over and crying. The grey shell of a woman she was in the ten years before she died.

After she has finished, she pulls up her underwear and straightens her skirt. She walks back down the aisle and sits again next to Simon. He is still asleep. She crosses her legs, reaches out and puts her hand on his knee. *Let me protect you for a change,* she thinks. She's calmer now, but there's still the landing to come and of course the return flight. *But I've got this far. It's not so bad.*

She gazes out of the windows to her left. The plane is tilting in the opposite direction, lifting up and away from the seascape. In his seat AJC is still asleep.

*

The knock on the door again. "Come in," Peter repeats, before realising that he's locked the door from the inside. He gets up from the bed and opens it.

Roisín stands in the corridor. Her hair is loose to her shoulders, and she is wearing a long bottle-green-and-red-squared dressing-gown. It's open just below her knees, and he can see the lace hem of her nightdress and below that her slim hairless legs and her feet in blue fluffy slippers.

"Roisín..."

"I couldn't sleep," she says. "There's - just something. I can't explain it."

"Come in."

Her words skitter from her mouth; she seems much less composed, much less poised than she is by day. He's only seen her once before like this - that night they made love.

She sits on the armchair, he on his bed.

"Is it just because it's a strange bed?" he says.

She shakes her head. "No, it's not that. It's not the nightclub on the ground floor. I've slept through worse than that, believe me. I just can't sleep."

"What's on your mind, Roisín? Tell me. Is it Seamus?"

She shakes her head again, more vehemently. "No. No. I don't know how to say it."

Peter's heart misses a beat. *It's about me. It must be.* He swallows, takes her hands in his. "Just try, Roisín."

"Last night I had a dream. I dreamed I was in the cemetery." Her hands grip his; she looks down at her lap. "And I saw a gravestone with your name on it."

Peter's stomach clenches.

"I woke up in a sweat. There were tears in my eyes. I realised how much I care for you. It scared the shit out of me."

"Shhh," he says. He takes her in his arms. She seems very small, very fragile. She slips her arms about his shoulders.

"Just hold me," she says.

He rocks her gently, as he would a young girl. As he's done to his own daughter. As to Helen, when something had upset her.

Tears track down from her eyes, down her cheek, drip onto his trousers. "Hey, come on," he says. "Don't cry." There's something about women's tears that strikes deep to the heart of him, reduces him to inner trembling. And something erotic. He gently pats her back; she holds her clinch tighter. He puts his hand under her chin, lifts her face, leans down to kiss her. He moves his hand down, undoes one of her dressing-gown buttons, slips his hand inside. He pushes the fabric of her nightdress aside, and runs his hand over her breast. He hears her breath, sharply indrawn, in his ear.

Once can be excused as a lapse, he thinks. *But not twice. Twice has to be deliberate.*

He sits on the bed and undoes his shirt. He watches her as she stands, undoes her dressing-gown and pulls the nightdress off over her head.

*

Statistically, dreams are most often dreamed in pairs. Ranging from a couple entwined in bed to two individuals continents apart who may never become acquainted. The strangest element in this already strange waltz of sleep rhythms and mutual mind adaption is that the partner leading the dance forgets the dream when waking, whilst the one twirled and led remembers it...perhaps forever.

*

Peter does not ask Roisín what she dreamed tonight, if she remembers it. In the darkest hour of the night, he feels her warm smooth flesh slide over his own, tender and sensitised by the memory, the dream, of their love-making. A faint kiss on the cheek, a soprano whisper *I love you* in his ear. A sleep-bleared view of her pulling her nightdress on over her head, letting it drop to cover her nudity, doing up her dressing-gown. Tiptoed steps, the quiet opening and shutting of the door. The memory of her words in his ear, her sighed and gasped orgasm, his final inward thrust.

Guilt. He should feel guilty. If it was casual dalliance, just a fuck, then maybe he wouldn't. When Helen rings him up first thing he'll be cheerful, he forgot to ring her just one of those things you know how it is had a bit too much to drink you know how business trips are. But he knows his mood is fragile, a shell. What he and Roisín have done goes beyond a mere lapse, and sometime soon they may have to pay the penalty. They have made a mistake by making love a second time; they've bound themselves together too tightly now, and he won't be able to free himself without leaving part of his flesh behind. And if Helen and the kids found out...

He and Roisín breakfast together. Next week they'll meet again in Dublin, her home town. Perhaps if he were to arrive the night before...she'll make some excuse to her boyfriend, say a girls' night out, and she'll stay with him in his hotel room... He nods; he knows he wants to, but he wonders what he's doing to his marriage to Helen. Poisoning it from within.

Roisín is in good form at today's meeting. Changed into a pinstripe suit, her hair gathered up at the back, her face subtly made up, she seems the model of a professional woman. But he can't think of her now without seeing the image of her, naked, walking towards him, arms outstretched.

He wishes he could leave. Be at rest. No more meetings. No more treachery. But then what would he do, with a wife and children and a mortgage? No, he's in a rut, no matter how comfortable it may be. What you regret most are the risks you don't take. A lifetime of if onlys, until you wake up one day to find it's getting dark and it's much too late.

*

In his seat AJC taps into his laptop. The woman opposite seems nervous...has been all flight. A phobia for flying: understandable. He taps a key sequence and her file is presented before him. No, it's not her time yet: there's still part of the long string left. She's only just got married; that's her husband next to her. What a tragedy if she died on her honeymoon. So much potential. Future generations sleeping inside her, silent eggs in a full ovary. Conception on her wedding night: the traditional way. How romantic. AJC hasn't been totally eaten up by cynicism.

He looks at her name, in bold type at the top of the file: **DAVIES, Jane Mary (née Crichton)**. There's something familiar about her, something he can't quite trace. He's encountered so many men and women, they all tend to blur into each other...

He presses another key and wipes the display. He calls up another file.

*

Jane is looking the wrong way when it happens. She is distracted by Simon's muttering something in his sleep, a disruption to his quiet snoring. So she hears a thump as something hits the floor and, as one with the crowd, turns to see what has happened. Behind her, wakened, Simon does the same.

At first something clenches in her stomach - *what's gone wrong something wrong with the plane am I going to die now like this?* But no, the plane is steady, nothing interrupting its serene onward journey.

She sees a pair of legs lying in the corridor, and Graínne

O'Hara's green-beskirted backside as she bends over him. The other stewardess helps her lift the man but he's too heavy for them; a male passenger helps out. Jane leans out into the aisle and watches as the three of them carry the passenger (collapsed? dead?) down the aisle out of sight. When they've gone, the passengers sit back in their seats, relax.

Jane sits back and closes her eyes. Silently she reaches out and clasps hold of Simon's hand. "What happened?" he says.

"Don't know," she mutters.

She leans out and attracts Grainne's attention as she passes. "Excuse me...is he going to be all right?"

"I hope so," smiles the stewardess. "There'll be an ambulance on the runway when we land. About ten minutes."

"Fingers crossed," says Jane.

Grainne smiles and walks past.

In a seat ahead, Jane can see an attaché case, lying unattended. Now she knows who the man is who has just collapsed: the one who used the toilet before her. A middle-aged man, balding, overweight. She can read the gold-embossed initials on the case: PHC. Jane thinks to call Grainne back, but doesn't. Someone will notice it.

Whoever you are, I hope to God you're all right.

"A heart attack. Or a stroke," Simon is saying.

Jane nods.

"He'll be okay." A voice behind her: male. She turns, to see AJC sitting to her left, watching her. "It'll act as a warning, that's all, Jane. He needs to slow down."

Jane says nothing, just stares in disbelief. *How do you know? How did you know my name?* But Simon didn't hear: he distracts her by tugging at the sleeve of her blouse.

"Look, there's Dublin."

In the wonder of the sight - the illuminated, nighttime city from the air, laid out like a gigantic jewelbox - Jane forgets everything else.

I've got this far. It's not too bad.

The plane banks - a huge dark kite - over the sleeping city. It is silent, as silent as most graves.

*

The man who collapsed - PHC - is let off first, carried by two ambulance men on a stretcher. Then the other passengers disembark, row by row. There's a buzz of conversation, brought about by the unexpected drama in the routine flight. Jane wants to confront AJC, ask him how he knew what she believed he knew - but she loses him in the crowd.

They collect their luggage and make their way out into Dublin Airport. They change some traveller's cheques for Irish currency, have a coffee, wait for the coach to Busaras, the central bus station.

On their way out, a woman comes up to them. She's about the same age as Jane, a couple of inches taller, in a sweatshirt and black leggings, with collar-length red hair and glasses. "Excuse me?" she says - and Jane notices her accent: she's a local. "Were you on the flight from Heathrow?"

"Yes we were," says Simon.

"Are you waiting for someone?" says Jane.

The woman nods, obviously glad for Jane's perceptiveness. A woman-to-woman exchange, excluding Simon for the moment.

"He's probably got lost," says Jane. "He might be wandering around the airport looking for you."

The woman smiles thinly, anxiety undercutting her goodwill. "Is this your first time in Dublin?"

Jane nods.

Simon says: "We're here on our honeymoon."

The exchange over, the woman smiles. "It's a beautiful city. I hope you have a great time."

"Thank you," says Simon. "Jane, there's our coach."

"Good luck," Jane says over her shoulder to the woman as they make for the exit.

Amber

"I used to play here when I was a girl," I said.

We were in the woods at the back of my grandmother's house, giving her dog Scamper, a barrel-chested black Labrador, his morning walk. Sunlight sparkled through the gaps in branches overhead, and pineneedles yielded spongily under my feet. We came out into a clearing, the sandy soil pitted with grey dried-out puddles. I bent down and let Scamper off his lead; he ran on ahead, sniffing at the scrubby bushes and bracken still damp with dew. A light breeze tickled the hem of my short-sleeved dress.

"It's a good place to bring up a child," said Ian. Hand in hand, we followed in Scamper's wake.

"It's Army land," I said. "But they let the public use it. I had a wonderful time, climbing trees, running about. A right little tomboy, I was."

And then I saw him.

I tensed.

"Toni, what's the matter...?"

I'd seen him only briefly, a quick flash of red.

"Over there. In the trees."

Ian turned. "I can't see anything."

"I thought someone was watching us."

"There's no-one there, Toni. God, you're jittery this morning."

"It was a little boy."

Ian laughed. "A little boy? He's only playing in the woods. Same as you did when you were his age. Why his parents let him out on his own is another matter..."

I said no more. Maybe I'd been mistaken; I didn't like to seem foolish. But in that brief moment, I'd caught a glimpse of his face. An eight-year-old boy. My cousin Thomas.

But Thomas had gone. In these woods, twenty years before.

*

"Eat up, Antonia dear," said Gran, as she served me a generous portion of home-made steak and kidney pie in rich gravy.

"Oh well, bang goes my diet," I laughed.

"You don't need to lose weight, Toni," said Ian.

"I can't afford to put it on – not if I'm going to fit into that wedding dress."

"Antonia always was thin as a rake."

"I have filled out a bit since then, Gran." I reached for the bowl of Brussels sprouts.

After dinner, Ian and I did the washing up while Gran went into the front room. Past seventy now, she walked with the aid of a stick. Scamper trotted dutifully after her.

"Nice old lady, your Gran."

"Yeah, she always was my favourite grandmother. At least she didn't assume you and I wanted separate beds."

"I did notice the hint about kids," he said. "We're not even married yet."

I sighed. "Let alone ready. The thing is, Ian: she'd love to see a great-grandchild before she dies, and I'm the only hope. Of her children, one's dead and the other one only produced me."

Another pause. "Toni...?"

"Hmmm?"

"Is something on your mind?"

"No. Why?" I smiled disingenuously.

"You seem a bit on edge."

"No, I'm okay." But I knew he wasn't convinced.

Coming back here, where I'd grown up, had brought it all back.

*

That evening, we sat in the front room with Gran. Scamper stretched out in front of the coal fire and fell asleep. Gran excused herself and went to bed at ten o'clock.

Ian yawned. "God, I'm tired."

"Tired? It's only just gone ten." In our London flat, we rarely went to bed before midnight.

"All this fresh air. I'm not used to it."

"You're too much of a townie, Ian. I'm a country girl. Big

lungs." Even if I'd left for the city as soon as I could, when I went to University.

"Don't you ever want to live in the country again?"

"I couldn't. Except as a visitor. I'm not sure I'd want to."

"It's a different pace of life. Less stressful. Safer. It'll be a nicer place to bring up children."

"Too many ghosts," I muttered.

"Pardon?"

"Oh, nothing. Let's go to bed."

Later, in my nightdress, I looked out of our bedroom window. The back garden was separated from the woods by a fence and a narrow unmade road, but at this time of night it was all a uniform blackness. All I could see were my face and the lamp, reflected in the glass.

"There's nothing out there, Toni," said Ian. "Come to bed."

I bit my lip. The moment had passed. I pulled the curtains shut.

"Aren't you hot in that nightie?" said Ian. He was naked, sitting up on one side of the double bed.

"No. I'm cold."

"Soon change that. Come on, come to bed." He patted the pillow.

I sat in bed with my arms looped about my legs, chin on knees. He rested his arm about my shoulders.

"Ian...?"

"Mmmm?"

"You were right. Something has been on my mind."

"Was it what happened this morning?"

"Yes it was."

"Then why didn't you tell me? You've been holding off on me all day."

"I wasn't sure you'd understand."

"Toni, I can but try. I'm not psychic."

"No, I'm sorry, Ian. It's just that it brought it all back to me."

"Brought all what back to you?"

This was my future husband: I knew I should have no secrets from him. So I told him. I hadn't told anyone since it had happened, twenty years before.

*

It was a sunny autumn day, a half-term Indian summer, when Thomas and I went into the woods. He was wearing a red T-shirt and jeans; I had on a new pair of dungarees over a lime-green top. My hair was in pigtails. I hated the style, but my mother always insisted. It was difficult enough for her to get me into a dress. Thomas liked to pull those pigtails whenever he got a chance, so I always had to be on guard. I was wary of him, ever since the last visit to his parents, when he'd put a frog into my knickers.

We were eight years old. He was two months older than me (which put him a school year ahead) and a boy, so he assumed the role of leader. It was for me to follow. We tramped through the woods under the trees, Thomas hacking a path through imaginary foliage with a stick.

"Come on, Antonia! Keep up!" He made an exaggerated drawing of breath and wiped his brow with the back of his hand. "God, girls are bloody useless!"

I scowled and poked out my tongue.

"Women! Can't live with 'em, can't live without 'em," he sighed, parroting something his father was fond of saying.

"Oh shut up, you."

"You must take your punishment for being slow," he said as I caught up. "Bend over."

"No I won't."

"And for being cheeky."

"What?"

"Don't say *what,* say *pardon.*" And he whisked me on the bottom with his stick. Not very hard, but it stung.

"Okay then, Private Antonia. Keep a watch out for the Jerries. I'm going for a piss. Don't look."

He liked to use coarse words in the school playground, to impress his friends and shock the more shockable girls. But I was made of sterner stuff.

As I waited for him to finish, I scratched an itch on my inside leg. Then suddenly Thomas made a lion-roar and charged towards me, head down. I shrieked as I was knocked forward and I landed on my face, tasting dirt and pineneedles.

Thomas sat on my back. He tugged at my pigtails. "Ride 'em, cowboy."

"Ow! That hurts!" I said as he tugged again, harder this time. Perhaps he wanted to make me cry, and was disappointed that my eyes remained obstinately dry.

"Repeat after me: you are in my power."

"You are in my power," I muttered.

He tugged at my pigtails again, harder still.

"I am in your power," I said.

"You will do what I say."

"I will do what you say."

He scooped up a handful of pineneedles. "Eat."

I shook my head.

He tugged again with his free hand. *"Eat."*

I shook my head again, my mouth pressed shut. He let go of my hair and clasped hold of my nose between his thumb and forefinger and squeezed hard. I had to open my mouth to breathe and he pushed the mass of pineneedles in.

I spat them out straight away. He stood up and so did I. My dungarees were dirty now: I knew I'd get into trouble for that.

"I'll get you!" I shouted at him. He'd finally succeeded: tears prickled my eyes.

He just laughed. "Come on then."

"No! I hate you! I'm not playing with you ever again!"

At that he hesitated. He knew as well as I did that we were only allowed to play in the woods away from the adults on condition that we stuck together. Maybe he realised he'd gone too far this time.

"Oh come on, Antonia."

I looked down.

"I'm sorry. I won't do it again."

"You better not," I pouted.

There was a pause, then he said, his voice brightening. "Okay then. Follow me, Private Antonia. We have to make the Secret City by nightfall."

I have very little memory of what happened next. I still can't make sense of it, but I see it somehow like this: In my first week at University, I made the break from home by having my hair cut short and becoming known as Toni instead of Antonia. As part of the process, I got very drunk for the first time in my life. Most of that evening beyond about half past nine is a blank. I have no idea what I said or did. I was led up to my room by a friend. What happened to me that afternoon at the age of eight was, in retrospect, apart from the alcohol, a very similar experience.

I remember my legs aching and I felt sluggish, as if walking through jelly. I called out Thomas's name and had no answer. I stumbled out of the woods and stood at the edge of the road. I glanced at my watch, the one I'd been given for my birthday. It said half past three, but I knew from the way the sky was purpling that it was much later than that.

"*Antonia!*"

A torch flashed in my face and I screamed. But it was my mother. She hurried over to me and hugged me. I burst into tears. "Oh darling, we were so *worried* - "

"Where's Thomas?" That was his father, my uncle Andrew.

"I don't know," I wailed.

"What happened?" said Mum. "It's nearly seven o'clock! We thought something had happened to you. You've been gone for hours!"

"Never mind that," said Andrew. "She's safe now. Where's Thomas?"

"I don't *know*."

"Leave her be," said Gran. "You can see she's upset."

"That's not the point," Andrew insisted. "Where the bloody hell is my son?"

Out of the corner of my eye I saw Thomas's mother, Aunt Jeanette. She said nothing. Her face creased and she sobbed into her hands.

Gran and Mum led me back to the house. Mum washed the dirt from my face and hands and put me to bed. She stayed with me awhile, then, when she'd turned the light off, I heard her say to Gran: "She's all right in herself. She's had a shock and she's a bit confused."

Andrew and Dad searched the wood with torches until it was

too dark. By that time, Andrew had called the police; they searched the woods next morning but found nothing. A policewoman went with me. I could point to the spot where Thomas had knocked me over: the pine-needles were still disturbed. I was questioned by the policewoman, with Mum present, for what seemed forever. I was very scared; I wasn't much help. I don't think they thought I'd killed Thomas. Even if that thought had crossed their minds, I'm sure they realised my confusion was genuine. If I had done it and was suffering traumatic amnesia (if that's the case – which I don't believe – I'm still suffering it), how had I disposed of the corpse so efficiently? Even if they did suspect me, they couldn't charge me: I was less than ten years old, and hence below the age of criminal responsibility.

Thomas was never found. There was no obvious motive for kidnapping, but even so no ransom demand was ever received. No item of clothing was uncovered. It was as if the woods had swallowed him whole. Eventually, in the absence of any further information, the police closed the case: Thomas was presumed dead. I went to his memorial service; we all cried.

The woods had always been thought safe, but that now changed. I was forbidden to go there unless I had an adult with me. Other parents did the same. People still walked their dogs there, but no children played there, nor did they eleven years later when I went to University.

The one who was hit worst was my aunt Jeanette. Her marriage had been shaky (as I'd gathered from what I'd overheard my parents saying, and from what I learned since), but the tragedy brought her and Andrew closer together. But the next time I saw her, she seemed much older. She'd let her hair go grey and seemed thinner, shrunken. She was always distant to me as I grew up: maybe, at some subconscious level, she blamed me for what had happened. It sounds callous, but I wonder if she'd have preferred me gone rather than Thomas. In some way my adolescence and adulthood were not rightly mine to have.

Jeanette was treated for depression over the years; during my second year of University, she took her own life. At the time I was sharing a house with no phone, so a message to ring my parents was left on the Faculty noticeboard. I didn't see it for a few days; when I was told the news I took the first train home. The funeral was the next day. If I'd got the message any later, I'd have missed it.

*

Ian listened as I told him this. When I finished, I said: "Hold me, Ian, please." He didn't need much prompting.

We made love: he was gentle, solicitous of me. Afterwards he slept. He had an enviable ability to do so, quickly, even in a strange bed. I lay, gazing up at the ceiling, listening to his breathing, past events turning and returning in my mind.

In the early hours of the morning I couldn't stand it any more. I climbed out of bed and dressed quietly so as not to disturb Ian. I tiptoed downstairs in my stockinged feet and put on my boots and coat. Scamper sat up in his basket. "Shhh, I'm not taking you for a walk."

I let myself out the back gate. The road was pale blue speckled with grey in the moonlight. I glanced both ways: there was no-one in sight. I went into the woods. I had a torch with me, but otherwise I wasn't thinking of my own safety as a city-dweller naturally would.

There were fewer trees than twenty years before: many had been blown down in the 1987 hurricane. So the gaps between branches were wider, black against deep blue, star-encrusted sky.

I shone my torch left and right. No-one there. I sat on a tree stump: it was cold through the fabric of my leggings.

"Thomas?" I said. Louder: *"Thomas?"*

I heard the tread of a foot. My stomach clenched and my heart beat fast. "Who – who's that?" I stammered. I shone my torch directly in front of me.

Thomas stepped into the light.

He was wearing the same red T-shirt and jeans, muddy now, as he had on the day he disappeared. He was still eight years old. He seemed small – but then I was a fully-grown woman now, and a tall one at that. Gone was his bravado: he was a frightened little boy.

"Thomas," I said. "What happened to you?"

"Antonia's left me behind. Where's Mummy and Daddy? Where's Antonia?"

I shone my torch upwards, so that he could see my face. "I'm Antonia."

He said nothing, just stared at me, bewildered. "What?"

I laughed. "Don't say *what,* say *pardon.* Remember you used to tell me off about that?" I held out my hand. "Come on, Thomas. I've come to take you home."

No sooner had I touched his hand than he snatched it away. "No! Mummy says I mustn't talk to strangers!" He turned on his heel and moved out of the torchlight.

I moved the beam to follow him but he was gone.

"Thomas! Don't be silly! Come back!"

I called his name several more times, increasingly desperately, then went back to Gran's house. Tears were running down my cheeks.

The kitchen clock said 3 AM. I looked at my watch: it said 1.30.

Whatever it was that had taken Thomas, it didn't want me. It hadn't wanted me as a girl; it didn't want me as a woman. Somehow time had wrinkled, but why it took Thomas and left me behind I will never know.

I tiptoed back up to the bedroom, undressed in the dark.

"Toni...?" Ian murmured sleepily.

"Sorry, did I wake you?"

"What's the matter?"

"I went downstairs. I couldn't sleep."

"Mmmm." He rolled over onto his side and went back to sleep.

It took me a long time to sleep myself, but finally weariness overtook me. I couldn't stop thinking about Thomas and that night I dreamed of him, caught in his time-wrinkle, never changing, never growing old, like a fly in amber.

Drowning

Blue, deep blue, my sister's eyes. I stare down into them, anxious for a glimmer of recognition.

"Beatrice?" I say. "It's me. Maria."

She gazes up at me from the hospital bed. I squeeze her hand. And remember.

Blue, deep blue, my sister's eyes. Her eighteen-year-old face, reflected in her dressing-table mirror, rapt in concentration as she leans forward, applying mascara. A tumble of Titian curls framing a long Modigliani face. There's something haughty about her as she pouts her lips to receive their offering of lipstick. Imperious beauty. Golden girl. Fallen angel.

"Beatrice...?" I say.

"Mmmm?" she answers, as she zips up her mid-thigh-length skirt.

"Is it Dave?"

"Yeah, it's Dave." Her answer is offhand, as if she knows already that Dave, her latest boyfriend, will be a minor character in the drama of her life.

Blue, deep blue, my sister's eyes. And beside them my own, nondescript brown. We're twins, but there's no resemblance. She's some maverick dredged up from our family's gene pool; one might suspect she isn't my father's child. But I am her twin, and clearly of my father's stock. Age me thirty years and I could be my aunt Celia, flat-faced plain, greying hair scraped back from her forehead, fumbling with rosary beads. Years of marital domination left a void behind at her husband's death. A worst-case scenario made flesh.

Now I sit by Beatrice's bed, holding her hand. Her skin is naturally fair, paled further by the greenish fluorescent lights. Her hair is shorter now, collar-length. When she was younger it went down to the middle of her back, devil may care; now, at age thirty, it denotes maturity, responsibility.

She squeezes my hand.

"Oh, thank God," I say.

I spend the night at Beatrice's flat and the following morning, Friday, I discharge her from hospital. We take the Tube first back to her flat to pack her overnight bag and then on to Paddington.

She shields her eyes from the sun with her hand. A bright day, and her eyes, even behind glasses, can't take the onslaught. Slender, deceptively frail-looking in a plain pale yellow top and long flimsy floral-print skirt, she seems very vulnerable, holding on to me as we're buffeted by the aimless crush of the crowd.

Questions hang in the air. No doubt she'll answer them as best she can. I know facts if not reasons. First there was the phone call, first thing Thursday morning.

"Could I speak to Mrs Maria Grant, please?" A distant male voice crackling at the end of the line.

"Speaking."

"I've, er, got bad news about your sister."

I go cold. "What is it? What's happened?"

"Yes, er... Miss Andrews was admitted to hospital this morning. She took some sleeping pills. Her condition is stable. As the next of kin, we had to let you know."

"Thank you. I'll come immediately."

I take the day off work and make quick arrangements for a friend to collect and look after James, my son, then I drive to Bodmin and take the Intercity to London. It's a journey of nearly four hours and I spend it gazing out of the window, unable to read my newspaper or the Mary Wesley novel or the magazines I brought along. I can only think of what Beatrice has done. As I get off at Paddington I'm at first disorientated - a mass of people milling about, held in by the walls, the high arched roof - that I clutch my handbag to myself, holding myself in, protecting. The sheer noise - a thousand people talking, shouting, the booming announcements - overwhelms my eardrums. It's years since I've been to London, first time since I moved to Cornwall, that I feel like a little girl again, alone, lost and afraid.

I discover a little more at the hospital. It was Beatrice herself who dialled 999, and gave her name and address before losing consciousness. The ambulance staff arrived to find the door unlocked.

Facts. As to reasons, only Beatrice can tell me.

Blue, deep blue, my sister's eyes. Often they flash with contempt, an implacable no. Everything she does is in reaction to me. If not to me, then to our father. I'm the studious one, she the rebel; I'm the kind of pupil the teachers take pride in while despairing of her. And of course the comparisons exacerbate the tension. Were we not conceived at the same time, carried in the same womb, born within minutes of each other, there wouldn't be that incessant making of examples.

And over the years her reaction against me continues. I'm the one who married, settled down, had a child: the fact that I'm divorced is irrelevant. On the other hand, she's never married, just had a succession of lovers, none of them long-lasting.

Eighteen years old, I lie on my bed, listening to Beatrice and my father argue. Their voices are low, but they carry through the ceiling to my room above.

"You are not to stay out till all hours," says our father. "You're far too young."

"I'm old enough. I can do what I like."

"When you're living in my house, young lady, you'll do as I say. When you're living on your own I don't give a damn what you do. Are you sleeping with this boy?"

"What's it to you?"

"I'm not having my daughter sleeping around."

"I do not sleep around!"

"Why can't you be more like your sister?"

That question. Asked many times, in many forms. And when not asked out loud, tacit.

On the train journey home Beatrice says little. She watches the countryside go past and smokes one cigarette after another. I try to hold a conversation but after a while I give up and read the copy of *Marie Claire* I bought at Paddington. I'm very tired, and I sleep awhile.

Back in Bodmin I drive to James's school to pick him up.

Although I spoke to him on the phone at my friend's house from the flat last night, I'm anxious to see him again; I feel half missing if he's not there. My son. Six years old.

"Won't be a minute," I say as I get out of the car. Beatrice nods. As I walk away I glance back at her, face greyed by the reflections on the window, chin in palm, fingers obscuring her mouth. I flash a quick smile.

It begins to rain as I cross the road; fat single drops spatter on my coat. I walk over to where James stands, under shelter with his class teacher.

"Sorry I'm late," I say. "I've just got back from the station, picking up my sister."

"That's okay, Mrs Grant," the teacher says. "James has been very good."

"Makes a change," I say. James grins up at me. "Come on, trouble." I take his hand and cross the road again.

"Hello, James," says Beatrice as I let him into the car. Her relationship with me has been sometimes fraught but she adores her nephew.

"Hello, Auntie Beatrice." He's picking up a definite Cornish accent, I notice. From his surroundings: he was born here in Bodmin. I was pregnant with him when my husband and I moved to this area.

"Your aunt's come to stay for a little while," I say.

And Beatrice smiles, for the first time today. With a child's unselfconsciousness James might stand a better chance of reaching her than I might. If I fail.

I put James to bed at half past eight then come back downstairs. Beatrice is in the kitchen, reheating the kettle for another coffee. The fluorescent light does her no favours. She seems older now all of a sudden, with a wide-eyed, over-awake look. Underweight. I realise how much she has been living on nerve-ends, coffee and cigarettes. Her nails are bitten. She has said she doesn't sleep well, and all that caffeine can't be helping.

We go back into the lounge. I sit on a chair, gathering up my legs under me, tugging at the hem of my dress. She sits opposite, legs set square, coffee cup held on her knees. Five cigarette butts lie curled and grey in the ashtray in front of her.

"You realise," I say, "you're welcome to stay as long as you like. As long as you need."

She nods. "Yes. I'm very grateful to you, Maria."

"Oh, it's nothing," I say, waving my hand. "What about your job?"

"That's okay. I'll call in sick on Monday." She puts the coffee cup down on a coaster. "Now, if I'm not being too rude, I'd like to go to bed."

"No, no. Sleep's a great healer." I lead her down the hall to the spare room where I've made up a bed for her.

I move to go, but she makes a sound which stops me. I turn and suddenly she embraces me. "See you tomorrow," she whispers.

"We can talk a lot," I say.

I watch her go into her room, shut the door. Silence. I gaze at the door for a while, but it yields nothing. I turn on my heel and walk back to the lounge.

Coffee-cup in hand, I gaze out of the window at the darkened garden, the silent country road. Penny, my cat, winds herself about my legs, then jumps up onto the windowsill. Absently I scratch her behind the ear as I continue to look out. She rubs herself against me and purrs.

I think of Mark, my ex-husband. It's so rare that I do this now, that when I do I surprise myself at it. It's now two years since he left me. I could no longer give him what he was looking for. So he went elsewhere. Perhaps it was simply that the love had died. We married too early, straight after graduation, and we'd both changed in the meantime.

I have to give as much as I can now. For my sister's sake, at least.

Blue, deep blue, my sister's eyes. Distorted by tears as she stands at our father's graveside. I hold her hand as the coffin is lowered into the ground. Those around us - Mark; Beatrice's then boyfriend - stand back, leaving us to our grief. Her hand is held up to her face as she sobs. Tears do not flow freely: they catch in her, and she trembles as they work themselves loose.

She was never close to her father; they were often in conflict. So why does she cry now, and so painfully? Perhaps there was affection, a grudging one born of respect for the opponent. Or maybe she is crying for herself, a lost soul with no-one now to react against.

In the morning I serve Beatrice breakfast in bed and sit with her as she eats.

"Slept well?" I say.

"Mmm," she says, nodding, mouth full of cornflakes. She sits up in bed, in a borrowed nightdress. It's loose on her, her small breasts hanging free as she leans forward. Penny has followed me in and sits purring on my lap, warm even through the padding of my dressing-gown.

"Anyway, get up in your own time," I say. "It's going to be a lovely day. We can take a walk, the three of us."

"Yes, I'd like that. Thank you very much."

After breakfast we walk down the lane to the village. Overhanging trees splinter the light; a high hedge on our right encloses a field. James runs on ahead leaving Beatrice and I to walk arm in arm. *We could grow old like this,* I think.

"This is wonderful," says Beatrice. "I'm envious."

"Mark and I set our hearts on living in the country," I say. "We couldn't wait to get away from the town."

"I'm a townie," says Beatrice, lighting a cigarette. "I need things to be happening, places to see. But this certainly makes a pleasant change. I'll have to drop by more often."

A pleasant change. It's said with a little too much edge, too much knowing irony, to be unselfconscious. A pleasant change from what? Although I didn't witness the scene, I see her collapsed on the floor of her flat, trying to vomit up the pills she swallowed, calling the ambulance before she blacked out.

"Do you still see Mark, Maria?"

I shake my head. "He's moved away now. He's got married again. James stays with them once a month, but apart from that Mark doesn't have any reason to involve himself with me too much. I get the odd phonecall, holiday postcards, birthday and Christmas cards, presents for James. That's all."

"Do you plan to marry again?"

I shrug. "I may do, I may not. Who knows? There's no-one in the offing. I've got my friends, I've got you, James, Mum. I'm quite happy on my own."

A pause, then she says: "You know, I envy you, Maria."

"Envy me? How come?"

"You've got your act together."

I laugh.

She looks hurt. "What's so funny?"

"I just feel all I've done is what's expected of me. I've played safe every inch of the way."

"Yes, but you're secure. Organised. I never am. I just go from one chaos to another. Just as if I've never stopped being a student, really."

"How do you mean?"

"Well, staying up late and going in early. Drinking and smoking too much, getting hurt. Did you know I had an abortion once?"

"You never told me! When was that?"

"Oh, about four years ago. I kept it quiet. Can you see me bringing up a kid, Maria? I'm just hanging on by my fingernails."

Although I'm not a creative woman, I can recognise the signs in Beatrice from the creatively gifted people I've met. She has that omnivorous attitude to experience, the taking of great personal risks - without as yet any sign of the talent to put it to good use. This may be her tragedy.

We make our way to The Cricketers for lunch. We sit outside as we eat, gazing at the pond in the beer garden, thick heavy green in the shade, ducks trailing through the water.

"You know," says Beatrice. "Do you remember that time when we were girls, Maria? We paddled in that river when we were on holiday?"

"Yes I do. I'll never forget that if I live to be ninety, Beatrice."

"I'm just reminded of it now. It wasn't too far from here, if I remember rightly." She smiles, eyes deep and inscrutable as pools.

We are ten years old. "Last one in's an idiot!" says Beatrice and runs down the slope to the riverbank. The grass has a toehold in the mud before giving out to the lapping water. We tuck our skirts into our knickers, kick off our shoes and socks and step forward. The water shocks in its coldness; the mud is grainy on my toes. Beatrice is already further out, waving at me.

"Coward!" she yells. "Maria is a coward!" She chants it again and again, like a litany.

"I'll show you," I mutter under my breath and step forward.

At that moment it happens. Beatrice slips and falls forward with a big splash and goes under. I see her face, hair ballooning out around her head, darkening as she slowly sinks.

I start to scream.

The next thing I know, my father is running down the slope, diving in. I go back to the bank and sit there, sobbing in fear. My mother holds me.

Through blurry eyes I see my father surface with Beatrice in his arms, her dress hanging sodden from her, her hair a mass of wet dark copper. He lays her down on the grass, head to one side. Water drains out of her mouth. I watch as my father gives her the kiss of life, see her pale face, her lips already going blue.

"Come on, Beatrice, *breathe*," my father whispers. Then he looks up at my mother. "Kate, get some blankets out of the car."

As my mother hurries up the slope I say: "Is she going to die, Daddy?"

He glares at me. "No, she is *not* going to die, you stupid child! Just shut up."

Beatrice makes a choking sound, then splutters up watery vomit.

"There's a good girl. Get it all out."

My mother hurries down the slope with an armful of blankets. Quickly she undoes Beatrice's soaking clinging dress. I'll never forget the brief sight of her body, lying there, frail and cold in her underwear before my mother wraps her up in blankets. Beatrice's teeth chatter. My father lifts her up - so easily, she must be so light - and carries her up the slope. I rub my eyes, reddened from crying; my mother turns and offers me her hand. I blindly take it and let her lead me up the slope to the car.

Beatrice is put to bed as soon as we get back, and she will go down with pneumonia. My father smacks me and sends me to my room without dinner. "Don't you ever do that again! Beatrice could have drowned!" I lie face down on my bed in the dark, my tears soaking into the pillow. It's not the pain of being punished that really shakes me, even though that's unnerving enough: this is the first time he's done that to me since early childhood and rarely then as I was seldom naughty. It'll prove to be the last time. It's more the unfairness: I have after all done nothing.

"Maria?"

My mother's voice. A blade of yellow hallway light cutting through the darkness. "Maria, can I speak to you?"

She turns on the light. I look up at her, dazzled.

"You've been crying."

She sits down on the bed next to me. Still unsighted by the light, all I can see is her silhouette, smell her perfume. I embrace her suddenly, by blind animal instinct.

"Daddy didn't mean to hurt you," she says. "He did it because he loves you. After all, your sister could have drowned..."

Now of course, especially as I am a mother myself, I see things her way. It was fear that caused my father to lash out at me, for really the only time in my life. Before and after this incident, I was the paragon among his twin daughters, invoked each time Beatrice defied or disappointed him. I have anxieties for James who is after all only six. But there are dangers in letting fear rule you. If I'm too restrictive towards him ten years or so from now, will he repay me with defiance, as Beatrice did to our father? So many mistakes I can make, with a human life at stake.

As we sit eating our lunch in the pub beer garden, Beatrice says: "I remember falling in. I didn't even feel the cold. It was like a sensory-deprivation tank: I couldn't see or hear anything. It felt so peaceful. I didn't mind it at all."

"Weren't you scared?" I say. "After all, you nearly drowned."

She shakes her head and lights another cigarette. "No, not at all. I knew someone would catch me."

Nighttime. James has been put to bed and Beatrice and I sit side by side by the fire. Tiny orange flecks leap up from the coals, and smoke billows up the chimney. There's a cordiality between us that we haven't had for years, if ever.

I say, at the risk of shattering this calm: "Why did you do it?"

She pauses before she answers, her skin glowing orange from the heat. So long that I think she hasn't heard.

"Beatrice...?"

"Yes, I heard you. That was really - you could really say that was the latest of my pathetic little bids for attention. A cry for help."

"How can you say that? You could have died."

She smiles. "Same as in that river. I knew someone would catch me."

"Why did you do it?"

She shrugs. "I don't remember clearly. It was just a lot of different things. I'd split up with Nick a few days before - that's one. I realised how desperate my situation was, financially - two. And I had that sense - you know, I'm thirty now, and what have I done? Can I continue to live this way? Three. I felt I was drowning, and I wanted someone to catch me. I just decided there and then to do it. Spur of the moment." She leans forward and takes hold of my hand. "You remember that day at the river, Maria? I just wanted Dad to be concerned for me for once. I didn't fall in deliberately, but it could have been subconscious."

"I don't understand."

"Well, you were his favourite. You can't deny that. I was forever being told to be more like you."

I nod. "It's not as simple as that, Beatrice. I do love you, but I wouldn't want you to be like me."

"But you've got everything going for you, Maria. You always did have."

I shake my head. "I do not. You always risked things. I've played safe all my life."

"It doesn't seem that way. I just seem to get hurt, really bruised. I put my all into an affair and it goes bad. I probably just attract shits, men as fucked-up as me."

"But at least you try things. It's nothing ventured, nothing gained otherwise. Let me tell you something, Beatrice. I've never said this to anyone before. The reason Mark left me was because he was bored with me."

"Bored with you? How come?"

"Bored with me. Just that. He said I was cold, I didn't give anything to him. And he was right, up to a point. Please don't put me on a pedestal, Beatrice. I *am* cold. I don't give because I don't risk anything." This takes an effort to say; as I do so, I feel a sting in my eyes and a tightness in my throat, the prelude to tears. I look down at my lap and glance back up at her. She watches me intently. I whisper: "It's not you who's fucked-up, Beatrice. It's me."

There's a pause, and Beatrice takes hold of my hands. The fire splutters, begins to die. Then Beatrice says: "Shall we go to bed?"

I gaze down at my hands and say nothing, exhausted.

"I feel very raw," she continues. "I don't want to sleep alone." Another pause, then she says: "Could I sleep with you, Maria?"

"Yes."

"Can I? Just for tonight. It'd mean a lot to me. We haven't done that since we were girls." And she kisses me.

*

Blue, deep blue, my sister's eyes. The windows of the soul. They show their history of hurt, of pain, of instinctual reaching out for something she can't name. Our orbits have diverged over the years, and I feel the ache of the string stretched tight to snapping point as the stone whirls round at its apogee. Now, thirty years on, the midpoint of our lives, we are revisiting a time when we didn't have these hurts. And starting again.

Half-Life

Just now Miriam, your wife – no, your widow – walked through you. She was vacuuming the hall carpet, and she went back and forth through the spot where you died.

You don't feel the cold, though January frost is on the ground outside. Come the summer, you won't feel the warmth either. By then Miriam will be gone, though you'll still be here.

Eat sensibly, they said. Take plenty of exercise. But everybody has 20/20 hindsight. When you felt the chest pains, you knew your time had come. A little part of you welcomed the inevitable. You were forty-five years old.

Is your soul forty-five? Or is it timeless? Maybe the latter, though there's no way of telling. You speak to no-one, and you have to answer your own questions.

Tick tick tick. The bleep of digital watches. Time is a treadmill. And now you're off it. You don't feel time passing. The clock hands turn, the leaves brown and fall, the ground is covered in white that melts to grey, but it's just a spectacle to you. You don't feel time's throb in your blood. You've shed the past and you have no future. A continuous present tense.

*

Miriam is on the phone to John, the eldest of your two children.

"I don't know," she's saying. "I did tell him to look after himself. But he wouldn't listen... Yes, I suppose you could call him pigheaded. I'd rather put it that he knew his own mind... Well, it's too late to do anything about it *now*."

The now is elongated, louder than the rest of the sentence. You watch as her face creases and she covers it with her hand. Her shoulders shake with dry sobs. Her eyes are red from crying.

*

This is your world.

You wander from the hallway into the kitchen, dining room and the study at the back. In another direction is the front room.

You can't leave the house. You're at your strongest in the hallway, where you died. If you roam the house, day or night (you don't sleep) you sense some loss of energy the further you move away from that spot. But you can't go out the back door. It's as if your house, your home, the network of associations it has amassed from your twenty years living inside it, holds you together. As if you're imprinted on it. You can't leave it: you've tried. Outside you'd simply disperse, scatter like ashes on the wind.

From the hallway you go upstairs onto the landing. Straight ahead is the bathroom. To your right is John's old room, then Georgina's, your daughter who's only recently left home. You were going to redecorate her room. Then there's the room you shared with Miriam for twenty years.

It's eleven at night, and Miriam is undressing for bed. You watch her put her clothes away, folding them with the instinctive neatness you used to envy. The woman you loved for twenty years or more is naked in front of you, and you feel nothing. You watch her pull a nightdress on over her head, smooth it down over her hips. She climbs into bed, puts on her glasses to read. But she can't concentrate, it seems, so she puts the book away and turns out the light.

*

Miriam answers the doorbell. On the step is Georgina in a pale orange padded coat, a scarf wrapped around her neck. When she speaks, her breath is visible; her cheeks are red. "Hi, Mum!" she says, and they embrace. On Georgina's right is a taller woman with long dark hair; she flashes a nervous smile.

"Mum, this is Sue," says Georgina.

"Oh yes," says Miriam. "Your..."

"The word is lover, Mum!" Georgina laughs.

Miriam invites them inside and takes their coats. Georgina has had her mouse-brown hair permed since you last saw her. You often wondered at her lack of boyfriends in the past, but didn't presume to ask her: she's always been attractive (if a bit on the short side) and looks especially good in leggings, which she's wearing at this moment. Now you know.

Later in the evening, Georgina says: "You remember when I told you I was a lesbian? Five years ago it was, now. Time flies." She and Sue are holding hands.

"How can I forget? It came as a total surprise."

"Did you ever tell Dad?"

"No, I didn't. I always said it was for you to do that."

"I never did. I was always meaning to. It's too late now. I – I...I know this sounds silly, but I had no idea how he'd react."

"Were you scared of him?"

A long pause. "I suppose you could say that."

"You shouldn't have been. He always thought very highly of you. In fact, he often asked me why he never saw you with a boyfriend."

"Well, he never bloody asked me!" Georgina's face is flushed; she gesticulates wildly with her cigarette in her right hand. "I'd have told him why if he'd asked! I've known since I was bloody ten!"

Sue looks on, not wanting to take part in this family altercation.

"You should have told him, Georgina," says Miriam.

Georgina is crying now. "It's not my bloody fault! It's his, for being so bloody distant!" She coughs, dabs at her eyes with her handkerchief. "I'm sorry. I'm sorry. I shouldn't have said that."

*

It's two in the morning. You look down at Georgina and Sue, sleeping in your bed. Miriam has given it to them: they need the space, not her. Miriam is in Georgina's old single bed.

Georgina lies on her side and so does Sue, facing the same direction, moulding her body round Georgina's.

You do feel something.

You feel pain.

I'm sorry, Georgina, you want to say.

But there's no-one to hear those words, asleep or awake.

*

The next morning John and his wife Donna arrive. Today is your funeral. Another family occasion. The last one was John and Donna's wedding. Donna's dress is rounded out at the abdomen. You were told you were to be a grandfather. You felt the pride you'd felt when he helped you from an early age in the garden or with the car; that pride when he grew up tall and strong, when he started to bring girlfriends home. You remember the evening when you came home one night (Miriam and Georgina were away) to find John and a girlfriend kissing and embracing on the front room settee, clothes loosened, oblivious. You smiled and closed the door, leaving them be. All that is in the past.

But now you'll never see your grandchild.

Miriam, John, Donna and Georgina kiss and embrace. John is pale and drawn; Donna, on the other hand, is blithe, the only one capable of smiling. Although she was always friendly to you (you always found her attractive, from the time when John first introduced her to you), she is perhaps most distant from today's event and with her pregnancy is otherwise preoccupied. Or simply putting on a brave face. John and Donna shake Sue's hand. Perhaps it wasn't wise for Georgina to bring her; she's out of place. But maybe their entwined roots go deeper, and her function here is to give Georgina support. And the time she does that is when they're together alone.

Miriam serves them all tea, then goes to change into her funeral dress, black with a veil. She climbs into the front passenger seat of John's car, Donna, Georgina and Sue crowding into the back. John starts the car.

*

The house is empty.

You are alone.

You do not know what will happen.

Have you been fated to last as long as the funeral? Will the action of putting your body in the ground, food for worms, put your soul at rest? You look at the lounge clock. They must be burying you about now. But you feel no dissolution of energy. Or will you just simply vanish, to go – where? And where are the other dead?

You don't know.

*

After the funeral, Miriam hosts your wake. In this room are people you haven't seen for years, distant relatives, old friends, some of them dating from your schooldays. How they've changed: put on weight, acquired lines, thinning hair. Parents and even, in some cases, grandparents. You listen to the conversation. How sudden, how unexpected, what a sad day. But further away, out of the earshot of your immediate family, darker notes are sounded: how you brought it upon yourself, didn't look after yourself, asking for a heart attack. They talk about Georgina too: how could she bring her lesbian lover to an occasion like this? Another comes to her defence: her father was very strict, took the news of her lesbianism very hard.

It's not true! you want to shout. *I didn't know about it!*

You want to cry, but no tears come. It's like you're watching a film; you can't change what you see. *I didn't know. I tried my best. You can't ask more than that. No-one can.*

In the centre of the room, Miriam stands next to John, talking to her sister Andrea.

"So what do you plan to do?" says Andrea.

"I'm going to stay with John and Donna for a while. They might need my help, what with the baby and everything." John puts his arm about her shoulder. "This place I'm going to sell, find something smaller. This is too big for me, and there are too many…memories."

*

A FOR SALE sign has appeared in the garden. John is helping Miriam pack her belongings into his car. Many items will be sold, as she won't have room for them in her new home; she's left a forwarding address by the telephone.

Finally Miriam is ready to go. The last suitcase is packed; the last box has been filled.

"Have you got everything, Mum?" says John.

"Yes, I think so." There's a slight quaver in her voice.

"Just one final look round?"

Miriam blinks. "Yes."

You follow her as she walks round one last time. She and John have done a thorough job; the house is bare. Nothing has been left behind.

Except for you.

As she stands on the doorstep, ready to leave, you reach out and touch her on the shoulder.

She looks up. Did she feel your touch? She mouths two words. And then she is gone. You hear the car turning on the gravel.

*

Like a radioactive isotope, you have a half-life. Eventually you will decay and die a second time.

*

Goodbye, she said. And then she said your name.

Straw Defences

There he is. On the doorstep. Older now – it's been fifteen years since that time and we wore school uniform then - but still recognisably the same man. The realisation of who he is hits me, a body blow. I clench inside. Sweat breaks out on my forehead and it takes all my effort to prevent myself from trembling. So much so I hardly hear what he has to say, his practised canvassing patter. I take none of it in, focussing all my energy on an urgent prayer to a God I forsook years ago – or rather who forsook me – not to let this man recognise me.

But I'm still forsaken. "Good Lord, it's Douglas Jellicoe, isn't it?" the man says. "If this isn't a coincidence! I'm Andy Joyce - remember me? After all these years...!"

Of course I remember you, Joyce. I'll never forget.

His words. So banal but so powerful too. Such is his skill in slipping in the knife. I taste fear again, cold and metallic at the back of my throat, a fear I thought was vanquished long ago. A fear that the love of men and the platonic love of women helped me snap the spine of, now returned fiercer than ever before.

*

Those events are before me again. The doorstep, Joyce standing there – the outward shell of the present-day world is thin and wavering, only just holding off the past. I only have to close my eyes and it'll overwhelm me totally.

A damburst.

I feel again Joyce, or one of his gang, twisting my arm behind my back. I squeeze my eyes shut against the pain. "Please, don't hurt me." I feel myself give way to tears, hot shaming sobs. Be a man. Boys don't cry. Only sissies cry.

"He's crying," one of the gang sneers.

"Don't it fucking make you sick?" says Joyce. "Boy of his age. Fucking poof."

Someone kicks me in the back of the knee. I fall to the ground, the pain huge and burning in my leg. I can't move it.

I hear again my father's voice: Just ignore them. When it was just taunting. Stand up to them. When it became physical. Hit them back. Be a man, not a little girl. You queer or something? My father was a very macho man, and queer was the worst insult in his vocabulary. It took all my courage to tell him I was gay. He never forgave me. Learned to live with it, but never forgave. Not deep down.

"This'll fucking give you something to think about." Joyce drags me across the floor by my hair. He takes the cigarette out of his mouth, waves it close to my eyes. He stubs it out on my hand. I hear myself scream, a high stuck-pig shriek.

"Shut up!" Joyce punches me on the side of the face. He grasps the scruff of his neck and pulls me upright. "You're fucking pathetic." And he spits in my face.

*

I let him in. I should slam the door in his face. But I let him in. I invite him into my front room. I serve him tea.

I watch him warily, as I would a wild cat.

"You got the day off work, then?" he says.

"I work from home," I say. "I'm a writer."

"Oh yeah, 'course, I read something in the paper about you. Now I remember. You wrote a novel or something, didn't you?"

Oh God, has he read it? Is even that, the product of the most private part of myself, not free from him? "Have you read it?" I ask.

He shakes his head. "Sorry. Never had the time. Never do have time to read. I was telling the wife, I went to school with the bloke who wrote that."

"It gave me some financial security. I do freelance journalism too. I couldn't stick the nine to five."

"So say all of us. You live alone?"

I nod. How much does he know? My homosexuality was mentioned in some of the reviews and features. It's no secret. You can guess it from the novel. I take it to be public knowledge. But how much of the literary world is public knowledge?

"Not married, then?" Very little, evidently.

"No, I'm not," I say.

"No kids?"

I shake my head.

"None you know about, eh?"

"No. No kids."

"Lucky you. Divorced, myself. That was a bloody disaster. More fool me for getting her pregnant in the first place. Don't get involved with women, Doug. Take it from me."

His assumed informality grates: no-one calls me Doug. I say icily: "Some of my best friends are women." This is true: they are so partly because I pose no threat to them. They know I'm gay so sex is not an issue, either overtly or as subtext. It's their boyfriends and husbands who are more wary of me.

He shrugs. "Not me. Only women I know are my friends' wives and girlfriends. I like it that way. The only thing women can give me men can't is sex. That's all I'm interested in them for."

"That's where we differ," I say.

"Not planning on getting married, then?"

I shake my head. "Not really. I'm not really the marrying kind."

He looks round the room, and notices the birthday cards. "Your birthday, then?"

I nod. "My other half's planning a surprise for me."

He chuckles. "Well, that's something to look forward to. Give her my regards."

My other half's name is Peter. I don't tell Joyce this.

*

Joyce and his gang take turns punching and slapping me, and kicking me when I slump to the ground again. One of my eyes is swollen closed. A warm trickle of blood down my cheek. They push my head deep into the toilet bowl and flush it so I'm gasping when they pull my head back out. They go through my pockets and take my money and my watch. Joyce grabs my hair and bends down, his face close to mine, his voice hissing in my ear. "You're overdue on your *payments* anyway. Don't do it again, that's a good boy." He shuts the cubicle door behind me, leaving me curled up in a corner. In the darkness I sob bitterly.

*

When Joyce finally leaves I watch him go down the footpath to his car.

Other homes, other victims. I stay at my front window until he's gone. Then I give way to trembling.

I hold a copy of his campaign leaflet in my hand. His picture stares up at me. *Andrew Joyce – Your Conservative Choice for the Council.* I screw it up and throw it as far as I can.

I lie on the bed, shaking. I feel all the poise, all the confidence I've shored up over the years, leak away, until I'm back to the fifteen-year-old I was, self-esteem in tatters, fearful to go out at night, petrified by intimacy, mistrusting any kindness. Even so much as a raised voice hurt me, broke through my straw defences.

What did I do to attract Joyce's wrath? Was it the contempt of the stronger for a weaker? I've heard he came from an unhappy background, but I can't excuse him for that. I have no forgiveness for him. Was it the conformism of school, which led anyone who was different from the norm in some way to be exposed to ridicule or worse? Perhaps. That would have been more fuel for him.

Did I give out signals of difference? I might have done. Friends who knew me then tell me I seemed to drift, not knowing what I wanted, trying hard to deny the fact of my sexuality. I had a girlfriend once, even went to bed with her. But that was a fraught episode all round, and cost me her friendship. It was only when I went to University and entered into my first proper affairs that I became more settled. I've never been effeminate, so that wouldn't have provoked Joyce to terrorise me. There was a boy there, Martin, who was very effeminate, and Joyce picked on him for that reason alone. Martin was the first man I had sex with; we were brought together by our shared status, as Joyce's victims.

Evil does not come with cloven hoof and forked tail, fire and brimstone. Evil is banal. Evil is a man in a grey suit, a rather pathetic man called Andrew Joyce. My very own demon.

And then I realise. The glue of my personality, what's held me together all these years.

Anger.

Anger at him, for what he did to me, for so many wasted years overcoming it. I was derailed for some time: what should have been forward momentum throbbing uselessly, stalled. Anger powers me. At first it was an uncontrollable blaze that flared up inside me at the slightest provocation, making me shake with its violence. Now it's damped down, controlled more, but it's never left me.

Anger. And with it, the urge for revenge.

He's never read my novel. He'll never know how much effect he had on it. Let alone the character who was based on him – but not so he'll notice.

It was anger that kept me up night after night, typing out chapter after chapter in white-hot fury, damaging my eyesight for evermore. Anger that etched the characters, pulsed within the prose: the sensitivity, the warmth, the wit, the life-enhancing qualities the critics saw were in their eyes only. It was no act of kindness. No act of love. It was written in hatred. Vitriol flows in my veins. Without that rage, my work would be hollow indeed.

I sit down at my word processor and switch it on. The screen stares back featurelessly green at me, and I start to type. But nothing comes and I switch it off again.

Without that novel I wouldn't have been able to give up the job I hated and make my living by writing. Without that appalling, negative rage, I wouldn't have written that novel.

And now I realise this, I cannot write another word.

Joyce's final triumph.

Miss Perfect

Steve, I can still see your expression when I accused you of being unfaithful to me. A mouthful of the flan I'd cooked made your cheeks bulge like a hamster's, and I thought for a moment you were going to choke. It was just like one of those scenes you see in the movies, when the wife tells the cheating husband that what he's just eaten has been poisoned.

Finally you said, "That's not funny, Catriona."

I'd said it lightly and I excused it as a joke, making sure for the rest of the evening to be extra attentive to you. Do you remember? You must do. That night you made love to me as if to prove beyond doubt I was the only woman in your life.

I didn't doubt it, most of the time. But you must admit you gave me cause, you and her. You and Miss Perfect.

I first heard about her the night you told me she'd been accepted for Simon's old job. You and Simon had made a pretty good team in Marketing, and had done so since before I joined the company. After I married you we'd had him and his wife round for dinner several times. So when he left for a new job there was quite a gap to be filled.

"She's from Leeds," you said, imitating her accent badly. "But seriously, she's very bright. Straight out of University."

I sat next to you, let you put your arm about my waist. You picked at a loose thread on my skirt.

"But that's not necessarily a good thing," I said after a pause. "You see these sorts of people all the time. They've got all this learning, they've been to University, but they don't know anything about life. They've had no experience of the real world. You have – you've worked your way up to where you are." And, although I didn't say it, so had I: I'd left school at sixteen to become a secretary. Now, at thirty-nine, I was still basically a secretary, if a better-paid one. (PA to the Finance Director was my job title, but I wasn't fooled.)

You thought for a moment, then said, "Well, there is that,

Catriona. But she can learn all that. She is a bright girl, as I said."

I moved in closer to you, rested my cheek on your chest. You put your arm about my shoulders, ruffled my hair with your fingers.

"I bet she's devastatingly good-looking as well," I said.

"Well, she is rather pretty," you said.

"I bet she's tall and slim with blonde hair and a nice figure."

"Erm, well...you're not too far from the truth."

"Mmmm, I hate her already."

You kissed me. "You'll meet her tomorrow. She's really nice."

"That makes it *worse*."

She is rather pretty, you'd said. Such an understatement. She was tall, five feet ten (six inches on me), and slim (I'm a size 14 on a good day), with shoulder-length fair hair (me: short mouse). She wore a charcoal grey suit and a white blouse and yes, she did have a very good figure.

You were showing her round and you introduced her to me. She shook my hand firmly.

"Hello, Steve's told me all about you," she said.

"Steve"? I thought. *That's a bit familiar, isn't it?*

"I'm his wife," I said.

She made a quick, thin smile. "I know."

About half an hour later, in front of me, she fished into her handbag on the desk for her packet of cigarettes. If I were a man I'd have instinctively glanced down, to catch a surreptitious eyeful of her breasts, partly exposed by the gap between two blouse buttons. I know what men are like, believe me.

Later that day I bumped into her again. She was coming out of the Ladies and I was going in. She smiled, said, "Hi, Catriona." I watched her back as she walked away. *Well, you've got to be polite to me, haven't you?* I thought. *I'm your boss's wife.*

I had to watch her. I knew how you and Simon had worked. You'd often had to work late on important jobs. What would happen between you and her in the same situation? Men and women working unsocial hours together get very close. That's how affairs start. And I wouldn't blame you, or any man, for failing to resist Miss Perfect.

You had nothing but praise for her. One morning as you were

shaving, you said, "You know, it's early days yet, but I think she's doing really well."

"What, better than Simon?"

"As good as. I did wonder what it'd be like working with a woman..."

I laughed. "Sexual tension, don't you mean?"

You chuckled, then winced as the razor made a small nick in your cheek. As I listened, I dabbed at the cut with tissue: it wasn't deep. "No, not really. She knows I'm spoken for and I know she is too. It's purely professional, just like you and your boss. And I'm not the only one who's impressed with her."

That went on for most of a year, as she settled in to her job. You told me about her progress. I didn't say so, but underneath I was waiting for Miss Perfect to fall flat on her immaculately made-up face. And of course she didn't. Life's hard when you're flawless, isn't it?

Once, when I had the day off, you rang me up. "Sorry to bother you, Catriona," you said. "Wally that I am, I've left my address book behind. You couldn't get it for me, could you? There's a phone number I need."

I fetched the address book and gave you the number. But when you'd hung up I looked through the small leather-bound book. There, under R, was her name.

I confronted you at dinner that evening. "Steve, why's she in your address book?"

"Why not? She's my partner. I might need to discuss something with her, when either of us is working at home. What's so suspicious about that?"

And then I said it. "You know, I could think you and her were having an affair."

You almost choked.

Later, you said: "Catriona, I think we'd better talk."

I nodded.

You paced up and down the room. "Look, I don't know what it is, but you've got some kind of downer on her. Otherwise you wouldn't keep making out we're having an affair. We're not, right? That's an end to it."

"I did say it was a joke, Steve. A light comment. I'm sorry you took it the wrong way."

You stopped pacing and sat down next to me. "Hey," you said, chucking me lightly under the chin. "Don't call me into question, please. She's a pretty kid, she's a bright kid, but she's still wet behind the ears. I'm eighteen years older than her, don't forget. It's purely professional, nothing more."

I nodded again, sighed. "I know, Steve. I'm a jealous cow, that's my problem."

You put your hands on my shoulders. "Look, tell you what, let's invite her over to dinner one Sunday. Her and her boyfriend. Then you'll see how nice she is."

Well, that dinner was a great success, as you know. We met her boyfriend, Murray. He wasn't anything like you (more hair – sorry to rub it in), and I did wonder how I could have thought you and her were attracted to each other. He was her age, and very trendy-looking.

You'd done a good job of easing my worries, but they weren't all gone. I was always very pleasant to her on the surface. However, I didn't like the way you looked at her. I knew I came off second best. I could see you were attracted to her, even though you denied it. Perhaps you weren't fully aware of it, can't step out of yourself to see yourself the way others see you, but it was obvious to me. Women notice these things. She kissed me goodbye, but I watched closely when she did the same to you. All credit to you, it was just a friendly peck on the cheek. I'm not blaming you, you understand: if I were a man, I'd probably fancy her. Was that why I hated her, while being oh so smiling and friendly on the surface?

I just thought she could do with being taken down a peg, that's all. I'm not making excuses for myself. I'm just trying to explain why I did what I did.

*

It was just over a year after she'd joined the company that she came up to me in the canteen. I was alone, as you had the day off.

"Hi, Catriona. Can I sit with you?"

A mouth full of food, I nodded. "Sure," I said, gesturing with my fork.

As she sat down several of the men in the canteen sneaked looks at her legs, as if no-one would notice. But I did.

She sat down, smoothing her skirt over her lap. "How are you?"

"I'm fine." I noticed she didn't say: "How's Steve?" She'd only last seen him the day before. "How about you?" I said.

"Oh, can't complain." She leaned forward, her cheeks glowing with excitement. "I told Steve this morning over the phone, but you're the first person I've told face to face. I've applied for a new job. Lockhart & Mason in Sheffield."

"Really? I thought you liked it here." Under the table, my nails were pressed into my palms, so much so that I thought I might draw blood.

"Oh, I do, I do. I like the work, I like the people, and it'd be a shame to say goodbye. It's a similar job, similar money, it's just that I wanted to go back up North."

"Why's that?" I was thinking: soon she'd be out of my life. I didn't doubt she'd get virtually any job she applied for. Any company in its right mind would snap her up.

"Well, I went to University down here in the South and I've worked here for over a year now. I just find the people friendlier there, that's all."

"You mean, you're homesick."

She smiled wryly. "Well, a bit of that as well."

"What about Murray, though?"

Her smile faded. "I was afraid you'd ask that. This in confidence, Catriona."

"Of course."

"Well, Murray and I, we've been going out since I started University. I've changed a lot since then. He hasn't. He doesn't realise I do have other responsibilities now."

"Have you told him this?"

"No, but I will. Soon. We'll still be friends, I hope. I think he wants me to settle down with him, get married, start a family. I'm not ready for that yet." Her fork stopped in mid-ascent. "Oh I'm sorry, Catriona. I'm so tactless sometimes."

"That's okay." So she knows, though who told her and in how

much detail, I don't know. Was it you? I suppose it isn't hard to guess, what with a nineteen-year marriage and no children to show for it. She probably knows where the problem lies, too: IVF hasn't worked, and we're too old to adopt now. I get very broody sometimes, especially when some proud mother brings a baby into the office.

As I drove home that evening, I thought about what she'd said. She was uncommitted now, or would be before long. All the more reason to be wary of her. If she didn't get this job she'd still be around you. No doubt I'd be rid of her sooner or later, but I'd hate to see her go without punishing her in some way. Just once. But how?

She sat her interview and a week later Lockhart & Mason rang to say the job was hers. She was overjoyed and went around the office giving everyone a big hug. She bought a bottle of wine at lunchtime and shared it round.

A day later, when you and she were in a meeting, the phone rang. I picked it up. "Hello, Blake & Steele."

A male voice answered and asked to speak to her.

"Who's calling, please?"

"George Evans, Lockhart & Mason."

I glanced quickly round the office and then the idea came to me. "Er..." I said, and fell silent.

"Is something wrong?" George Evans said.

"Can I call you back?" I muttered.

"Certainly," he said, puzzled. "I'll give you my direct line."

I signed out of work early and went into an empty office at the other end of the building, where no-one would see me. I rang George Evans.

"Hello, this is Celia Denton of Blake & Steele," I said. This was to cover myself: there really was a senior manager of that name. "I'd just like to make you aware of an unfortunate incident where some money went missing. We decided not to involve the police at the time. But we thought you should be aware of it."

"I see. You needn't go any further, Mrs Denton, I get the picture. But I don't understand why you gave her such a glowing reference. That was what swung it for her."

"It's not Blake & Steele's policy to give bad references, Mr

Evans. But we thought you'd better know that she isn't quite so trustworthy as you may have been led to believe."

"I follow you."

"This is in confidence, you understand."

"Of course. Thank you for the information, Mrs Denton."

"You're welcome."

When he hung up I pressed my thighs together and clenched my fists, my nails digging into my palms, almost drawing blood; my heart was beating very fast and I almost wet myself with excitement. I'd done it! That'd show Miss Perfect!

I went home and changed. I cooked your favourite meal.

You were appreciative. "Have I forgotten my birthday or something?" you said when you saw the table I'd laid, with candles. You'd always liked my cooking, and I'd made your favourite meal.

"I thought I'd give you a surprise," I said.

"You certainly have. And you look ravishing, Catriona. Good enough to eat." You couldn't take your eyes off my breasts – anticipating the moment when you could put your hands on them, no doubt – and I was in danger of falling out if I leaned forward. When, later that evening, I stood before you naked, I was triumphant.

That night I took your penis into my mouth. It's not an act I enjoy, in fact I hate it, but giving you this treat was the finishing touch.

Does Miss Perfect like to suck your cock?

The next morning I made some excuse to go into your office. You had your arms about her shoulders; she was sobbing into her handkerchief. It was the first time I'd ever seen her cry.

"God, what's happened?" I said. "Why are you crying?"

"It's bloody well not on," you said. She just shook her head and burst into tears again. "It's thoroughly unprofessional," you went on.

"What is?" I said.

"They've just sent her a fax saying they don't want her. After accepting her, as well!"

"That's terrible," I said. I turned to her. "I'm really sorry for you! Is there anything I can do?"

"Some other bastard's been given the job. And they didn't even have the common courtesy to say why."

I went over to her and put my arm about her shoulders. "It doesn't matter. If they're going to do that sort of thing, they're probably not worth working for anyway."

"I'd be inclined to write a very strong letter of complaint," you said. "I'll do it myself if you won't. I'd check the legal position too. Has Evans gone completely mad?"

That lunchtime I bought her a bunch of flowers. As I gave them to her, her lip trembled and for a moment I thought we were going to get more of the waterworks. But she didn't cry; she put her arms about me and hugged me tight.

I was satisfied. I'd had my revenge.

Well, as you know, she stayed on with our company a while longer. I thought she might apply for other jobs, but to the best of my knowledge she didn't. Maybe the experience had taken something out of her, and had had the side-effect of curing her homesickness. Even so, I was glad to see you didn't sing her praises quite so much. Perhaps you'd had second thoughts about her yourself.

For a while you didn't say very much to me; you were in a strange, distanced mood. You worked late a few times, and when you were away on business you didn't ring home quite so often. You had absolutely no evidence, but I do wonder if it had crossed your mind that I'd had something to do with Miss Perfect's job rejection. You should have asked, if only to clear the air. I'd have denied it hotly, of course. But maybe you didn't know how to broach the subject. I can understand that.

Or maybe there was another reason. She'd just broken up with Murray. It had been more fraught than she'd hoped. You were good friends, and so she turned to you for consolation. And the inevitable happened. And she was soon going to leave your life and hurry back to Yorkshire (you thought) – perhaps you really had fallen for her. Anyway, the possible departure added poignancy to the occasion. It was inevitable, really.

Well, Steve, congratulations – you achieved what many desired but few accomplished. You slept with Miss Perfect. Was the experience all you imagined it to be? You're living with her now – she's not pregnant yet, is she?

To your credit, you didn't try to hide it. "I'll be honest with you, Catriona," you said. "I find this very difficult to say – It's better I tell you than you get it by rumour."

You might have expected me to scream, or swear, or cry, or plead with you, in some way make a scene. But I didn't; that would be degrading. I stayed calm, as stiffly formal as you. You must have wondered why. I held it all inside, didn't let any of it out in front of you.

I nodded, looking down at the floor. "You'd better go then, hadn't you?"

When I was alone, I burst into tears.

Sometimes I wonder if I could cut myself open, from the neck to the navel. What would I let out then? I've given blood enough times: I know it's not difficult to penetrate a vein. Miss Perfect's veins are quite visible, close to the surface of her flawless porcelain skin.

It would only take one cut.

Eggshells

1

Today I read about a woman who gave birth to a boy whose left arm was swollen and discoloured. The doctors urged that the baby's arm be amputated. This was done. On examination the arm was found to be riddled with cancer.

And now I'm dreaming of an arm gone bad. It lies in the hollow in the bedclothes between our legs, bent slightly at the elbow, hand partially closed, clutching at nothing. Brown veins of corruption run the length of its bruise-stained flesh.

I open my eyes. I lie in bed, listening to my alarm clock tick. It's six o'clock, an hour before it's set to wake us, but I know I won't get to sleep again. Beside me lies my husband Noel, oblivious, his face away from me, breathing evenly in sleep.

It's been a hot night; there's a fine film of perspiration over my body. Good move, Vicky, I think. Just the thing for a pregnant woman to read. Serve you right if you get bad dreams. I lie on my back and run my hand over my swollen abdomen in a slow circular movement. You won't be like that, baby, I think. I'm seven months pregnant but look further advanced. Weak stomach muscles, the doctor said. No two pregnancies are the same; every woman is different.

Half past six. I climb out of bed and pad barefoot to the washbasin. I splash water over my face to wake myself. I gaze at my reflection in the mirror. My features have rounded out recently; I've got a double chin now. I'm not tall, but I'm big-boned: broad shoulders and large hands. Country-girl stock.

Noel's face: he came back one day, tiredness lines etched into his face, pepper-and-salt hair in disarray, strands stuck to his forehead, glasses rain-spotted. And then I told him I was pregnant. His face was transformed. That seems so long ago. He already has a daughter,

Hannah, eighteen. But her mother was his first wife.

His first wife. Pauline. Not a subject to bring up.

I never met Pauline. Noel married me a year ago, to some eyebrow-raising as at twenty-three I'm twenty years his junior. People said it wouldn't last, but I'm determined it will, and this baby will be proof of our intent. It's difficult to get Noel to discuss Pauline. I know only the bare minimum: they were unsuited to each other, a situation made worse by depression on her part. Soon after Noel married me, Pauline drove her car out into the countryside, sealed the windows, attached a tube to the exhaust pipe, fed it in through the one open window and started the engine. A jogger found her body the next morning. Noel and I went on a short holiday to Paris to help him get over it. It was there, I believe, that I conceived.

I ease myself back into bed so as not to disturb Noel. But he's awake.

"Sorry, Noel, did I wake you?" I say.

He shakes his head. "My own accord." He squeezes my hand. "Good morning."

*

It's cold in this room. I wrap my arms about myself. The heating isn't on, of course, not in July. But it's going to be a cool day; we're expecting more hot weather later in the month. I'm wearing a T-shirt over a pair of trousers with an elasticated waistband, though I wonder just how far it will stretch.

I'm alone in the house: Noel has gone to work, Hannah to her holiday job. I was at work until last Friday, as a PA. I'll serve out my maternity leave before I hand in my notice. I don't want to go back.

Housework occupies me this morning: vacuuming, bedmaking, ironing. I hate ironing.

At ten o'clock I'm bent over the vacuum cleaner. Don't do anything too strenuous, said Noel. Get someone else to do it. You've got to *be careful,* Victoria. Perhaps what he's trying to say is *be sensible.* I used to rush around recklessly, lift heavy objects, climb up ladders. *Now be calm.*

The doorbell rings.

"Hi, Vic!" It's my friend Maeve. "You're looking well." We kiss.

She sits opposite me at the kitchen table. She's a good head taller than me; slim, legs crossed under a short skirt, she's recovered her figure very quickly after the birth. She's cheerful, though obviously tired: her four-month-old daughter Graínne has kept her awake most of the night. The future, I think grimly. Her boyfriend has the day off, so Maeve, back part-time at her PR job, has come to visit me. She shakes her shaggy honey-blonde hair out of her eyes.

I settle in my chair, shifting my bottom by inches to get comfortable.

"Looks like you'll get the nice weather in first." She leans forward, elbow on the table, chin in palm. "Careful, though. Stretchmarks don't tan."

I gaze down at my cup, at the lightbulb's distorted reflection. "Everyone's telling me to be careful."

"I know Noel is."

"Well, he can be a bit of an old woman at times. I do love him, but he acts as if I'm a piece of china. Fragile."

"It obviously means a lot to him, Vic. This baby."

"I know it does. He's said so himself. Our marriage isn't complete without a child of our own. His exact words."

"Sentimental old eejit."

"I wanted it too."

"Yes, I noticed you getting broody when I had Graínne. You didn't hang about, I'll give you that." There's a pause, then she adds: "How's Hannah?"

"Still difficult."

"That's a shame."

"Sometimes we'll talk a bit, but we never go below the surface. Other times, she won't give me the time of day."

"She's at an awkward age."

"She's bloody awkward, full stop. Plus what happened to her mother. She never really got over that. Sometimes she acts like I *stole* Noel from her."

"Which is bullshit."

"I know. *She* knows that. I just can't seem to break through with her, though."

I see again Hannah's eyes, flashing contempt at me. Her voice, taking delight in sarcasm. This morning: the way she looked me up and down as she went into the bathroom as I came out. Dressed only in a T-shirt and knickers, showing off her slim figure, long smooth pale legs. Attractive to boys, who call for her at all hours. I've asked her to call me Vicky, but she hardly ever addresses me by name. When she does it's *Victoria,* accent heavy on the second syllable in mocking emphasis.

I don't hate her. I try not to dislike her. I try to ignore the way she acts, as she's my stepdaughter. And she's wounded, I can see that. Her wounds must run deep: Noel has told me of an shoplifting episode when she was thirteen. Or the time when he and Pauline came home to find Hannah in bed with a boy. Hannah was fifteen at the time.

I'll say this about my husband. He always thinks things are for the best. Until he's confronted with the worst. Perhaps that's why he's so cautious – so he can keep up this vision of the best.

*

I make Maeve a salad lunch, then we go out. As I spend much of my time at home now, the noise and crowds are overwhelming. Although it's cool it's humid; I'm short of breath and I tire quickly. I sit down on a bench. Maeve stays with me, until I regather my strength.

"Look, Vic, if you don't feel up to it, say so. I'll take you home and finish your shopping for you."

That's what Noel would have suggested I do. But I shake my head. "No, I'm all right."

"Sure?"

I nod.

A woman in her late thirties, a girl of about six in tow, comes up to us. "Is she okay?" she says to Maeve.

I nod. "I'm okay." I smile. "Just a bit tired."

"Well, you don't want to overdo it, love. Not in your condition."

I nod again, smile thinly. "Thank you."

The woman lingers. "It's your first, isn't it?" Evidently I don't look old enough to have already had one. I've always looked young for my age – being short helps. "Make the most of it, love. It's worth all the effort."

"I hope so," I say. "Or else I've been badly conned. I think I'm okay to carry on now, thanks." The woman says nothing as I stand up.

As Maeve and I walk away, I mutter: "Silly cow."

"She was only trying to be helpful, Vic."

"I guess so." I shrug.

Perhaps I shouldn't have been so sharp with the woman. But I can stand that sort of bland all-is-for-the-best talk less and less. Why do I feel such foreboding? I should be very happy. But something, something cold and dark and black, nags at my mind. A canker in what should be my happiness.

*

When Maeve's gone, I unwrap the shoulder of lamb I bought. A treat for Noel. I have no hope of winning Hannah over: that's a victory to be won by increments.

The paper is slippery as I peel it away from the raw meat.

The first thing I notice is the smell.

As I peel the last of the paper away I gasp and clap a hand to my mouth, trying hard not to retch. I back against the wall, trembling.

The meat is rotten. Maggots seethe around the bone.

*

I'm preparing the dinner when Noel comes home. He comes up behind me and puts his hands on my hips, kisses the nape of my neck.

"Mmmm, that looks wonderful, Victoria."

I lean my head back as he lightly massages my shoulders. He's one of those men who become more attractive as they age: the lines of character, that distinguished touch of grey at the temples. I was a PA at a company he was liquidating – that was how he met me. I felt at ease with him straight away, as if we'd known each other for years. "A right song and dance I had with it," I say. "The first one I brought home was alive round the bone."

He grimaces. "Charming."

"So I rang Hawthorne's up. He didn't believe me at first."

"Didn't you notice at the shop?"

"I'd have noticed, you'd have thought. It looked perfectly all right."

"Report him. I'm sure the Environmental Health people will be interested."

"He came out and got me a new one. He was worried about his reputation. That's after I refused to bring it back. 'I'm seven months pregnant, there's no way I'm getting behind the wheel of a car.' He obviously values my custom."

"There must be someone else you could use in future."

I touch his elbow. "Oh, it's over and done with, Noel. Let's forget it."

As I continue with the dinner, Hannah comes home from her clerical-assistant job, dressed in a sweat-tired white blouse and a plain blue A-line skirt.

"Hello, Hannah."

She glances at me, then walks into the hallway.

"Don't talk to me, then," I mutter. Hannah doesn't come back downstairs until Noel and I are eating dinner. She's put on some make-up and changed into a short black dress, her feet in two-inch-heeled shoes.

"Where are you going?" says Noel.

"Out."

"You haven't eaten, Hannah," I say.

"Not hungry," she says. "I'll get something, don't worry. Thought I'd leave you two in peace for an evening."

"Look, it'd be nice to see you once in a while, Hannah," I say.

She glances at me. "I need to get out of the house. If you haven't worked it out yet, I've had a really shitty day. Don't wait up for me, right?"

I begin to say something, but feel the pressure of Noel's hand on my arm.

After she's gone, Noel says: "Well, it'd be nice to know why she's had a bad day."

"Oh, leave her be," I say, wearied by my attempt at friendliness. "She's right. I wouldn't mind not seeing her for another evening."

*

The next morning I go up to Noel's study and take out some old photo albums. Noel doesn't understand this urge I have to find out about his life, what this collection of artlessly-posed snapshots has to tell me. *Pauline's dead and gone. It's all past history, Victoria.* That's what he'd say. But even so, I want to know. I had boyfriends before Noel, slept with some of them – although Noel is the first man I've ever gone so far as to live with, let alone marry and fall pregnant by – but Noel doesn't want to know about them either. *Irrelevant,* he says.

I leaf aimlessly through albums hardly opened in years. Pauline, in a white summer dress, kneels on the grass, squinting at the camera. She wore her mid-brown hair in a tight perm then – it was fashionable at the time – and it's before she wore glasses. In front of her Hannah, naked and grinning, her arms held by her mother, stands in a paddling pool. It's a bright day, and looks hot. Hannah I'd say is one year old in this picture, which would make me six. What was I doing at this time, when my future husband was taking this photograph?

Another photo. Pauline in some woodland. She's smiling, but the lines under her eyes undercut her happiness.

I close the book and go downstairs. These old photos sadden me. I think of the seeds of Pauline's depressive illness germinating in her mind at that time, unknown to anyone, perhaps even to herself. The illness that destroyed her marriage and finally her life.

What caused it? What triggered it? As if these photos will tell me.

I draw my legs up under me on the chair, huddle myself with my arms. God, you're a bundle of laughs today, Vicky. Noel's right: you're just being morbid. It's cold in this room. Not my hormones mucking me about, is it? There's no reason why it should be cold: the temperature outside is thirty degrees.

Perhaps I'd be better off outside. I'm beginning to get stir crazy. Make the most of it - you won't have time to yourself when the baby's born. Sleep will be a luxury then. Should I ring Maeve up? I've an antenatal class to go to this afternoon.

The second post arrives. A plain envelope, addressed to Mrs. V. Sutton. The postmark is too faint to make out, and I don't recognise the handwriting. A fluid looping script, probably a woman's.

I open it.

There's no address and no date.

Dear Victoria,

So you're the second Mrs. Sutton. I'm sorry I never met

>you. I hear you're quite a bit younger than Noel. And you're expecting a baby, too. I know Noel and I wanted another one. Pity I couldn't produce it. I hope you have a boy: Noel always did want a son. (Not that he wasn't overjoyed when Hannah came along.)
>
>Please take care of Hannah. She has been hurt, one way or another. I know it's hard, but do persevere.
>
>It's certainly good to make contact with you.
>
>Best Regards,
>
>Pauline (the first Mrs. Sutton)

*

"It's someone's sick idea of a joke," says Noel.

"Who would do this sort of thing?" I've recovered now, but earlier I had to sit down from trembling so much. I rang Noel at work. His secretary took a message: she's known Noel longer than I have and she's always had a supercilious tone towards me, as if she didn't quite approve.

"I have no idea. If you get another one, call the police. That'll stop it." There's a pause, then he says: "I wonder if this is Hannah's doing."

"What's my doing?" says Hannah from the kitchen entrance. We haven't noticed her there.

Noel holds out the letter to her. "Are you responsible for this, Hannah?"

"Let me read it." She takes it from him, scans it briefly, then drops it back on the table. "Of course I didn't do this. It's sick. Who do you think I am, Dad?"

"Hannah, this has upset Victoria and if you're lying to me..."

"She didn't do it, Noel," I say.

"Thank you," says Hannah. "I'm glad to see *someone* believes me round here."

"Well, who did then?" says Noel.

Hannah looks over my shoulder at the letter. "It does look like Mum's writing."

"It's similar, that's all," says Noel.

"*Very* similar. Almost exactly the same."

Noel sighs. "Don't be stupid, Hannah. Your mother's dead. She's not sitting writing letters from beyond the grave, for Christ's sake!" He screws the letter up, walks over to the bin and throws it in. "There! That's an end to it!"

*

That night Noel and I sit side by side on our bed. I'm wearing only my dressing-gown; Noel is naked, his arm about my shoulders.

"Penny for your thoughts," he says.

"I'm still thinking about that letter."

He snorts. "Oh, *that!*"

"It *scared* me, Noel. How could she – whoever wrote it – know so much about us?"

"Oh, it's not *that* difficult, Victoria. We're all on record somewhere. I mean, God help me, I *look* twenty years older than you. And you're obviously pregnant."

"But why would someone do it?"

"Sssh..." he says, drawing me to him. "Just put it out of your mind. All it is, is a prank."

"You're right, as usual."

"I know I'm right. I just don't want you to worry, Victoria. That's all."

"I'm still cold. I've been cold all day."

"It must be your hormones. It's sweltering."

I stand up and walk to the window, look out. A calm scene: no cars passing, no-one walking outside at this time of night. A streetlight overlooks the tarmac, washing it orange. What we aspire to: peace and quiet.

I turn away and slip off the dressing-gown. I watch in my dressing-table mirror as Noel walks up behind me, rests his arms on my shoulders. The baby kicks.

"What's the matter?"

The surprise on my face has given way to a deeper smile of delight. "He kicked me."

Noel rests his chin on my shoulder, rubs his stubbled cheek against mine, nuzzles my earlobe. He moves his hand down, holds one breast in his palm, caressing it, lays his other hand on my solid-seeming bump. He likes to feel the baby moving.

*

A week later, Hannah brings her boyfriend Patrick home for dinner. They've been going out together for a month now: Noel and I have spoken to him briefly on the phone, but this is the first time we've met him.

As Hannah answers the door to him, Noel takes my hand in his. No formalities. After all, it's not very long since I was in Patrick's position, being introduced to boyfriends' parents, hoping I'd make a good impression. Poise, tense and fragile as an eggshell. And just as easily broken. So we'll be casual. No standing on ceremony this evening.

Patrick is tall, over six feet at a guess, with dark brown collar-length hair and steel-framed glasses. Hannah takes his hand in hers. "Patrick, this is Noel, my Dad." He and Noel shake hands. "And this is Victoria, his wife."

Later, as I'm finishing preparing the dinner (Noel is a dreadful cook), Hannah comes into the kitchen. "Need any help?"

"Yes, please. Could you get the chicken out the oven? It's a bit heavy for me."

As she does so, and I spoon the vegetables into their bowls and place them on the table, I pray silently I haven't made some awful mistake. What if Patrick's a vegetarian? No, that was the first question I asked Hannah. I'm sure everything will go well, but a fear that something will go wrong lurks in my mind. Maeve tells me I still act as if I'm on sufferance, and my relationship with Hannah has been sometimes fraught. Today, and recently, she's been calm, but sometime soon I know she'll show me the sharp edge of her tongue. On the other hand, I was accepted without reservation by Noel's friends and relatives, some of whom have told me I've done him a lot of good.

"Dad and Patrick are talking shop," says Hannah.

What does Patrick do?"

"He's a computer programmer."

"A subject close to Noel's heart," I say. Noel doesn't work with computers as such rather than use them – he's an accountant – but they are his hobby. A new PC has pride of place in his study.

I sense Hannah wants to know what I think of Patrick; and at the same time she couldn't care less. An ambivalence. She rests her hands on the back of one of the chairs, leans forward slightly. "How are you anyway?"

"I'm okay, thanks. Marking time, really. I'll be glad when it's over."

"It'll be odd having a brother or sister. Even a half one."

"I'm looking forward to getting back to my old sylphlike shape. Will I ever. I just feel fat."

She glances at my bulge. "Well, you are very big."

"Thanks a bunch!" I laugh, to show her I haven't taken offence. "I sometimes think I'm carrying an elephant."

"Or twins."

"I'm not, thank God."

"Anyway, are we ready? I'll get Dad and Patrick."

I glance across the sideboard one last time to see if everything's in order. Then something catches my eye. In the corner, next to the framed photographs is another one, unframed. A Polaroid, creased at the edges: Pauline, in a long white dress, sitting in some grass, her bare legs crossed. How did it get here? I've never seen it before. I pick it up, glance at it closely. Did Hannah put it here, as a joke, or as a baleful reminder? No, of course she didn't. But who did? This shouldn't be here. Noel doesn't deny his own history – he won't destroy those old photo albums – but he keeps it private. There are no pictures of Pauline on display.

I look at it closely. Pauline's blue eyes, wide open, hold my gaze. It was a hot summer day when this was taken. How real the grass seems. I can feel it tickling against my bare legs. And the sunlight, the heat...

I hear the others coming back into the kitchen. I blink, rapidly, as if I've suddenly come from darkness back into light. I cover my confusion by guiding the others to their chairs. Hannah and Patrick next to each other, Noel and I at either end.

I'm not naturally unfriendly, but something inhibits me this evening. I always thought I could get along with anyone – if I was ever shy, I overcame that long ago – but somehow I find it hard to chat to Patrick. Noel senses this, and covers for me, engaging him in conversation, drawing on his practised affability, the mask he adopts with clients. As they talk, Hannah takes Patrick's hand in hers, leans her shoulder against his.

"Where did you meet?" says Noel.

"At a nightclub," says Patrick. "I was standing at the bar and I saw this beautiful girl..."

"Brown-nose," says Hannah, and pinches his forearm. "But thank you anyway, that's nice."

"...leaning against a pillar..."

"My boyfriend at the time. You could see the resemblance."

"...and I said..."

"'Do you come here often?' Something original like that."

The three of them laugh.

It's cold. The fine hairs on my arms are stiff as needles. I blink. There's a tightness in my head like G-force, as if I'm receding at great speed from this room, this scene. The voices decline into murmurs. I clutch at my stomach, hoping I'm not going to faint or be sick. A prickling on my scalp, like tiny claws scrabbling.

The photo on the mantelpiece. Pauline.

— *Say cheese, says Noel.*

I smile, blinking as I look into the sun. A click. The camera extrudes a wide white tongue, the photograph. I stand up, shake the grass out of my skirt, walk up to him. I put my hand about his waist and watch over his shoulder as my image rises up from the white square.

Noel puts his arm about my waist, slips his finger in the space between the white top and skirt, kneads the flesh. He wants sex, he wants it now. The garden wall is high enough to thwart onlookers, and Hannah is asleep. Now. His hand moves down, rides up the hem of my skirt, and I blink.

"Are you all right, Victoria?" says Noel. He's leaning forward, concern on his face.

I nod, perhaps too forcefully. "Yes, I'm okay." The sick feeling is receding as I gulp at my glass of mineral water. Everyone else is drinking wine.

"You were miles away."

"No, I'm okay."

He nods, and after a short pause changes the subject. But I know I'm not telling the truth. For a few moments I wasn't me, Victoria, but Pauline. I saw things through her eyes, felt what she felt, thought what she thought. I was her.

*

After Patrick goes home, Noel and I go to bed. A little later, we hear Hannah walk up to her room.

"I was very impressed with him," says Noel.

I murmur agreement. "He tried a bit too hard to be ingratiating, though, don't you think?"

Noel considers this briefly and says: "I suppose he did."

"I think he might do Hannah some good. It was nice not being made to feel two feet tall for a change."

"Hmmm."

"Well, you could intervene."

"It's difficult for all of us, Victoria. She *is* my daughter."

"And I'm your wife."

"I wish you too would get on better. I really do. But she's eighteen years old. How can I tell her what to do? She might be an adult in the eyes of the law, but she's still a child as far as I'm concerned. It's very very difficult, Victoria."

I rest my head on his shoulder. "I know. I knew this when I married you."

"You knew it wouldn't be easy. I never pretended otherwise. Anyway, changing the subject – what did happen at the dinner table?"

"I don't know."

"I thought you were going to faint."

"I keep feeling cold."

"I think you'd better check with the doctor. I mean, it could be nothing, but it's best to be sure."

"Yes, Noel, I know."

He's sensed the weariness in my voice, for he adds, louder: "It's not a crime to be concerned about my wife. Especially now."

"I'm only pregnant, Noel. It's a condition, not an illness."

"Yes, but you're vulnerable. You should take care of yourself. As I said, it could be nothing," he adds in a lighter tone. He kisses me

145

on the cheek. "Good night. See you in the morning."

Soon he's asleep. I lie awake, not even tired. I can't discuss what happened. It would sound absurd, however lucidly I could describe it.

After at least an hour I climb out of bed, and put a dressing-gown on. I'm still cold. I go downstairs into the kitchen and make myself a cup of drinking chocolate.

As I sip at it, I hear a noise. I tense. A key turning in the outside lock.

I can't scream. Noel and Hannah are both sound sleepers. They won't hear me.

I silently put the cup down, and tiptoe over to the sink, out of sight of the door leading into the porch. As quietly as possible, I open a drawer and take out a kitchen knife.

A rustling.

I stand behind the door, holding the knife flat against my chest. I'm trembling now. If this is a burglar, will the sight of me with a knife deter him? If he attacked me, could I use it? Visions of rape and murder in my head. What did they say in the self-defence classes I took so many months ago? Just when I need to remember, I can't.

A key turns in the door. I grip the handle of the knife even harder, steeling myself to strike if I have to, trying to stop my teeth chattering.

The door opens.

Hannah comes in.

I gasp out loud. "*Shit,* Hannah! Don't fucking *ever* do that to me again!"

But Hannah doesn't answer. She stands in the middle of the room, clad only in a dressing-gown and slippers.

"Hannah...?"

She looks round at me, and I realise she can't see me. She's sleepwalking.

I know better than to try to wake her, but even so I'm worried. What causes her to get up at night and walk outside the house? Does she even know she's doing it?

Hannah turns into the hallway. I follow her up the stairs. She goes into her room and shuts the door behind her.

Normally, I wouldn't dare go into Hannah's room uninvited, but my curiosity is too great. I open the door as quietly as I'm able.

Her room is a mess, clothes and magazines lying scattered on the carpet. She stands in the centre, facing away from me as she unbuttons her dressing-gown, hangs it up on the hook on the door. She's wearing nothing underneath. It's the first time I've ever seen her naked. She turns, stares directly but blankly at me. Guilt, at intruding on her privacy, overcomes me and I back away. She climbs into bed. I go out onto the landing and shut the door.

*

Two days later, I'm alone in the house when the post comes. Amongst the letters is one that's familiar. The blue envelope, the looped handwriting. It's from Pauline. This time I can read the postmark: local.

I open it.

Dear Vicky,

(hope you don't mind if I call you that),

Here I am again. It's nice to see Hannah's found someone. She needs that. She needs love. I couldn't give it to her. I should have been close to her, and I regret to say I wasn't, especially near the end. She was at an impressionable age when my illness started, when I felt things go bad inside me. I was scared, feeling things crumble (excuse vagueness), under my fingers. I couldn't help it. I couldn't do anything. God only knows what effect it must have had on her.

I'm very very sorry. That's all I can say, but it's probably nowhere near enough.

You can't do much for her. You can't help her, though you can do your best. You can always do your best. You're a stranger at the feast, you came late. Hannah's learned to be friendly to you but there's always been a wall between you and her. Deep down she thinks you stole Noel from me. Of course you didn't, but there's a difference between perceiving things intellectually (Hannah's a bright girl, no doubt about that) and emotionally. Also, she finds it a little obscene that Noel finds evident sexual fulfilment in a woman young enough to be his daughter, in fact only five years older than his actual daughter. It's like incest. But she'll accept you, I think and hope. Give her time.

Love,

Pauline x

As I read this letter, I feel everything outside it recede, blur into a uniform daub of colour. The writing on the paper expands in my sight, takes on a life, becomes three-dimensional. I sense images pinned down like butterflies behind the words, struggling to come out, to break loose inside me. As I finish reading, I have to shake my head to free myself from the hold this letter has on me.

I lean against the wall, eyes lightly closed, as the swimming in my head subsides.

Somehow Pauline is watching me. Is she still alive? No, Noel saw her body, had to identify her. There's no doubt she's dead. Or is it her ghost, some little bit of her that's left behind, not gone wherever it is dead people go?

*

Afternoon. Maeve and I are sitting in the kitchen. I made her lunch, and we're talking over coffee. Gráinne lies on her lap.

I like Maeve for her frankness. She says what she thinks, and won't spare you. We discuss subjects we certainly don't discuss with anyone else, such as each other's sex life.

"...you wouldn't think it, looking at him. I mean, he's an accountant. He even looks the part."

"What's wrong with accountants?" says Maeve. "I mean, I've shagged a few accountants in my time."

"But you know what I mean... People have this image of accountants..."

"What, weedy little grey men in suits with bottle-end glasses and little willies?"

I laugh.

"You mean he's got a healthy libido, put it that way," adds Maeve.

"Yes."

"And so have you. You two are well matched."

"Oh we are. We still do it."

"Really...?" She raises her eyebrows. She reaches over to the fruitbowl for an apple. Suddenly I feel cold, and I tighten my arms across my chest. I know there's something wrong, and I want to tell Maeve to put the apple down, not to eat it. But, as if in slow motion, I see her bring the apple to her mouth, bite down. The flesh of the fruit gives way under her teeth.

"*Shit!*" She throws the apple onto the table. The apple is hollowed out inside, black. A long pink worm uncoils itself.

I clap my hand to my mouth. "I'm going to be sick."

"*You're* going to be sick? It was me who bit into the fucking thing!"

"Maeve, *I'm sorry!*" Tears sting my eyes.

"Just get me some water, please."

I pour her a glass of Evian. She gulps it down. I pour her another, which she drinks more slowly.

"I'm sorry, Maeve. I don't know how that got there."

She puts her hand on my upper arm. "It's all right. I'll live."

"I should've seen it was bad – "

"It's not your fault. Best get rid of it."

With newspaper I scoop up the remains of the apple, and the worm, oozed out five centimetres from the hole made by Maeve's teeth. I jam it into the bin as far as it'll go.

"It makes me feel ill, just thinking about it."

"Just forget it, Vic. It couldn't be helped." She slips her handbag onto her shoulder. "I'd better be going now. Come on, trouble." She picks up Grainne. "God, you're a heavy lump."

I walk with them to the door. "Well, I'll see you next week," I say.

Maeve laughs. "For our usual gossip session. Take care." We kiss. "Come on, Grainne, say bye-bye to Vic." She holds Grainne's hand and makes her wave to me; the baby makes a gummy smile. I kiss Grainne on the cheek.

When they're gone, I pour myself a glass of water. I look at the remains of our lunch: scraps of salad, slices of quiche. But I'm not hungry anymore: the thought of that wormy apple makes me queasy.

I'm still cold. Pauline, if it's her, hasn't gone away.

I stand facing Noel. I can't believe he's said what he's just said.

— You stand there and tell me this. You've got a fucking nerve, you have. You bastard! You've just stabbed me in the back.

— Look, Pauline, it just happened. One thing led to another.

— You're a bastard. I don't know what that makes her.

— Keep her out of this.

— I don't see why I should.

— This is between you and me, Pauline.

A flush rises in my cheeks.

— I don't want to know about her, Noel. I don't really want to know what you did together. You can go to hell for all I care. And you can take her with you.

And I turn on my heel and walk away.

Pause, a beat. Time passes, in reverse as well as forwards.

And now I'm facing him. I sit on our bed, still in my work clothes, white blouse, charcoal-grey skirt ridden up under me on the duvet. Noel has his hands on my shoulders, his lips against mine. My blouse is half undone.

— Noel, don't!

— *Come on, Pauline.*

He tugs at the hem of my skirt, slips his hand underneath, reaches all the way up.

— You're as cold as ice, you are. What the fuck is a man supposed to do?

He tugs my knickers down, undoes the belt of his trousers. His erection bulges out his underpants.

— I've had enough of this crap. You're going to do it, Pauline, like it or not.

I'm lying on the landing. How did I get here? I climb uneasily to my feet, and suddenly all the blood drains from my head. I clutch onto the banister to save me in case I faint. I begin to shiver, and something turns over inside me. I hurry to the bathroom, and lift up the toilet lid just in time to be sick.

"Oh, brilliant," I say. "This is all I need."

For the rest of the afternoon I lie in bed. The vision nags at me.

Did Noel have affairs when he was married to Pauline? Did he rape her? If he did, I'd find it hard to forgive him. But how much can I believe? If this is really Pauline I'm in touch with, then it's only her side I'm seeing. Noel would say differently. Or my unconscious could be making all this up. There's no way I can prove anything.

*

The sickness has passed when I wake up the next morning, but I'm still shaky. As I dress, Noel says: "Are you better now, Victoria?"

I nod. "I'm a bit wiped out."

He rests the back of his hand against my cheek. "You're still a bit hot. You take it easy, now."

"It was something I ate, Noel. It must have been."

I spend the morning in the garden, in a shortsleeved dress, reading my book through sunglasses, the radio on low. I feel my strength return. Perhaps I come from strong stock: in any case, I've not had a difficult pregnancy, compared to Maeve for one. She was sick for almost the whole nine months and had very high blood pressure, being hospitalised twice. I've had only the morning sickness early on, and the swollen ankles more recently. The baby seems at peace inside me now – at least he (I think it's a he) isn't kicking me.

Did Noel really rape Pauline?

I can't believe it. Maeve said herself he has a healthy libido, and so have I. Sex is a vital part of our life together. And consensual. There have been times when I've refused him, when the time wasn't right. But I can't imagine Noel forcing me to have sex with him. He never has done. He never will.

*

In bed, I say to Noel: "Did you know Hannah's been sleepwalking?"

"No. How do you know?"

"I saw her. The other night."

Facing me, Noel rests on his elbow. "What happened?"

"She'd been out the back. She let herself back in. I was scared – I thought we were being burgled, Noel."

Noel rests his hand on my shoulder, rubs it in gentle circling movements as we speak.

"How long's she been doing it?"

151

"I don't know. That was the only time I saw her do it. I called her name and she didn't answer."

"Ah, well. You mustn't try to wake her."

"I wish she'd say what's on her mind, don't you think?"

"She will when she's ready. She's had a lot to get over." And with that he puts his hands on my shoulderblades and pulls me to him. Gently he nuzzles my earlobe.

"Noel...?"

"Mmmm?" His hand has slipped under my nightdress, between my legs.

"Noel, don't, please. You're hurting me." I close my legs on his hand, forcing him to withdraw it.

"Does it hurt too much now?"

"Yes it does. The baby doesn't like it."

"We'll have to find another way." He sounds disappointed.

I nod.

He climbs out of bed and I watch him pad naked over to the window. His penis is still erect. There's a tension, visible, in his shoulders, as his hands press down on the sill and he looks out.

I can feel that familiar coldness descend on me like a mist. The metal taste of fear in my mouth. *Pauline, what are you going to do to me now?*

"Is something the matter, Noel?"

"No, Victoria. I'm just thinking."

"What are you thinking, Noel? Tell me."

"I think there's something you're not telling me."

"What, because I don't feel like having sex?"

"No, of course not. I've been here before, remember. I know what it's like."

"I want you to make love to me, Noel."

"Maybe it's me, but I just get the feeling there's more to this sleepwalking business."

"Lots of people sleepwalk."

"I'm worried about her. She is my daughter."

"She's my *step*daughter. And if anything we're going through a good patch at the moment."

"I'm glad to hear it. If anything else happens, let me know."

"Of course I will. Noel, come to bed."

He turns away from the window and climbs into bed next to me. And we do try "another way" as Noel put it. It's an activity Maeve and her boyfriend tried when she was pregnant. It's not comfortable for me. It's soon over, and we sleep as well as we can in this hot weather.

*

The next evening I'm wide awake. There's that coldness again, that metal taste in my mouth. It's been clinging to me all day, and even seems worse – baleful, putting me on edge – though there have been no more visions. After an hour of listening to Noel's even breathing, I go downstairs, not bothering with a dressing-gown over my nightdress this time.

It's like the anxiety of being close to sickness, not mine but others'. It's the quivering tension inside me that I felt in the hospital, visiting every day, watching my father die of cancer. I was seventeen years old; he was only forty. The disinfectant smell, the hushed voices, the agony etched into his face as his body rotted from within.

I sit on a kitchen chair, stretching out my feet, dangling my slippers from my toes, sipping a cup of hot chocolate. I command myself to relax.

There's a sound of feet on the stairs. Noel, woken up and wondering where I am, worried about me? Touching, if sometimes infuriating. But I know his tread, and this isn't him. So it must be Hannah. But it doesn't sound like her either.

I walk over to the hallway entrance, to see Hannah, in a dressing-gown, walking towards me.

"Hello, Hannah," I say.

No answer.

"I know you can't hear me. You're asleep." I laugh nervously. "So I'm talking to myself, really! I don't know if you're registering me at all. Can you hear what I'm saying?"

Silence.

"This is bloody stupid. It's like trying to hold a conversation with a zombie."

Hannah steps to one side to avoid me.

"That's right, Hannah, walk round me. I'm big enough." And then I pause. The layout of the stairs, hallway and kitchen must be committed to memory from her waking existence. But I can't be. "Hannah, *you know I'm here*. You'd have walked straight into me otherwise."

She walks on, turning left towards the porch.

"Hannah, stop." I rush round in front of her, taking hold of her arms. Calmly, she lifts her arms out of my grasp. "Hannah..."

Then I see a blue envelope poking out of her pocket. I take it. On it, in neat looped handwriting, the words *Mrs. V. Sutton* and this address.

I begin to tremble. "Shit, Hannah. It was you after all."

Hannah snatches at the envelope but I hold onto it, each of us trying to tug it away from the other. Then, suddenly, she slaps me hard across the face. In surprise, I let go of the envelope and it slips from Hannah's fingers to the floor.

I put my hand to my cheek. "Hannah...?"

She slaps me again, stingingly, with one hand, then the other, as she walks towards me. Her face is blank, a sleeping person's. I back away from her until I can go no further, against the wall. She reaches her hands up and closes them around my throat.

I grasp her wrists, trying to break her hold. Perspiration trickles down from my forehead with the effort. But her reactions are numbed with sleep, and eventually I force her fingers open and push her firmly away. She staggers back, trips over her feet and falls, her head hitting the floor with a thud.

I hurry forward. She looks blankly up at me.

"Hannah, I'm sorry. I didn't mean to do that – "

She starts to quiver. First her hands shake, then her eyes blink rapidly, then her arms and legs twitch. Her mouth falls open, and a bead of saliva runs out of the corner. She moans, as her whole body shakes. Her hands and feet thump heavily on the floor. I put my foot under her head to keep her from banging it against the tiles. Her seizure ends as soon as it's begun; she lies there inert, like a broken doll.

"What am I...I don't know, nothing...I've wet myself...Victoria..." Her voice is a low thin moan. And then she bursts into tears.

I hold her to me. "It's okay, Hannah. You've had a fit. You've been walking in your sleep."

She clings to me with surprising strength. "I don't understand..."

"It's okay. You're all right now."

Gone is the hard late-teens sophistication. She's revealed now for what she is, a lonely, confused and hurt young girl.

"I've wet myself."

"Doesn't matter."

I hold her until she cries herself out.

I walk upstairs with her. "Go in and get changed."

She nods, her mind still blurred by sleep.

I go downstairs and wipe up the mess with paper towels. The letter is still lying on the floor; I put it away in a drawer. I make another cup of hot chocolate, then go upstairs and knock on Hannah's door.

She's sitting up in bed in an old T-shirt, her arms wrapped about herself. She has goose-pimples on her arms.

"I made you some hot chocolate, Hannah."

"Thanks." She takes the cup from me.

I sit down on the end of the bed.

"Are you better now?" I say.

She nods. "How long have I been sleepwalking?"

"I don't know, Hannah. I've only seen you do it once before."

"When was that?"

"A few days ago."

"What did I do then?"

"I think you must've been out in the garden. I just saw you let yourself back in."

She laughs. "Wonder what I was doing."

I chuckle. "I don't know. People do funny things in their sleep. Walk, drive cars, operate machinery..." I don't say what I know she was doing: posting the letter I received two days later.

"I dunno."

"Well, it's harmless. Nothing to worry about."

She smiles.

"Hannah," I say. "Have you ever had an epileptic fit?"

She shakes her head vehemently. "No."

"Are you sure?"

"Yes, I'm sure."

"Not blackouts?"

"No. What are you getting at?"

"Hannah, I know what an epileptic fit looks like. I just saw you have one, or something very much like one."

"I don't remember. All I know is I woke up to find myself on the kitchen floor."

I sigh. "Oh, let it be for tonight. But I think you'd better see the doctor. Just in case."

"Okay." A pause. "Are you going to tell Dad?"

"Not if you don't want me to."

"Please don't."

"He knows you've been sleepwalking. That's all I've said." I stand. "I'll leave you in peace."

As I walk out, she says: "Thanks, Victoria."

I haven't told her, nor will I tell her, the whole of what she did tonight. The violent behaviour, the attempt to strangle me. I don't want to disturb her more than she has been disturbed already.

*

I don't read the letter until the next day.

Victoria,

I am VERY VERY angry with you. How could you let him do it? You must have wanted it too. Do you like being buggered? Does it turn you on? Did you come?

Let me make it absolutely clear you are a disappointment to me.

Pauline Sutton

I screw up the letter and throw it away.

I go upstairs to Hannah's room and find what I'm looking for in her dressing-table. A pad of blue writing paper and matching envelopes, packed away in a corner of her knickers drawer.

I hold it up to the light. Yes, it's the same paper, the same watermark.

The paper and envelopes are in Hannah's room; she was carrying the letter when she came downstairs... Hannah wrote those letters.

It makes sense. If anyone has reason to resent my presence in this house, in Noel's bed, it's Hannah. She seems to have come to terms with my being here, become friendlier to me, but maybe somewhere deep down she still can't accept me, and these letters, needling and taunting, are an expression of this.

But... This isn't her handwriting: it's large and neatly looped. Hannah's is a thready scrawl. I wish I had a sample of Pauline's writing to compare with this.

Also, the wording of this latest letter couldn't come from Hannah. It's certainly possible Hannah can hear the sounds of Noel's and my lovemaking from her room, but how could she know precisely what we were doing? No, the only person who knows that, apart from me, is Noel, and he certainly didn't write this letter. It's not his writing either, and Hannah was carrying it. It originated in this room.

Pauline wrote it. Through Hannah.

Hannah's seizure was caused by Pauline leaving Hannah, throwing her into turmoil. She's used Hannah as much as she's used me. But Hannah isn't, mentally, as strong as me.

A flash of anger inside me. I open the pad and write:

Pauline,

Why are you doing this to us? Tell me that. Leave Hannah alone. If you want to tell me something, tell it to me straight. I don't want you using Hannah.

Victoria Sutton

I don't think about how to explain this if Hannah (her wide-awake self) finds this note. Also, I don't know how dangerous "Pauline" can be. If I'm mentally stronger than Hannah, physically I'm more vulnerable.

I close the letter pad and slip it back where I found it.

*

It's the next day and no letters have come. Well, they wouldn't, would they? I think. I intercepted the one that was meant to come today. I wonder if Hannah posted another last night?

When I'm alone in the house, I go up to Hannah's room and take out the letter pad from her drawer.

The note I wrote yesterday has gone.

*

The next day there's no letter. Maeve visits again, with Grainne.

"Thought I'd see how you were getting on," she says.

"It's like I'm an invalid."

"Well, you are, sort of. You can't do all the things you did before, not when your body starts acting funny."

"You're my lifeline to the outside world, Maeve. I don't go out much now. Do you want a coffee?"

"Sure."

"I'll try not to poison you this time."

Maeve smiles wryly as she sits. I watch as she breastfeeds Grainne. "It's like having this little madam." She pats Grainne on the back; the baby's tiny hand reaches up the slope of Maeve's plump breast. "You remember how my blood pressure shot up – if you'd wired me to the National Grid, I could've powered Doncaster. What I'm saying is, you get something worthwhile in the end. Not like breaking your arm, say. That's pain to no good purpose. It's something men can never appreciate."

"Noel just acts as if I'm a danger to myself."

"Oh, he'll go all gooey over it when it comes, don't you worry. But he isn't the one who's putting in all the work. I hope you appreciate that, young lady," she adds, looking down at Grainne.

"She's lovely," I say.

"Isn't she just." Maeve beams. "And I'm sure yours will be too."

*

Another day, and still no more letters. I haven't felt that coldness in days. Noel blames it on my hormones in turmoil, but I know it's Pauline's presence nearby. I haven't sensed her recently, let alone had another vision. Has she left me?

2

It's the middle of August, and very hot. Noel and I are going away on our own for a weekend in Cornwall, the last excursion before the baby's birth. As Noel drives through heavy motorway traffic I sit in the back, as the front seatbelt is too uncomfortable for me now. I have the window open: inside the car it's close and stuffy, made worse by the blankets draped over the back seat. When I was younger, I used to be able to read in cars – the trick is to look out of the window as you do it – but I know if I try now I'll make myself ill. I'm queasy from the heat, the humidity, the smell of exhaust.

We stop off at a service station for lunch. I'm hesitant that if I have too much, or something too rich, this afternoon I'll be sick.

Noel notices this. "Victoria, are you all right?"

"I'm okay. I'm not very hungry, that's all."

"So much for eating for two. You look a bit pale."

"Cars and me don't get on, Noel. Not at the moment."

He smiles, lets the subject drop.

Noel waits for me as I go into the Ladies. I smile, shrug, in resignation at him as I join the long queue winding back through the foyer and outside.

And I feel cold again.

Pauline, I think, are you here with me?

But there's no answer, only the deepening cold. A chill biting into my bones, stiffening the fine hairs on my arm; a chill that no heating, natural or artificial, can eradicate. My teeth begin to chatter; I wrap my arms about myself.

Finally I reach the head of the queue. I feel a tingling in my scalp, like tiny claws scraping at my head.

After I come out of the cubicle and wash my hands and face in the basin, I hear a contralto voice, American, to my right say: "Hi, when's it due?" I turn; a tall big-built black woman, aged about thirty, grins back at me, an open lipstick tube in her hand.

"Two months, two and a half." My voice is far away and echoey, as if I'm hearing it down a tunnel.

"Your first, is it?"

I nod.

She laughs. "Make the most of it, hon."

I smile back at her.

"When I had my first, I thought – Say, are you okay?"

I hear myself say: "Yes, I'm fine, thank you."

I go back outside.

Instead of the heat, the sunlight glancing dazzling bright off the parked cars, the open glass and steel, the space, I'm in a long grey corridor, closed in, small windows. Overcast day outside, weak sun. At first I feel a lurch of shock, fear. I look back: I've just come out of a door marked LADIES. The American woman smiles at me; the door shuts. But then I feel acceptance, a growing curiosity. If I'm in this world I may as well explore it. I make one step, then another. It's like walking through water: a weight, a dragging pressure at the back of my head, slows me.

I pass a window and look at my reflection. Pauline's face, puffy, bag-eyed and double-chinned, looks back at me. My abdomen bulges hugely, straining at the thin cotton of my maternity dress. This must be Hannah inside me, I think, but the thought is tough and slippery, resisting my efforts to think it, saturated as it is with future knowledge.

"*Give her air!*"

My body weighs me down. Hollows in my shoulders from my breasts, heavy with milk. My eyes, haunted with the knowledge of the course I'm taking, the sleepless nights to come, the pain of labour, the stress of a messy, noisy, demanding and totally dependent child.

"Look, get out of the way, someone's fainted in here!"

I blink, wondering why my bedroom ceiling's different. But I'm not in bed. I'm lying on the ground outside the Ladies'. The American woman's large face, staring down at me.

"Are you okay, hon?" she says.

I nod.

"Not going to be sick?"

I shake my head. "I don't think so."

"Are you with someone?"

"Noel."

"Noel?" says the woman, puzzled.

"That's me. I'm her husband." I look up at him. "What happened?" he says.

"She fainted," says the woman.

"She didn't hurt herself?"

"No, I caught her. It's okay, guys," she says to the circle of people that's formed round me. "She's okay."

"Could you help me up?" I say quietly.

The woman and Noel put a hand under each armpit and lift me. I clamber to my feet. Fully upright, I loop my arm through Noel's.

"You want to be careful," says the woman. "I know. I've had three myself."

"It's probably the heat," I say.

She nods.

"Well, thank you for all your help," says Noel.

"You're welcome. Well, all the best, hon. Hope it goes well." She puts out her hand and I take it. "Maxine."

"Vicky."

Noel and I walk to the car. I'm conscious of people's eyes on me, either curious or concerned. I grit my teeth: I've made a spectacle of myself, embarrassed myself and Noel. The cold is receding from me, but it leaves a trace behind. Pauline is still here, still near me.

In the car, Noel adjusts a pillow behind my neck. "We won't get there before the evening as it is," he says. "You'd better go to bed soon as we do."

I nod. "I don't want to ruin the holiday," I mutter.

"You're not ruining it," he says, a little testily. "You can hardly help it."

*

The sky is darkening as we arrive at the small bed-and-breakfast. We've been here before, and know the owners, Jim and Anne, well. They're about ten years older than Noel. They've known him from when he was married to Pauline, but have always made me welcome. Anne is taken aback by my size: "You said you were expecting but ...dear, you're *huge!*" She kisses me. Noel holds my hand, pride evident in his face.

"Anne's gone all broody again," says Jim.

"Well, I always did want another one and it's too late now," says Anne in her strong Cornish accent. She has a strawberry birthmark under her chin. When I was a little girl I used to think a birthmark was where someone's face had gone mouldy – and once said so, to my mother's embarrassment.

"If you'll excuse me, I'll go to bed," I say.

"What, no dinner?" says Anne.

"Victoria's not been very well today," says Noel.

"I fainted in the service station Ladies." I make a nervous giggle. "And, thank you, but I don't think I'd better have too much to eat."

"I'll make you a little something, dear," says Anne. "You're having dinner, aren't you, Noel?"

"For your cooking, Anne, anything."

She touches his arm. "Oh, you do know how to flatter me, Noel!"

Noel escorts me upstairs and helps me unpack. I wash and change. He sits on my bed and puts his hand on my forehead.

"You're a bit hot," he says.

"I've got a headache."

"I'll get you something for that. Just have a good sleep. I want you fresh for tomorrow."

"I'm not going to be walking up hills this time, Noel..."

He chuckles. "I'd better be going down for dinner. I'll be back up soon." And he leans forward and kisses me. I rest my arms on his shoulders.

"I love you, Noel," I say in a low voice.

He holds me to himself for a while, then pats me on the back, stands. "Sleep well." He walks to the door. "Do you want the light off?"

"Please."

I lie here in the darkness. I don't see Noel coming back upstairs after dinner: when I open my eyes he's lying asleep beside me. I glance at my watch: twenty past midnight. No dreams. Good. Pauline already intrudes into my waking life; I don't want her invading my sleep as well.

*

I'm much better the next morning, and I eat a full breakfast.

"That didn't touch the sides," says Anne.

"That was lovely, thank you," I say. "I am eating for two, and I didn't have very much yesterday..."

After breakfast, Noel says: "I'm going for a walk. Anyone coming?"

"It's a great day for it," says Jim.

"I'll catch a bit of sun," I say.

"Sunbathe?" says Noel.

"Well, I was going to go topless, actually, you know? I'll spare you all that right now." I squeeze his hand. "Enjoy your walk."

I sit on a wooden bench, at the edge of the field behind Jim and Anne's home. I take out my paperback copy of the latest Margaret Atwood and begin to read.

I'm alone now. I can see no-one from here to the hills on the horizon in any direction. With the one exception of Anne. I watch her carry a bucket of kitchen waste and empty it onto the compost heap. Carrot ends, sprout leaves, potato peelings, eggshells. I close my eyes and picture them lying there for days on end, slowly decomposing in the sun.

The last time we were here, Noel and I walked for a day in the hills. I got my jeans muddy. We took a picnic lunch with us in our backpacks; we must have covered about twenty miles. We got back at dusk, weary and footsore, and went straight to bed after dinner. Sex was drowsy, warm and blurry, not sharp and urgent that time.

When Anne goes back inside, I'm completely alone. I concentrate on my book, and it's a while before I notice a cool breeze has sprung up. Then I realise: it's not the wind making me cold. It's Pauline.

"What do you want, Pauline?" I mutter.

I sense her presence building inside me: chill and a sick speeding-car feeling in the pit of my stomach. She's pouring into me, filling me up. I know I should be afraid but I'm not, not deep down. I know if I close my eyes she'll take me over completely. I'll be in her body, see through her eyes, feel what she feels.

I close my eyes. *And open them again.*

163

I'm in a white nightdress, lying on my back. I grit my teeth. The nightdress is pulled up over my hips. My legs are bent with my knees in the air, apart.

— *Push, Pauline! Push!*

And I push. My eyes are tight closed, and the nightdress is damp with sweat.

— *I can see the head!*
— *Push!*

And I push. Tears run down my cheeks. I open my eyes, look down the length of my body, to where the baby is emerging, red, wrinkled and wet. The midwife takes hold of her, pulls her slowly out. I close my eyes again, and after a long moment I hear a gurgling cry as the baby draws her first breath.

— *It's a girl, Mrs Sutton. It's a beautiful baby girl.*

My eyes stay closed.

I open my eyes. I can see Jim and Anne's wide field, and in the distance the hills. The view is blurry, as if suffering interference.

But I'm in control this time. The experience is intensely vivid but, unlike at the service station, I'm not totally swallowed up in it. There's a clear divide between my normal state of consciousness and this other state, and I can come back at will. A lucid dream, not a passive one any more. A coming to terms with Pauline, in a way.

I close my eyes, and let Pauline take me again.

Noel says little to me. I lie on my side away from him, my legs firmly closed to him. I don't want him to touch me. In a cot in the next room baby Hannah starts to cry, for the third time tonight. I can't sleep for the crying, and bags disfigure my eyes. I shut my ears with my hands against the noise, but Hannah won't be denied. I hate the smell of soiled nappies. Has she done it again?

I open my eyes.

I think: Pauline, I'm sorry for you. Really I am.

But there's no answer.

I close my eyes again.

As I take Hannah to her first day of school, I hold her hand. My only child. I won't have another – so much pain. And I won't let Noel near me – well, hardly ever. Sometimes I let him do it, as a sort of reward. I know he's seeing other women. He couldn't deny it. They tell me Hannah is a spiteful child, that she torments those weaker than her, that she steals, she intimidates. The headmaster writes to us when she's expelled. We know Hannah has problems, she's disturbed. Is it something we did wrong? All the many decisions you make, that shape the life of your child – and one of them is the wrong one? I don't know. Hannah is all that holds Noel and me together. Our marriage is a shell, form no content.

    Noel and I return from an office party. I played the dutiful wife tonight. In my Laura Ashley dress and my make-up, I swapped anecdotes, empty chatter, over the wineglasses with the other office wives. You couldn't spot the seams. But it was a sham. Everyone knew it was. Everyone knows Noel is sleeping with another woman: she was there in the room with us. They pretended not to know each other so well, to be colleagues. We open the front door. There's a powerful smell of cigarette smoke in the air. We go up the stairs. Hannah's door is open.

    — Hannah...? says Noel.

    She looks up from the bed. As does the boy, who must be about twenty. The sheets are gathered at their waists; both are naked. The boy takes his arms away from Hannah in surprise.

    I watch Noel's face whiten, his fists clench.

    — She's fifteen years old, you little bastard!

    — Dad, leave us alone, says Hannah.

    — You shut up! You've done enough damage already!

    — Hey, leave it out, says the boy.

    — Get the fuck out of my house. I'll call the police. Get dressed and get out.

    He grasps hold of the boy's shoulder, drags him out of bed.

    — Dad!

    The boy dresses hurriedly.

    — What do I care? he mutters. Everyone's had her. You don't know nothing.

    Noel punches him under the chin, causing the boy to slump back against the wall. The boy tenses, clenches his fists, but relaxes.

    — Okay, I'm going. I'm fucking going.

Hannah's seeing a psychiatrist. I hope it's having an effect. She lives with me now, though Noel sees her at weekends. We try to be civilised, keep our arguments behind closed doors.

My eyes sting, and tears trickle down my cheeks.

Something is eating me, gnawing inside me. Noel can't feel it, and I don't know if Hannah does. It gets me when I'm alone and most vulnerable. It puts a chill in me. It rots away at my life, kills all the good in it. It has done this, and more.

I sit up, tense. I rest my hand on my abdomen and I feel the baby kick inside me.

It's after dark that I drive out onto the Common. No-one will see me here. No-one comes here at this time. I walk outside the car, stretching my legs to break the knots in my muscles. Winter ice in the air. I've practised this so many times now, I could do it in my sleep. I fix the vacuum cleaner hose to the exhaust, run it back into the car. All the windows are shut except this one, and I've padded the space around the hose with old newspaper.

I sit in the front seat and start the engine.

I know it won't be long before I die.

I close my eyes.

"Still a bit tired, bless her," says Anne.

I blink. "Sorry...?"

"Sleeping like a little baby."

I look up to see Jim and Anne leaning over me.

"Sorry, I must have dozed off."

"You were well away," says Jim. "Snoring."

I climb to my feet, aching all over. Warmth returns to my body; Pauline's cold retreats. I feel numb, scraped raw. The merest touch – Anne's hand on my arm – hurts me.

I walk back to the house and up to my room. I shut the door behind me, lie on the bed. I press my face into the pillow and silently give way to tears.

*

Something that ate away at Pauline, destroyed her, formed itself into her image that is now threatening me. It has affected Hannah as well. And Noel? Does it only affect the female members of the family? Is it a female spirit – are there then male spirits? Or does it affect Noel in different ways that I can't see? He's a very rational man: perhaps he can reject it better than most. Or is he some kind of psychic Typhoid Mary, infecting others but remaining unscathed himself?

*

At mid-morning on Bank Holiday Monday, Noel and I drive home. There's a long tailback. It's not so hot as before, and I don't feel queasy today. The breeze from the open back window cools me pleasantly, without that bone-chill announcing "Pauline's" presence. It's as if a pressure has lifted; I feel easier, lighter than before. As we packed this morning I made a slow, elephantine-graceful twirling dance in the bedroom.

"You're in good spirits," Noel said.

"I feel really great today."

Noel's features crinkled into a smile. "Good. You lighten us all up."

I put my arms about his shoulders. He held me briefly, patting me gently on the shoulder-blades, resting the point of his chin on the crown of my head.

At other times we might have made love. But not then. It was a brief, precious moment.

"I wonder how Hannah's been this weekend," says Noel, as he gazes out the front window at the long line of traffic. We spoke to her over the phone on Saturday.

"Probably had a party," I say.

Noel's knuckles whiten on the steering wheel. "I expressly told her not to. If I find out that she had – "

I laugh. "Oh, come on, Noel, lighten up. I did that sort of thing when I was her age. At the very least Patrick must have stayed the night."

Noel sighs. "Victoria..."

"Anyway, she's not like she was. You have to give her credit for that."

"Give the shrink credit for that, you mean."

"*And* her. She's not a robot, Noel. She'll be going to University soon. She's a lot more at ease. Patrick's done her a lot of good."

"I bet they're sleeping together."

"I'm sure they are. So what?"

"I know that. But this is my own daughter we're talking about."

"Look at it her way, Noel. I certainly didn't want to think about my parents having a sex life. And look at me now – that's a constant reminder that we have one."

There's a pause, then Noel says: "I see it from a different perspective to you, Victoria. You didn't see it the way I did. You weren't there. You didn't see the way she was."

But I did, I think.

"Sure she's made a lot of progress," he says. "But she's not there yet. As in many things, I take a lot of convincing. She's let me down so many times."

I say nothing. The silence is filled by music from the radio, on low. When Noel speaks again, it's to change the subject.

Late in the afternoon, we arrive home. Hannah is sitting in the lounge in an armchair, her legs gathered up under her. She's playing a *System of a Down* CD. Her hair is freshly washed, tied back in a ponytail. As we come in she climbs to her feet, kisses and embraces each of us in turn.

*

As we lie in bed, I say: "Noel...? Tell me about Pauline."

"I don't want to talk about Pauline." He rolls onto his side away from me.

I put my hand on his shoulder. "Noel, you said we'd be honest with each other. You made me say that."

"Hmmmm?"

"So talk to me about Pauline. You never talk about her."

"What a time to ask. Do you really want to spoil the weekend?"

"No, of course I don't."

"You don't want to hear about Pauline. Believe me, you don't want to hear about Pauline."

"Let me be the judge of that, Noel."

At the tone of my voice, he looks up.

"I'm serious. I want to know."

"Why? Why do you want to know?"

"I do. You remember that letter?"

"I should've called the police. Did you get another one? Why didn't you tell me?"

"No, I didn't get another one. But it brought home to me that I don't know what went on."

"Why should I tell you what went on?"

"Because I'm your wife. I'm very serious."

"I never ask you about you and your old boyfriends..."

"Ask me. Ask me anything. I'll tell you all you want to know. Who I went out with, who I slept with, what we did in bed together. I won't hold anything back. Just ask me."

Noel sits up, his arms hanging forward over his lap. "This is very difficult for me, Victoria."

I slip my arm about his shoulders. "Tell me."

He sighs. "Well, the basic thing that was wrong was, we weren't suited to each other. Another man would've been ideal for her. Not me. We weren't compatible."

"Sexually?"

"Yes. Sexually. Particularly sexually. When she got pregnant she wouldn't let me near her. And after she had Hannah."

"So you went elsewhere."

"Yes. I had affairs. I'm not proud of it. Our marriage had pretty much broken down by then. Which of course damned me even more in her eyes. I was breaking the sanctity of marriage. Which didn't help her. I could see she got depressed. She once said something was eating away at her. I suppose I'm at fault for not paying much attention at the time. I'm not proud of the way I behaved. But I could see she'd go off the deep end eventually. She seemed fine during the divorce hearing. That's why they gave her Hannah. I knew she wasn't stable. You know the rest of it."

"Did you still have sex together?"

"Hardly ever."

The question - *You didn't force yourself on her?* - is on the tip of my tongue. But I don't ask it. I can't ask it. Instead I settle into the warm circle of his arm.

He sighs, and pats me on the shoulderblades. "I don't know

why you've got this fixation about Pauline, really I don't. But I hope I've put your mind at rest now."

"It's not a fixation. I just wanted to know."

"Whatever it is."

He could be lying. He could be telling the truth. It's his word against...what? Nothing, really. He is my husband, the man I live with, the father of my unborn child. He is the one I choose to believe.

3

My pregnancy advances, weighing me down more and more. My ankles are swollen, and I'm permanently tired. I rarely leave the house now; Hannah gets the shopping for me, or sometimes Maeve does it on a day off from work, calling round to keep me company. There's only a month to go but I wish it could be over soon.

*

Before he goes to work, Noel gives me breakfast in bed. From our room I listen to him drive away.

I've never been one to linger in bed in the morning, always mindful of unperformed tasks. Even now. Slowly I wash and dress.

I walk out onto the landing. Silence. I'm alone. But no – Hannah's downstairs: I simply can't hear her.

A low sound in the distance, like a scraping. A chuckle.

And then that cold descends on me.

Oh no, not you again...

I wrap my arms about myself, the fine hairs on my arms needle-stiff.

I blink, expecting every time I open my eyes to see a different picture to the one I see now. But this time, there's no change.

A quivering inside my stomach, like the vibration of a car or a train.

I walk slowly until I reach the top of the stairs. I look down.

A steep staircase, twenty steps.

So fragile, I think. So easily broken. So simple to put an end to it. One foot in front of the other. Just step into space and it'll soon be over.

I grip the banister with my hand. A pressure building inside me, impelling me forward. Panic, thick smoke coiling round that pressure, those thoughts. Was this what went on in Pauline's mind in her last moments? Did this cause her to kill herself?

My knuckles whiten on the wood of the banister.

"Hannah..." I gasp. "Hannah, help..."

Everything slows, thickening like jelly, impeding my thoughts. Hannah in the hallway fifteen feet below me, walking slowly, so slowly, mouth opening in an O. Her voice, thick and distorted: *"Victoria...?"*

I push back with my mind, resisting. In the thick air in front of me I see the outline, faint at first but increasingly clear. Pauline's face. Her expression is blank, a solidifying grey blur, her body a nebulous outline hanging below it.

I close my eyes.

I reject Pauline with all the energy I can muster.

My mouth opens and I scream: "*No!*"

The scream, a bursting, as if I've blown every fuse. Something snaps and recoils inside me and I gasp, stagger back, as if I've been hit in the face. I blink rapidly, as I slump against the wall, slide into a sitting position.

A pain, dull and thick and black, in the small of my back and low down at the front of my abdomen.

Hannah hurries up the stairs. "Victoria, what's the matter...?"

I'm breathing heavily as I speak. "I think it's started."

At first she's uncomprehending, then she takes hold of my arm and leads me back to my bedroom. "Come on, lie down."

"No, I'm all right."

"No, you lie down. I'll call Dad."

As I lie on the bed, I hear her speak on the telephone in the next room. Noel has impressed this on her many times: "When Victoria goes into labour, I don't care where I am, I don't care how important the meeting is, you're to tell me at once." Now the time has come.

"Dad, Victoria's just gone into labour... Yes, I *know* it's two weeks early, Dad..."

I still feel coldness, but less of it now. Has it finally gone, or don't I feel it any more? I lightly close my eyes.

Noel comes home half an hour later. My contractions are twenty minutes apart. By late afternoon, they're five minutes apart and acutely painful. Noel drives me to the hospital. The coldness rests lightly on my skin.

Pauline, I think. Do what you like with me. But don't harm the baby.

And as I lie there, there's a light-headed sensation and a

quivering in my stomach as if I'm going to faint or be sick. As if I'm floating... And I see my body, in the back seat of the car. My eyes are lightly closed; I look very peaceful. As I watch myself, as I float up up up

and I blink. I feel calmer now. The cold is virtually gone, only a trace in my bones and my blood. I tighten my hand about Noel's.

The midwife notices this; she turns to me. "Your first time, love?"

I nod, and wince with the pain. But I've done this before, although that was in another body, a different size. I haven't yet become accustomed to this one.

I'm in a hospital bed, changed into a light blue nightdress that I brought with me. Noel stays with me, now and again going outside to use his mobile to call Hannah, who has Patrick with her.

After the second call, Noel comes back and squeezes my hand. "She seemed ill-at-ease."

"I'm not surprised – this is new to her. New at first hand, I mean. It's hard to get used to."

A pause. "How do you feel?"

I sigh. "I've carried it so long, I just want to get it over with now. You know, out of my body and done with. You know what I mean?"

He says nothing. He squeezes my hand again, encloses it with his other hand, bends his head so I can't see his face. Then he says, so low I can barely hear him: "This is the greatest day of my life, Victoria."

He said that last time.

I chuckle. "One day I might agree with you, Noel. But not at the moment. It's too fucking painful." He continues to hold my hand as the next contraction comes. My eyes close with the pain, my teeth grinding together. *"Fuck."*

His skin is white under my nails, until the pain passes. I'm in tears now, and I blindly clutch hold of him. His muscles are tight with worry, helplessness at seeing me, the woman he loves, in so much pain. All he can do is pat me gently on the back. "It's all right, Victoria. I'm here," he says, a little stiffly.

I sigh. Somehow I find it in myself to chuckle. "Well, that was the worst yet, wasn't it?"

*

By the time midnight comes, I'm drenched with perspiration, my cheeks wet with tears. The midwife who has been with me up to now is at the end of her shift, and hands over to the night staff.

"Hello, Mrs Sutton," says the new midwife, whose name is Mary.

"Vicky," I gasp. Another contraction, pain white-hot, worse than before. Tears roll down my cheeks as I scream.

"It won't be long now, Vicky."

It's as if I'm being torn apart inside. "Fuck you, make it *stop*. You got me into this! Make it stop!"

I lie there, the baby inching itself towards life outside my body.

"*Push,* Vicky," says Mary. "I can see the head. Just one more."

Noel squeezes my hand again. "Come on, Victoria. I love you." He kisses me on the cheek. A reprieve, then another contraction drags me down again.

"One more push, Vicky. Once more, you're doing great."

And I push, and something moves inside me, squeezing itself out from between my legs. I strain, my eyes closing, my muscles taut, one more push and it'll all be over – and it's gone.

A miracle. A perfect baby boy.

"Congratulations, Vicky."

Noel kisses me and cuts the cord. I lie back, utterly exhausted. "Can I hold him...?"

He's handed to me. Noel looks over my shoulder at his new son, Daniel James. I can't see Noel's face but I sense his happiness. As I look down at my child, run a finger across his tiny nose, his lips, his hot red and wrinkled face, I feel inside me a swelling, blossoming love.

Daniel stares up at me. Then he screws up his eyes and begins to cry.

City 101

Anna can see a woman standing in the window opposite, the same height above the ground in her towerblock as Anna is in her own. It's a hot night, sweet sickly city smells in the air. The woman is wearing a pair of khaki combat trousers, but above her waist all she has on is a white bra. In her right hand is a wine bottle, and from time to time she takes a swig from it. Her black hair is long, spilling over her bare shoulders.

Anna wonders if this woman has been a soldier of some kind. She is certainly fit; Anna can see that she has no superfluous fat on her, and her abdomen is taut about the shadow circle of her navel. She doubts that the woman jogs, as that could be dangerous around here, though she certainly looks as if she could take care of herself. Perhaps she goes down to the dilapidated gym two blocks away.

The woman turns, as if disturbed in her reverie. Has she seen Anna, staring at her? Anna turns away, backs into her own flat. She doesn't want to make herself conspicuous.

It'll soon be time to go to work. Anna is hungry again, so goes into the small kitchen and heats up soup from a can on the small gas ring. Then she changes into her uniform; the skirt is tight on her.

I like big girls. That's a voice, a male one, but she no longer recognises its owner. It's separated from other memories by blanks on either side, and she wonders sometimes if she dreamed it one night. She is overweight, she knows, but she's on her own now, and has no-one to please but herself. She works in the supermarket from midnight to eight, then sleeps as best she can until four or four-thirty, then stays in until her shift starts, munching snacks and gazing at a television set with the sound turned down low. Night-time suits her: the daylight is too bright, the streets too noisy and claustrophobic.

She takes the lift down to street level. She must walk briskly, meet no-one's eyes. There is a short cut, but it's narrow and unlit and she can't go down there. She did once, stood poised at the entrance to the alleyway, but the rest of it is blank too. Best to stick to the main roads, even if it doubles her journey. She passes the brightly lit all-night takeaways, wrappings strewn over the pavement. The deep bass pulse of the nightclub. By the side of the old foursquare building, a woman in a short black dress bends over a litter bin, and a man in a grey jacket holds her hair out of her eyes as she vomits.

Anna walks determinedly on.

She arrives about ten minutes early, so sits in the staff room and makes herself a coffee, leafing through the magazines strewn over the table.

Sometimes, on the way home, she's stopped at the railway station and had breakfast there, watching the trains disgorge all the men and women in suits ready for a day's work. *Where do you want to go? Anywhere I can get to for ten pounds.* Someday she might do that again, take a destination at random, leave here and start again somewhere else.

The clock ticks round to midnight, so she puts her cup down half-finished and walks back down to the shop floor.

The supermarket aisles are sparse at this time of night, the greenish fluorescent lights only emphasising the gaps in the shelves. They'll be restocked with the morning deliveries. What remains is old, what hasn't been sold during the daytime.

One night, a man had an epileptic seizure right here, in this aisle. One of the other staff had the presence of mind to put his shoe under the man's head so that he didn't hit it on the floor tiles. The man had bitten his tongue, and a thread of red wound its way into the froth spilling from his mouth.

Anna finds her position and sits on her chair, switching on her till. She's the only cashier on duty at the moment, though Michael can operate another till in the unlikely event of it being busy.

Michael is the only other staff member in the shop at the moment; tall, thin, long-haired and acne-scarred, he's working nights during college vacations. As he mops up a milk spillage, he looks up. "Hi, Anna. It's going to be a quiet night tonight."

He wants to make small talk but she answers his words with monosyllables. She senses his eyes wandering, and she tenses. He's suggested in the past that they go for a coffee and breakfast once their shift ends. She's put him off before, but will he ask again?

Cold hands on her back. Another gap. *34E – how come you're such a big girl all of a sudden? A* gap. *Hands lifting her skirt.* Gap. Gap. Gap.

Anna closes her eyes.

"Excuse me, Miss?" A woman in her thirties, at the end of her shift perhaps, or insomniac – she doesn't look like a clubber. Anna busies herself with checking out tinned fruit, frozen meat, a two-litre container of milk: a routine she's practised so long now.

"Bet you don't get much custom at this time of night," the woman says. "They probably pay you more than they take in."

Anna smiles thinly.

"Still, I'm glad it's here when you need something after all the other shops have closed." She arranges her purchases in a bulging carrier bag. "Thanks, love."

And the shop is empty of customers again. "She comes in every night," Michael says, nodding at the woman's back as she goes out through the doors. "Probably hasn't got much of a life. Still, rather her than the drunks." Anna has to step over their sleeping bodies in the doorway at the end of her shift.

Another customer comes in. Anna's stomach clenches as she recognises her: the woman from the flat opposite, the maybe-soldier. She's wearing the same pair of combat trousers, her hair gathered up under a cap, a denim jacket over a T shirt.

Has she followed Anna here? Did she see Anna watching her?

As Anna watches, the woman turns, flashes a brief smile, then walks out of sight behind the first set of shelves. Michael is also watching her, as she appears briefly again at the end of the row, then disappears again, not breaking her straight-backed stride.

And then she's walking towards Anna, a shopping basket full of groceries. Anna concentrates as she checks out each item in turn.

"Hey," says the woman. She has an American accent. "You're from the flats opposite, aren't you?" Close up, Anna sees more detail of her face: the high cheekbones, the wide mouth, the hint of olive in her complexion.

Anna nods, struggling to retain her composure, not to go red. Does this woman want a confrontation, an explanation as to why she's been spying on her?

But the woman doesn't ask this, merely says: "Can you sleep at night? The *noise*. Jeez. But then you work at night, don't you?" She lifts up her two carrier bags. "See you."

At the end of her shift, Anna signs out and walks home. The sky is a thick industrial red-orange; a scrap of paper tumbles end over end, kicked into the air by a passing car. Anna feels very tired, longing for home, a cleansing shower, bed.

In the entrance of her flat, she notices something in her mailbox. There's usually nothing in there except circulars and letters addressed to The Occupier, so she often lets days go past before checking. But now there's a note, folded in two. She stuffs it into her skirt pocket.

Anna steps into the lift. She's always worried that it might stall, trapping her inside. Or the light, buzzing and crackling, will fail, sealing her in darkness. Up the lift goes, ten floors, twenty, finally opening to let her out.

Once inside her flat, Anna locks the door behind her. She yawns; soon, hopefully she will sleep. She pours herself a cup of milk and sits down at her table and opens the note.

Hi, it says. *I'm new here. Maybe you can show me around. Call me* (a telephone number). *A.* It's in a large, fluent, rounded script, probably a woman's.

Anna stands, and gazes out the window to the flat opposite. The curtains are drawn. Maybe A, the woman who lives there, who stands in the window at night-time – it must be her, it can't be anyone else – is trying to sleep. As Anna will be soon: her eyes are heavy, wanting to close, and dreams are flickering like flames at the edges of her consciousness, waiting for her.

As Anna climbs into bed, she leaves the note by her bedside. When she wakes, she will make that call.

Migraine

Penny has a migraine.

She's suffered from them since her early teens, enough to know their onset: the sick feeling in her stomach, the one-side-of-the-head ache, the visual disturbance. "I'm sorry," she mutters. She gets up from her VDU and hurries to the Ladies'. She leans against the washbasin, gazing at her reflection. Someone has cleaned up in here; the air is sour with disinfectant. Penny's face is pale. But despite the churning inside her, the dizziness, at least she's unlikely to vomit.

She holds her breath and counts to ten, then strides purposefully back into her office, past her desk and up to the end of the room where Pam, the supervisor, sits. Pam looks up, eyes large behind her glasses. "You don't look too well, Penny."

"I'm not," says Penny, rubbing at the pain, over her right eye.

"Another migraine?"

Penny nods.

Pam tuts. "You really ought to see a doctor."

"I've seen a doctor." Several, in fact. The first, a man, was inclined to blame it on PMT. But the headaches don't coincide with her periods, more like halfway between them. *My fertile time.*

"How are you going to get home?"

"My bus goes at half past."

"You will be all right? You don't want me to drive you home?"

"No, I'll be all right, thanks."

As the bus tails through the outskirts of Birmingham, Penny lightly closes her eyes. A hazy winter sun glares painfully through the window. The noisy chatter of schoolchildren assaults her ears. When she got on this bus, she made sure she sat alone. She wrapped her arms about herself, folded one leg over the other, tugged at her skirt to cover her knees. Self-contained, untouchable. Contact hurts. But the bus has filled up with children returning home; she now has a boy of fifteen sitting next to her, leaning across to chat up the girl across the aisle. The girl is laughing at what he says. Penny is not impressed, but then she's twenty-five now, not fifteen any more.

She lets herself into the house she shares with four others. In the kitchen she eats nothing, drinks only water. She doubts she could keep anything else down. She goes to her room, shuts the door, draws the curtains. Silence, apart from the creak of a loose floorboard. She's the only one in the house. That's the way she likes it: Mark across the corridor has been known to play high-volume heavy metal in the evenings. Normally it's an irritant; now it'd be like needles raking her skull.

She undresses down to her bra and knickers. She shivers in the cold air and hurriedly climbs into bed, pulling the sheets and blankets up to her neck. She closes her eyes and tries to sleep, the only relief from the thick pulsing inside her skull.

She sleeps fitfully, if at all.

Today was the day one of my colleagues, Sarah, left to go on maternity leave. Another colleague, Sammi, who had done likewise a year before and never came back, also called in to visit, baby in tow. Sammi and Sarah and other women in the office who'd had babies - and a few broody non-mothers as well - compared pregnancy notes, admired Sammi's young son. At the centre of it all Sarah sat, self-evidently happy, full, fat and blooming.

My name is Peter. I was one of three men in the office. One of the others, who couldn't stand young children, took the opportunity to go for a coffee. I, on the other hand, stayed and watched, in between phonecalls glancing up.

Envy is a destructive emotion. And inaccurate: I didn't envy Sarah. Not her happiness, at least. But in a way she took her good fortune for granted. If, as I ardently hoped, I could live as a woman - the operation being the final stage of it - I could never be pregnant, never have a child of my own. It is, quite simply, medically impossible.

And babies were back in fashion, of course. Farewell to the careerist Eighties, welcome to the brand spanking new green caring sharing Nineties. Hail the 1992/93 birthrate bulge. If the Eighties were symbolised by the yuppie, than the key figure of the Nineties was the Earth Mother.

Oh cruel nature. Stick in the knife and twist it home.

In the evening I went home. I was tired - I was always tired after work now. There were not enough staff to answer the volume of calls that came in day after day, so we all went home mentally poleaxed, often with a stress headache.

I shared a house in Aldershot with four other men. One of them was rarely in and, when he was, he was more concerned with fucking his girlfriend than with socialising. It wasn't a household as such, just five individuals under one roof. I kept myself apart, and was content to keep it that way. No-one came into my room unless invited. For there I kept my secret. I had never told my mother (my father died five years ago), nor my elder brother Richard, living in Southampton. And speaking of fashion...Richard's wife Michelle was soon to produce the first of their 2.4 children.

Consider: if I revealed all to any of them (housemates or relatives), how would they react? Would they think I was gay? I was not, though I'd had one (and only one, thoroughly unsuccessful) homosexual experience. That I was a transvestite? No, a transvestite knows that under the lacy bra and frilly panties, the schoolgirl dresses, the wigs and makeup, is a fully-functioning masculine body...with an erection. Many drag queens despise women, and no transvestite wants to be one. There is a divide between acting and reality.

A male transsexual wants to close that divide. To be a woman. I am a male transsexual.

Often I stood naked in front of a mirror, the full-length one in my wardrobe. However much I tried to rationalise it, I looked wrong. My mind and my body were out of phase. Where were my breasts? (In my imagination I had magnificent breasts, say 38D.) What was that useless knot of tissue, like a twisted sock, hanging between my legs?

My clothes. I had quite a collection, carefully gathered over the years. I'd shopped for it, an item at a time, different shops in different towns so that no-one might recognise me as a regular. Often the assistants would offer to help; perhaps I looked like the man buying his girlfriend/wife a present for her birthday or - at the appropriate time of year - for Christmas. A bra here (which I'd pad out with socks when I wore it), a pair of knickers there, some tights, some pairs of one-size-

fits-all stockings. Some old skirts I'd bought at a jumble sale. Lipstick, eyeshadow. When I wanted to feel sexy, I had a black suspender belt. And the pride of my collection: a long lavender evening dress. When I was alone in the house and knew I wouldn't be disturbed, I'd put them on. And for a while I'd cease to be Peter and I'd become...Marie. She is me and I am she.

In the morning Penny comes down to breakfast swathed in a nightdress and dressing-gown. Lorna, the only other woman living under this roof, is sitting at table in her pinstriped suit, applying lipstick: a secretary. Soon she and her boyfriend will be buying a flat of their own. A good time to do it, with prices depressed.

Lorna glances up. "Hi, Penny." Then she looks up again, for longer this time. "God, you look *awful*."

"I feel awful."

"Then why'd you get up out of bed, you silly cow?"

"I had to eat something."

"You really ought to see a doctor. You keep getting these migraines. It could be something you're eating. You may have to change your diet. I know about these things."

"I know. I've seen a doctor. It's like my head's fucking splitting open."

"By the way, your brother rang up last night. I said you weren't well."

"I'll ring him back. It's probably Mum again."

"Remember to log the phone call, won't you?"

Shortly after one o'clock Penny rings her brother. A chartered accountant, he often works from home. But it's his wife, Michelle, who answers: Penny can hear the ping of a microwave oven in the background.

"Can I speak to Richard, please?"

"I'm sorry, he's with a client. Who's speaking, please?"

"It's Penny."

"Penny, hi! Why didn't you say? How are you?"

"Not too good. I'm just getting over a migraine."

"Oh, poor you. You get them really bad, don't you? It's about what Richard rang you up about, isn't it? I can tell you what that was all about. It's your mother, I'm afraid. She's taken a turn for the worse. He wondered if you'd like to come up here, stay with us a while...? Not if you're not well enough to travel."

"No, I'll come. I'll get the train tomorrow. I should be better then."

As soon as she puts the phone down, it rings.

"Hi, Penny!" It's her boyfriend Malcolm. "Lorna said you were feeling better." Lorna had introduced them to each other six months before.

"Better than I was last night. I've just found out Mum's taken a turn for the worse. I'll be going down to Southampton tomorrow."

"I was just wondering if I could come over tonight. Not to go anywhere. Just to see you."

"That's sweet of you, Malcolm. Sure."

After she puts the phone down again, she goes back to her room and into bed. She dozes fitfully. In her waking moments, she imagines Malcolm's visit tonight. They'll talk, they'll play music, watch TV or a video. They'll make love.

And tomorrow she'll travel south.

At midmorning, I left my desk. I glanced across at Isobel, who looked up at me and nodded. When I first started working here, I knew what it was like to be left out of a clique: everyone knew everyone else better than anyone knew me. Conversely, I had an early reputation for being aloof. Now, of course, I was accepted, part of a team; cordiality reigned, at least during working hours. Twenty years older than me, Isobel was the first to befriend me. As we both smoked, we took a midmorning coffee break together. When she was on leave or unable to leave her desk for some reason, I'd take a science fiction novel with me.

The staff lounge on the sixth floor had been partitioned in two when the company passed its no-smoking policy. The left-hand half was officially the only place in the building where you could smoke (the fire-escape stairs were used unofficially). As there were a lot of smokers in the building (those who weren't, were often drinkers), a permanent smoke-haze hung over the room.

183

Isobel and I sat down next to each other and she offered me a cigarette. "What a morning, eh?" she said.

"I got involved in this big complaint case. Someone rang up wanting to know when we were doing this job. He'd been told this week. No-one had done bugger-all about it."

She shrugged. "Bloody typical. He probably spoke to this phantom man or this phantom lady we have about."

"Jenny seems to be getting it hard." This was someone who had joined our department three months before.

"Poor girl. She told me, every time she gets in her car at five o'clock she just bursts into tears. Still, it could be worse. I spoke to someone in the London office yesterday and she told me there's somewhere in the country where people are being treated for depression. It was just the same at my last job. They just squeeze you dry and use you up. And of course, you can't go anywhere else. You're lucky you've got a job at all. That's what they'll say."

In many ways, if I'd been born twenty years earlier I'd have wanted to be her. I found her attractive, as did others. She had children, and was kept young by her boyfriend (ten years her junior); she had a young outlook on life, generally. But I knew this was another pipe-dream. I hadn't told her I was a virgin (heterosexually); I hadn't told her about my homosexual experience (which was nearly aborted when he found I was wearing a pair of knickers under my trousers - he wanted to have sex with a man, not a woman manquée). Most of all, I hadn't told her about Marie. But if I were to confide in someone, it would be her.

We went back down to the office. In amongst the memos to ring certain customers was a message to ring my brother. I went over to the clerical assistant's phone (we were no longer allowed to use the office switchboard phones for personal calls, though many still did) and dialled his work number. He answered on the second ring.

"Hello, Richard," I said. "You rang. How's things?"

"Oh, fine," he said. "Listen, Peter, the reason I'm ringing - it's Mum. She's taken a turn for the worse. She might not last the week."

"Oh shit."

"She's had false alarms, but I don't think this is one. Do you

want to come down? Michelle and I could put you up."

"Yeah, sure. I'll speak to my boss about it. I'm sure I can get leave. In the circumstances." *Said with an involuntary grimness.*

"Yes," said Richard. "I'm sure you can."

So there it was. My mother was finally dying. And when the moment came, she'd have her two sons next to her. She had no daughters - if you discounted myself.

The following morning, Penny boards the Intercity from Birmingham to Southampton via Reading and Basingstoke, a journey of close to four hours. Faint glimmerings of her migraine are still present; she wears tinted glasses to cut down glare.

She's grown accustomed to living in Birmingham: she went to University there and stayed on after graduation. She'd never been inclined to drift aimlessly like some of her friends, or go round the world in a year. She wanted a job and after a couple of months found one, with an insurance company. Since then, apart from Christmas and odd weekends and more significantly her father's funeral, she's never been back to Southampton, where she was born and brought up and where her mother and brother still live.

She finds an unreserved seat and tries to lift her suitcase up on the luggage rack as the train pulls out of New Street Station. She almost stumbles, and sweat breaks out on her forehead and under her arms. She looks frustratedly up; she's just that couple of inches too short to manage to push her case up all the way.

"Excuse me, Miss, do you need any help?"

She turns. A man in his early forties, hair greying, is standing in the aisle to her left. She nods and he reaches up and pushes the case in.

"Thanks," she says. "It's not easy when you're five foot two."

He smiles. "You're welcome." And walks past her, his copy of the *Daily Telegraph* under his arm. She watches him go. He's obviously sensed she wants to be alone. But he seemed quite safe, not the type to try it on. She's not *dressed provocatively,* as a rape-case judge might say: a loose peach-coloured top that doesn't show the shape of her small breasts, and black leggings. And that Miss jarred: she's always insisted on Ms.

Her concentration is too fragile for reading. She changes trains once, then twice. She sits back for the last forty-five minutes of her journey. But as the train pulls out of Winchester she becomes aware of a growing sense of unease. She realises that it's been with her since she got on this train at Basingstoke. A lowering disquiet, as if someone is staring directly at the nape of her neck. Once or twice she turns round but there is no-one there. Apart from her, the carriage is empty.

I left the train at Southampton and exited the station by the north side, near the Mayflower Theatre. I glanced round the carpark and saw no-one I recognised, so I sat on my suitcase and waited. Five minutes later, Richard and Michelle pulled up.

Richard helped me put my case in the boot. Michelle came out to watch. She was petite and pretty, her round face framed with a black pageboy cut. Her abdomen had rounded out a little: I'd known from Richard's phonecalls she was four months pregnant, but this was the first time I'd seen her that way. She wasn't unfriendly to me, but there was a distance between us. Maybe the aloofness was in me, or in the signals I gave off.

"Did you have a good journey?" Richard asked me.

"Yes, thanks." It had been an hour and a half's journey from Aldershot, with a changeover at Woking. I'd moved away, and found lodgings in Aldershot, when I found a job in Guildford; later I got my present job, walking distance from where I lived.

"Keeping well?"

"Uh-huh." I looked up; Michelle flashed an awkward smile at me. Richard and I got on fine over the phone; face to face we became incommunicative. It took us time to penetrate each other's carapace, to seem like the brothers we were.

Richard drove up to his house in the Portswood district, just behind the shopping centre. As we approached, I became aware of a disquieting sensation, a back-of-the-head throb: I'd had it in the train, but it had disappeared once I'd got into the carpark, leading me to suspect it was caused by the stuffiness of the train compartment. But it returned, and intensified during dinner. I thought it might be some unusual kind of headache, but it never developed into that.

We sat and watched television then I, claiming tiredness, went to bed just after ten o'clock. I spent half an hour unpacking. I'd brought some of Marie's clothes with me, but I knew I'd never have a chance to wear them, except possibly a pair of knickers under my trousers. I saw myself as others, not understanding, might see me: frivolity in the presence of death. Perhaps that was the source of the anxiety I felt, that near-headache I still had. Normally I'd get through the day knowing I could lock myself in my room at night and shed Peter to let Marie out. Like a snake sloughing its skin. But I didn't have that relief now.

I was still feeling edgy, so I locked myself in the bathroom and masturbated into a sheath of toilet paper. I felt better; at least the anxiety was gone. As I was kneeling down, wiping away some semen that had spilled despite the care I'd taken, I heard Michelle's low voice outside: "He doesn't say much, does he?" Then Richard's voice, shushing her.

I went back into my room and lay down in the dark.

And then I heard the voice in my head.

Penny arrives in Southampton. She goes into the car park, where Richard and Michelle are waiting for her by the car. She embraces, kisses them both. She's always got on with Michelle, who today is even more animated than usual. This is the first time Penny has seen her since she became pregnant; the small bump rounds out Michelle's figure nicely.

The three of them prepare dinner, eat it and wash up. Penny phones Malcolm and they talk for twenty minutes. Penny, Richard and Michelle sit in front of the TV in the small front room until ten o'clock when a bout of yawning prompts Michelle to urge Penny to go to bed. "You've had a long day."

"Yes, you need to be fresh tomorrow," says Richard.

Penny nods, and yawns. "I think I'd better."

"You're picking up the Brummie accent," says Richard.

"Am I? I haven't noticed. I must've lived there too long."

"Anyway, we'll see Mum tomorrow."

"It's terrible. It's not so long after Dad died."

Richard shrugs; he always has been fatalistic. Michelle mutters: "It's such a terrible shame."

As Penny wanders down the hallway to her room, she realises how tired she is. She undresses slowly, having to search for places to drape her clothes; natural tidiness forbids her to drop them on the floor. The light is weak, the wardrobe crowding out much of it. The bed is harder than she's used to; she never sleeps well in strange beds. She lies in the darkness, tossing and turning, bone-weary yet unable to sleep.

And then she hears:

- *Such a shame can't Marie not here oh shit...*

"Who's there?" she says aloud.

- *What's that?* It's a male voice: not in the room but inside her head. *Who are you?*

She begins to tremble. She thinks: Am I going mad? It's the first sign of schizophrenia, hearing voices. Soon she'll begin to hallucinate.

- *What's your name?* says the voice.

"Who are you?"

- *I asked first.* More peevish than threatening; she begins to relax. *What's your name, please?*

She's poised to say it aloud, but she pauses, then thinks it:

- *Penny.*

A thought with a little extra thrust, so this other person can hear it.

- *Hello, Penny. I'm Peter. Now, what are you doing here?*

- *What are you doing here?*

- *You tell me first.*

- *I'm staying in this room in my brother's house. We're going to see our Mum in hospital tomorrow.*

- *Hang on, something's just clicked. What's your brother's name?* Peter asks.

- *Richard.*

- *What does he do?*

- *He's a chartered accountant.*

- *Is he married?*

- *Yes. His wife's called Michelle. They've been married two years.*

- *Have they got any children?*

- *No, but one's on its way. Where's all this leading to?*
- *I've only got one more question, the voice in her head says. Just one more, Penny. When and where were you born?*
- *7th July 1967, in Southampton. Why?*
- *So was I. It's all coming into place. I've also got a brother called Richard, a sister-in-law called Michelle, and a dying mother. You're me. You're the person I'd have been if I'd been born female.*
- *I've never heard such shit in my life,* Penny thinks. *You're just a voice in my head and I'm going mad. Now fuck off and let me sleep.*

She buries her head in the pillow and resists any further attempts of the voice to communicate with her.

The following morning I could still feel Penny's presence in my head. It was like having a second pair of eyes. The view from her head was faint; she was holding me off.

It was tantalising. I must surely be imagining this: or maybe God was being generous for once. I wanted, more than anything, to be a woman; now He was presenting me with just that possibility.

If I could only look through her eyes, just once. To be a woman...

Her voice inside my head: - Fucking forget it. You're not getting inside my head.

But I knew I'd only be disappointed. I knew, even if I had a sex change, that I could only ever be an approximation of what I wished. For most purposes a close, even indistinguishable, approximation, but still an approximation. I'd never have periods, never be able to have children. I'd been cheated of girlhood and a proper adolescence.

- What are you so worried about? There wasn't anything special about my adolescence. Nor my girlhood. It was quite ordinary really.
- *But you're taking it for granted,* I said. *You haven't been cheated. You fit.*
- What did I do? I smoked a few fags, got pissed a few times, had sex on Saturday nights. I was no different to anyone else.

At least we could talk together. During breakfast, the phone rang, in her world only. But I heard it, so vividly that I started.

Richard looked up. "What's the matter, Peter?"

189

"The phone's ringing."

"No it isn't." He laughed. "Wake up."

(In Penny's world, Michelle got up to answer the phone. In mine, she stayed put, reading the tabloid section of The Guardian.)

"I could have sworn it was."

Michelle looked up at me and smiled. "Hearing things, are we, Peter?"

"I must be."

(In Penny's world, Michelle was saying: "Yes, I'll go and get her." She walked back into the kitchen and said to Penny/me: "It's for you. Malcolm.")

I ate my cereal and didn't say anything, but in my head I was with Penny as she went to the phone.

("Hello, love of my life," she said.

("Hi, Penny. How you feeling?"

("I'm a lot better, thanks. We're going to see Mum today.")

As they talked, I made a little mental push and sank deeper inside Penny's head. Her flesh was ghostly-solid now, the telephone receiver a faint pressure on my ear. But memories and thoughts floated up, about Malcolm, and Penny's relationship with him. And memories of their lovemaking. Their first time, in her flat, after a nightclub. And the most recent, when she tried oral sex on him; I could feel the sensation inside my mouth. I could hear the creak of the bedsprings, her gasping loud in my ears. And then brief snippets of sensation: his penis entering her, the whole-body fuse-blowing of her orgasm.

To my embarrassment, I had an erection.

- Will you get out of my head!

More forceful than ever before: she pushed me away, so much so, that contact was broken for a few seconds. When it returned, I was back to the usual arm's length contact.

("Have a good day," Malcolm finished his conversation. "Love you."

("Love you," Penny said.)

Penny sits in the back as Richard drives to the hospital.

The voice seems so convincing, so reasonable. It (he) even has a name - Peter. So logical and yet so absurd. She thinks: My name is Penelope Jane Walsh. Less formally (more usually), Penny Walsh. I am female, single, twenty-five years old. I do not have a male alter ego.

And yet she does. According to Peter, if nature's dice had landed another way, and she were a man, she would be him.

And Peter wants to be her.

- *Tell me*, she says to him. *Why do you want to be a woman?*

- *I don't know. I always have. Ever since I was little, I've had this sense I was in the wrong body. When I was at school, I had to prevent myself from going into the girls' toilets. I did once, and everyone laughed at me.*

- *I'm sorry for you. But I still think you're exaggerating. I don't think I'm very feminine. I only wear a skirt because I have to for work. Outside work, I slop around in leggings or jeans. I don't wear makeup. I've got one posh dress I never wear, except to weddings.*

- *It's all very well for you to say. That's your choice. You have that choice: you're a woman.*

- *I know I am. I wouldn't want it any other way.*

- *You can't imagine it any other way.*

- *Well, no. I wouldn't want to be a man. That's the last thing I'd want.*

- *Then how do you think I fucking well feel? I can imagine it, but I can't fucking have it!*

She can feel tears prickling his eyes, a band about his throat. She feels his iron self-control. If Michelle and Richard weren't in the front seat, he'd be crying. Or maybe he wouldn't be.

- *Then why don't you do something about it?* she says. *It's no good wallowing in self-pity.*

- *What do you mean?*

- *You can get a sex change.*

- *You can't just "get a sex change"! Do you know what's involved in that?*

- *Well, no. I can't say I do.*

- *You've got to get a psychiatrist to certify you're genuinely transsexual. If he doesn't believe you, you can't get the operation. You've got to live as your chosen gender for two years. I'll have to have electrolysis treatment to get rid of my facial hair. I've have to take hormones. And then, if I'm lucky, they'll let me have the operation. That costs a lot of money if you get it done privately. Do you know what they do there?*

- No doubt you're going to tell me.

- They cut your penis off. They fold the scrotal tissue into a hole they make between your legs: that's your vagina. The glans becomes the clitoris. They restructure the urethra. Only an expert can tell the difference between that and the real thing.

- Stop it! You're making me sick!

She breaks contact. It's her own fault; she asked him for details and she got details.

She's still feeling queasy when they reach the hospital.

I lay in bed that evening talking to Penny. From time to time she complained I was keeping her awake: I could feel her weariness.

- I'll let you go to sleep if you'll let me do one thing, *I said.*
- What? *Sleepily.*
- Let me get into your head. Just for a minute.
- What do you mean?
- Let me be you. Come on, only a minute.
- Isn't that dangerous?
- We won't know until we try! Come on, Penny, *please.*
- You sure you can get back into your body?
- Yes! Look, I can feel what you feel, hear what you hear, see what you see. But it's only little bits. I want to go all the way.
- That sounds like a chat-up line. *I could hear her chuckle.*
- But you will?
- Oh all right. But just for a minute. I don't want you stuck in my head.
- Thanks, Penny. You don't realise what this means to me.
- Oh, cut the sycophantic bullshit. Get on with it.

And I pushed.

There was no other word for it: just an extra mental effort, a flexing of a new muscle.

For a moment I thought it hadn't worked. I was still gazing up at the same ceiling.

"It hasn't worked," I said out loud.

And then I froze. I began to tremble. My voice was not the same. It was quite deep, but lacked the gravel undertow of a male voice.

I looked down at myself. It wasn't easy to move my head; it was as if my neck muscles were resisting me.

I was wearing a nightdress. It was loose on me, and I could see the shadowy gully of my cleavage. I slid my finger up the side of the breast, touched the areola and the nipple.

Then Penny's voice inside my head:

- Your minute's up, matey. I didn't say you could have a feel as well. Go on, back to your own body.

I broke contact. I was in my own body again. Overweight. Male. But for a minute or so, I had been a woman. The thrill of that minute had given me an erection. I climbed out of bed and locked myself in the bathroom and masturbated.

I knew that that minute would tantalise me, maybe for the rest of my life. If I went ahead with a sex-change, I would look the part: breasts, smooth soft skin, broader hips, a vagina. I could have sex with men who could bring me to a woman's orgasm. But I wouldn't have that sense of rightness, that sense of **womanliness** *that I'd experienced just then, just for a moment.*

*

Penny sits at the breakfast table, reading Richard's newspaper. Michelle is eating toast. Penny sends out a thought:

- Can you hear me?

No answer. She shrugs. Normally he's only too keen to converse. It gives Penny pause, to be the subject of such obsessive curiosity. She remembers the night before: she'd let him inside her head, fully inside, for a minute. She'd felt his fascination at being inside a woman's body at long last. Different to what he'd been used to.

I suppose it might be, she thinks. I'm built differently. Shorter, for one. I've got breasts; he hasn't. My body fat is stored in different places to his. My weight would be distributed differently. I was lying in bed: just let him try and walk.

But if he's done it once, he'll want to do it again...

- *Morning,* she hears inside her head.
- *I tried to call you a minute ago. Where were you? Ignoring me?*
- *No, I didn't hear you. I've just come downstairs.*
- *I've been here all the time.*
- *I wonder if that's it. Hang on, I'd like to try something.*
- *You're not getting into my head again, are you?*
- *No, nothing like that. Stay right where you are. I'll just break contact.*

She feels him go. She tries to read the newspaper but can't concentrate. A minute passes. Then she hears:
- *It's me again.*
- *Where did you go?*
- *I just walked round the room. I tried to get back into contact with you but I couldn't. It's only when I sat down. Same seat as you're sitting in.*
- *What are you driving at?*
- *I can only get in contact with you, Penny, if we're in the same place at the same time. That's why we've never spoken before this week. We lead different lives. We live in different places. It's only because we're down at Richard's place, because of Mum being ill, that we've got into contact.*
- *But you went with me down the hallway...*
- *We were in contact at the time. We didn't break contact then. This is fascinating stuff.*
- *I'm sure.* She sniffs. *I'm still not convinced I'm not going mad.*
- *You're not. Unless you're a figment of my overactive imagination.*
- *Oh, I'm real all right.* She chuckles, aloud.

Michelle looks up.

"Sorry," Penny mutters.

Michelle returns to her toast.

- *I heard that,* says Peter.
- *I couldn't give a shit if you did. 'Bye for now.*

Penny breaks contact.

Michelle took the phone call. Richard was out with a client. She picked up the receiver. "Hello...? No, he's not here. Can I help, or take a message? Oh, I see..."

I stopped listening at that point, and only recovered my attention when I heard her put the receiver down. The heavy slap of her slippers on the wooden hallway floor.

"Peter...?"

I looked up. She was bending over, the lines framing her mouth deeper than before.

"It's your Mum," she said. "That was the hospital. She died during the night."

I'd known it would happen. It had been inevitable, and I'd had six months to prepare for it. But there was still a lump in my throat that I couldn't swallow.

Michelle put a hand on my shoulder. "You may want to be alone. I've got to let Richard know."

I nodded.

As she rang Richard's mobile phone, I tiptoed past her up to my room. I was trying to make contact with Penny, but couldn't. Was she somewhere else, or was I unable to do it any more? I wanted to speak to her. She would be hearing the same news as me. We could comfort each other - we were the same person. But she wasn't there.

I shut the door behind myself and lay face down on the bed. I wanted to cry, but tears wouldn't come.

Penny has gone to the newsagent to buy a paper; when she lets herself back in, Michelle tells her that her mother has died during the night.

"Oh shit," Penny mutters.

"Look, sit down," says Michelle. "I'll make you something."

Penny puts her face into her hands and bursts into tears. Michelle brings over a box of tissues and dabs at Penny's eyes. Blindly, Penny reaches out and embraces her.

Half an hour later, Penny goes up to her room to read her newspaper. She can't concentrate. It all seems so trivial. Why am I worrying about things - Mum was dying all this time, she thinks. In her sleep - I'm glad she didn't have any more pain. All I'm worrying about is so unimportant compared to that.

    - *You speak for yourself,* Peter says inside her head.

    - *What are you doing? Can't you leave me alone?*

    - *It's my grief too. You are me, after all.*

    - *No I'm not. We're different people. We lead different lives. Don't you try to make out we're the same. I'm not a -*

    A pause.

    - *Not a what?* says Peter.

    - *Nothing. Forget it.*

    - *Not a mixed-up pervert, you mean?*

    - *Don't put words into my mouth. I wouldn't say things like that.*

    - *You are so fucking smug, Penny! Do you think I want to be a transsexual? You think yourself lucky for once!*

    - *Look, I'm sorry, Peter.*

    - *So you should be. You owe me.*

    And he breaks contact.

It was a few days later, the evening of the day of the funeral, that I asked Penny the question. After the last outburst, we had stayed on friendly terms, holding mental conversations as we walked down the High Street, or around the Ocean Village shopping centre.

    I'd wanted to ask her, but I didn't know how she'd react.

    After the funeral, Richard and Michelle had hosted the reception. I'd assisted. Later, when everyone had gone home and I was helping clear up, I knew I had to ask it. I was going back to Aldershot the next day - presumably Penny was taking the train back to Birmingham - and I'd never have another chance. We might never come in contact again, after that. Here, Richard's house, was the most likely place - if we were ever here simultaneously again.

    I had to ask her. And that night, as I was lying in bed, I did.

    - Penny...?

    - Hmmm?

    - Tomorrow - I know this sounds silly, but I don't know how to put it - tomorrow, can we swap bodies?

    - Can we what?

- Swap bodies. I be you, you be me. Only for half a day.
- You're mad.
- *Please.* I'd be very grateful.
- If you think I'm going to let you run rampant inside my body, you're very much mistaken.
- Don't you want to know what it's like - to see the world through a man's eyes? Know what it's like to be male?
- Frankly, no.
- But it'd mean a lot to me, Penny.
- Why? It'd only make things worse for you. It'd only show you something you could never have. Even if you had a sex-change, it wouldn't be the same.
- But just to say I was a woman, a genuine, real, functioning woman, even for a few hours... Isn't it better to have had something and lost it, than never to have had it at all?
- That's a matter of opinion.
- You'd be doing me a great favour.
- I'm aware of that. I'm not sure. Let me think about it. Don't go away.

She broke contact. I lay there, tossing and turning in the dark. I wanted to know where she was - somewhere in the room - but I didn't know. I wanted to know what she was thinking.

- How do you know it'll work? *she said.*
- It worked before.
- That was just for a short while, and I was still about. I didn't go into your body. What'll happen if we break contact with our bodies? How do we know it won't kill us?
- I'm prepared to take that risk.
- That's big of you. What about me?
- I left my body and went back, that time. It didn't kill me.
- Let me think about it again.

She broke contact a second, shorter time.

- Okay, *she said.* I'll do it. But I'll make the conditions.
- Fine.
- My train goes at half-past ten. You can catch it too - I change at Basingstoke, you change at Woking. I want you at the station at

twenty past sharp. We'll meet at the Quicksnack. We'll swap back then.
- No problem.
- Do you promise?
- I promise.
- Fine. I'll do it, then. Just this once. Just for you. For three hours only. I don't know what I'm letting myself in for, but somehow I trust you. You're right, I would be curious to know what it's like to be in your body.
- I'm very very grateful, Penny.
- Don't get all mushy. I can't bear it. Now, before we go to sleep, let's both write a few things that we'll each need to know. Like, where everything is. See you tomorrow.

She broke contact again, for the final time.
I hardly slept that night, for the excitement.

Penny opens her eyes at half past six, from a half-remembered dream that fades on waking. At first she's disorientated, then she remembers. Today she will change bodies with Peter, for three hours. At half past seven. For three hours she will be a man.

A queasy nervous sensation in the pit of her stomach. She sits on the side of the bed, dangling her feet, her toes just touching the carpet. She hugs herself through the thin fabric of her nightdress. It's cold. For a moment she wonders if she'll be sick, but she fights back the bile rising in her throat.

Couldn't she just back out, not go through with it? But she promised, and she's prided herself on always keeping her word, if it's in her power to do so. She's sensed what this exchange means to Peter. But he has no existence in this world, she thinks - who could prove I did anything? But she has no existence in his world either; they are each equally unreal.

She has made a list for Peter's information. She felt ridiculous writing it out - what would she have said if someone caught her doing it? The instructions range from the informative - which toiletries in the bathroom are hers - to the admonitory - *don't spend anything - I'm nearly overdrawn as it is* - to the very personal - *I NEVER wear yellow!!* (redundant, as she has no item of clothing of that colour in her suitcase).

What has kept her awake - apart from anxiety about the whole process - is the fear that it may go wrong, she may be stuck in Peter's body forever. Then I'll know just what he feels. And he'll get his wish. She shudders.

- *I'm ready when you are, Penny.* She can sense his excitement.
- *I might as well get it over with. Remember, the Quicksnack at ten-twenty sharp.*
- *Understood.*
- *How do you do this?*
- *It's easy, just* **push.**

She chuckles. - *Like giving birth.*
- *I wouldn't know about that.*
- *Neither would I.*

And with her mind she gives a *push*

and blinks.

At first nothing has happened. The same bed, the sun coming in the same window.

But something's different. Something. The first intimation: clothes. They hang differently. Look down. The nightdress is gone; pyjamas instead.

Stand up. A moment of dizziness; a brief lurch inside the head as Penny breaks contact.

Everything seems different, but the room is just the same. He realises why soon enough: he's five foot eight. Six inches taller than Penny. He tests this by reaching for the top of the wardrobe. He can do this; Penny never could, and always had to stand on top of a chair.

I've always wanted to be taller.
And then: What do I look like?

He opens the wardrobe and looks in the mirror. Peter's face stares back at him. Recognisably the same - the family resemblance is there - but the hair is shorter, the face less soft, and there's stubble that needs shaving. Also a double chin: after all, Peter is overweight. He pinches folds of flesh about his stomach. And then, he takes a deep breath and unbuttons his pyjama top, slips off the bottom half.

He cups his penis and testicles in his hand. It is strange to hold, this limp mass of tissue attached to him. The absence of breasts and vagina is less disorientating than the presence of a penis. Penny has seen them before: limp in occasional foreign films, erect in the *Lover's Guide* video she and some female friends watched one giggly tipsy evening, erect and inside her for Malcolm and the four other men she's had sex with. But then it had been other to her - a focus of desire, an object of amusement, a *willy*, something men were preoccupied with. But not so commonplace as this, not part of her. Perhaps men felt the same way about breasts *(boobs, tits, knockers),* as objects of mirth in seaside postcards and *Carry On* films, or objects of lust - but to Penny simply part of her body, something she has in common with all other adult women.

At the memory of Penny's sex life with Malcolm, he feels a tingling. His penis becomes warm to the touch and begins to stiffen. Embarrassed, he turns away and dresses hurriedly. Putting on men's clothes is not strange: with the exception of underpants, there's nothing that Penny hasn't worn at some time.

He goes downstairs. Richard and Michelle are already sitting down; Richard has finished breakfast and is reading his newspaper.

"Morning."

"Good morning," says Michelle.

"Got to go," says Richard, getting to his feet and folding his newspaper away in his briefcase. He extends his hand. "Well, safe journey home, Peter."

"Thank you." He is taken aback that Richard doesn't kiss him; but then, he thinks, he's not Penny now.

After Richard has left, Michelle leans across the table. "What time's your train?"

"Twenty past ten. It's actually twenty-two, but - "

"Give it plenty of time, I know." Michelle is curter now; he wonders if it's because she's in a bad mood. But then, he remembers, she simply doesn't get on with Peter as well as she does with Penny. Not so friendly. Well it's only his fault, she thinks: too shut in on himself. "I'll drop you off."

In mid-morning, he leaves the house to get a *Guardian.* At first it's not so easy to walk; the weight distribution is all wrong. He wonders if everyone is staring at him. But they don't notice; they won't notice him. He, Peter, is nondescript. What he wears, how he looks, is not being judged.

Back at home, as he is reading the newspaper, Michelle glances over his shoulder as she passes by on her way to do the dusting. "You don't usually buy a paper," she says.

Something clenches inside him; he feels his cheeks burn. "I - I just felt like it. Something to read on the train." Inside his head he's thinking: What? What paper does Peter read? Doesn't read any. Watches TV news.

Michelle says nothing. She glances at her watch. "If you're ready I'll drop you off."

They hardly speak in the car. He misses the girltalk Penny often had with Michelle. He wants to start such a conversation, but something inhibits him. He doesn't know where to start. There seems to be some barrier between them; perhaps it's in the nature of the relationship between Peter and Michelle. Some archness.

Michelle pulls up in the station concourse, and turns to him. "Okay, then. Have a nice journey home."

"Th-thanks for everything. For putting me up."

"You're welcome. Any time. Hopefully next time it'll be in better circumstances."

"It'll be nice to get back to my flat. To see Birmingham again."

"*Birmingham?*"

"Sorry. Aldershot." He blushes. "Don't know why I said Birmingham."

Michelle chuckles. "I think you need a good night's sleep. You look all in. Anyway, plenty of time on the train to do it."

They don't kiss, which disappoints him. Penny and Michelle would certainly kiss. She leaves him at the station entrance with his suitcase. He buys his ticket, a single to Aldershot. There's a delayed earlier train, but he purposefully doesn't rush to catch it. He makes his way to the Quicksnack to wait for Peter to return to reclaim his body.

When I opened my eyes I knew something was different. The air was clearer, and I could feel the morning cold on my skin. I looked down at myself.

I was a woman.

I shook my head to feel the ends of my hair tickling my shoulderblades.

I stood up, and at first almost toppled over. I was shorter now, five foot two at the most, and my weight was differently distributed. I could feel the weight of my breasts. I pulled my nightdress off over my head and looked at myself in the wardrobe mirror, running my hands over my breasts. The tangled triangle of hair at my groin; I touched my clitoris and vagina, inserting a finger.

The tingling sensation felt good. I lay back on the bed and masturbated, slowly at first, then faster and more vigorously as I approached orgasm. It was a different climax, not a simple spurt, felt only in the penis, but whole-body, and in waves. I bucked and moaned, my back arched; I gasped out loud as I came.

Penny had left some clothes out for me. I ran my hands through them: they were disappointingly **ordinary**. A light blue long-sleeved top and black leggings. For my one day - one morning, few hours - as a woman, I wanted to wear something a little more striking. I rum - maged in the suitcase and took out a black miniskirt and a white blouse. I put on her pair of low-heeled shoes. I applied lipstick and eye-shadow.

I went downstairs. I had to be careful walking: not only was I unused to heeled shoes, which caused an ache in the small of my back, but I had to get used to being five foot two instead of five foot eight. It was as if the whole world had shifted upward by six inches.

Richard, dressed for work, was reading his newspaper. He glanced up at me as I came in the room. His eyebrows lifted momentarily, then he said: "Hi, Penny."

"Hello," I said, and smiled. I sat down, and crossed my legs. Perhaps I had overdone it: did I look too made-up, too tarty? More to the point, too much unlike Penny?

Michelle was sitting opposite me; I hadn't noticed her until now. She smiled at me. "All ready to go, then?"

I nodded.

"It's a long journey," she said.

"About three hours," I said, guessing. "I've got things to

read..."

"You must be glad to get back to Birmingham," she said. "Not that we haven't been glad to have you here. You must come down again sometime, under better circumstances. Once I've had the baby. You must bring Malcolm."

Malcolm? I asked myself. Then I remembered: Penny's boyfriend. "I'd love to," I said.

Richard sat bolt upright, and folded his newspaper into two, slipping it into his briefcase. "I'd better be going." He stood up. "Goodbye, Penny." He stood, expectant - of what, I didn't know at first. Then I realised: I stood up, and we kissed. He hugged me, patting me on the shoulderblades.

It was strangely pleasurable, to be kissed by my own brother. As a woman, by a man. Apart from my mother in hospital, I'd never kissed anyone in a long time. The last time was by that other man, as prelude to his fucking me (to be crude about it - it was a crude occasion).

After breakfast, I helped Michelle wash up.

"I'll run you down to the station, if you like," she said.

"That'll be very nice," I said. I paused. "I'd like to go down to the shops for a bit, though."

"A few things for the journey?"

I nodded.

"You look very nice this morning."

"Thank you," I said.

"I wish I had your legs. I couldn't get into a skirt like that."

I wanted to go outside for other reasons. I wanted to put myself on public view. I'd convinced Richard and Michelle. Now I wanted to convince strangers. One fantasy I had was to appear in public in full drag, spend a day or more as a woman, without my biological sex being discovered. I'd never had the courage to try. Now of course, I couldn't be detected. I was in a woman's body, the right body, for the first time. And the only time: even a sex change wouldn't make me as complete a woman.

Penny had been right. My experiences today would only tantalise me for the rest of my life. In an hour or two, Penny would reclaim this body, and I'd return to Peter's.

Unless, I thought as I walked down the road to the shops, unless I didn't. If I could avoid Penny at the station, there was nothing to stop me staying inside this body. Granted, there were things I'd have to get used to. Penny's job, Penny's home, Penny's circle of friends. Not to mention Penny's body. But that would be the easy part.

I walked down Portswood Road. The wind was chilly on my legs: it had been a mistake to wear such a short skirt and thin tights. Lack of experience showing. Some men stared at my legs as I passed. The wind was cold on my face, too. It was as if I were a skin thinner: sensations were sharper and I felt the weather more. The crowd noise was a degree louder than I'd have expected it to be.

I did my shopping quickly. I wondered if people thought I was ill. I had a permanent low-level headache muzziness and I must have seemed distracted. It was also strange to be addressed as "love" by the middle-aged shopkeeper.

I got home and busied myself packing. I had achieved my fantasy: to be seen in public as a woman. I would have wished it to be better: but we can never live up to our imaginations. It would improve with practice: I hadn't had a lifetime's training in femininity. And what was femininity anyway? Penny wasn't necessarily how I saw myself.

Michelle drove me to the station. I was quiet, and she remarked on it.

"I'm always like this before long journeys," I said.

She nodded. But I wasn't being truthful. It was more disappointment: I would be leaving this body soon, before I could get used to it. I would be returning to Peter's body, and the torment of a mind-and-body mismatch. Penny had been right: all I'd achieved was a lifetime of frustration. Unless.

Michelle pulled up in the concourse, and walked with me to the ticket office. She stood behind me as I bought a single to Birmingham New Street.

I heard a distant announcement: "...train now standing ...delayed Inter-City..." I didn't hear the rest.

"Penny!" Michelle tugged at my sleeve.

I turned.

"Penny, that train's going to Basingstoke."

"It's not due for twenty minutes."

"It's the previous one. It's been delayed. If you're quick you might just catch it!"

We kissed and embraced hurriedly.

"Give us a ring when you get back," she said. "Let us know you got back safely."

I nodded, then hurried away. My suitcase was heavy, and it was difficult to run in heels. But I went as fast as I possibly could, willing my body forward to catch the train. Over the station bridge, my heels clicking on the tiles. The guard blew his whistle and for a moment I thought I'd missed it. But there was a shout in my ear - "Hurry up, love!" - and I jumped the last few feet, and scrambled through the door. A man sitting opposite me smiled as I slumped into my seat, panting heavily. The train pulled out of the station.

It took me a few minutes to recover my breath. The train had picked up speed before I realised what I'd done.

At first I felt bad about it - I'd gone back on my word to Penny, after all. But there was nothing she could do about it. I didn't exist in her universe. No body, no crime. And nothing she could do about it, short of coming to Birmingham after me. But there were ways of avoiding her: I could move to another flat. Move in with Malcolm, even.

As the train sped through the Hampshire countryside, I sat back and smiled. Of course I had a lot to learn. I had to accustom myself to a new life. But I knew I could do it. I was looking forward to meeting Malcolm, too. I only hoped he wouldn't find me changed by my stay in Southampton. If it all worked out, perhaps one day we'd get married, have children...

I was looking forward to my new existence.

It was ironic, I thought; we had returned, after a fashion, to our original states: a woman, and another woman trapped inside a man's body...

Slowly, surely, Penny returns to her body. A slide, a greased slipping from one to the other, the ungainliness melting away as she returns to the form she knows of old. Standing outside the Quicksnack, she stretches her legs, breaking the knots. The headache-muzziness she had as Peter is already going.

- *What took you so long?* she asks.
- *I was...delayed.*

She doesn't question him. She's simply relieved to be Penny again, her gender and her physical form in unison.

- *How was it?* he asks.
- *It was an experience.*
- *No more than that?*

She shakes her head. - I *don't want to do it again. I'm quite happy with my own body, thank you.*

- *You're fortunate.*
- *I suppose.*

The train they'll both catch has arrived; the PA announces it.

- *Well, this is my train,* she says.
- *It's mine as well.*

They stay together as far as Basingstoke. There, they part: Penny to Reading and Birmingham, he to Aldershot via Woking.

- *Well,* she says. *If you were here in front of me, you'd get a kiss. I don't know when we'll meet up again.*

- *When we visit Richard and Michelle again. I know what I've got to do now.*

- *I wish you luck.*

- *Thank you. Touch the banister, at the top there.*

She does so, and for a moment, she feels his hand there, warm, sharing the same space as hers.

- *Goodbye.*
- *Goodbye.*

And then he's gone. Penny walks through the tunnel towards her platform.

Over the station bridge, my heels clicking on the tiles. And suddenly one heel slipped and I went crashing to the floor. My suitcase slid away from me.

"Shit!" I said out loud. "Fuck it!"

"Are you all right?" A man was standing over me. I realised

with a sudden embarrassment that my legs were splayed and he could see up my skirt.

I stood up. Fortunately I'd done myself no damage. I dusted my skirt with my hand.

"Running for the train, were you?"

I nodded. I glanced through the bridge windows down at the platform. The train had gone.

"I'll be all right, thanks," I said. I began walking back the way I came. Towards the Quicksnack, where Penny was waiting.

He stands by the Quicksnack, waiting. The train he planned to catch leaves, and he waits half an hour for the next one. But still Peter doesn't return.

Peter has left. In Penny's body.

I should have fucking known, he thinks. I should have known I couldn't trust him. I gave him the opportunity of a lifetime. How could I have been so fucking *stupid?*

Finally he gets on board the train. By now there is a tight band about his throat. There is no-one else in the compartment. He gives way to tears.

If anyone asks why he's crying, he'd have no explanation. None that would make any sense.

He glances out of the window. Peter's reflection stares back.

I'm not Peter, he thinks. *I'm Penny. Penny. Penny.*

But repetition doesn't help.

I'm not a man. I'm a woman.

With the passing countryside, mile by mile, the trap deepens.

A Night Away From Home

They took a taxi from the airport to the hotel. Already the clouds were clustering over Glasgow, and Patrick knew it would rain soon. Lindsay paid the fare and took a receipt for her expenses claim. The hotel was a tall, foursquare, high-windowed stone block of a building perched at the top of a hill in the West End, just by an Underground station.

A porter took them to their rooms. They'd been booked next door to each other - someone in the company must have had a sense of humour.

"I'll see you in a while," said Lindsay. She smiled: he wished she wouldn't do that. She made a little wave, a finger-wiggle.

Patrick had a shower. He'd been sweating: large damp circles under the armpits of his shirt. He dried himself off, and sat naked on the end of the double bed, for a moment at a loss. It had been a long journey, their flight from London delayed. He changed into casual clothes and made himself a coffee. He switched between channels on the television, but nothing appealed. He gazed at the wall separating his room from Lindsay's. He couldn't hear her.

Two nights away from home. The following day, Friday, they had a meeting at the company's Glasgow branch that would last into the evening. They'd spend most of the Saturday looking round Glasgow, a city they'd never previously visited, before taking the last flight back to London.

Two nights away from home. And in Lindsay's company.

Patrick knew about the rumours. None of them were true: they'd never kissed (except once, under the mistletoe: a brief peck on the cheek), let alone slept together. Just good friends, that was all. He rationalised the situation this way: when they'd met, Lindsay had been in a relationship with someone else. Not a platonic one: she'd actually been living with the man, which had made the breakup all the messier. So Patrick had understood when she'd said she didn't want any involvement, although he'd been disappointed. They worked together well, often shared a drink outside work, went to films, shows and concerts together. They had similar tastes. Many people assumed they were an item, despite their denials. Patrick found Lindsay attractive but knew she was out of reach.

I'm holding a torch for her, he thought. *And I'll do so until I find someone else.* It had been nearly a year since he'd split up with his last girlfriend: his workload had been a major reason, and it was probably why he hadn't been able to meet anyone.

He knocked on Lindsay's door. She opened it, wrapped in a large hotel towel, her hair straggly from the shower. "Hi. Come in."

"Perhaps I should come back when you're ready...?"

"Oh no, that's all right. Come on in. Take a seat."

Five feet six, she was half a head shorter than him. He forced himself to maintain eye contact, not to glance at her cleavage pushed up by the tightly-wound towel.

He sat on the bed as she went back into the shower. He sneaked a look at her back as she turned away, the curve of her slim hips outlined by the thick blue-and-gold towel. Drops of water clung to her legs and squeezed out of the ends of her short brunette hair.

Her room was much the same as his: ensuite bathroom partitioned off by a mirror-fronted sliding door; double bed with small units either side; a dressing table and cupboards; a trouser press; three framed still-lifes hanging on the wall. Lindsay talked from inside the shower as she dried herself.

"...I rang the office first thing I did. Just to let them know we got here okay."

"Anything happening there?"

"No, nothing worth bothering about."

Phoning the office. Commitment. He hadn't bothered to make the call - truth was, it hadn't even occurred to him to do so. There was no rivalry between Lindsay and himself, but he knew they'd both be up for promotion soon. In many ways there wouldn't be much to choose from between them, so those little things would make the difference. And they might want to promote a woman, if only to be seen to be politically correct. Not to mention a woman who was intelligent (upper second degree) and good-looking. He wondered if tomorrow's meeting, when they'd both have to give presentations, would be a test of their mettle.

"Patrick...?"

"Hmmm?"

"Would you mind closing your eyes for a moment? I'm coming out."

He obeyed. He heard the door slide open behind him, the quick pad of her feet - he pictured her damp footprints fading into the carpet - drawers opening, clothes rustling.

"Okay, you can open your eyes now."

He turned round. Barefoot, black leggings pulled tightly up to her waist, Lindsay had just fastened her bra. She trained the dryer on her hair.

"Sorry I'm taking so long," she said as she pulled on a powder-blue sweatshirt over her head. "It's been one of those days."

They had dinner in the hotel restaurant. As she poured out their second glasses of wine (they could claim half a bottle each in expenses), she leaned forward, chin resting on interlaced fingers.

"Patrick - I noticed the hotel's got a nightclub in the basement. Fancy going along there later?"

He said nothing. He used to go to nightclubs in his late teens and early twenties: he associated them with quick fumbles in semi-darkness. Sometimes he'd got laid; more often than not he hadn't.

She frowned. "Don't pull a face. It's better than spending a night in front of the TV. There's bugger-all on, anyway."

"Haven't you got a presentation to prepare?"

"Been there, done that. I went through my notes on the plane."

He sighed. "Nightclubs aren't my thing anyway."

She poked out her tongue. "You really are a boring old fart, Patrick. You'd think you were forty-eight instead of twenty-eight. I'm just suggesting we have a good time, that's all."

"Okay, I'll come with you."

"Well, don't force yourself, you know..."

"All right, all right. You win. I'll go."

Lindsay knocked on Patrick's door at ten o'clock. He'd spent the last couple of hours rereading his notes, checking his slides, the radio on low in the background, tuned to Classic FM. He was still in the clothes he'd worn to dinner.

"Are you ready then?" Lindsay stood in the hallway in a black minidress and sheer smoke-grey tights. He'd never seen her wear high-heeled shoes to work, but she was wearing them now. She held out her arms. "How do I look?"

"How many clothes did you bring with you?"

"Enough. Come on, how do I look?"

"You look very nice, Lindsay."

"Well, I did want to look my best..."

They took the lift to the basement and walked round two corners to the nightclub. They showed their room keys: the club was complimentary to residents. In the semi-darkness, Patrick could see it was already half-full - mostly with locals, he suspected. Most of them were dancing. The club was close and sweaty, and Patrick could feel the sound system's bass in his teeth.

Lindsay claimed a table and two chairs by depositing her handbag. "I'll get the first round. What do you want?" As she leaned forward to retrieve her purse from her handbag, he could see most of her breasts. She wasn't wearing a bra. His gaze followed her as she walked up to the bar and bought the drinks.

She handed him his (a pint of Foster's lager), sat down and crossed her legs. She sipped at her drink, a bottle of Diamond White. Strong stuff. On his round, she asked for the same again.

Patrick wondered what she was playing at. Tomorrow's meeting was important, and he knew she had the sense not to arrive there hung over. Women had a lower tolerance of alcohol to men: that was a scientific fact. He couldn't work out why she wanted to prove it, tonight of all nights.

She tugged at his sleeve. "Come on, let's dance." She held on to his elbow as they both stood up. On tiptoe, she whispered in his ear: "Guess what? I'm not wearing any knickers." She giggled.

You really are pissed, Patrick thought.

Lindsay kicked off her shoes and nudged them under the seat. She was a little unsteady on her feet. But when she was on the dancefloor, all that changed. He sensed she had a lot of energy pent up inside her: she leaped and turned, twirled so vigorously that already people were glancing across at her.

She was out of control. Patrick guessed all she'd wanted to do was let her hair down, as a relief from all the hard work, all the long hours she'd put in. Fair enough, though surely it would have been better the following night, after the meeting, than tonight. She'd had enough of being respectable and dutiful; she wanted to be outrageous - hence the words she'd whispered in his ear. But the drink had unlocked something inside her, something dark and agonised, that couldn't be contained. Some pain, so deeply-embedded that even he, her friend, hadn't been aware of it.

Patrick wondered how it would end. If she drunk much more she'd be sick. He saw himself holding her head over the toilet bowl while she threw up. If she passed out, he'd have to put her to bed. He'd lift up her skirt and part her legs, slipping down her tights carefully as not to ladder them. He'd enter her while she lay insensible...

What the hell was he thinking? Lindsay, despite her behaviour, was still his friend - so why was he fantasising about raping her?

"What's the matter?" Lindsay shouted in his ear.

"Nothing."

"Come on. Lighten up. Enjoy yourself. Dance with me."

So he did. Soon after there was a slow song and the flashing lights became a wash of ultraviolet. Lindsay slipped her arms about his shoulders. He rested his hands on her waist.

"Come on - hold me *tighter.*"

So he did. Her clinch tightened. She rested her cheek on his shoulder. He could hear her sigh in his ear.

Was she coming on to him? No, of course not - it was just friendliness. They wouldn't ever be more than just good friends. No more than that. And no less. She'd set him straight on that very early on. He'd told himself that time and time again. They wouldn't ever be more than just good friends.

More than ever, he wanted to fuck her.

"Thanks for the dance," she said, as the song finished.

She didn't even kiss him.

His bladder was full from his two pints. As he went to the poky, poorly-lit Gents, his erection slowly subsided.

When he went back into the nightclub, he couldn't see Lindsay at first. Her handbag and shoes had gone from where she'd left them. Then he saw her.

She was sitting on a barstool, one leg folded over the other. She had another drink in her hand. Next to her, resting his elbows on the bar, was a dark-haired man. As he watched them, she laughed at something he said.

He strode over to them, wondering why he was doing so. If she wanted to be picked up - and his feelings for her had blinded him to this - who was he to stop her? He had no claim on her. She was an adult woman and could make her own decisions.

She waved at him.

"Hi, Patrick. This is Jim." She was seemingly looking through him, so unfocussed was her gaze.

"Hello, Patrick." Jim shook his hand. He must be about thirty, Patrick reckoned; he spoke with a Glaswegian accent. He was wearing a work shirt, the sleeves rolled up, collar undone and tie removed: a professional type, at a guess.

"I work with Lindsay," Patrick said. Jim bought him a drink and soon after he and Lindsay went back onto the dancefloor. Patrick held back, as he guessed was their intention. Lindsay had stayed with him as long as politeness had demanded. Whatever followed was no longer any of his business.

Well, fine, he thought. Whatever it was that Lindsay wanted to prove, whatever it was she wanted to expel from her system, he had less and less inclination to indulge her. If she turned up at the meeting hung-over and bleary from lack of sleep, that would be her lookout. She'd only have herself to blame.

A slow song had started, and he watched Lindsay and Jim clung together, slowly turning. He was running his hands over her buttocks.

Patrick didn't like what he saw. Jim was taking advantage of Lindsay's drunkenness. She was so far gone, it would be easy for him to manipulate her into bed.

He cursed himself. Why hadn't he made a move on her before now? But she had been the one who'd made it clear they could only be just friends. But now she was allowing herself to be picked up by the first man who passed by.

They kissed.

Why him? he thought. *Why not me?*

As they returned to the bar, Patrick could stand it no more. "I'm going to bed. See you at breakfast."

She hardly reacted. It was if he wasn't there. Jim waved goodbye; she, laughing, copied him.

Well, if you regret it in the morning, don't come crying to me.

He locked his bedroom door behind him.

He lay in bed but couldn't sleep. He never slept well in strange beds, and the night's events were turning round in his mind. He should never have gone with Lindsay to the nightclub. But would she have gone on her own?

His stomach clenched as he heard the door of Lindsay's room open.

The walls were less soundproof than he'd thought. He could hear their footsteps - the flat slap of his shoes, the more staccato *clip* of hers. Their voices, but not the words they said. The clap of the toilet lid; flushing. If he strained, he could hear the zip of her dress being unfastened.

To his horror, he was becoming aroused.

There was silence from the next room.

He closed his hand around his penis. It was fully erect. He ran his hand slowly up and down the shaft.

He heard the creak of bedsprings. High-pitched female gasps.

He masturbated faster, his eyes closed. He climaxed with a gasp, spilling his seed over his thighs, the sheets.

He opened his eyes. The tightness in his chest was gone now. He could see the wallpaper, close up. He turned his head and saw -

- his own body on the bed. His mouth was open in mid-gasp. His erection, still held in his hand, was wilting now.

At first he panicked. Vertigo. But when he realised he wasn't going to fall, he became calm. And then he felt himself moving, towards the wall. *Into* the wall. And out the other side.

He was looking down at Lindsay's bed. Their clothes were strewn on the floor. They were both naked. Jim was lying on his back, the sheets about his knees. Lindsay was straddling him, and Patrick could see his condom-clad penis moving in and out of her. Her face was flushed, leaned back, mouth partly open; as Patrick watched, Jim moved his hands from her hips up to her breasts, her stiffened nipples.

Patrick could see every detail: the dimples in her buttocks, her brown coinsized areolae. Her breasts were smaller than he'd thought.

She looked as if she was about to come.

The edges of his vision were blurred and dimming; darkness filled in his sight.

After they'd made love, Lindsay and Jim lay in bed, holding each other and talking for an hour. They made love again, less energetically this time. Finally he put his clothes back on and left for the night, just after one o'clock.

She slept soundly, woken by her alarm. She'd forgotten how much sex, or at least good sex, relaxed her. She'd been carrying a packet of condoms in her handbag but hadn't used them before now. *Well, a girl can dream, can't she?* That's what she'd said to Anne, her oldest and best friend, when she'd rung her on the mobile phone yesterday. There was now one left in the packet.

At least it shows my responses aren't dead. The break-up with Patrick, the way he'd turned nasty, had devastated her. She couldn't forget the evening he'd beaten her up and raped her. Anne had helped her through the worst of it; she knew everything. Next time they spoke, Lindsay would tell her about Jim.

They'd see each other tonight, after the meeting. Perhaps they'd go out for a meal, go to the theatre maybe. Lindsay had no illusions it would be more than a two-night stand. She'd take it one stage at a time: she still bore Patrick's scars and they were still painful. Whatever happened with Jim, she hoped they would still keep in touch. There was a tightness behind her eyes. Was it the loud music, or had she misjudged the drink? She took a couple of paracetamol.

Today's meeting was important. She knew her presentation by heart now, but that didn't prevent - as she'd described it to Anne - butterflies performing dogfights in her stomach.

Lindsay showered, dressed in her pinstripe suit, went down to breakfast. That man from last night - she thought he had the room next to her - wasn't in the dining room. Just as well: he'd sat near her at dinner the night before and spent much of the time staring at her chest. He hadn't said a word to her: he gave her the creeps.

After breakfast, Lindsay doublechecked her handbag and attaché case, refreshed her lipstick.

"Wish me luck," she said to her reflection in the dressing-table mirror.

As she left the hotel, she caught sight of the man from the next room. He was watching her as she went out the revolving door. Who did he remind her of? *Memory's getting worse.*

Lindsay walked across Sauchiehall Street, earmarking shops for visiting later, and up the steep hill to the company building. She commanded the butterflies to be still.

Four A.M.

A woman is sitting in the corner of the cafeteria, smoking. From time to time I glance across at her as I serve what few customers there are at this time of night. She's late thirties at a guess, lines under her eyes and framing her mouth, crow's feet. She's wearing a dark blue jumper with a hole worn into its elbow that reveals an off-white shirt. A pair of jeans fits tightly over thin boyish hips. She has an old pair of trainers on her feet. Her collar-length mouse-coloured hair is straggly, dull with grease. Homeless, is my first thought, but when I glance at her there's something about her that suggests otherwise. Something in the way she sits, the way she stares ahead of herself, indicates a spirit that hasn't been blasted by alcohol nor hardened by years on the streets. At times she seems to be falling asleep where she sits, then she jolts herself awake again.

  Over in the other corner are three men, long-distance night drivers, seated round a table, their elbows spread so they cover most of the surface and no-one can intrude on their space. Men, none older than thirty, tattooed arms bulging out of T-shirt sleeves, jeans ridden down to display the top of the crack between their buttocks. Normally one of them might walk across to the woman, try to chat her up, even - if their luck's in - entice her to go with them to the back of their lorry. The youngest - he must be no more than twenty-one, with a skinhead crop - tried it on with me. But they spend most of their time drinking coffee, talking loudly and profanely, playing cards. Eventually they get up and leave.

  Shortly afterwards, the woman comes across to me and asks: "Excuse me - can you tell me where the Ladies is?"

  "Through that door, across the corridor to the right."

  "Thanks." She smiles. "Thanks..." squinting at the namebadge pinned just above my left breast "...Louise."

*

I took the job at the motorway services the summer before the final year of my English degree. When I applied, the interviewer told me how the place was run: "We're open twenty-four hours a day, three hundred and sixty-five days a year. We never close." I was given the option of working nights and immediately took it. There was extra money in it and somehow the thought appealed to me. Quiet. Peaceful. A space all my own. They were worried at first about a woman being on her own in the cafeteria all night, but there's Mick most nights by the petrol pumps in case anything happens. Sometimes when it's slow I'll dial his extension and we'll chat. There's nothing to read into that: Mick's forty-six, married with two teenage children. It's simply friendliness. In any case, I've just broken up with my boyfriend and certainly don't want to involve myself with anyone else for a while. At least not before the new term.

When I'm alone, it's as if I'm travelling in a bubble, lit with a greenish-white fluorescent glare, floating in the darkness, captain and crew and sole passenger of my own ship. Sometimes there's the nightclub crowd, coming in for coffee until three or four in the morning. They know my name and, boys and girls both, chat to me. I hear all the gossip from the evening: who's scored with whom, who's fallen out with whom, whether so-and-so is pregnant. There are the long-distance lorry drivers. And occasionally lonely souls like the woman who's just gone to the Ladies.

*

She's gone five or ten minutes. The radio is on low. Before now, I've often wondered what's played during the night. If daytime is mainstream, and the evening is more offbeat, then maybe the night-time features sounds that are truly strange and exotic. Now I know the truth: languid ballads to soothe shiftworkers and lull any insomniacs who may be listening to sleep.

I rub my eyes. There are times when I wish I could be tucked up warm in bed. *Think of the money.* Using the glass front of the sandwich counter as a mirror, I renew my lipstick.

The woman comes back into the cafeteria. She has a cigarette in her hand, lit. She sits down where she was before; the ashtray in front of her is smeared grey with ash and full of stubbed-out ends. She must be chain-smoking: I haven't seen her use matches or a lighter or ask anyone else for one.

I'm wiping the tables clean, emptying the ashtrays into a rubbish sack, collecting the dirty plates. As I see her, I straighten, instinctively wiping my hands on my skirt. I go back behind the counter.

"Have you got the time please, Louise?"

"Just gone four."

She sighs. "Four A.M. When only the sad and lonely are awake. I couldn't have another coffee, please?"

"Sure." I set the percolator going. This'll be at least her third, and our filter coffee you can stand a spoon in. No wonder she needed the Ladies.

"How long have you worked here, Louise?" she says. Her voice is firm, glassy-grave, with the sort of standard English accent that could have come from anywhere.

"A couple of weeks. It's a summer job."

"Uh-huh." She nods, and takes another drag at her cigarette. "They pay you well?"

"It's okay."

"Any job's better than none, eh? In this day and age."

"I suppose." I draw the line at cleaning toilets. And as for stories of female students reduced to stripping or escorting or even prostitution to make ends meet...I shudder.

She turns to face me directly. Her eyes are pure deep blue.

"You don't get lonely, all alone in here?" she says.

I shrug. "No, not really. It's nice and calm. I'm alone with my thoughts."

"Your thoughts?" She sits back in her chair. "What do you think about, Louise?"

"Oh...things." The conversation has gone far enough; I can feel my cheeks burn. *Mind your own business,* I want to say, but don't. I don't want to be reported to the management for rudeness.

She sits back and glances at the side wall opposite her.

"I'm making you uncomfortable, I see."

"No, no."

"I am. Don't try to lie to me, Louise. I can spot a liar."

A pause. It's up to me to restart the conversation. "I'm sorry, I don't know your name...?"

"I haven't got a name."

"I'm sorry...?"

"I don't have a name. It's irrelevant. I left it behind with everything else. I'm nobody's daughter, nobody's wife, nobody's mother."

"I told you my name."

"No you didn't. It's on that badge, part of that uniform you wear. You wouldn't have told me otherwise, now would you?"

I bite my lip.

"How about you, then? It just says LOUISE. You have got a surname, haven't you? You're somebody's daughter."

"Jackson," I mutter.

She leans across to me, takes hold of my left hand. I tense, ready at the slightest signal to snatch it away. "No ring. You're not married. You don't have a child either, not that that necessarily follows these days." She smiles and takes another drag.

I shake my head.

"You see? That was a good guess. Do you have a boyfriend?"

"No..."

"No? You're full of surprises, Louise Jackson. I would have thought a pretty girl like you - you could have your pick..."

"If you must know, I've just split up with my boyfriend."

She sits back. "I'm sorry to hear that, Louise," she says, her voice taking a more conciliatory tone. "It's really sad when that happens. You'll still be friends...?"

"I - I hope so."

"He didn't hurt you or anything? Didn't beat you?"

At that, something flares inside me. "Of course he bloody didn't! It's none of your business!"

"Of course? There's no *of course* about it, Louise." She half-stands and lifts her jumper and shirt at the side. About her waist is a bruise, six inches wide, its colour changing from pink to yellowy-puce, to purplish-black at the centre.

I grimace.

"Makes you wince, doesn't it? Makes you sorry for me. My

husband did that."

She lets her jumper fall back into place and sits down.

"How could you let him do that to you?" I say after a pause.

"I didn't *let him,* Louise. I could have got help. But I did nothing about it for years and years."

I guess what she's done: she's escaped, disappeared, somewhere where her husband can't find her. You can do that - just not turn up for work one day, simply vanish. A new life somewhere else. She's only recently escaped, too: that bruise is fresh.

"You just hope that he'll change, that he won't drink so much. That he'll improve. You say, do what you like with me but leave the child alone. Sometimes you think it's *you,* your fault, you've somehow brought it upon yourself. And then you wake up and you say to yourself, listen you stupid bitch, he's like this, he's always been like this, he always will be like this and there isn't a single fucking thing you can do about it." She grinds out her cigarette in the ashtray and almost immediately there's another one, lit, in her hand. "And all the time that hate, that resentment, just grows and grows inside you like a knot in your stomach, it just grows and grows until you want to *burst.*"

She holds up her hand, palm outwards, and at that instant five small blue flames shoot up, one from each of her fingers.

"How did you do that?"

She smiles and blows out the flames one by one, sucking on her fingers to douse the smoke. Her fingers are clean, freshly washed pink, unscorched and unblistered.

"That's a trick," I say. Something must be protecting her fingers - some jelly, the kind that film stuntmen use.

She shakes her head. "It's no trick. I was five when I learned I could do that. I used to show it to the girls at school until a teacher caught me and sent me to the headmistress. She didn't understand how I'd done it. She just gave me a lecture on the dangers of playing with matches." She chuckles. "She never understood anything, the silly bitch."

I say nothing.

She reaches inside her jumper and takes a flat square out of her handbag. She holds it out to me. A Polaroid, taken on a sunny day. It's of her - younger, hair permed, but recognisably her - kneeling down on some grass, towelling a naked boy who must be about three years old.

"That's you," I say.

"And my son."

"How old is he? He's ever so sweet."

She snatches the photo back from me. "He's dead."

I stare at her.

"Yes, that's what I said. Dead. Do I have to spell it out for you?"

"I'm so sorry. What - what happened?"

"It was an accident. He - he got burned."

"*Burned?*" As the implications of that sink in, something clenches inside me. Behind the counter, my hands begin to tremble.

"You see," she goes on. Her voice is calm, but I sense from her body language that she's holding herself in very tightly. "I thought I could control it, you see. But there was too much smoke, it was too hot. My husband was asleep but I'd meant to get him. But I couldn't fetch my son. I had to press a wet handkerchief to my nose. I couldn't breathe. I barely got myself out before the roof collapsed."

She stands up, stubbing her cigarette out violently into the ashtray.

"You're mad," I say.

"Mad? I'm not mad." She stares back at me. "Or if I am, I was made that way." She pauses, then says: "I'm sorry if I've disturbed you, Louise. I thank you for the company. For the chat. It was nice to have met you. But I really must go now."

She turns on her heel out of the door. From behind the counter I can see her walk across the half-empty carpark.

I sit down heavily and put my head in my hands. I shudder. *Jesus Christ,* I think. I should have called Mick on his extension. But this woman made no indication of wanting to hurt me.

As I sit there, watching her small figure walk away, I think: *You really blew it, Louise. The woman was crying out for help. And you turned her away. You're no Good Samaritan.*

And I get up from my chair. I hurry across the cafeteria, my heels clicking on the tiled floor, and out into the cold night air.

The woman is at the far end of the carpark, by the fence leading down to the motorway.

I don't think about the consequences of leaving the cafeteria unlocked and unattended. I run as fast as I can towards her.

"Come back!" I shout. "Come back! I'm sorry! Come back!"

She turns for a moment, then climbs over the fence.

By the time I reach the fence, she's scrambled down the grass verge and is standing on the hard shoulder. She glances to her right, then steps out onto the motorway.

"Don't be bloody stupid!" I yell.

To my right there's a bright light in the distance. It resolves into two, close together. A lorry. Travelling very fast.

The woman stands directly in its path. She holds up her hands, palms facing the oncoming vehicle.

Its horn blares.

Ten small flames shoot up from the woman's fingers. They are stronger this time, and the flames quickly spread down her arms.

I scream -

When the lorry hits her, her hair is ablaze.

A Giant Amongst Women

Portia drove a Porsche. A terrible pun, as she would have been the first to admit, but it was the gesture that counted, suitably flamboyant. It was her signature.

I remember sitting in that car (Bessie, she called it), as she drove. The windows were open; her headscarf, holding her collar-length dark-brunette hair in place, blew out like a banner.

She had an innate gracefulness, despite her size. At six feet five inches, she was the tallest woman I had ever met. She was the only woman I ever had to look up to, to meet her gaze. She was broad-shouldered with large hands and a heavy bust. Her chin was pointed, her lips full, her brunette hair thick and shoulder-length: but she had the most delicate shade of blue eyes. I sensed at once she could have been, indeed almost certainly had been, deeply hurt.

I remember sitting with her in the front room of her flat one wintry night. The gas fire was on. She sat opposite me, smoking a cigarette. She was wearing a thick off-white woollen jumper and black leggings, her long legs crossed at the ankles, dangling one size-eleven shoe from the ends of her toes.

"What I liked about you, Graham, when we first met," she said, "was that you didn't mention my height."

I told her: "Because I knew you'd be sick of it. I mean, I got this tall early on and stopped. Other boys caught up with me and overtook me. But I was the one who got 'Isn't he tall?' all through my teens."

"Well, you're not exactly short, Graham."

"I'm six feet one. That's taller than average, I suppose. But I'm not Very Tall. Not for a bloke, anyway. It's different for you."

She said nothing, merely smiled.

*

I first met Portia in a hot London summer; she was twenty-nine, three years my senior. When I first arrived in London as a student, I soon noticed that it was warmer than where I'd come from: London is built in a natural bowl, while my parents' house in Hampshire – not especially urbanised, but not rural either – was built on a gently sloping hillside. In London, the summers stifle, with the crowds, the noise and the pollution. I stayed on after graduation and had several temporary jobs – which shows you how far an English degree gets you – while struggling to make ends meet as a freelance journalist, film material mainly. I rented a room in a house in Tottenham and was often short of money between the intermittent paycheques. In what little spare time I had, when I wasn't too exhausted, I worked on a novel. The going was hard and I was slowly facing up to the fact that I had no real talent. As well as the novel I'd written some short stories, but rejection followed rejection with disheartening frequency.

That summer, the bedsit's deficiencies had become less and less bearable and relations between me and my landlord were souring. Heidi, my girlfriend of a year's standing, left me, due to my own stupid fault. I'd struggled along for five years with nothing to show for it. Something had to happen.

I saw the advertisement – room to let in Camden – in *Time Out*. I was reluctant to apply, as I was sure it would have gone almost as soon as it saw print. I rang the number anyway and left my message as directed by the well-spoken female voice of the answering machine, briefly stating who I was and what I did, as requested by the advertisement. Then I forgot about it. I went to the pub and downed four pints of John Smith's.

When I arrived home, there was a message for me. The same female voice, stiff and pedagogical, as if unused to speaking to a machine. "This is Portia Martindale," she said. "I got your message. Yes, you're welcome to see the room. Call me and we'll arrange a time to look around."

So I did, and visited her one morning before she went to work. Her flat was a few minutes from Camden Town Tube, part of a terrace. Within sight were a Greek taverna, a snooker hall and a modern-design Roman Catholic church.

She shook my hand. All she said as introduction was: "Hello, I'm Portia. I hope you don't mind cats." (There were two: a tabby,

Phoebe, and a tortoiseshell, Sophie.) Her brusqueness would have put many off, perhaps intentionally, but I wasn't so easily deterred. She showed me round her two-bedroom flat. It was clean and tidy, though not entirely spotless. It looked like a place I'd want to live in, and was certainly better than where I was now. Portia had on a cream-coloured blouse and a long floral-printed skirt. She seemed nervous and she frequently dragged on her cigarette. I tried to make conversation, particularly when she made coffee, but it wasn't easy. I sensed she was wary of me.

I left having written that one off. No doubt others had visited before me; the room had gone already, and she'd only shown me around out of politeness. I was self-employed, didn't earn very much. But when I arrived home my answering machine's message light was blinking. "Hello, Graham, this is Portia. The room's yours if you want it. When can you move in? Call me back."

"Who's Portia, then?" asked Claire, a toothbrush in her mouth as she walked past my open door, drying her loosely-permed light-brown hair with a towel. Claire worked nights for BT Faults and had only just got up - it was three in the afternoon. She often went barefoot around the house dressed as she was now, in a baggy T-shirt and an old faded full-length skirt that had worn almost to transparency at a point just below her knees. We'd gone out to the pub and film previews now and again, and had kissed under the mistletoe at Christmas, but she'd made it clear to me and to others that she wasn't interested in a relationship.

"My new landlady," I said.

She stopped and blinked, the toothbrush at right-angles, her gaze unfocused without her glasses. She knew I'd been looking elsewhere. "Oh. Whereabouts?"

"Camden."

"Very nice. She sounds quite posh. What's she like?"

I described her, and mentioned how tall she was.

"Shit." Claire looked up at the ceiling. Portia would dwarf Claire: she was five feet two and a half ("and don't forget the half"). "Like one of those basketball players on the telly."

"You get the picture. I didn't ask her if she played."

"Anyway, good luck. Keep in touch." She walked past my door

to her bedroom.

I found out (much later) that I'd been the only one to visit Portia's house. Everyone else who had called had been told the room was taken. So why had I been the exception? I asked Portia this; she told me she'd had a feeling I was the right person. Gut instinct, intuition: she would say no more than that.

That evening, I was back in Portia's flat, writing a deposit cheque. "Who do I make it out to?"

"'Mrs P.J. Martindale'."

I glanced up. She had no wedding ring on her finger.

"I'm divorced," she said. "I don't want to talk about it, if you don't mind."

"Sorry."

"Don't be. It's past history. Dead and gone. Sealed away."

That was my introduction to the strange world of Portia Martindale.

*

Claire and her brother helped me move in on the Saturday. Portia was out, but I had a key by then. Come late afternoon, there was a pile of my belongings on my bedroom floor. Just as we finished, Portia returned.

"Hello, Portia," I said. "This is Claire, my ex-flatmate. She's helping me move in."

Claire, I noticed, had been put on the defensive by Portia's bearing and accent. When Portia opened the door, Claire had been wiping her glasses on the legs of her dungarees - she'd dropped her hands to her sides as if standing to attention.

But Portia put her at ease, shook her hand and offered us all coffee.

When Claire finally left, she said: "Keep in touch." We kissed and hugged.

"Is Claire your girlfriend?" Portia asked as we put the cups away in the dishwasher.

"No, just good friends."

"You can never have enough friends," she said.

*

I didn't sleep well that first night: I never do in strange beds. One of the floorboards outside my door – after a while I could locate it exactly, five feet to the northwest – squeaked every time Portia walked past. I'd gone to bed early, exhausted by the move. I lay aching, as if I'd pulled every muscle it was possible to pull, unable to sleep. It was a hot humid night.

At sometime after midnight, I gave up trying to sleep. I pulled on a T-shirt and a pair of underpants and tiptoed onto the landing.

"Hello, Graham."

I started. Portia stood in the middle of the hallway, her hair sidelit by the small top window, in a thick burgundy dressing-gown over a white nightdress.

"Can't sleep," I muttered.

"Can I get you something?" she said. She stepped forward, fully into the light. "I'm going to make myself a cocoa. Do you want some?"

"Oh...yes please." I swallowed.

"And then we can chat." She smiled. "I'll see you in a minute." She turned around. I watched her walk away down the hall.

I shouldn't have stared. I certainly found her attractive – but she'd given no hint she was available. How did I know she didn't already have a man in her life?

I went into the kitchen. Portia was sitting on a stool, bent forward over the table, a steaming cup of cocoa resting between her large hands. Her legs were crossed and the dressing-gown fell open below her knees.

The kitchen seemed sparser than it did by daylight, with the curtains shut, the bright light shining off the cream-coloured walls, the glossy covers of rows of cookery books. Portia's face was partly in shadow. I sat down.

"I expect it's all a bit overwhelming for you," she said.

"Well, they do say moving house is the most stressful thing there is. Next to divorce, that is."

She made a moue. "I've been divorced. I can believe that."

I said nothing. I'd never even been married, but splitting up with Heidi had been painful enough.

"You're a writer, you said."

I sighed. "Well, I like to think of myself that way. I'm sort of making my living as a journalist."

"But you write fiction?"

"I try to. I'm working on a novel but I'm not getting very far." Thirty pages of longhand in a W.H. Smith's A4 jotter pad: it lay unpacked at the bottom of a box.

"How about short stories?"

"I'm written several. No-one's accepted them."

"You should keep on trying. I work for a magazine, by the way."

"I – you never told me that."

She chuckled. "You never asked. We don't publish fiction unfortunately. I'm a sub-editor – I do some freelance proof-reading and typesetting. That Apple Mac over there is for when I work at home. But yes, I'd like to have a look at your novel if I may."

"It's only rough. First-draft stuff."

"It will still give me some idea, Graham," she said. "Show me tomorrow."

*

A few days later, I came home from a lunchtime preview. I let myself in and went into the kitchen to make myself a coffee.

A man was sitting at the breakfast table. He was wearing a T-shirt and jeans; a leather jacket, with a red AIDS ribbon pinned to the lapel, was draped over the back of his chair. He looked up as I came in. "Oh hi, you must be Graham." We shook hands. "I'm Steve. I'm here for dinner – Portia's just gone out to get something, she'll be back any minute. You're a writer, so I'm told."

"Journalist."

"I'm an illustrator myself. Book covers, magazine interiors, kids' books. Portia likes to surround herself with the, er, more artistic sort of person." I said nothing, and he continued: "You'll meet them all eventually, no doubt. Uh-oh, speak of the Devil. It's the woman herself."

Portia let herself in, a bulging shopping bag in each hand.

"Hello, Graham," she said. "How was the film?"

"Dire."

"Oh dear. I see you've met Steve. I'm just making dinner. You're welcome to join us."

"You won't regret it," said Steve. "Portia's cooking's out of this world."

"Flatterer." She touched him briefly on the elbow. He slipped his arm about her waist and gave it a friendly squeeze.

Steve and I helped her. As best as I could in my case - I was no cook. When dinner was ready, Portia had changed into an ochre dress, cut low enough to display two inches of cleavage. She'd renewed her lipstick and put on a pair of gold pendant earrings. When she leaned forward past me to light the beeswax candles, I could smell her perfume. It was like a romantic dinner for two. But for her and Steve: I was an afterthought. I felt like an intruder.

Portia served her home-made vegetable soup. As we drank it, she asked Steve: "How's Max?"

"Stable. Stable at what he was, that is. Sometimes he doesn't remember who I am."

"It's such a shame," said Portia. "I could cry. He was so talented."

"My lover," Steve explained to me. "He's got full-blown AIDS."

"I'm sorry," I said.

Something in my expression must have begged the question, for Steve went on: "In case you're wondering, I'm negative. Max was positive before I met him and we, er, played it safe."

"I introduced him to you, didn't I, Steve?" said Portia, pouring out three glasses of Soave.

"That's right."

"I knew you two would get on."

"We did. House-on-fire stuff. In the early days, when we weren't working, we were in bed, fucking like the proverbial rabbits." He turned to me. "Sorry – does that make you uncomfortable?" I shook my head; he'd probably said it just to see how I'd react.

"He was an illustrator, just like Steve," said Portia.

"Freelance graphics designer, please."

"He painted me once."

"Nude," Steve said in an aside to me.

Portia reddened.

"He's the only man who's got your clothes off recently."

"Steve!" She batted his elbow. "You can be so rude sometimes! That was really below the belt."

Steve blew her a kiss. "You're beautiful when you're angry." He raised his glass to her. "But seriously folks, you're a great matchmaker. The best."

Portia sat back, smiling broadly. The candlelight gave her skin a deep honey glow as the red flush faded. Steve was right: she was beautiful. "Yes, I am a good matchmaker, aren't I?" She touched me on the forearm. "I ought to match you with someone, shouldn't I?"

"Portia! How do you know he wants to be matched?"

"You're not with anyone, are you, Graham?"

I shook my head. "I don't have a girlfriend at the moment."

"You see?" said Portia. "I was right."

"You've never done matchmaking for straights," said Steve.

"Yes I have. I've got plenty of female friends, I'll have you know."

"Some, I'll grant you, and a few of them are dykes. But how come I always see you with gay men?"

"I split up with my last girlfriend not long ago, actually," I said.

"Oh dear," said Portia. "Is it still sore?"

"I guess not. It was stumbling along for a while anyway. Neither of us was strong enough to end it."

"What was her name?" asked Portia.

"Heidi."

"What did she look like?"

"Tall – well I thought she was at the time. Not as tall as you. Five ten."

"Well that is tall, for a woman."

"Says the giantess."

"I beg your pardon, Steve. There's a woman in America who's seven feet seven. I'm not the tallest woman in the world."

Steve blew her another kiss. "Five ten's not exactly short for a man either."

"She had red hair and very fair skin and freckles," I continued. "Slim build. She had a great sense of humour."

"She sounds very nice," said Portia.

If I closed my eyes I could picture Heidi: posing in front of a statue, her face shaded by her sunhat, for a holiday photograph; in her bikini under a shade on the beach; naked in my arms, as we made love. "Then two things happened. I got drunk at a party and did something I shouldn't have done with another girl. And she got a job transfer, back to Newcastle, nearer her family. We still write to each other, phone now and again."

"Oh good. At least you'll stay friends."

"Until you drift apart," said Steve.

"Steve!"

"Shit happens."

"Oh Steve, you're such a cynic."

"It's my shell. I'm all soft and vulnerable inside." This was said so flatly, I wondered if he were being sarcastic.

"You and me both, Steve," Portia sighed. "You and me both." She got up to serve the main course, Thai green fish curry.

After dinner, the three of us washed up, then sat in the front room to talk and listen to some CDs: Tori Amos followed by Portishead and then Radiohead.

"Well Mrs Martindale," said Steve as he left, "thank you for a pleasant evening."

"You're very welcome." They kissed. "Love to Max."

"Of course." He shook my hand. "Nice to meet you, Graham. Now I know who's the new man in Portia's life. Or her house at least," he added laughing as she thumped him on the upper arm. "I do so love winding her up."

*

A few days later, I rang Claire; that evening at eight o'clock I called at the house where I used to live.

She let me in. Her hair was still straggly from the shower; her glasses magnified her blue eyes. The first thing I noticed was how short she was. She was not especially undersized, but somehow living under the same roof as Portia had accustomed me to tall women. Also the house was different, strange; I'd been living here only a few weeks earlier, but since I'd left it seemed to have changed in many subtle ways. Perhaps I and the house had been part of a pattern; now I'd stepped out of it, the pattern had reformed without me and was different, and I was also seeing it from outside.

She grinned. "Hi, come in." I followed her into the kitchen.

"How are you getting on with – what's her name? the big woman," she asked as she filled the kettle.

"Portia." I told her about the dinner with Steve. By the time I finished, we were sitting on opposite sides of the old chipped-varnish breakfast table.

"She likes queers, then," said Claire.

"And arty types."

"There you are then," she laughed. "You're well in. Have you had something to eat?"

"I had a Burger King on the way over."

"Oh don't. I'm on a diet."

"You don't need to go on a diet, Claire."

"I do," she pouted. "I can't get into any of my pairs of jeans. I'm popping out of my *bra,* for God's sake."

"Now that I'd like to see."

Her face clouded. She kicked my shin under the table, solidly enough to act as a warning. "Oh, you. Don't."

We went out to The Garden Gate, a small unpretentious pub half a mile down the road. We'd often gone there as a cheap way of getting out of the house. But even this old haunt seemed changed: more down-at-heel than I remembered, the wallpaper peeling in places, the few regulars more miserable-looking.

I bought the first round: a pint of John Smiths for me, a Bacardi and diet coke for her, a packet of cream cheese and chive crisps which we shared.

"You're not your usual ebullient self," I said.

Claire was resting the point of her chin in the palms of her hands. "I've had a really shit day." The few times Claire swore it always sounded forced, and was defused by a quick thin half-smile, as if to say:

Naughty girl, for using such words. "You get people who want their line fixed now. They want enhanced maintenance but don't want to pay for it."

"You're just there to be shouted at."

"That's right."

After three rounds – three pints which made me pleasantly insulated – Claire walked me to the Tube station. She was to my side and slightly ahead, her handbag swinging gently against her hip, her heels clacking on the pavement.

We kissed goodbye at the station entrance and she gave me a hug. With other women I might have gone further – embraced her tighter, moved up a hand to her breast – a possible prelude to sex. But there was a rigidity to Claire that underpinned her warmth: *this far, no further.* We were friends, very good friends, no more than that. And no less.

We parted. "Keep in touch," she said. "Look, I've got my lipstick on you."

"Where?" I put my hand to my face.

"There. Let me." She wetted the tip of her finger and dabbed at a spot just above my upper lip. "All gone."

We waved to each other as I went down the stairs to the platform.

The train was nearly empty. The scowling, punky-looking young woman on the opposite side of the carriage was wearing a badge that said EVERYONE CAN SEE YOU STARING AT MY CHEST.

Camden High Street was almost deserted. During the day you could hardly move for the press of people, the noise of the market (almost entirely human-generated - there was little or no music playing), roadside stands selling cheap cassettes, the clashing colours of the bustling shops, the sizzle of hot dogs and burgers. All that had gone, leaving its detritus behind: scraps and twists of paper stirred by the evening breeze, splashes of unidentifiable liquid, the lingering smell of joss-sticks.

I let myself into the flat. Portia, sitting in the front room, stood up as I came in. "Oh, it's you, Graham." Her voice was lower-pitched than usual, deliberately enunciated; she had a heavy-lidded tired look.

I guessed she'd been drinking. "How was Claire?"

"She's fine."

"She's a nice girl."

"We're just good friends."

She nodded, and made a gesture that could either be waving away my quibble, or a beckoning. Possibly both. "Come in here, we'll have a chat."

She sat down again, slipping out of her sandals and tucking her legs under her in a way I didn't think would be comfortable for someone her size. She smoothed out her long blue-green batik-style skirt. Phoebe, disturbed, clambered up to sit on her lap and imperiously leaned her head back to be scratched under the chin.

The television was on, playing a video of *Breakfast at Tiffany's*. I'd seen the box on the shelf so when Portia said, "This is one of my favourite films, Graham," it came as no surprise. I had come in at the scene where Audrey Hepburn tells George Peppard that she gets the "mean reds".

"Do you want some wine, Graham? Pour yourself some. There's a new bottle in the fridge and glasses in the cabinet behind you." This last sentence was spoken in an unbroken monotone. There was an empty bottle of Chablis on a small table next to her, with a half-empty lead-crystal glass next to it on a coaster. I wondered how much she'd drunk.

I collected the new bottle from the fridge and refilled her glass, filled mine. I sat down in the armchair opposite her.

"How much have you had, Portia?"

"Second bottle." She held the glass in her hand and agitated it gently, the meniscus travelling up one side then the other. She gazed at the movement of the wine, seemingly hypnotised by it.

"You're pissed," I said.

She shook her head. "Not pissed. Just tipsy. What's it to you?" Her tone had suddenly hardened.

"Nothing, nothing. No offence." This was a side of Portia I hadn't seen before and I didn't like it. It worried me, even scared me.

But she wasn't angry; her mood subsided as she sat back on the settee. "It's like, some days things just get to you, don't they?

Sometimes you just have to switch it off."

"I don't understand. What do you mean? What's happened?"

"You wouldn't understand."

"Try me."

She didn't answer that, just said: "Come and sit next to me. I'm grateful for your company."

My heart was beating faster, through nerves more than anything else. She swung her legs away from the settee, planting her feet squarely on the floor, for me to sit next to her. Phoebe perched herself on my lap and began licking the underside of her leg; Sophie emerged from behind the armchair and entwined herself about my legs.

I didn't know what to say or do. So I said nothing.

"Graham," she said. "Could you do me a favour, please?"

"Yes, sure."

She blinked. "Could you please give me a hug? I'm going to cry."

I took hold of her awkwardly; she slipped her arms about my neck, clinging tightly to me.

Then she burst into tears.

Her body shook with each sob. All I did was hold her until she cried herself out. She sat bolt upright, dabbing at her eyes with her monogrammed handkerchief. Whatever had hurt her was out of her system.

"Are you all right now?" I asked.

She nodded, blowing her nose. She put the handkerchief away in her blouse pocket. Then she leaned across and kissed me on the cheek. "Thanks for that, Graham. A good cry always does me good."

"You're welcome."

She smiled. "I do that sometimes, you know, but usually on my own. Better that than bottling it up, don't you think?"

"I guess so. I can't say I do that."

"Yes, but you're a man. It can't be easy for you."

"I suppose not. When I cried as a boy, my Dad always told me not to be a baby."

"It's one of those things. I've been hurt once too many times. I saw Max in hospital today. It's so sad – he's a shadow of himself now.

Every time I see him could be the last."

"You must have been very close friends."

"We were." She reached over to the mantelpiece and handed me a framed photograph. "That's him – or rather, that *was* him." She patted me on the elbow. "I'm going to bed now. Good night." She went out, ducking her head to avoid hitting it on the top of the doorframe, as she'd done more than once in the past. She left the video running.

I looked at the photograph. It had been taken on a hot day, in a garden. Portia, in a sleeveless summer dress, was taken from waist height, and next to her was a dark-haired, thin-faced, bespectacled and bearded man, a couple of inches shorter than her. He had his arm about her shoulders; she was smiling and inclining her head against his, her eyes lightly closed. I would have said they both seemed very happy: if I hadn't known better, I'd have said they must have been in love. But it was a rootless image, out of its context. Where was Steve, as Max's lover? Was this before they had met? Or was he the one behind the camera?

I put the photo back in its place, flanked by family pictures, surmounted by a framed seascape painted by Max. I stayed in the front room. Perhaps I should have done some work, but I didn't feel up to it. I switched the video off and rewound it, skipped channels several times and settled on *The Late Show*. I couldn't concentrate; what had happened that night was going round and round in my mind.

*

The following Thursday evening, I went with Portia to the Renoir to see *Ma Saison Preferée*. I hadn't seen the preview of this film: most multi-media screenings were of commercial fare that wasn't to Portia's taste (which was why Claire often got to use my second tickets). I saw her dabbing at her eyes near the end. Afterwards we took the Piccadilly Line to Leicester Square and went to a pub. We bought our drinks and stood outside in a walkway; in front of us was the side wall of the Wyndham Theatre, stuck over with posters.

Portia lit a cigarette – her first that evening – and alternated puffs with sips at her vodka and orange. I was conscious that people were staring at her. She must have known better than I did that she could turn heads solely because of her height; she must have learned to ignore it. She said nothing, but I sensed she was taut as a singing wire.

"Crowded tonight," I said. We continually had to step aside for people passing back and forth, many of them couples I'd describe as yuppies. It was a hot summer night. I'd showered before going out, but I'd rapidly become sweaty again.

"It's not as crowded as Camden gets at weekends. The market's London's number four tourist attraction, you know."

"Really? I didn't know that."

She smiled. "You'll get used to it."

"Why did you move there?"

"I liked the area. I still do."

Perhaps it was her well-spoken accent that was misleading, because I knew she wasn't as straitlaced as she might first appear. However, the idea of Portia living a couple of hundred yards away from a bustling market offering everything from tarot readings to fetishwear, from right-on bookshops to ethnic eateries, gave me pause.

"It's hardly the most genteel part of London."

"I'm hardly the most genteel sort of person. You either find the place immensely stimulating, or you run a mile at first sight. I think you can tell which camp I fall into."

"Not to put too fine a point on it, it's very studenty."

"I wouldn't know – I wasn't a student."

"Why not? You're more than intelligent enough."

"Thank you. I don't know, really – perhaps I should have gone. Maybe I will some day. At the time I'd just got married – not that I'm going to talk about that."

"I notice you don't."

"No, I don't. Let's just say it wasn't the happiest time of my life, but it's past history. We all have mud at the bottom of our pools – what's the point of stirring it up?"

Quite right, I supposed: but there was something too practised, too pat, about what she said. It was as if she had a phrase for every level a questioner persisted to. I might have tried further, but at that moment I sensed she wasn't listening to me.

What had caught her attention were two men sitting at a corner outside table. They had been staring at Portia, in an increasingly hostile manner, since we arrived. I followed Portia's gaze. There was too much noise for me to hear what they were saying, but it wasn't too difficult to work it out: *Fucking freak.*

Portia rapidly finished her drink. "Let's go, Graham. I'm very tired."

As we walked away, she slipped her arm through mine. A spontaneous gesture – or maybe not: it would be a deterrent to any further harassment.

As we waited on the northbound platform, sitting side by side, she said: "Oh by the way, I've read your novel."

"What did you think?"

At that moment, the train arrived. There was one free seat, which Portia took; I stood, holding onto a strap.

"I've written out some notes, they're at home. We'll sit down one evening and go over it in detail, shall we?"

"But what did you think of it on the whole?"

There was a pause. "It's not bad," she said. "It's not good, mind you, but it's not bad. I think you're trying too hard."

"I see."

"It's the oldest advice in the book, but write about what you know, things you see around you. What's happened to you."

"What's happened to me? Nothing much. I haven't travelled the world or swum the Channel."

"There must be something. Those are my initial thoughts, anyway – I'll go over it in more detail, as I said."

"Thank you."

"Not tonight, though." She yawned. "I'm tired. Anyway, Graham, you've achieved something by getting that far. Take it from me, I've tried and failed."

"How do you mean?"

"I don't have that talent, Graham. You have, though it's not fully formed. There's a spark there. You've got to work at it."

"One per cent inspiration and ninety-nine percent perspiration."

"That's right."

We left the train at Camden Town and walked home, not hand in hand this time. Just inside the front door, she turned to me.

"Well, Graham, thanks for taking me. I enjoyed that."
"You're welcome. We'll do it again sometime."
"Yes, I'd like that."
And she kissed me.

It was a small tentative peck on the lips, but a kiss nonetheless. I put my hands about her waist and in the absence of any resistance tightened my grasp. She slipped her arms about my shoulders in a clinch. My grip tightened; so did hers. I moved my hand up to her breast.

She froze.

Her grasp on my shoulders loosened. "No, Graham," she said. "Please don't." I held her, ignoring her. I had an erection. She must have known I had.

She pushed me away.

Very hard: she was taller and heavier than me. She put a lot of force behind it. I stumbled backwards and hit the wall with a thud, more startled than hurt.

"Portia – "

She stood in the middle of the hallway, stooped slightly forward. Her hands were fists. Her mouth was a thin line, and her eyes blazed.

"Portia – "

"Don't touch me. Don't you *bloody* touch me."

"Portia, I'm sorry, I thought you – "

"Don't you dare tell me what I'm thinking. You haven't got the first idea, Graham."

The use of my name told me she was coming down from her peak of rage. But I was still astonished by that fury. I'd overstepped the mark. I should have backed off when she'd told me to. But I hadn't seen that reaction before. In any woman. Ever.

"I'd better go."

"I think you'd better."

As I lay in bed that night, I thought about what had happened. Portia's anger had unnerved me. I'd come to value her friendship – would I now have to find somewhere else to live?

I was woken by Portia's knock on the door. She was standing

in the doorway in her dressing-gown. "Good morning, Graham. I've made you a cup of tea."

She placed the cup on my bedside table. I sat up to drink it, aware that I was naked between the sheets. She sat on a chair. I suspected she had an ulterior motive other than bringing me a drink, and I was right.

"Graham, we have to talk."

I nodded, wondering what I was in for. She seemed too calm to be about to deliver a tongue-lashing, but how could I tell? She was nervous and looked down, toying with the hem of her dressing-gown as she spoke. "I – I find this difficult to say. You have become a friend and I'm glad of that. But I don't want to get involved with anyone just now. I hope you don't mind."

It's not up to me, is it? I thought. "I understand, Portia. I'm sorry about what happened."

"It's not your fault. You weren't to know." She stood up. "I'll see you later."

*

Just over a month later, on an early September Saturday, Portia turned thirty and she marked the occasion with a party. During the day Steve and I helped with the organisation. I arranged the food: chicken portions, drumsticks and nuggets, sausages, flans and quiches, vol-au-vents, dips, samosas, onion bhajias and pakoras, fruit-in-filo-pastry parcels, salads. I speared cheese squares (both vegetarian and non-vegetarian cheddars) and pineapple chunks with cocktail sticks until my fingers were slick with juice and I'd pricked myself several times. Steve, as I knew and Portia didn't, had arranged for a chef friend – former lover – to produce a birthday cake (laced with Irish poteen) with thirty candles.

The previous weekend I'd been alone in the flat. Portia had been away, at the annual convention of the Tall Person's Club of Great Britain, held in a Docklands hotel. It was news to me that such an organisation existed. As a male of six feet one I wasn't one of the 1.3 million tall people in the country (I'd have to be two and a half inches taller for that), merely of above-average height. Statistics like that really put me in my place. As we shared a coffee and Portia smoked a cigarette, her stuffed-to-bursting overnight bag at her feet, Portia put it this way: "It's nice not to be different for a change. Even if it's only for one weekend."

I'd been glad for the time to myself. Since the incident in the hallway, I'd noticed that Portia had cooled towards me. She was never less than cordial and was often genuinely friendly, but we were never as close as we had been. I blamed myself, for misinterpreting simple warmth as something more. We had never gone out again: when she went to the cinema (for example, *Thirty Two Short Films About Glenn Gould*), to the theatre, to art galleries and concerts, she went with others, most often gay men from her circle of friends. A month had taken the edge off my embarrassment, but it hadn't gone away. Of course what I was really experiencing was the twinge of wounded and scarred-over pride.

After a while the silence of the flat had become oppressive, and the usual warding-off strategies had ceased to work. I'd been bored by TV, there'd been nothing on at the cinema I hadn't already seen that I'd wanted to watch, and I'd had enough of playing Portia's CDs. (I certainly didn't share her taste in modern classical music.) I'd called Claire and she'd come over for the evening.

Now, as I helped Steve arrange the music system for the party, I wondered if I was being self-indulgent: this was a man whose lover was near death. In the light of that, my problems were very trivial.

As party-time approached, Portia changed into a long classic-style black dress. She'd gathered up her hair and had on a pale-coral lipstick. Heels added an inch to her height. Gold peardrop earrings hung from her earlobes.

Steve said what was on my mind: "Portia, you look stunning."

The three of us sat in the front room, waiting for the first arrival. I remembered that scene well from many times before, such as when I'd held my twenty-first birthday party at university with my then girlfriend. The waiting, apprehension that no-one would turn up... And, from a guest's viewpoint, the wish not to be early.

Portia had suggested I invite a guest of my own; the only candidate was Claire, but she was away visiting her parents for the weekend. So I was alone.

The first guest to arrive was Murray, a film and TV director (commercials, mostly). He was in his early thirties, but looked older: puffy-faced, balding and overweight. With him was his girlfriend Kerry, a petite blonde with fire-engine-red lipstick. Her hand seemed glued to his, and I never heard her say much.

I helped the guests with their coats, which I laid in neat rows on Portia's bed. I'd seen her room briefly before, but this was my first really good look. It was unmistakably a woman's room, warm, comfortable and pastel, with no bachelor-pad austerity and untidiness. (I plead guilty to this stereotype.) The bed was a double: perhaps she needed the space. A medium-sized teddy bear sat on the pillow. One ear had been torn and stitched back on, and the bear was so old that it had been virtually worn bald in places. Its boss-eyed stare seemed to object to my trespassing.

Celibacy. The last time I'd had sex had been months before, at a party not dissimilar to this one. I and a German girl called Ulrike, a visiting student if I remember rightly, both of us drunk, had staggered into a room which we at first thought was empty. But it wasn't: there were two men there, both asleep. Or, I was certain, pretending to sleep while they watched Ulrike and me fucking (as best we could, considering our alcoholic state) on the bed between them. I don't remember much of this: I hope we put on a good show. Heidi, who had missed that party due to flu, didn't need their eyewitness account to dump me: Ulrike and I had been all over each other before then.

I doubted much would happen tonight: these were Portia's friends, predominantly gay men. That was a lifestyle that held no attraction for me.

When I went back to the front door, the gathering had grown and had spilled out of the front room into the hallway. There were two men in drag and another man, well into his forties and clad in leathers, red handkerchiefs hanging out of both back pockets, with a companion barely out of his teens. Steve introduced the newest guest to me. Joshua was an operatic bass, whom Steve had mentioned once or twice previously. He was enormous, six feet six plus and very fat, with thick fair curly hair and a beard. He shook my hand and kissed Steve on the lips.

"Where's my darling birthday girl?" His trained voice cut through the hubbub.

"Joshua! How are you?" Portia stood there, beaming. Joshua made two strides and they embraced and kissed. He presented her with a bouquet of flowers; she flushed with delight and kissed him again.

Joshua was the only man I'd ever seen who made Portia look normal-sized. "What's it like being thirty, precious child?" he asked.

"It's no different than twenty-nine was, yesterday."

"They say her thirties are a woman's prime." And he patted her bottom, a gesture that would have got me a slap in the face had I made it.

"I'd like to hope so. It's wonderful to see you, Joshua. No party's complete without you."

He bowed. "At your service."

They went into the kitchen to put the flowers in some water.

Steve said: "There's straight-acting gay guys, there's queens and there's screaming queens. The only place Joshua could act straight is on stage."

"You've slept with him?"

He nodded. "Yeah, virtually every gay man here has screwed him at one time or another. Or been screwed by him. Bucket-arse."

I wondered if Portia's friends were all connected sexually. "The gay scene's totally alien to me."

"There's no reason it should be otherwise. You're straight."

"That's not what I meant."

"It's not exactly well known to Portia, either. To use a phrase she hates, she's a fag hag. She knows we're all gay, but all those messy little details of exactly how we fuck each other she doesn't want to know about." He smiled thinly. "I've taken her along to the Black Cap round the corner a few times. Because she's so tall and big-built, everyone thought she was a man in drag. Someone tried to grope her. 'You look very convincing, darling.' She was really pissed off by that."

Later, I was standing behind Murray, queuing for the toilet. Murray had been drinking, and his speech was slurring. Earlier in the evening I'd heard him talking about his current projects. Now, under the influence of alcohol, his East End accent was slipping: born-again working class.

"You fancy Portia, don't you?" he said. "You want to shag her."

"I'm sorry?"

"I've seen you staring at her. Don't pretend you haven't been."

"I'm her lodger." As if that were a mitigating circumstance.

"Good-looking girl," he said. "Nice big tits, nice arse, too fucking tall. Hangs around with too many queers. Fucking cobwebs between her legs."

"How do you know her?" I couldn't see what Portia saw in him – certainly not this side of him.

"Kerry – used to work in the same fucking office. You know you and me are probably the only fucking straight guys here. Let me tell you something – Kerry really likes it up the arse. When she comes, she *squeaks*."

I grimaced. "Do you mind?"

His face clouded. "I'm just being honest. Don't be so fucking prissy." Had he been boasting, or was it just man-to-man sex talk? He turned to the toilet door, and muttered: "How long's this fucking bint going to be in here?"

As if on cue, the door opened, and a young woman, mid twenties, emerged. She had short fair hair and blue eyes, in a white top and black leggings. Murray slipped past her and slammed the door.

The woman smiled at me. "Bit of a wanker, isn't he?"

I smiled in return.

"Enjoying the party?"

"Yes thanks," I said.

"Good." She walked past me towards the kitchen and the hallway; I glanced behind me, watching her retreating back. Yes, she was attractive but knowing my luck she had a boyfriend or was a lesbian. She probably assumed I was gay like almost every other man here.

Around the plughole of the washbasin were a few speckles of white powder. It wasn't too hard to guess what it was.

I went back into the front room. Everyone – about thirty people – was sitting in a half-circle on the floor. Steve had Phoebe on his lap and was stroking her; Sophie, always more nervous, had fled. "This cat will do anything for attention," Steve said to me as I walked past. "She's an utter tart."

"Unlike her owner, I hasten to add," Portia called out from where she was sitting in the middle of the room. Sitting next to her was Joshua. Another man was at the piano.

I sat at the back, next to the fair-haired woman I'd met earlier. She was sitting with her arms wrapped about her legs, her pointy chin resting on her knees. She smiled briefly at me. There were few other women in the room. Portia and Joshua were comparing knee problems. The knee is a fulcrum which, for both of them, wasn't designed to support the weight it was being asked to, a common problem amongst the very tall. Joshua's would be operated on soon; Portia's simply hurt.

As she sat there, one leg demurely folded over the other, I sensed she was very happy. She was seeing out her third decade (not an altogether pleasant one, I guessed) surrounded by her friends. Her face was flushed from the wine and she was laughing a lot. I thought she was beautiful.

The pianist began to play "Bridge Over Troubled Water". Portia sang the Art Garfunkel part. She had a quite serviceable mezzo-soprano voice, perhaps a little thin and occasionally erratically pitched (compared to Joshua's, who sang the Paul Simon part). This singalong was apparently a repeat of one from a previous party and it wasn't unpleasant to listen to, though Portia wouldn't make a career out of her voice.

At the end, we all applauded. The two singers kissed, then Joshua went over to the pianist, Portia towards me.

"I see you've met Lucie," she said.

"Well, sort of," I said.

The fair-haired woman smiled and extended her hand.

"This is Graham, my lodger. He's a writer. Lucie's an actress."

"It's Lucie with an I-E," she said.

"My mother did a lot of amateur dramatics," said Portia. "That's how I got my name. She was in *The Merchant of Venice* when she met my father. She'd come over here from Australia as a student. He was English."

Something else about her I didn't know: she seemed much less guarded in company. Or maybe I didn't ask the right questions.

"Do you see your parents?" I asked.

"My father died of a heart attack when I was ten."

"Oh, I'm sorry."

"My mother went back to Australia. We email each other a lot, speak on the phone about once a fortnight – I'm her only child, after all. I'm hoping to visit her next year. Anyway, that's enough of me. I'd better circulate."

So there it was. I'd learned more about Portia tonight that I'd ever done. Everyone here knew her better than I did. How presumptuous I'd been.

"Penny for your thoughts," said Lucie.

"Nothing much." I shrugged.

"Are you gay, Graham?"

"Pardon?"

"Well, I'm staring at a roomful of gay men. It's a fair question to ask." She giggled. "That's one way of breaking the ice!"

"No I'm not."

She made a double-take. "Good God, a straight guy! How do you know Portia?"

"I'm her lodger."

"I know that, Graham. How did that come about? She's quite particular – well, not that particular. She did have me, after all."

"I just answered her ad, that's all."

"That's not what I'm getting at, Graham. She said you're a writer, didn't she?"

"Freelance journalist."

"Do you do other writing?" She cocked her head to one side, waiting for my answer.

"Short stories. I'm trying to write a novel."

"Then that's why you're here. Portia goes for artistic types, creative types. Murray may be a complete arsehole, but he's got talent. That's his saving grace. Do you see what I'm getting at?"

"Well, I hope I'm not a complete arsehole..."

"No, you're not. But you must have some talent, or Portia wouldn't be interested in you – you'd be too ordinary for her otherwise. God, that sounds really snobby. She isn't like that at all."

"Portia said you were an actress..."

"I try to be. I do a lot of resting."

"What have you appeared in?"

"Oh, Fringey sorts of things. *Time Out* noticed our latest effort. It's on in Notting Hill, above a pub. I play an artist's model. We thought we'd bring in the punters if I got my tits out."

"And did you? Bring in the punters?"

She laughed and nodded, so vigorously that her earrings jingled. "Yes, both of them. Have you seen it?"

"No, I don't do theatre reviews, I'm afraid."

"Would you like to see it?"

I paused. "Yes I would." And maybe I'd get to know Lucie more...if she wasn't committed to someone. The old Graham was waking from his slumber.

"Remind me at the end of the party. I'll leave your name at the door. Complimentary, since you're Portia's friend. She's seen it already."

"Okay. Thank you."

She turned away and paused, one foot balancing on the other, a ballerina's pose. "Am I making you nervous, Graham?"

"No..."

"Could have fooled me. I'm nothing to be scared of."

And she was gone in the crowd, leaving me with a red face. She hadn't been far from the truth.

I'd thought I knew it all. Back in my mid-to-late teens, I'd thought I knew the right things to say to girls, what to do, the most effective flatteries, the tried-and-tested ways into their knickers. Said crudely as it was a crude process. I'd been particularly good at prising the shy ones from their shells. Perhaps they appreciated the attention, I don't know. Such as the girl who took my virginity, and I hers. I was fifteen and big for my age; she was eighteen, skinny and as tall as me, with a complex about her height. So yes, I thought I knew it all.

But I knew nothing. Why did Lucie make me seem so clumsy and naïve?

Even at age twenty-six, I was still an adolescent. I had been one when I'd made that unsuccessful pass at Portia, and I was one now. Not an adult.

Steve interrupted my self-critical reverie. "We're going to get the cake."

At first I didn't know what I was expected to do. I gazed at the bottom of my empty wineglass.

"Come on, give me a hand, will you," he said. "While Portia's distracted."

I followed him back down the hallway through the kitchen and into the utility room. One man winked at us as we passed: I realised with some discomfort he assumed we were going to some quiet place to have sex together.

Steve and I lifted the cake – heavier than I'd thought – out of its box and onto a trolley. It was a large square fruit cake with white icing and *Happy Birthday Portia 30* in blue calligraphy. Steve lit the thirty candles and we pushed the trolley back into the front room. Silence, a wave breaking from the door to where Portia stood in the corner. When she saw the cake she let out a high sound, a laugh and a shriek combined, and clapped her hands to her cheeks. Her face was scarlet.

We pushed the trolley into the centre of the room as people made way for us. Lucie smiled at me as I passed.

Joshua's voice boomed out: "Portia Martindale, *come on down*!"

Portia kissed me and then Steve on the cheek. I scratched idly at the spot, as if she'd left some of her lipstick behind.

"Come on, Portia, blow them out in one!" someone in the crowd shouted.

Portia obliged: tipsy or not, she had powerful lungs. We clapped and sung "Happy Birthday".

"Speech! Speech!"

Portia laughed. "Oh, you know I'm no good at making *speeches*." Pause. "Oh, come on!"

"There are writers present. How could I do better than them? Perhaps I should have asked them to write a speech for me. But you've got my miserable efforts instead. I'd like to thank all of you who've helped organise this. All of you for coming and making today the best day of my whole life." Some people began to applaud, but she held up her hand to still them. "There's not a lot to say. I wish my father were here. I wish my mother could have made it over." She paused: were those tears in her eyes? "But what the hell, there's nothing better than celebrating with my friends. Thank you again, from the bottom of my heart. I really appreciate it. And do have some cake – it looks absolutely scrummy."

And we all applauded.

I heard Lucie's voice in my ear: "'From the bottom of my heart'! Pee-*yuke*. That's such a cliché."

"It sounded like she meant it," I said.

She stood beside me as we queued for a slice of cake, which Steve and Portia were cutting. "She probably did mean it," said Lucie after a pause. "Don't get me wrong: I like her a lot and I'm glad she's happy. But she's got more actressy mannerisms than anyone I know, and I'm the actress. It's not always easy to tell where she's coming from."

When we reached the head of the queue, Portia smiled at us both. I wondered whether there had been a purpose behind her introducing Lucie to me. I was straight, Lucie apparently unattached – maybe I'd divert my libido towards her and away from Portia.

The cake was sticky and very rich: the poteen gave it quite some kick. After we'd all eaten, someone dimmed the lights and slipped a CD into Portia's system.

Portia was at the centre of the floor. She'd kicked her shoes away and was dancing vigorously. Steve quickly joined her, then Joshua, then many others. Always a hesitant dancer, I stood at the side.

Lucie grabbed hold of my arm. "Come on, you're not getting out of this!" She tugged, and I followed her onto the floor. She twirled energetically, her hand in mine.

When the slow numbers began, soon after, Lucie was the obvious woman to ask. She smiled and slipped her arms about my neck.

"Tighter," she whispered. "You can hold me tight, can't you?"

So my grasp tightened about her waist. She sighed, loud in my ear. She pressed herself against me, her breasts on my chest, her crotch grinding slowly against mine. I was becoming aroused, and she knew it. I smoothed my hands over her bottom, clutching at the flesh of her buttocks through the fabric of her leggings and knickers.

Portia was dancing with Steve, then with Joshua. A new song had begun, and I hadn't noticed. A few men were dancing together.

"Thanks, that was lovely," said Lucie at the end of the second song. She kissed me on the mouth. "See you later." And she was gone, leaving me standing in the middle of the floor. My skin tingled, sensitised by her touch. I stood in the semi-darkness, hoping no-one would notice my slow-subsiding erection.

Next I danced with Portia. She'd sobered a little but was still on her adrenalin high. Ours was a more decorous dance – we kept our distance.

"You and Lucie seem to be getting on very well," she said.

"Mmmm."

"I knew you would."

"I think I must be the only straight man here...except Murray – where is Murray?"

"He's gone home. Kerry isn't well. She's pregnant, you know."

"I wouldn't have known."

"She's not very far advanced, only a month or so. Rather her than me."

The rest of the evening passed quickly. I was introduced to two journalists, a man and a woman, both writers for the gay press. I vaguely recognised them: I must have seen them at screenings before. The man asked me what I thought about New Queer Cinema of a year or so before. (I'd sat through the likes of *The Living End* and *Swoon* without batting an eyelid but feeling my opinion of them to be irrelevant: they clearly weren't aimed at me.) My reply must have been too blandly diplomatic, for the two of them debated amongst themselves: he excoriated *Philadelphia* as Hollywood sentimentality at its sickliest; she advocated *Go Fish,* the lesbian film of the moment. There was some debate as to how reactionary *Forrest Gump* was.

Portia and Lucie danced a tango, Portia leading and Lucie following. In my alcoholic state I found it hilarious and I wasn't alone.

Two men in the hallway, kissing deeply. One of them had unzipped the fly of the other's jeans and had his hand inside.

A fortyish film critic I'd seen at press screenings, one of a crowd I'd often gone to the pub with. He was married. He was intent on one of the men in drag: he scowled as he saw me.

The end of an argument: "Look, you can fuck right off now if you're going to be like that!"

Searching for the toilet, my bladder full and urgent, I opened the bathroom door. Steve was standing in the corner of the room, one arm resting on the cistern, the other on the towel rail. His trousers and underpants were about his ankles, and a leather-jacketed man with heavily gelled fair hair was kneeling on the ground, energetically fellating him. Steve looked up at me while the other man continued his ministrations unawares.

(Later) I heard Portia shout, "It's midnight! It's not my birthday any more!"

(Later still) I was dancing with Lucie. I held her tight, my palms flat on her haunches. In the darkness she put her hand on mine and, with no resistance on my part, lifted it up to her breast. I heard her sigh in my ear.

(Finally) It was over, and the lights were on, far too bright. I was standing to one side while the guests were putting on their coats, saying goodbye to Portia. Lucie slipped her arm through mine and whispered in my ear, "Are you all right?"

I nodded. I needed to sober up. "Come this way," she said, and led me into the kitchen. I filled the water jug to brimming and waited patiently while the water trickled through the filter into the hopper. When there was enough, I poured it into a glass and gulped it down. And again. It sat coldly on my stomach and had some effect, but not much. I had a long way to come down.

"We're not going to be able to have sex if you're in that state," said Lucie.

I blinked. Had I heard her right?

"Come on. Lucie's patent hangover cure." She opened the fridge and took out a couple of eggs.

"They're Portia's. Free-range."

"Does your hangover give a shit what they are?" She cracked open the eggs and spilled the whites and yolks into a glass. She mixed the liquid with a fork. "Here, drink this."

I did. "I think I'm going to be sick."

"Not in the sink, please. Use a binliner if you must."

I found one just in time. "Sorry about this." I stood up and wiped at my mouth with a sheet of kitchen towel.

Lucie touched my elbow. "Don't be silly, Graham. We've all been there."

She rested her hand on my shoulder, just at the moment when Portia and Steve came in.

Portia laughed. "We wondered where you two had got to."

"Are we interrupting something?" said Steve.

Lucie and I parted. I went red.

"Lucie," said Portia, "do you want me to call a cab? I'm in no state to drive you home, I'm afraid."

"That's okay, thanks, I'll do that myself. Graham said he'd show me my old room."

Actually I hadn't – her old room was my present one – but I said nothing.

"Nostalgia isn't what it used to be," said Steve.

"Okay, but can you help me clear up?" said Portia.

"You're surely not going to wash up tonight, Portia?" said Lucie. "Not at two in the morning?"

"*Clear* up, not *wash* up. That's tomorrow's job. We'll just load the dishwasher for now."

So we all helped, mopping up food spills, retrieving discarded plates.

"You know what I found in the utility room?" Steve said to Lucie. "A condom. Used."

Her face wrinkled. "Ugh, gross. When I have sex with a guy I do expect him to clear up after himself."

Between the four of us, we finished quickly. We were standing in the hallway, Lucie and I hand in hand.

Portia yawned. "I'm going to bed."

"Me likewise," said Steve, who was sleeping in the front room before he went back to the hospital the next day.

"Well, Lucie," said Portia. "I'm sure we'll keep in touch."

They kissed, then Steve and Portia went away down the hallway.

Lucie turned to me. "Okay, Graham. Let's go to bed."

"They know," I said.

"Of course they know. Portia and Steve know me very well. They know how much I like sex."

We went to my room. Lucie kissed me, then said: "I'll just be in the bathroom." She rested her hand briefly on my crotch.

I laughed. I sat on the bed, wondering why I wasn't more excited: I was about to get laid, after such a long time. Perhaps the drink had put a damper on my mood.

I opened my eyes to darkness. I had a throbbing headache and was naked; so was Lucie, sleeping on her side away from me. My watch said 3:55. I'd fallen asleep before Lucie had come back. But how could I have undressed myself? Or had Lucie done that for me?

I put on my dressing-gown, tiptoed shakily to the kitchen where I swallowed a couple of paracetamol and drank a glass of milk, then I went back to my room. I'd tried to be quiet, but Lucie was awake. When I got back into bed, she whispered, "Graham...?"

"Uh-huh?"

"How do you feel?"

"Better."

"Good."

And she placed her hand on my thigh.

"Your hand's freezing."

"Cold hands, warm heart." She stroked my inside leg then toyed with the head of my penis with her thumb and forefinger. I was suddenly, fiercely aroused. Lucie smiled. "Mmmm, you *are* pleased to see me." She closed her hand about my shaft and tore open a condom packet with her teeth, carefully unrolling it over my penis. She kissed me on the lips, then slid her body on top of mine, lifting her buttocks to position herself, lowering herself to take me in fully. I reached up and placed my palms over her nipples. The bedsprings creaked as she pushed down on me. But then I felt my erection wilt and panicked as I tried to prevent it, but of course I couldn't.

Lucie's expression was unreadable as I slipped limply out of her.

"I'm sorry, Lucie."

"Does that often happen?"

She was still kneeling astride me. I looked away, in shame: I couldn't bear it.

"I mean, I'd hardly started. You can't just stop there. Graham, look at me." I obeyed her. She was holding her hands upright, palms flat on her breasts. "Honestly, *men*. I have to do everything sometimes." A quizzical smile played on her lips. "Don't look so hurt. It's just one of those things, can't be helped."

She lay on her side next to me. I rested my hand in the incurve of her waist. She stroked my penis with her fingers and tried to work on it with her mouth; it responded a little, but not much.

"Let me," I said.

I moved my head down her body and between her legs. I'd only performed cunnilingus once before, on Heidi, and it hadn't worked out – she hadn't liked it or at least not me doing it, I'd been too clumsy. But this time it was much better. As I did it, I glanced up along Lucie's body. Her head was turned away, her eyes were closed, her mouth was open and she was moaning aloud, her fingers clawing at my scalp. She pressed her feet firmly down on the sheets, her ankles clasping my sides; her back arched. She came with a gasp.

I lifted myself away from her. She embraced me silently, then said: "That was good. Thank you." She kissed me.

We talked until we fell asleep again, and woke up at 7.30. Lucie shook me awake. "Graham, I'd better be going."

"Stay for breakfast."

"Thanks, but I'd better be off. My folks are taking me out to lunch."

"I'll walk down with you. Are you sure you don't want a coffee?"

We dressed, then went out to Camden Town Tube. The market would open soon, and some traders were already setting up their stalls.

"Where do you live?" I asked.

"Notting Hill. I share a house. You'll have to see it sometime."

"Sure."

"You're coming to the play? Come on, you promised."

"I'd love to. Is Tuesday okay? I've got a screening on Monday night."

"Tuesday's fine. It starts at eight. I'll leave your name at the door – hang around afterwards, we'll go out somewhere."

"Looking forward to it."

We kissed goodbye at the top of the stairs. I walked back to the flat. There was no sign of Portia or Steve. I made myself breakfast, then went back to bed and slept until noon.

*

On Tuesday night, I took the Tube to Notting Hill Gate. I'd rung Lucie for directions, so I wouldn't look like a tourist by checking my A-Z every three minutes. I still got lost. The pub was down a back street; I found it almost by accident.

I went in. It was small, quiet and sparsely-furnished; a landscape print partly hid a damp patch on the back wall. I bought a pint and stood by the bar. Three men, two white and one West Indian, huddled in a corner to my right; two solo drinkers sat to my left. One of them averted his eyes as I glanced in his direction. He'd been staring at me, sizing me up. Did he want to fight me or pick me up? There was an underlying silence – only emphasised by the West Indian's loud voice – that, with the spartan surroundings, lent the place the opposite of conviviality.

The only woman was behind the bar, plump and fortyish with mousy permed hair. I sensed this wasn't a place a woman visited on her own, so I wondered what Lucie went through to come here. Maybe she was good at self-defence.

"You come for the play, love?" said the barmaid.

I smiled. "You guessed." It was probably obvious.

She didn't return my smile. "It's upstairs."

At the side of the bar was a flight of stairs. I finished my pint and went up them. There was a doorway at the top. Just inside was a big black man, obviously hired for his size. He said nothing, so I stammered, "Lucie said just give my name."

"Which is?"

I gave it; he glanced at a handwritten list. "Yeah, Lucie's guest. Take a seat, any one."

It was only a nominal amount, £2 or so, but I had the freelancer's mentality by now: never pay when you can get in for free. I sat near the front, a legacy of student days when I could only afford cheap cinema seats. (The theatre had been totally out of my price-range then.) I glanced round briefly at the audience: two or three student couples, a scattering of Fringe-theatre devotees male and female, a group of three women whispering earnestly to each other, and two or three men who I guessed were here for the female nudity. There were about twenty in all.

I glanced through the programme, four pages of dot-matrix print. The play had a cast of three, and had been written by the actors and the director. The lights dimmed and the play began.

It started naturalistically if minimalistically, with The Model (Lucie), dressed in everyday clothes, auditioning for The Artist. In alternating scenes, we saw The Model's relationship with The Boyfriend, and The Model's conversations with The Artist as she posed for him. Lucie was naked for most of her scenes with The Artist, but was dressed when she was with The Boyfriend. At one point she walked away from The Artist (as his lighting dimmed) and put on her underwear before stepping up to The Boyfriend and the next scene. Towards the end, The Model and The Boyfriend, both fully clothed, mimed having sex. The play's (didactic) thesis was that The Model – and by implication, women in general – was not a person but a construct. She was defined by the meanings and roles imposed on her by others: artist's muse, girlfriend... subject matter. The play lasted an hour but felt longer.

As the audience left, I waited behind for Lucie. She came out from backstage with the two other actors and a redheaded woman in a T-shirt whom I presumed (correctly) to be the director. A denim miniskirt showed off Lucie's legs. Lucie greeted me with a kiss on the cheek, then introduced me to them. The two men soon made their excuses and went down to the bar. The director, whose name was Vanessa, shook my hand and asked me if I was going to review the play. "I just came to watch," I said.

"We'd be very grateful if you'd give us a mention. We need all the coverage we can get. Lucie's very talented, don't you think?"

"Aw shucks," said Lucie.

Lucie and I walked Vanessa to the Tube. "Nice to meet you,

Graham," she said, and shook my hand again. She kissed Lucie on the cheek and said: "See you tomorrow, Luce." They embraced.

As we turned away, Lucie said: "I live just down that way. Do you want to come back?"

Both hungry, we bought takeaway kebabs and ate them as we walked.

"What did you think of Vanessa, then?" said Lucie.

"Seems all right."

"I saw you sizing her up."

"Was it really that obvious?"

"If you want the God's own honest truth, yes."

"Sorry."

"Don't apologise, Graham. She's a lovely girl, but I wouldn't hold out your hopes."

"She's spoken for."

"Yes she is, but more to the point she's a lesbian."

"I didn't realise."

"She's on her way to her girlfriend's as we speak."

I chuckled. "I've met enough gay people over the last few days to last a lifetime."

"That you know of."

We reached the house she shared, and disposed of our used kebab-wrappings in the dustbin outside. In the kitchen she washed out two cups and put the kettle on for coffee. She leaned against the sink, facing me.

"What did you think of the play?" she said.

"Not my sort of thing, really."

She shrugged. "I got the impression you didn't like it."

"You don't mind?"

"I'm not offended. I'd much rather you be open with me – don't try and spare my feelings. Was it really crap?"

"To be honest, I'm sure some of the audience were just there to see you naked."

She shrugged again. "I don't give a shit. If I worried about what other people thought of me I'd never get up in the morning." She glanced at the kettle. "Oh, bollocks to the coffee. Let's go to bed."

*

I stayed the night. Lucie made me breakfast the next morning: sausages, bacon, black pudding, scrambled eggs and fried bread. I hadn't eaten such a full breakfast since the last time I'd been at my parents'. I needed the energy, as I hadn't slept well in Lucie's double bed. We'd had sex twice that night.

We ate at a bare-wood, paint-spotted table: Lucie moved a pile of envelopes, money-off vouchers, mailshots and local takeaway leaflets to one side. After breakfast I helped her wash up.

"What are you doing today?" she asked.

"Not an awful lot. Shall we go out somewhere tonight?"

"I can't, I'm afraid. I've got the play tonight, remember. I've got another performance to give tomorrow as well – the dole office." She pursed her lips. "You're welcome to hang around, Graham. I've got something I need to talk to you about."

"What?"

"Not now. Let's finish this and go into the front room."

Ten minutes later we were sitting facing each other, I on the fraying sofa, she on a single chair. Lucie rubbed her eyes and yawned: she was as tired as I was. Then she sat bolt upright. "Graham. This isn't easy to say. I do like you a lot but we'll have to stop seeing each other. Sexually, that is. We'll still be friends."

I hadn't expected this; my stomach clenched, as if in reaction to a bodyblow. "Why?" I said in a strangulated voice.

"Dan comes back tonight."

"Who's Dan?"

"My boyfriend."

"Your boyfriend?"

"You must have known."

"I did not."

"Portia must have told you."

"She did not."

"Oh fucking *shit*." She stood up and faced away from me, out of the window. She said after a pause: "I'm sorry about this, Graham. I thought you knew about Dan all along. Are you really really pissed off at me?"

"In a word, yes."

"I hate it when this happens. You stupid bitch, Lucie. Stupid stupid *stupid*." Her hands clenched into fists, then relaxed. She sighed. "Basically, Graham, Dan lives here when he's in London but he's away a lot. He's been in Edinburgh with his theatre group. We're a couple, but we don't expect each other to be faithful when we're apart. As long as we're careful, neither of us minds."

"That's very cosy."

"Well, it's a bit much to ask us both to be celibate, Graham, isn't it? Anyway, that's how it is. I'm sorry you're hurt but I can't help that."

I glanced down at the floor. Any anger I'd felt had passed now, replaced by a sense of foolishness.

"I think I'd better go," I said.

Lucie accompanied me to the Tube station. It was midmorning, and Notting Hill had come to life. We didn't speak much. At the subway entrance she said: "Well, Graham, thanks for the two-night stand."

"Well, it was nice while it lasted," I said.

Lucie kissed me. "Give my love to Portia."

"I will."

As I went down the steps she waved goodbye.

*

When I got home the flat was empty: Portia was at work. On the noticeboard above the telephone was a Post-It note in her ornate, looped handwriting:

Graham,

    Clara [sic - or maybe I misread it] *rang. Please ring her back.*

    P.

I called Claire. No reply. She wasn't at work at that time: she must have been out somewhere. I let the phone ring seven times. "You've forgotten to turn the answering machine on, you silly cow," I shouted into the receiver.

I was in a foul mood, but I had work to do so busied myself with that. Writing page after page of copy, with Virgin Radio blasting out as an accompaniment, kept my mind off Lucie. I made myself lunch, dozed for an hour, wrote some more, then faxed it all to the magazines I wrote for. (I had an extension in my room into which Portia let me plug my phone/fax.) I tried without success to do some of my own writing, flicked through the book I'd been asked to review, then left the house for an evening screening. The film was awful, which didn't improve my mood. I didn't stay behind for a drink; I went straight home.

Portia was standing in the hallway, her arms folded.

"Hello, stranger," she said.

"Hi."

"Well, Graham," she went on, her voice sharpening, "you disappear for more than a day and all you can say to me is 'Hi'."

"Sorry, Portia. I've had a really shitty day."

"Well don't take it out on me, will you? I'm not the cause of it, am I?"

"No you're not. I spent the night at Lucie's."

"Really?" She raised her eyebrows.

"Yes, really, and it was what you're thinking. And on that point, I want a word with you."

"Don't talk to me like that, Graham. Don't be so bloody rude."

I shook my head, looking down. "I'm sorry. I really ought to just bury myself for the rest of this evening."

"I was going to say, Claire rang about an hour ago. She seemed quite concerned you hadn't rung her. I said I had no idea where you were."

"I did ring her – she wasn't in. She'd forgotten to switch on the fucking answer machine."

"Ring her *now*."

"No point, she'll be at work."

"Ring her now. Leave a message. And when you've done that come into the front room and we'll share a bottle of wine. For what it's worth, I've not had the best of days either." And she turned on her heel, so quickly that her long grey skirt belled out about her ankles.

I called Claire. The phone rang and rang – no answer machine again. I was just about to hang up when someone picked up the line. It wasn't Claire but Darren, a student who'd moved in just before I'd left. He sounded half asleep or (more likely) stoned. I left a message but doubted Claire would get it.

Portia was sitting in the front room, Phoebe on her lap, Sophie stretched out at her feet. The latest issue of *Granta* lay open on the table, on top of last month's *Cosmopolitan*. I sat next to her. Phoebe shifted herself to my lap and nuzzled my armpit. Portia poured out two large glasses of wine.

"So how's Lucie?" she said.

"Very well. No-one told me she had a boyfriend."

"I thought she would have told you that."

"That's what she said to me about you. This morning. After we'd slept together twice. 'Oh by the way, my boyfriend's coming back tonight'. So I really fucking end up in the shit."

"I'm sorry, Graham. It's obviously been a big misunderstanding."

"That's putting it mildly."

"I can't say I approve of her lifestyle. But she's very talented, so I can excuse her quite a lot."

"That's a matter of opinion. I thought her play was a piece of shit."

"I wasn't impressed much by it myself. It was too politically correct for me. Dan's gay, by the way – well, apart from Lucie that is. That's how he knows Steve and that's how he knows me."

"This gets worse."

"He's with a gay men's theatre group – a few lesbian friends play the female roles sometimes. Lucie was in one of their productions."

"Lucie's not a lesbian."

"No, she's bisexual."

"You're kidding."

"I'm serious. Didn't she tell you that either? She slept with Kerry once – that's quite something, as Kerry's straight. Keep that to yourself, by the way: I don't think Murray knows. Actually Lucie's slept with him too, I think Kerry knows that. Lucie made a pass at me once."

"And did you?"

Portia chuckled. "That would be telling! Actually, no I didn't."

I thought of Lucie's farewell kiss and embrace with Vanessa: I wondered if they had been (or were) lovers.

By now we'd had two glasses of wine each. Portia sat back. She seemed more relaxed now, more at ease.

"Anyway," she said, absently stroking Sophie, who had jumped up onto the chair beside her, "what's happened is that – you know Steve's at the hospital with Max?"

"You did say that."

"Well, Max was given the last rites today."

"Oh shit."

She gazed down at her lap. "It's so sad, I want to cry. I just well up every time I think of it."

There was a long pause, then I said, "Why don't you cry?"

She slowly shook her head. "It's sweet of you, Graham, but I'm okay. He was the kindest, sweetest, most talented man I've ever known, and he's not going to live to see his thirtieth birthday. What kind of world is it where that happens?"

I said nothing for a while. Then I said: "Talent counts for a lot with you."

"Yes it does, doesn't it? They say I hope it'll rub off on me. They could be right." She scratched Sophie behind the ear; the cat purred. "I have tried, you know. I've tried very very hard. But the hard brutal fact of it is, I don't have any talent. Not like you: you can write, but it's up to you to apply yourself, hone your talent. You've got that spark – don't waste it. Not like me. I have the ideas and God knows I've been through enough to draw from experience. But I can't express them, they just die inside me."

"How can you be so sure?"

"I am sure. I can see other people's talent so very clearly, and I know I'm not that way. I just don't have that gift." She sighed; I saw tears glistening in her eyes. "I'm sorry, you don't want to hear all this. I get maudlin when I drink. It's the mean reds. I'm sorry."

"You don't have to apologise."

"Graham, could you hold me again? I really am going to cry."

She rested her chin on my shoulder as she sobbed. I felt pity for her: Nature, God or whatever, had played a cruel trick on her. She could never pass unnoticed. She couldn't help but stand out in a crowd, but not in the way she wanted to. With her deep, quite painful sensitivity, she had the temperament of an artist to an almost parodic extreme, but not the talent to back it up.

She sat upright. She poured out another glass of wine for herself and me, which finished the bottle. "There's another bottle in the fridge, Graham. Let's get really really sloshed."

"Second time in two days."

"What kind of lightweight are you? Are you doing anything tomorrow?"

"There's always something to do when you're a freelance. But I'm up to date, more or less."

"Well then. I've got the day off. What the hell." And she emptied her glass in one gulp.

So I fetched the next bottle. I knew I'd be hung over in the morning, but I'd had such a bad day, I didn't care.

"Portia," I said, emboldened by the alcohol, "something I've been meaning to ask you..."

She looked up. "Hmmm?"

"You're obviously happy to be divorced...how come you've still got his surname?"

She gazed down at her glass again, smiled tightly. "That's a good question," she said after a pause. "I just didn't feel right in calling myself Miss Bromwich again... I *had* been married and although it was a disaster it has changed me. I can't go back. I suppose *Mrs Martindale* does stop some men trying it on."

"You never do talk about your marriage."

"It really isn't very interesting. I was young and foolish and naïve and I made a mistake. I married a child and I was a child myself. You have to realise I was this tall at fourteen, I was taller than anyone I knew and no man would come anywhere near me. I just thought the first one who did must be that special person. I was wrong. All he wanted to do was put me down, with his fists if necessary. That's all."

"Have you met anyone since?"

She shook her head, a sluggish movement. "Who'll have me? I'm not the type men go for. Women aren't meant to be my size."

I said nothing.

"You know, I look around myself and I see – " She was blinking away tears. " – I see *couples*. I see them and I ask myself *Why can't that be me?* Is it written on my forehead or something? Am I someone God has pointed to and said: 'You, Portia, are never going to be in a lasting relationship'? Am I going to go to my grave with no-one to care for me, no-one special in my life, no-one to love me?"

"Portia, don't talk that way. You're only thirty."

"No, Steve was right. He said all he sees me with are gay men. They're very good friends, but – "

"They're not interested in you as more than that?"

She shook her head. Tears were running down her cheeks. Her voice was barely a whisper: "And they won't hurt me."

We finished the bottle between us. I was lightheaded; her speech was slurring and she was unsteady on her feet. We went to our beds: she kissed me then went into her room. I lay in my bed unable to sleep for a while.

She had this great sensitivity but no productive use for it. I wondered if her drinking was her way of numbing it, shutting it down now and again.

When I opened my eyes in the morning Portia's face filled my vision. "I didn't mean to disturb you," she said in response to my surprised grunt. "I was just watching you sleep." She was wearing a dressing-gown partly buttoned over her nightdress. "Did you know you snore?"

"Yeah. Heidi did too, that made us even."

She smiled. "I just wanted to say thank you for listening to me last night. It helped a lot."

"You're welcome," I muttered. I was uncomfortably aware of my nakedness between the sheets; I still had the erection I'd woken up with.

Neither of us said anything for a moment.

Portia stood up. "Well, I'd better let you get dressed. I'm going to go for a drive today. Would you care to join me? It's going to be a lovely day." And she turned and walked out of the door. I climbed out of bed and pulled on a pair of underpants.

Could it have happened? If so, I'd just experienced a turning point in my life – but, unusually, I'd known it at the time. If one of us had made the first move... But I'd been too wary. As for Portia, who knew? Assuming that had been her intention, perhaps past hurt had weighed too heavily on her. But we hadn't seized the moment and it had gone, probably never to recur. But what if we had made that vital step and had become lovers instead of just good friends? It might have worked. Or we might have been totally unsuited. But now we'd never know which.

Bessie was parked in the garage at the back of the house. Portia had bought the car, a Porsche 924S, second-hand, and lavished a lot of care on it. It was a windy day; she was wearing a headscarf tied under her chin with a best Girl Guide knot. The pointed end of the scarf flapped free behind her. I thought it made her look frumpy, but I kept quiet.

We drove south, slowly through London and on the M25, faster once we left it, spending a couple of hours driving aimlessly through Surrey countryside. We parked outside a pub and walked around the tiny village – I didn't know its name – before returning to the pub for lunch. It was a different pace of life: less of the adrenalin-hassle of London, the metropolitan sophistication that often masked a deep seen-it-all cynicism. But on the other hand it was small; I wondered if there was anything to do in the evenings apart from the pub.

As we sat waiting for our ploughman's lunches, Portia undid her headscarf. She had just opened her handbag to renew her lipstick when there came a beeping from inside. It was her mobile phone, which she kept in case of emergencies. Normally she'd have set the answering machine but today she'd diverted the home phone to the mobile in case Steve rang with news of Max. She frowned.

"Hello, Portia Martindale." There was a pause, then her expression tightened. She handed the mobile to me. "It's for you. Claire."

"Hello, Claire."

Her voice seemed tiny and far away, crackling with static. "This line's awful."

"I'm on a mobile. Portia's diverted the phone."

"Has she indeed? I was wondering if you still wanted to know me, now you're living in the land of 0171 phone numbers." It was a Claire I'd never heard before: her voice was sharp.

"I don't understand."

"Well I mean. You don't return my calls – what am I supposed to think? You don't want to know me any more."

"I called you back yesterday. You weren't in – I left a message with Darren."

"He didn't say anything to me."

"Well he wouldn't. He's stoned out of his fucking brain most of the time."

Portia looked up sharply from her makeup mirror. So did the couple two tables away.

"There's no need to swear," said Claire.

I glanced round. "Listen, are you in this evening?"

"Yes, before I go to work."

"Can I come round?"

"I suppose so. Will seven do?"

"I'll be there. Promise."

I handed the phone back to Portia. She had lit a cigarette, one elbow resting on the table.

"You should never keep a woman waiting, Graham," she said.

"All right, Portia, don't lecture."

"I never understood why you're not a couple. You're obviously close."

"We were. Now I'm not so sure."

"She's hurt. That's a good sign: it shows she cares."

"I suppose."

"You'd forgotten her. You were carrying on with Lucie."

"Yes, mother."

"Don't be sarcastic: it's unworthy of you. You don't always realise how what you do affects others. I can understand why Claire's hurt."

"As one woman to another."

"I'm *a* woman, Graham. I'm not *all* women. Why aren't you two a couple, anyway? She's a nice girl – pretty, too."

"Well, when I first knew her I was with Heidi – this was about five months before we broke up. I don't know – maybe I'd got to know her as just a good friend. I couldn't see her as anything more than that."

At that moment the food arrived. As we ate we talked about less personal subjects. I sensed she was withdrawing from me, or had that closeness earlier today been only in my imagination? I glanced sideways at her as she drove back to London, her headscarf flapping in the wind, flicking cigarette ash out of the window, Classic FM on the radio.

When we got home Portia locked Bessie in the garage. She turned the call diversion off, then rested her hand on my shoulder. "I'm going to have a shower. If the phone rings and it's for me, come and get me."

"Even in the shower?"

She laughed. "Well, maybe not that. See you later."

The phone didn't ring. I went out for the evening.

Claire met me at the station exit. She was wearing a black leather waistcoat over a white top and black leggings. She was thinner about the face than I remembered: she'd lost weight. Her hair was shorter and she wasn't wearing glasses – contact lenses, presumably. "Hi, Graham," was all she said.

"You look very well," I said.

"It's my new look. What do you think?" She twirled round on her feet, arms held wide. "I've lost four pounds. Aren't I a good girl?"

"Well done. I can't remember the last time you weren't in a skirt."

"How about it, eh?" She ran her hands over her hips. She had a good figure, and had decided to display it.

"It suits you. Shows off your figure."

We went back to her house and sat in her room. I rested my back against the wall, underneath a Tom Cruise one-sheet film poster I'd bought her as a birthday present. "Do you want to stay here or go to the pub?" she said. "I've got to be at work at eleven, remember."

"It's up to you, Claire, but I think I've drunk enough over the last few days."

"Oh, really? Do tell."

So I told her everything that had happened: Portia's party, my affair with Lucie. I didn't spare her anything.

She sat in silence for a while, chin in palm. Then she said: "Part of me says you deserved everything you got, Graham, to be quite frank."

"Only part of you?"

"I do care for you, Graham."

"Thank you, Claire. I'm sorry for taking you for granted."

She waved that away. "Don't worry about it. Let me tell you something now. Did you know, when you were with Heidi, I could hear you two doing it through the ceiling?"

"Oh God, were we that noisy?"

"The headboard of your bed kept hitting the radiator. None of us wanted to be the one to tell you."

"How embarrassing."

"And you remember, I was at that party where you got off with that German girl."

This was worse and worse. "What are you saying, Claire? I'm led too much by my prick?"

"I wouldn't put it quite that way."

"I don't think you'd be far wrong."

"No, I was thinking: you and Heidi were very well suited. And somewhere it all went wrong. And you were sleeping together – that made it worse. I'm not involved with anyone at the moment, as you know. It wasn't always that way. It's partly my job: I work nights, so I can't have much of a social life. But partly I don't want to. I don't want to go through all that crap I used to have to put up with. Am I doing the right thing, Graham, or am I just being a coward? I sometimes feel I'm shutting off a part of myself – or maybe I'm just being made to think that."

"You should chat to Portia. She seems to feel the same way as you. That's probably why so many of her friends are gay men."

"I wouldn't know about her, but there's another thing: I was raped when I was nineteen."

"Jesus! *Claire!*"

She waved that away. "It was a man who followed me home

from a nightclub. I didn't do anything about it: I'd danced with him, I wasn't a virgin, and I was in a low-cut minidress and heels. Provocatively dressed, as they say. I didn't want to have my reputation dragged through the mud in court. I've only told a few close friends this. That includes you now – you're the first man I've told."

"I'm sorry, Claire. I didn't realise. All this time, and I didn't know."

"So of course that does colour my opinion of men. I know you better, of course."

There was nothing I could say. She seemed calm about it, but I had to wonder what damage that incident, six years earlier, had done. I'd thought I'd known Claire very well but I evidently hadn't.

"Anyway," she said after a pause. "Do you want to go out for a drink or stay in?"

"Up to you. I'm easy."

She smirked. "Ooo-*er*. Wouldn't say that too often if I were you. Certainly not around some of Portia's friends." She glanced at her watch and shrugged. "Let's go out – I've been cooped up in here all day."

We walked down the road.

"I don't like losing friends," she said.

"You lose touch with people."

"Yes, yes, I know that. But when I find someone I really like I do want to hang on to them. Is that being selfish, Graham?"

"No, you just value your friends. Nothing wrong with that, that's good."

"But people change. I know I have."

"Well, they do say the friends you make in your twenties are those you tend to keep."

"Do you think we'll still be friends in twenty years...?" She smiled awkwardly.

"I hope so."

She looked away. "Maybe if we...if we both get involved with people with the same interests...we could go out as a foursome...?"

I didn't reply to that. Friends we were, just good friends, no more but no less. That was what she was telling me.

We went into the next pub along. I bought the first round: my due, as I'd been the guilty party. She had a malibu and pineapple then switched to diet coke. "I can't get pissed – I've got to go to work, remember." I stuck to halves of bitter. We stayed until ten, then walked back to the Tube.

"What are you doing tomorrow?" she said.

"I've got a lunchtime preview. That's all, really."

"Why don't I meet you afterwards? I'm not working tomorrow night. We could go to a show or something."

"Mmmm, sure."

"That'll be nice."

We kissed and embraced, with some warmth on her part. I stood at the top of the stairs; she half-turned and waved. I watched her go: the lazy swing of her handbag against her side; the leggings moulding her curves; the slow flat slap of her ankle-boots on the pavement.

Now I knew why it was so difficult for a man and a woman (assuming both heterosexual and unattached) to be "just good friends". At some point, sex had to be addressed. I was attracted to Claire – had I always been? Up to now we had managed that difficult feat. And there was no reason why we couldn't continue to do so, I told myself.

The lights of the flat were on, so Portia was still up. I let myself in. She wasn't there: normally she'd be standing in the hallway at the sound of the door being unlocked. The free copy of the *Camden New Journal* was still sticking out of the letterbox; Portia, scrupulously tidy, would normally have collected it and filed it in the magazine rack. She wasn't in the front room either – maybe she'd fallen asleep. If she hadn't had one earlier that evening, I would have guessed she was using the shower. She wasn't in the toilet: that door was open. Maybe she had gone out – but she would have left a message on the noticeboard. Had she gone to bed without turning out the lights? That would be unlike her: she was always parsimonious with electricity.

"Portia...?"

No answer.

It was then I knew something was wrong. She would at least have acknowledged me. Unless she was asleep, and something told me she wasn't.

There was only one room left, and its light was on. Portia's bedroom. I was hesitant to go in there uninvited. I knocked on the door. No reply. So I turned the handle and looked inside.

Portia, still in the kaftan she'd been wearing earlier, lay full-length, clutching her teddy bear to herself, her bare feet hanging off the end of the bed. Asleep, I thought at first. But she wasn't in her nightdress, nor between the sheets. I knew something was wrong from the way the cats were behaving: Phoebe looked up as I came in and let out a fearsomely loud yowl. Sophie was mewing plaintively and was dabbing at Portia's arm with her paw.

"Portia – ?"

I went up to Portia. I shook her shoulder. A snail-trail of saliva had run out of the corner of her mouth leaving a damp spot on the duvet.

"Portia, wake up."

On her bedside table was the bottle of pills she occasionally took to help her sleep. And it was empty.

"*Portia!*"

At first panic rioted inside me. But I thought: *No. Think. What to do.* I used the extension phone in her room to dial 999.

While I was waiting for the ambulance, I sat on the bed beside her. Her pulse was faint. I wanted to cry. There was a tight band about my throat, and a pain in my chest as if I'd swallowed a fishbone.

"Portia, why did you do this? What the fuck were you thinking of?" Sophie was dabbing at my arm, as if to say: *Come on, do something.* And then I said it: "Portia, please don't die."

I let the paramedics in. As they pushed a tube down Portia's throat, she vomited.

I rode in the ambulance to the hospital. "Is she going to die?"

One of the paramedics, a short Indian woman younger than me, smiled. "No, I don't think so. We got her in time."

I sat back in my seat. I felt utterly helpless, all my twenty-six-year-old sophistication stripped away. I was like a little boy again, scared of a world so much bigger than me, needing to be reassured.

I gave Portia's details to the A & E receptionist. "What relation are you to her?" she said.

I was about to say *lodger.* "Friend."

"Do you want to take a seat?"

It was nearly midnight but there was no way I could go home to sleep. I felt totally alone. I'd done my bit to save Portia, but what would have happened if I'd stayed away longer? She could have died. And now I was powerless. I thought of her now, lying on a bed while they pumped her stomach.

I wanted to talk to someone. Anyone. But who? Claire was at work. I didn't want to call Lucie. So I did nothing; I just sat there. The receptionist got me a coffee.

"Graham..."

I looked up. It was Steve. He sat down next to me.

"Steve...?"

"Thank Christ you're here." And he embraced me. I was surprised – and normally I'd be reluctant to be embraced by any man, let alone a gay one – but I didn't resist. He was unshaven and red-eyed with lack of sleep and, I suspected, tears.

We parted. I said: "How did you know?"

"Know what?"

"It's Portia. She's swallowed some sleeping pills."

"Oh fuck. I was afraid of this."

"What are you talking about?"

"Well, she's not the most stable person around, is she? Haven't you learned anything or are you just naturally stupid? She shouldn't have been left alone. Where the fucking hell were you?"

"Now hang on a minute – I'd gone out. I didn't know she was going to do this."

He put his hand to his eyes and shook his head. "Sorry, it's me. I've been in a state all day. Max died earlier this evening."

"I'm sorry, I didn't know."

"She was the first person I rung. I could hear her crying on the other end of the line. It's my fault, I shouldn't have let her be alone. I wasn't thinking right."

"It's not your fault, Steve. It's no-one's fault."

"You don't know how close they were."

At that moment a doctor called my name. I stood up. "You

came in with Mrs Martindale?" she said. Her Scots-accented voice was grave and I felt a blow to my gut. *Portia had died.*

But she was saying: "...she's out of danger, but we'd like to keep her in for observation. You'll be able to visit her tomorrow. Anyway, I think you'd better go home to bed: there's nothing more to be done tonight. Do you want us to call a taxi?"

"It's all right – I'll take him home," said Steve.

I had a further revelation to come. As Steve drove, he told me precisely how close Portia and Max had been. Max had been Portia's first friend when she moved to London after her divorce, and Portia's social circle had formed around the two of them. They had even been lovers for a while, but Max's homosexuality had put paid to that. He had tried his best, but the sexual part of their relationship had been forced and unnatural. Portia had even proposed marriage to him, on the understanding that he could continue to lead a gay lifestyle on the side.

"...but that would've been living a lie," said Steve, "and Max didn't want to do that. Portia was hurt, but deep down she did respect that. Shortly afterwards she introduced Max to me."

"What sort of behaviour is that?"

"A gesture of love." There was an edge of wistfulness to Steve's voice. "She only wanted Max to be happy." There were tears in his eyes; he pulled up by the side of the road and turned away from me. "I'm sorry, I'm embarrassing you." He pressed a handkerchief to his face.

"Don't worry." I rested my hand on his shoulder for a few minutes.

"I should be used to this," he said. "I've been expecting this day ever since I met him. I lose a friend every fucking fortnight. Why doesn't it make it any easier?"

He dabbed at his eyes, then started the car again. Neither of us spoke until we got back to the flat. "I'll pick you up at twelve. I won't hang around."

He drove away, much too fast. I let myself in and went to bed, but I didn't sleep at all that night.

*

Steve called promptly at noon. He had taken charge of the situation: I wanted that. More urgently, I wanted something to distract me from the yawning black helplessness that had opened up before me. I'd phoned Claire at five to twelve, leaving it as late as possible to let her sleep. As it happened, she was awake. "Are you all right?" were the first words she said: my voice had been trembling. I told her what had happened, where I would be and to meet me there. I also rang to cancel my place at that afternoon's film screening.

Steve said little, and I wasn't inclined to start a conversation. When we arrived at the hospital, Steve said: "Do you mind if I go in first? There's a couple of things I want to speak to her in private about. Do you mind? Give me ten minutes."

So I sat in the waiting room. Possibly because I've always been healthy, I find hospitals depressing. There was a strong smell of disinfectant in the air. With nothing to do but wait, I was reduced to glancing round at the few others around me.

Finally the ten minutes were up and it took me another five to find Portia's ward. She was sitting up in the corner bed, in a pair of hospital pyjamas: presumably the nightdresses didn't fit her. Steve sat on a chair the other side of her, holding her hand.

"Hello, Graham." She was very pale, with bags under reddened eyes. She lacked any kind of animation, as if it were a considerable effort to do anything but lie in bed.

"How are you?" I asked.

"Not good," was all she said in reply.

Steve leaned forward. "Graham, we'd like to ask you a favour."

"Ask away."

"Would you hold the fort back at the flat? Portia's not going to be out for a day or so and when she does, she'll be staying with me for a while. We thought it'd be better that way. At least until Max's funeral's out the way."

"Sure. Anything I can do to help."

Portia squeezed my hand and made a small thin smile. "Thank you."

Politeness hung like a pall over the entire conversation. No-one was going to ask her *Why did you do it?* I supposed I knew the answer, if only in outline. But I didn't know, wouldn't ever know, the complex of circumstances that finally tipped Portia over the edge. Do you grit your teeth and carry on, waiting to see that light at the end of the tunnel? And at what point do you think there is no light, only more tunnel? I couldn't answer my own question: I'd never been there. How long do you continue, how long does hope last? *As long as it takes.*

After ten minutes or so, we were joined by Lucie and her boyfriend Dan. He was black, as tall as me, but fuller faced and bigger built. He looked as if he'd be useful in a fight. Lucie introduced him to me and we shook hands; he probably knew I'd slept with his girlfriend, but I didn't dare ask.

Lucie sat to my left, hand in hand with Dan, one fishnet-clad leg folded over the other.

"How's things, Graham?" she asked.

"I'm absolutely shattered."

"You look it."

At the end of visiting hour, we went back to the waiting room. Claire was sitting near the back reading a Stephen King paperback; I attracted her attention by nudging her shoulder.

"Hi, how long have you been here?"

"About half an hour."

"You should have come in."

"I was waiting for you." She shrugged. The subtext was obvious: she felt herself out of place. Apart from me, no-one here knew her.

"Who's this, Graham?" said Lucie.

For a moment I wanted to slap her: she sounded so full of herself. I introduced her to Claire. Claire smiled, was polite, but when Lucie went back to Dan and Steve she muttered to me: "Did you really sleep with *her?*" I nodded.

Steve held out his hand. "You must be Claire. I'm Steve." His voice was terse; they shook hands. "Look after Graham, won't you? He's all in."

"I will," said Claire, and took my hand in hers.

Lucie and Dan left, Lucie giving me and Steve a kiss. Steve drove Claire and me back to the flat.

"Well," said Claire, puffing out her cheeks and sighing. "That's it, then."

"That's what, then?"

"All the drama over."

"It's only the afternoon. It feels like bloody midnight."

"What do you want to do?"

"Catch up on my sleep. Have a siesta."

She smiled. "You're getting old before your time, aren't you? But you do look as if you need it."

I dozed for three hours in Portia's favourite armchair. Meanwhile, Claire went home and came back. In the evening we shared a pizza delivery and sat side by side in the front room, watching television and listening to music. By mid-evening I'd become bold enough to slip my arm about her shoulders. She made no objection, and settled into the crook of my arm.

When we went to bed, we were both nervous, like bashful teenagers. We undressed in the dark; the light from outside picked out the curve of her haunch. We held each other between the cool sheets, kissing and touching and stroking, before I moved on top of her at last. She slid her legs apart and up to clasp my hips, and I entered her.

*

While Portia stayed at Steve's, she came back to the flat to pick up the post. These short visits – not always when I was there – made me realise how much I missed her company. Still, Claire called over most days, or at least phoned, and we went out a couple of evenings. She spent the night on her evening off; now we were a couple, my routines and hers were changing to accommodate the new person in each other's life.

The morning of Max's funeral, I went out from my room, where I'd been working, to find Portia sitting in the kitchen, chin in palm, watching the kettle boil. I hadn't seen or heard her come in.

I made coffee for the two of us. I remained standing; she sat in her chair and smoked a cigarette.

"Graham...?" she said after a while.

"Yes, Portia?"

"I feel really bad. I can't help thinking what I must have put you through..."

"Don't worry about it, Portia."

"And to think, you saved my life... If you hadn't been there, I'd have been dead – "

I rested a hand on her cheek. She looked up at me.

"I'm sorry, Graham," she said.

I leaned forward, slipped my arm about her shoulders and kissed her on the forehead. I said: "Portia, *it's okay.*"

*

She moved back home a week later. I was glad to see her around again, but I knew she had changed. She'd lost some of her flamboyance with Max's death. I'd never met him, but I sensed Portia had in some way energised herself from him. Steve had been right: they should have been a couple. Without him, she was paler and quieter; thinner too, having lost weight.

So I wasn't surprised when, in late October, she announced she was taking a fortnight's leave. She packed her bags and drove away in Bessie on Sunday morning. She kissed me goodbye and also Claire, who'd stayed the night and would go with me to the preview of *Mary Shelley's Frankenstein* later that morning.

I had a phonecall later that day from a service station outside Stafford; two days later, a postcard from the Lake District; then finally a call from an Edinburgh phonebox. That was the end of her journey: a city she'd always wanted to visit.

I heard nothing more for a week. In the meantime, I kept the flat in good order and fed the cats. Apart from Claire, I didn't see Steve or anyone else: I sensed that with Max's death and Portia's absence, her group had fragmented. For a few years that Camden flat had been a place where her friends, all creative people in their way, could gather. If she herself had no artistic ability, despite her most ardent wishes, then she at least could create an environment where those so gifted could flourish. She had even seen a spark of talent in me, at a time when I'd begun to despair of it. Perhaps that was her real gift: to be a catalyst. Her tragedy was that she didn't realise this. Or if she did realise it, she didn't accept it. Either way, the mean reds had a way in to her mind. I looked for the *Breakfast at Tiffany's* video one evening, but I couldn't find it.

Then she sent me a letter.

As it turned out, she'd had a plan behind her journey north. She had applied for, and been accepted for, a job in Edinburgh. So in effect I'd been given notice, while she sorted out the complexities of buying one flat and selling another four hundred miles away.

By this time Claire had changed jobs, transferring to Croydon and daytime working hours. She'd left the bedsit and moved into a four-woman shared house nearer work. I'd stayed the night a couple of times and everyone there was happy for me to move in. "That's if you don't mind being the token male," said Claire with a wry smile.

I helped Portia pack for her move; in the evenings, Claire and her brother assisted. Portia would stay in rented accommodation in Edinburgh while the flat was sold. The removal van was loaded, and finally there were Portia, two catbaskets, and what she had loaded into Bessie's boot. We kissed and she hugged me tightly, promising to keep in touch, write, phone, visit if possible.

And then she drove away. She was gone.

Previously from Elastic Press

Open The Box by Andrew Humphrey

With quiet understatement and beautiful characterisation Andrew Humphrey examines the complex link between relationships and abandonment, resulting in an important collection of 13 stunning stories.

A rising star in the independent press - Trevor Denyer, Roadworks

Forthcoming from Elastic Press

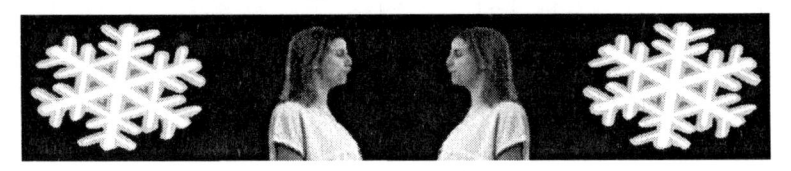

Sleepwalkers by Marion Arnott

In her first collection of short stories Award Winning author, Marion Arnott fashions ten contemporary slow-burning tales which dig deep into the human psyche, spreading unease and unsettling fears.

Includes *Prussian Snowdrops* - CWA/Macallan Short Story Dagger Winner 2001

For further information visit:

www.elasticpress.com